1 Percent

Misti Cain

This book is a work of fiction. All names, characters, places, organizations and incidents are either the product of the author's imagination or are used fictitiously, and any resemblance to actual persons, living or dead, business establishments, events or locales is entirely coincidental.

dedication

For Byron Campbell, Tara Hodgens, Stephanie Burns and Dad
(the angels are lucky to have you). Words will never be able to
express my love and gratitude.

contents

prelude

~April 26 ~

"So, do people ever call you 'J' or Jess or anything?"

Is this an interview or a Girl Scout initiation? "No."

"Oh, I see. OK then. So, just Jeslyn?"

Blank stare.

"Right. OK then. Shall we get started?"

Silence.

"OK then. I'm going to be..." The interviewer glanced quickly at a sheet of paper in her hands. "Uh, what I meant to say is...would you mind if I recorded this?"

"No."

"OK then."

If I hear 'OK then' one more time...

"Please, um, please state your name for the record."

"Jeslyn Kennedy."

Another hurried glance. "Any relation to...?"

Cold glare.

"Right. OK then."

"Stop." Katya froze at the forcefulness of Jeslyn's one word command. "Give it here." Jeslyn's thin arm gracefully extended itself toward the nervous young woman, and her hand gestured sternly for Katya to relinquish the paper that her clammy fingers gripped firmly.

"Well...I...I usually don't –"

Jeslyn's hand, seemingly with a mind of its own, immediately became rigid, palm up, waiting. Katya timidly handed the single sheet over then watched, with what looked like longing, as her interview questions floated away. Jeslyn saw the young woman grit her teeth in frustration; an action that appeared to be directed inwardly.

Why the girl had handwritten her questions on a piece of notebook paper was anyone's guess. In Jeslyn's opinion, it only made her appear even more inexperienced. Her nervous squirming wasn't doing her any favors either.

In all honesty, it wouldn't have mattered if she'd transcribed the questions onto expensive linen note cards, carved them onto stone tablets, or written them in her diary. It wouldn't have stopped Jeslyn from doing exactly what she'd just done. There were few limitations that prevented her from requesting (or obtaining, for that matter) what she wanted.

Katya's brows furrowed in contemplation, no doubt a reflection of her thoughts. Thoughts that were apparently so all-consuming that she failed to realize she was being scrutinized. When she finally happened to glance up, she looked startled to see Jeslyn's chocolate brown eyes boring holes into her.

"Sorry...I...did you –?"

Jeslyn's eyes remained fastened on the fidgety figure sitting opposite her. She certainly wasn't what Jeslyn had expected; although, Jeslyn wasn't entirely sure what she'd been expecting. Sensing her scrutiny had lasted too long, she dropped her eyes back to the paper.

It took serious mental effort for Jeslyn to keep from twisting her own face into a reflection of her thoughts. The result would have been an exasperated grimace. Instead, she remained expressionless and silently ran down the list of questions the young, entry-level reporter had prepared.

The questions ranged from juvenile to ridiculous. A pang of irritation began to rise in Jeslyn's chest and spread like warm tar. She quickly skimmed through the list of twenty-eight bulleted items while an analog clock, previously unperceived, counted off the seconds with loud ticks.

Katya's open-mouth breathing and random knuckle popping added to the cacophony of dissonant sounds.

Question 24.

The warm thickness of irritation lost its heat as Jeslyn read then re-read it.

24.) What is your relationship with Forbes Keith?

Not that it hadn't crossed her mind before, but it was then that Jeslyn realized with absolute certainty this interview was going to be more difficult than she'd originally planned.

1

"Katya, line one."

Sitting in her cubicle, one of many in the So-Ho inspired modern offices of CMT Publishing, Inc., home of *Gray Flannel Suit Magazine*, Katya's delicate features took on an expression of bewilderment.

Marcy, the office receptionist, had given no indication of who was holding for her. It was Katya's first week as Assistant Reporter Level I. She had been officially hired on at *GFS Magazine*, after interning there for the past nine months, and she hadn't ever received a call. Not even from friends or family. They would have first tried her cell. She looked at the characteristically silent device now – no missed calls, texts, emails or voicemails. Being that she had just been issued a phone and personal extension from HR not more than two hours ago, a call on line one for her specifically was unexpected.

She had read somewhere that a smile could be heard through the phone, so she tacked one on before picking up the receiver. It didn't quite feel natural, but she was sure it would let the caller know she was pleasant and capable of handling whatever inquiry they might have.

"*GFS Magazine*, this is Katya." A mute reply greeted her. "Hello?" More of the same.

The blinking green light kindly let her know there was a caller waiting to speak with her. "OK then, let's see here," Katya murmured to herself as she carefully pushed button after button on the phone's keypad. "Hello?"

Nothing. Well, this was awkward. As she stared at the phone, the light blinked faster. It was now firmly informing her that the caller, who had specifically asked for her, was being kept waiting longer than acceptable.

Come on, Kat, you can do this. You can answer a phone.

Except she couldn't. Her internship had been a disappointment from what she thought she'd be doing compared to what she had actually been assigned to do. She thought she'd be writing articles, helping to track down leads, learning the ins and outs of the publishing world, that sort of thing. What she actually did was a lot of filing, fetching and data entry. Towards the end of the internship, her supervisor had given her a few sympathy writing assignments, but nothing major and obviously nothing at all to do with *GFS's* intricate phone system. It was like it was a prized piece of technology too valuable and sophisticated for an intern's unworthy touch. With the light now flashing an angry burnt orange, she considered the possibility of that being true.

"Hello?" No matter what she did the phone refused to unlock the caller from the blinking light prison they were trapped in.

In receptionist angel form, Marcy appeared from around the corner of the cubicle, took the receiver from Katya's inept hand and pressed the one button that had beaten Katya in the game of hide-and-go-insane-trying-to-find-me.

"Thank you so much for holding. Ms. Houston will speak with you now." Marcy tossed a sweet, undeserved smile Katya's way before handing her back the receiver. "Happens all the time," she mouthed before disappearing as benevolently as she'd appeared. Katya did not believe her.

With less assuredness than before, she re-greeted the mystery caller. "Thank you for calling *GFS Magazine*, this is Katya."

"You were just hired on as a writer, am I correct?" The voice that came through the line was feminine, sultry and authoritative, but not familiar.

"That's...well," Katya stammered. Technically she was Assistant Reporter Level I. That's what had been typed on all of her new-hire paperwork and published in the staff directory on the magazine's website. To be deemed a writer for *GFS* at this juncture was a severe overstatement, "Ah, yes, that's correct," but none of the caller's beeswax. "I'm sorry, may I ask who this is?" Katya's puzzlement couldn't be contained.

"I'd like you to interview me." The female caller spoke as if this was a discussion they'd been having for quite some time and a decision had just been reached.

"I see." Katya was slightly unsure of how to proceed. She looked around cautiously, yet absolutely convinced she'd see a group of co-workers conspiratorially enjoying this first-week-on-the-job prank.

Her cubicle, which was comprised of three, four-foot high taupe and chartreuse walls, topped with clear Plexiglas communication dividers, was located on the east wall of the Creative Pit – a moniker for the lower-floor work area that was home to all the lower-level staff. Like 'open communication dividers', Katya had always felt the name Creative Pit was somewhat of an oxymoron. She was not alone. In an act of solidarity, or perhaps it was more passive-aggressive rebellion, she and her fellow grunts had begun calling it the Crap-tative Pit or simply the Pit.

Similar cubes decked out in complimentary earth tone shades and less complimentary personal posters, knick-knacks, and photos stood in the center and along the west wall. A flight of stairs, made of light-hued bamboo wood floors and a metal cable railing, ascended to a loft area. This was the domain of the executives and higher-level staff. It boasted a mix of glass-enclosed offices, swanky modern decor, hi-tech open work stations, a well-stocked break room and an extremely spacious game room. She could see people milling about all around her, but no one seemed to be paying her any particular attention.

"And you said your name was...?" Katya allowed a slight hint of amusement to play into her inflection.

"I didn't," the caller replied, very matter of fact. "My name is Jeslyn Kennedy."

There is a fairly well known saying in the publishing world: Stop the presses. Prior to now, Katya had felt that saying was merely an antiquated cliché used in black and white films and advertisements that predated her by about thirty or forty years. Now, she wanted to stand up and scream it at the top of her lungs. This simply couldn't be.

"And by Jeslyn Kennedy, you mean, *the* Jeslyn Kennedy?" There would be no question as to which Jeslyn Kennedy either of them was referring to.

"The very same." Katya thought she heard a smirk in the woman's voice.

"I'm sorry, would you mind if I placed you on hold?" Katya's mouth went dry. She could feel the color draining from her face and moist anxiety pooling in her armpits. She was thankful this had not been an in-person visit, because as clammy as her hands were just from hearing Jeslyn's name over the phone, she was sure she'd be nothing more than a puddle at the woman's feet had the interaction been tete-a-tete.

"Sure." Jeslyn's formality had taken a momentary vacation.

Katya squeezed the receiver in her palm and glanced down at the phone. The keypad once again became her nemesis. For pity's sake, was it that hard to simply put the word 'HOLD' on a button and call it a day? She contemplated the icons and decided to go with the red button that displayed a graphic of a phone's receiver off the cradle. Mercifully, when she pressed it, line one went silent and the steady red light reverted back to the cheerful green blinking from minutes before.

What am I supposed to be doing? She felt like she'd been bonked on the head and left dazed in a cloud of confusion. She stood up to rise above it. As if by destiny, David Sims, Senior Features Editor, walked by. Katya snapped to attention and called his name in a hushed whisper.

"Hey'ya, Kat, what's going on?" David's smile revealed too many teeth and his over-shellacked, under-styled hair seemed to form a protective helmet.

Katya looked him square in the eye as if she were about to report a serious emergency and urgently needed his undivided attention in order to avert an impending tradgedy.

"David,"

"Yes, Kat?" His 50-bajillion watt smile and overeager active listening skills were grating. She needed him to just shut up and listen.

"David, I need you to listen to me." She left out the 'shut up' part.

"Mmmhmm. OK. What's up?" Perhaps she should have included it.

"David," Katya felt that if she said his name enough times, he'd take this seriously. "On hold. Right now. Is Jes-a-lyn Ken-ne-dy." Katya heavily enunciated the entire sentence, then staccatoed Jeslyn's name in an effort to up the ante on communicating the gravity of the situation.

Mission accomplished.

"Katya, are you shittin' me?" David suddenly became very serious.

"N...n...no, sir." *Sir?* His sudden taciturnity caused her jitters to return in full force. David pulled violently on his plaid, sea-blue and tangerine tie, loosening its hold on his throat but tightening the triangular loop into a strict knot that would undoubtedly be a pain to undo later.

"Well, what does she want?" *Was that a snap?*

"Sh...she wants me to interview her."

"You!?" It was a mix between a scoff and a bellow. Would that be a 'belloff'? No, wait, a 'scoffellow'? Katya contemplated how to merge the two words. Whatever it was, her pride had been wounded. Maybe she, too, had been taken aback by the possibility that Jeslyn Kennedy would not only call and ask to speak with her, but ask that Katya interview her on top of that. She wasn't going to lie, the word farfetched had come to mind.

But really, David? Did it really warrant an unadulterated scoffellow to my face?

"Yes. Me." Katya's not-so-delicate frame straightened. She pushed her shoulders back and raised her chin a few imperceptible millimeters. The adjustment bolstered her confidence a few imperceptible degrees.

"Well, how long has she been holding?" David asked.

"Um, not very...only..." Katya glanced back at her desk with trepidation. The angry orange light was giving her the middle finger.

"Are you going to *answer* that?"

"Y...yes." Katya scurried over to the phone and snatched up the receiver, her jitters replaced with indignation at David's sudden, bossiness. "Ms. Kennedy?" Katya peeped, not expecting her to still be holding.

"Yes."

And just like that, the jitters were back. Every first date/new experience/pop quiz/ public speaking butterfly that had ever lived descended on Katya with a fury; it was officially monarch season in her stomach.

"Hi. OK then. Yes, I'd be happy to speak with you about the opportunity to –"

"April twenty-sixth. Three-o'clock p.m. The Hotel Del Coronado. At the front desk, ask for Jennifer Yen. Any questions?"

"I –" Katya frantically tried to open her desktop calendar and simultaneously take notes. "OK then. April...um..."

"I'll wait." Again, Katya could practically feel Jeslyn's brazen superiority etching its way through the T3 phone line.

As if anyone needed to be reminded of how brazen or how superior she was.

Jeslyn Kennedy, founder of Foxxy Red Apparel and Accessories, had made quite a name for herself. Seemingly overnight, she'd become part of the self-made millionaire society. But that wasn't what had tongues wagging. A steamy letter, a risqué photo, a high profile venture capitalist who had been in a coma for the past nine months, and who was currently on life support, and no trace of the woman who appeared to be the only link tying those three things together is what had everyone's attention.

She was the topic of nearly every conversation these days, the only problem being the conversations were full of threadbare suppositions seeing as how Jeslyn had yet to come forward and voluntarily or involuntarily make a statement. Law enforcement had nothing on her that would warrant them hauling her into court or, what most people were secretly expecting, off to jail. And although a slew of major magazines, newspapers, blogs, news stations and an equal amount of non-major news outlets and rags wanted face time with her, no one had been able to get an interview.

Who was she? How had she made it to the upper half of the wealth pyramid so quickly and without so much as a blip on the radar beforehand, as if she'd simply materialized? And what was her role in the series of events that had resulted in Matt Coleman – founder of Coleman Ventures and a notable corporate magnate – falling into a coma that doctors weren't sure he'd come out of? The publishing and digital media world was sick with Kennedy fever.

Now, like a mysterious entrepreneurial Loch Ness Monster, she'd surfaced from unknown depths only to reveal herself to the most unlikely of sources – Katya Houston, Assistant Reporter Level I (as of approximately four days, two hours and 15 minutes ago) for *Gray Flannel Suit Magazine* – who couldn't even properly answer the phone but was requested by name by one of the media industry's hottest

7

interview prospects. This same enigmatic "it" girl wanted her to conduct one of the media industry's most sought after interviews.

"No, Ms. Kennedy, I have it. April twenty-sixth, three p.m. at the Hotel Del. I should ask for Jennifer Yen at the front desk."

Thankfully, there were two things that Katya did very well. The first was remember and the second was keep information confidential. She never forgot a face, a name, a place, a number, a time, an appointment, an author, a movie title — the list was endless. If it involved memory or confidentiality, she was a bona fide encrypted data server.

It was at this time that her phenomenal memorization capabilities kicked in and she remembered David Sims had been snippily hurling questions at her. But where was he now?

She briefly scanned the Pit and the Loft and caught sight of him flailing his arms in the face of Sara Jensen, Editor-in-Chief, the woman responsible for overseeing the magazine.

Sara, for her part, was raking her fingers through her short, spiky, brown hair, which only served to increase the spikiness of it. Her face was intensely stoic in comparison to David's over-animated one. Katya had been studying their exchange for a few seconds when David pointed in her general direction. Immediately, Sara's head snapped her way. Katya could see Sara's face contort into a look of absolute horror (or perhaps bewilderment, it was difficult to tell from her vantage point), then watched as Sara leaped into action. She pushed her way past David, threw open the door to her office and made a beeline toward the cubicle where Katya sat mesmerized at the sheer velocity of Sara in motion.

"Good." Jeslyn's cucumber-cool voice stole back Katya's attention. "I have a few other requests as well." Katya quickly reached for the nearest writing utensil and positioned it over the note-taking journal that lay to the right of her mouse.

"Continue." If Jeslyn was going to play hardball, Katya was going to have to suit up and at least look (sound) the part. She tried to blot out the human hurricane that was barreling toward her, but knew the storm would strike with a vengeance in a matter of seconds.

"When I say you do the interview, I mean you. Come alone." A hard-as-granite tone seeped into Jeslyn's voice. This sounded serious. Katya's mind began to race:

What if she's crazy? Is she going to try kill me or torture me? How did she make her money? What if she's tied to the mob or drugs or murder? Even as the various scenarios played out in her overactive imagination, each one more improbable than the next, Katya began jotting down a list:

1. Come alone.

"OK. Got it. Next." Before Jeslyn could continue, Sara and David were inside her cubicle. Sara immediately began using rudimentary sign language for her to do five things at once.

"This interview is yours. Not your boss', not your editor's, not any other reporter in your office. That means you come up with the questions, you conduct the interview and you write the story with your byline appearing as the author. No exceptions."

Katya was silent. Was that even possible? There was no way Sara would allow her to have full creative rights to the most exclusive story of the moment. That was no with a capital F. She tried to develop the most appropriate choice of words that would convey this impossibility to her caller – *the* Jeslyn Kennedy.

"I...I see. Would you mind if I placed you on hold one more time?" was all that came out. Katya cringed. Would Ms. Kennedy hold...again?

"Holding." It was delivered with what could only be described as sufferable patience. Katya, who had unknowingly been holding her breath, released it.

"Thank you. I won't be long." Before she could even turn around Sara's hands were on her shoulders.

"Tell me *everything*." Sara's eyes became two, intense rays.

Katya took a deep breath before running down the list of Jeslyn's requests. Sara's expression never changed as she absorbed every syllable spilling from Katya's lips. When the brief recount of events was complete, she waited for Sara to react. She imagined laughter or a Tourette-inspired diatribe. Instead, Sara bowed her head as if in prayer. Katya watched her expectantly.

Sara was a soft kind of thin; the type of thin that was more likely attributed to good genes or a fast metabolism rather than a healthy lifestyle. Her short hair accentuated the angular, hard lines of her worn facial features. The description, rode hard and put away wet, wasn't altogether inaccurate.

At long last (10 seconds had never taken so long) Sara spoke three words; three words that filled Katya with dread and elation all at once.

"Make it happen."

Katya responded immediately, practically sprinting the two-foot distance to her phone and successfully bringing Jeslyn out of the on-hold black hole. She felt as though she had resuscitated a dead person.

Tuning out David, who was quietly muttering his shock and disapproval, Katya did her best to exude confidence and poise as she collected the final pertinent details from Ms. Kennedy. Her fingers already itched to begin extensively researching her journalism talisman. This was sure to be a turning point in her fledgling career. Most seasoned professionals didn't get this type of opportunity, yet here it was, literally in the palm of her hand. It hadn't yet crossed her mind to contemplate the *how's*, *why's* and *what the hell's* of the whole thing; she just temporarily basked in it.

Sara stood beside her throughout the remainder of the call but graciously dismissed her Debbie Downer Features Editor. Once the call concluded, the two women went over everything.

"You know this is going to be huge." This statement followed on the heels of a brief moment of silence while Katya added notes to her never-been-used Moleskine writing journal.

Thank you, Captain Obvious. "Yes, it will...be...huge." What was there to say to that? Of course it was going to be huge.

"Do you think you can handle it?" Sara's steely gaze locked on Katya.

Before screaming out, 'yes, of course I can handle it,' Katya took time to actually mull the question over.

This was going to be *huge*. The weight of everything began to materialize. It was heavy, heavier than she'd stopped to consider. If things went well she'd be an 'it' girl herself. If things went poorly...oh, if things went poorly.

Katya let her thoughts graze in the field of possible failure. It gave her indigestion. Failure was simply not an option.

"Sara, I'm going to do the very best job I've ever done at anything in my life. I can't promise I won't make mistakes during the process, but what I do know is, I will do *GFS* justice, conduct an amazing interview and write a Pulitzer Prize-worthy article. I'm ready. Yes, I think I can handle this."

Maybe the *I Have a Dream* response was a bit overboard, but it was heartfelt and seemed appropriate given the circumstances.

In return, Sara gave a weak smile, one that seemed to say, 'I hope you're right.' Then, without much enthusiasm, she raised her hand like she was holding a wineglass, or perhaps a shot glass, and gave an imaginary toast. Katya reciprocated with a pantomime cheers of her own right before Sara excused herself to go 'collect her thoughts.'

Her boss hadn't even hit the Stairway to GFS Heaven when Katya once again had company. Fellow Pit coworker, Brandon Seltzer, who would've been better suited for a viper pit, slithered his way over. Katya tried to remember the last time that Brandon had so much as spared a fleeting look in her quadrant of the office; nothing came to mind. She had been intern pariah to him previously, and figured he either didn't know or didn't care that she was an official *GFS* employee (as of four days, four hours and twenty-five minutes ago.)

That's because Brandon was interested in only one thing. Brandon.

How to enhance his career and image, how to move up to the Loft, how to score brownie points with senior management, how to score, period, with Sara's Executive Assistant – who was most commonly referred to as the Loft Hottie. Not only did Brandon have a singular focus, he also had the moral aptitude of Rhoda Penmark. It bordered on disturbing the way he worked to appear admirable, like he was an all-around great guy, while polishing the handle of the blade that protruded from your back. Katya trusted him as far as she could see – if she were a blind woman trapped, in the dead of night, on the eve of a new moon, in a windowless, door less, concrete room tucked away beneath a mine shaft.

"Hey there, kid." Brandon, along with a so-strong-it-was-nearly-visible cloud of nauseatingly musky cologne, drifted into her cubicle as if a welcome sign had been erected there. Katya considered not saying anything to him at all, but knew this would not do. *GFS* was a huge place in terms of physical square footage, however, it became oh-so-small when it came to office politics.

"Hey'a sport." She managed a thin grin and watched his feathers ruffle. Brandon was used to being fawned over, in some form or another, by practically every office person with XX chromosomes. In Katya's opinion, his egotistical attitude and rude demeanor made him grossly unattractive. Besides, who did he think he was addressing her as kid? She was sure he couldn't be more than two years older than she was, if he was a day.

"There seemed to be a little commotion this a.m. around your general area." He moved his hands in a circular motion, like he was casting a spell. "I thought...did I see the Big Cheese and you gettin' kind of cozy over here? I think I did."

Did he just ask then answer his own question? I think he did. Katya stopped herself from shaking her head in disbelief.

"So, anything I, you know, should be aware of?" He lightly stroked his baby-smooth chin and tried to give off an air of casual indifference as he pressed his nose firmly into her business. Katya addressed him in a completely unaffected tone.

"Nope. We were just talking about a few business matters. Thanks for stopping by and checking on me, though; that's really nice of you." Katya watched his eyes glint with annoyance. She exhaled audibly before continuing. "Unfortunately, I'm really swamped at the moment in this general area." She, too, worked her hands in a spell-casting circular motion. "So, perhaps we can chit chat later when, you know, things slow down for me." She allowed her demi-grin to grow into a full one before standing and facing him full on.

Katya applauded herself for wearing four-inch heeled wedges on her first official day of employment, a dress code she normally shied away from. She came eye-to-eye with Brandon thanks to their assistance. Allowing the tension to warm just one degree past uncomfortable, she then edged past him.

"Just gonna go – " An awkward two-step ensued as Katya maneuvered around him, leaving her sentence and their interaction deliberately unfinished.

2

Katya's already light *GFS* plate had been completely cleared so that she could direct all of her attention to the colossal Jeslyn Kennedy entree she would be serving up in less than a month. Her eight-day window until the interview had already been whittled down by nearly 24 hours, and she felt no more prepared than she had nearly 24 hours ago.

Adding to her stress was the fact that this feature was scheduled to run in the June issue, which in actuality, dropped May 20th. That meant the proofs would have to be back from the printer no later than May 10th for final review and approval; which, in turn, meant her submission had a drop dead date of May 1st. All those dates combined meant Katya would have exactly five days post-interview to write, edit, rewrite, re-edit and deliver the complete, Pulitzer Prize-worthy article she'd promised Sara on, perhaps, the magazine's most explosive story of the year.

No pressure.

The June layout was already being put together. The editors and designers were having a field day analyzing article and advertising submissions, and rearranging like mad to accommodate this sudden change.

'Do you know how long the article will be?' They asked.

No.

'What about accompanying graphics and photos?'

14

Great question. I'll be sure to let you know...as soon as I know.

Just thinking about the possible directions the interview could take caused a heavy mist of fear to hang on Katya.

What was Sara thinking? She was an Assistant Reporter Level I, for crying out loud. Did Sara really have the confidence that she could pull this off, or would it be snatched from her after she'd completed the preliminary grunt work? What if the story was given to Brandon Seltzer? Katya shuddered at the thought. Worse yet, what if this was all just a dreadful ruse?

Not one prone to entertaining conspiracy theories, Katya tried to let those thoughts fall by the wayside. She was a nobody in the media and journalism world; there would be no point in ploys or ruses. Also, she had no enemies to speak of, neither in nor outside *GFS*. The little regard she was given around the office was genuinely amiable in nature by those who gave it. Besides, *GFS* was not the type of place that would waste manpower hours and resources on a bait and switch. If they were going to give this assignment to someone else, they would have already done it. The way it was looking, Sara probably would've given the story to her dementia-ravaged mother if it meant getting the exclusive scoop on this media lynx.

Yet and still, she couldn't let it go that this had all happened a bit too easily. Generally, things that were too good to be true were exactly that. Katya herself wondered if the caller was who she said she was – *the* Jeslyn Kennedy. Unfortunately, wondering was useless. This required action. It was now up to her to answer the question that had been purling through the halls and offices of many a newsroom over the past few months.

Who is Jeslyn Kennedy?

*　　*　　*

Over the next few days, Katya set to work trying to scrape together anything she could on Jeslyn and her possible association with the Matt Coleman scandal. Scrape being the operative word. It was as if new-fallen snow had covered the tracks of her past.

Katya started with a simple online search. Some random gossip blog posts offered sketchy back stories that hinted at mafia ties and Ponzi schemes. A WhoIs search on Jeslyn's business domains all came up private. Her LinkedIn page was photo-less and had only one connection – Jennifer Yen, Jeslyn's pseudonym, or perhaps alter ego? When she clicked over to the Jennifer Yen profile, it at least had an image of a Stradivarius cello as the profile picture. However, everything else mimicked Jeslyn's profile almost verbatim. One exception was that Jennifer's page listed biochemistry as an interest. Nothing else of note seemed to exist for either of the names.

Any news or press on Jeslyn's business ventures referenced quotes from, and contact info for, the company's VP of Communications, Tracy McGillan. It appeared that Tracy, for her part, did not believe in returning calls or emails. She seemed to be the VP of non-communication as far as Katya was concerned.

Being that this was the very beginning phase of the research process, Katya did her best not to become too disheartened by the lack of progress she was making. It was just extraordinarily peculiar that there were so few ripples out there for someone making such big waves. She made calls and pecked around online a bit more, looking over, under and in-between every rock, crevice and html cranny she could find or think of. Still nothing. Then, the smallest of breakthroughs accidentally, but quite literally, fell into her lap two days after the Jeslyn bomb had landed there.

It was fiesta Friday at the office – an event randomly concocted the previous morning by upper management seeking to boost morale. At least that was the reason given in the memo.

Katya's appetite was uncharacteristically low and had been for the past couple of days; the smell of greasy Mexican food did little to revive it. That being said, she hadn't packed on 19 pounds in the past four months by way of osmosis. She headed to the break room and loaded a paper plate with chips, salsa and two churros – the perfect midday meal of sedentary champions. Once she arrived back at her desk, after casually chatting with a few coworkers and absentmindedly consuming one of the churros (which meant she had to grab a third), she typed out notes on her computer with one hand while scooping salsa onto her tortilla chips with the other.

Overloading a chip and underestimating her left-handed dexterity resulted in a blob on her knee-length, khaki skirt. Not thinking to grab a napkin along with her calorically dense snack, Katya found herself staring objectionably at the red mess on her thigh.

"It's probably not the best solution, but it's all that I've got." If Brandon Seltzer was the office demon, Ethan Peters was its demigod. There he stood, less than a foot away, with attractiveness clinging to him like a tween to Justin Bieber.

"Oh, OK then." Katya, although not a deer-in-the-headlights wreck, was certainly blinded by science anytime Ethan was in the vicinity. She reached for the square envelope he extended her way.

"Whoops, let me just – " Ethan casually removed, what looked like, an invite from the envelope then offered it to her again, this time with an actual handoff. As she scooped chunks of tomato, onion and cilantro off of her with the makeshift trowel, he stood by making idle chit chat and increasing her resting metabolic rate. "It's some charity thing. I covered it a year or two ago, so they keep inviting me."

She caught only the tail end of his explanation, everything else had been drowned out by her daydreams starring Ethan.

"Cool. That's awesome, Ethan. Very cool." Katya, having taken on the challenge of using the word cool as many times as possible in one sentence, was spent. She'd come to the end of her communicating capabilities, thereby relegating herself to the position of gawking mute.

"Thanks...I think." Ethan's casual smile caused the heavens to open, allowing pure ecstasy to rain down onto her. "Well, I'm going to get back to my side of the Pit and try not to lose my lunch."

"Ha!" Make that a monosyllabic gawker.

"Oh, and let me know if I can help you out with anything. Marcy told us this is your first week as an employee. Congrats on officially becoming a *GFS* inmate."

All she heard was the word mate. A million tiny red fire engines crept up her neck and parked all over her face. She tried to cover it with humor. "Thanks...I think." Katya gave, what she hoped was, a come-hither grin; it probably looked more like indigestion. Ethan did not come hither. He tucked a chunk of golden brown, chin-length hair behind his ear then bid her adieu using the invite as the brim of an imaginary top hat and tipping it to her.

As soon as Ethan's back was turned and she deemed him a safe distance away, Katya dumped the salsa chunks into her wastepaper basket then examined the envelope. It was addressed to Ethan Peters using the office address (not a home address, sigh) and it was from a Heroes & Helpers non-profit organization. She put her search engine to use to look up details on this sliver of Ethan's life, and found information on the company's website in their About Us section:

Heroes & Helpers is a non-profit organization committed to the betterment of youth ages five to fifteen. We work to recruit, train and connect caring, committed, positive role models to serve as mentors, heroes and helpers in the lives of at-risk children and adolescents. Through uplifting engagement opportunities with empowering support figures, troubled kids and young adults are able to find a sense of purpose, interact with great leaders and establish a new life path.

Katya clicked the site's Events tab.

JOIN US!
DANCE UNDER THE STARS AT THE 'HEROES & HELPERS' CONSTELLATION BALL
MAY 2ND
7PM - 11PM
(Doors open at 6:30PM)

She wondered if Ethan was actually going to be attending this Constellation Ball, or if he only supported the organization monetarily. Perhaps there was information on that, too. With no idea what the search would yield, and less of an idea of what she would do with the information if anything worth knowing happened to come up, she did a search using keywords 'Heroes and Helpers Constellation Ball, donors, sponsor, attendees.' In 2.6 seconds, 1,725,063 search results populated her browser. However, it was the third listing on the page that caught her eye.

In her haste, Katya had failed to clear her last query. To that end, she'd inadvertently typed, 'Jeslyn Kennedy Heroes and Helpers Constellation Ball, donors, sponsors, attendees.' The result read: ***Heroes & Helpers*** *would like to thank...****donors*** *for their generous...****Kennedy, Jeslyn****...Kensington, Eve.*

Katya's pulse quickened once again, albeit for an entirely different reason. She clicked the url above the search result and found Jeslyn's name in a rather lengthy list of donors and supporters.

There was no way of knowing whether this was *the* Jeslyn Kennedy. There was also precious time being wasted contemplating this uncertainty. Katya decided it was more prudent to put her investigative skills to a more appropriate use — one that didn't involve e-stalking her colleague — and pay a visit to the Heroes & Helpers headquarters. She quickly browsed through a roster listed on the site to familiarize herself with the organization's staff and board members, then pinged Sara on the office's internal instant messaging system letting her know she would be out following up on a possible lead.

As she made her way from *GFS* to H&H, she went over her spiel; how she was going to get whoever it was she met to give her the skinny on Jeslyn — if it indeed was the same Jeslyn. The plan would have to be made on-the-fly. Katya wasn't a fan of on-the-fly. She preferred having time to think and prepare for a situation beforehand.

Too bad cupcake, she tried tough-talking herself. *This is journalism, not a freaking meditation clinic.* It was too tough, and she ended up apologizing to herself for the rest of her commute.

After finally scoring a parking spot, Katya made her way into the nondescript H&H building. An older woman with a kind face set down her crochet project and smiled at her warmly.

"Welcome to Heroes and Helpers. How can I help you today?"

"Hi there, I'm Katya Houston and I was wondering if I could..." Katya's mind began whirring. "...see some..." her eyes panned the area. "...material on do...donating to your organization." The words tripped and fell out of her mouth.

"Oh yes!" Ms. Crochet sprang to life, leaping out of the chair and making her way around the desk. "Let me introduce you to Patty. She's just great, you'll love her. Patty can explain all about our program and get you set up, dear." The woman placed her hand on the small of Katya's back and guided her down a spacious hallway with large windows on one side and battle ship tough, wooden doors with tarnished nameplates running along the other. The lack of window coverings created a perfect opportunity for the bright April sunlight to make itself at home in the broad linear space.

They came to an office that smelled of lavender and dusty books. Hunched over a desk, scribbling ferociously on a pad of paper was a very disheveled looking person of interest that Katya assumed was Patty. She didn't remember seeing that name on the roster she'd skimmed through (a lot of help that had been). The woman from the front desk stood in silence, still smiling, with her hand still lightly affixed to Katya's lower back. After a few seconds she cleared her throat softly, almost as if she feared a loud noise would send Patty completely over whatever edge she was veering towards.

"Patty? Dear?" It was said like a lullaby.

"Huh? Oh, yes. Hello there. Oh, I'm sorry." Patty seemed to address four different people before awkwardly pushing her chair back and standing to greet her two guests. "I was just working away, didn't even see you there. Come in, come in." Patty motioned excitedly for the two women to enter the office.

"Patty, this is Cara. She wants to make a donation." The older woman spoke in an eye wink, elbow nudge tone. Donations must have been few and far between.

"Oh! Oh, how wonderful. Very good, very good. Thank you, Irma. I'll take it from here." Patty was all smiles and hand flurries, like she was competing with the sun for a sunshine award. "Sit, Cara, please." Patty took her own advice and plopped back down in her office chair.

"Actually, it's Ka-" Katya tried sitting and correcting Patty on her name; two attempts that were thwarted by a sharp object jutting into her backside. "Yow!" She spun around to face her inanimate assailant.

"Is everything alright?" Patty furrowed her brows but otherwise made no movement to come to Katya's aid, as if a surprise assault were an everyday occurrence.

"Yes, it's just there's a...OK then." Katya removed the clear acrylic file stand and placed it on the desk on top of a pile of scattered folders, thinking that the folders might not be in such disarray if the stand was put to a use other than impaling people.

"So, how did you hear about us?" Patty's eyes gleamed.

"That's a great question, Patty."

In the world of sales, there's a technique called mirroring where a salesperson will mirror a person's body language and style of speech – a tactic designed to loosen their guard and make them feel comfortable. Katya amped up her smile and leaned forward, placing her hands on the desk, and mirroring Patty's posture.

"A friend told me about you guys, actually. He also mentioned that Jeslyn Kennedy is a supporter – I'm such a fan of hers – and I thought, 'If Jeslyn's on board, it must be a great cause.' So, I came out to see for myself."

Patty beamed as she leaned back in her chair and clasped her hands together. "Oh, that's spectacular! Well, let me tell you what we do then show you around."

Katya leaned back and pressed her own hands together excitedly. "Oh, you don't have to do that. I've done my due diligence and feel really confident in what you all have going on here." Then it was time to turn the boat around back to its intended destination. "After all, it's Jeslyn Kennedy we're talking about here." Katya toned down her enthusiasm in order to convey her deep awe. She crossed her legs demurely and placed her hands in her lap.

There's a second half to the mirroring sales technique that lets the salesperson know if he's winning over his prospect. After mirroring the customer for awhile, the salesperson will stop and execute a completely different yet subtle movement. If the customer feels comfortable, they will then begin mirroring the salesperson. It was at this time that Patty's huge smile fell to a serene grin and she angled her body forward, ever so slightly, crossing her legs at the ankle and allowing her hands to drift towards her lap.

"Isn't she remarkable?" Patty's voice was tinged with wonderment.

"She *is*," Katya breathed. "Have you spent much time with her?"

"Not as much as I'd like, I'll tell you that. We were just so surprised when Forbes brought her to the gala. Well, first we were surprised Forbes came to the gala, period, but then when we saw he'd brought a date and it wasn't that floozy he'd been dating – no one liked her much – well, we were just shocked. In a good way, mind you." Patty's words came out in a constant stream as if someone had turned a water hose on inside her. "So, I said to Irma, 'Irma, will you look at that. Forbes is here *and* he has a girl with him!' Irma was just as shocked as I was, I'll tell you that. Well, it was only appropriate for me, you know, being the new Development Director and all, to go and introduce myself. So, that is just what I did."

Katya didn't butt in to ask any questions even though she had plenty. *What gala? Forbes? Floozy?* Instead, she just watched and listened.

Patty's plump frame filled her worn office chair. Her shoulder length brown hair, made up of random waves and curls that didn't quite fall into any sort of a style category, bounced along her jaw line as she spoke. Her hazel pupils were filled with mirth even though they struggled to be seen through droopy eyelids and thin, mascara-caked eyelashes. She couldn't have been on the other side of 45, however, deep wrinkles laid claim to the areas around her mouth and neck. Sun-aged skin, smattered with freckles, played the role of canvas to coral and beige baubles that hung from her necklace and lay unceremoniously over her décolletage. To complete the frumpy look, trace amounts of blonde dog hair clung to her black, cotton, v-neck top. While her appearance murmured dowdy, her personality screamed vivacious.

She continued. "She's very pretty, you know, but very kind. And, we hear, quite wealthy now, too. Even if it might come with a bit of trouble," she whispered the last word. "That's a shame she's wrapped up in that mess. You know, with that senator and all." He was actually a venture capitalist, but Katya let the error slide. "I don't know if she always was — wealthy, that is. I've heard she comes from pretty humble beginnings, but I suppose that's a different story. All in all, she's just a really sweet girl. Well, once you get to know her. At first she can be a little standoffish, but she just warms right up with a smile, I'll tell you that." Patty gazed off into the distance, lost in her own reverie.

"So, did she ever discuss her work or family or anything like that?" Katya made an attempt to marry an air of neutrality with a tone of genuine interest.

"Oh, no, nothing like that. Come to think of it, she never really spoke about herself at all. Listen to me, talking as if we were the best of friends. I really only saw her a couple of times. One of our other donors did mention something about her, though. She works in the same building with that judge; you know, the poor man who's in ICU now. Anyway, *she* said she could've sworn she saw Jeslyn coming out of his office a few days before that accident." Patty stopped suddenly. "Whoops! Gossip. That's enough of that. Uh oh, I've done it now." She then proceeded to giggle like a Catholic schoolgirl experiencing her first buzz. "Ah yes, but other than that, no, I can't say I've heard much else about her."

"I see, I see." Katya smiled warmly as if she too had been sipping from the same cup and was just as giddy as her Heroes and Helpers informant.

"So, Cara, what type of donation are you looking to make today?"

And this was how a seat-of-your-pants strategy sometimes fell apart at the seams. Katya was now perfectly fine with everyone calling her Cara.

"Oh, yes, well, you see," she knew even before she said it that it was the absolute wrong thing to do, but that did very little to stop her. "I seem to have forgotten my purse." She bounced a palm against her forehead. "However, maybe you could mail me information. I'd like to stay in touch with the organization."

"Of course!" Patty's enthusiasm was back. She turned to a large, black brick on her desk. The laptop looked so ancient Katya wasn't sure it would work; it looked more like an artifact. "What's your mailing information?"

Katya, requesting that any correspondence be addressed to Ms. Houston as the intended recipient, rattled off her parent's home mailing address. She was sure her mother would make some sort of donation. It seemed like a cause the older Houston woman would support.

After finishing up their goodbye's, which included hugs from both Patty and Irma, Katya left the Heroes and Helpers offices feeling better than she did before. Finally having some relevant information gave her hope.

Figuring she'd concentrate better at home than at *GFS*, Katya made the trek back to her Carlsbad studio. Her first order of business was looking up who this Forbes character was. And look up she did.

Katya found herself wishing the interview was with him instead. Aside from the fact that he belonged on a Times Square billboard in his underwear, there was a motherload of information on him. Forbes Keith, renowned biochemist. Something instantly clicked. Biochemist. Biochemistry. Jennifer Yen's LinkedIn profile. Her hobby.

Well played, Ms. Kennedy.

Maybe clues that were as obvious as the nose on her face were everywhere – if one knew where to look. The gauntlet had been thrown and Katya accepted the challenge. She'd play Jeslyn's game whether Jeslyn had actually initiated a game or not. In any event, Katya planned to be one step ahead of her interviewee. This piece *would* be Pulitzer-worthy. The world of Jeslyn Kennedy darkness was about to be shown the light.

3

The morning of the interview, Katya awoke before six a.m. without the aid of her alarm clock. She had a debriefing with Sara and a couple of editors and designers at nine a.m., and a noon lunch she'd foolishly promised to her best friend, LeAnn. It was poor timing and it stressed Katya out that she'd allowed herself to be guilted into spending the few precious hours she had before possible career sovereignty (or suicide) stuffing her face with her best female confidante. But LeAnn wouldn't have it any other way.

"It's not my fault you've been too busy playing Walter Cronkite to meet with me." LeAnn sidled into the cozy, oversized booth at BJ's Restaurant. "I already know what I want, so make it snappy. I almost picked a fry off of an ugly stranger's plate on our way to the table, I'm *that* hungry."

Katya smirked as she perused the Encyclopedia Brittanica of menu options. LeAnn Cairling was bossy, stubborn and the best friend a girl could have; a sister, really. It had been ages since they'd seen each other, seven days to be exact. In Katya and LeAnn's worlds that was practically a lifetime.

"I'm hurrying, I'm hurrying."

All Katya wanted was dessert. She knew she should have a salad or something equally light and healthy, but her fingers flicked past the more prudent options to the back where the sweets were listed. She reasoned that if she had dessert now, by the time her blood sugar levels dropped she'd be in the interview, which would cause her adrenaline to spike. That spike would, in turn, not only combat the effect of her low blood sugar, but also burn calories. It was a sound argument; dessert for lunch it would be. Katya completely pushed aside the fact that she'd also had kid cereal and buttered toast for breakfast. It was never good to dwell on the past.

"Oh man, so many RMs to go over." LeAnn began looking through their texts from the past week.

'RM' stood for 'Remind Me'. If something happened that couldn't be expressed in 140-180 characters or less, the two women simply texted 'RM', and a few words to remind them what needed to be discussed in detail later. For example, Katya already knew she'd be sending a text that said, 'RM-the Jeslyn interview.' Previous RMs had ranged from, 'RM-the guy behind me in the grocery store' to 'RM-2am panic attack abt penises.'

After a day or so, or sometimes even a few hours after seeing each other, they'd get together to go over all the RMs – the system was flawless. That was unless, in an attempt to not divulge too much and waste the point of sending an RM, there was too little info in the clue or too much time had lapsed and one or the other forgot what their RM was even about.

"OK, but can we go over them later? I have to be in Coronado at two o'clock." Katya set the menu on the edge of the table.

"Seriously? It's only twelve fifteen, Kat. What the hell am I supposed to talk to you about while we're sitting here? Should I take a vow of silence for the next hour?"

"At this point, that'd be nice." Katya turned to the waitress that had approached their table and placed her order. She could hear LeAnn muttering under her breath, her lips forming words better suited for a frat house than a lunch table.

"So, are you nervous?" LeAnn propped her elbows on the table and stared intently at Katya.

"Does Pinocchio have wooden balls? Yeah, I'm nervous."

"About what, exactly?"

"Well, for starters, this chick could be a lunatic. I'm actually not super worried about that, but it's not out of the realm of possibilities. Two, for a rock star entrepreneur turned possible murderess, there's very little information about her anywhere; that's just really weird. And C, let's say she's this perfectly normal multi-millionaire who has nothing to do with this Coleman scandal everyone's talking about, I still have to write an insanely brilliant article about her, and I'm not even sure she'll tell me anything all that interesting." There was a brief pause before LeAnn spoke

"Yeah, you're screwed," she said glibly before gulping down her water.

"Thank you for that. Honestly, exactly what I needed right now." Katya sighed.

"You're welcome." LeAnn noisily crunched the ice cubes from her glass. "I'm kidding, Kat. Hey, look at me. You're going to do great. You know it, I know it, that woman over there who can't seem to get enough of our conversation knows it," she turned her head to the right and stared down the eavesdropper, forcing the lady to become overly engrossed in the utensils on her table and the napkin in her lap. "You're just doing the thousand deaths things again. Don't do that."

"I know, I know." LeAnn was referring to Katya killing herself with worry a thousand times over instead of just dying the one death that everyone faced eventually. "OK, I'm stopping now."

"No, you're lying now, but that's OK. I love liars, they're my favorite type of people."

"You're right, I am lying now." Katya dropped her head onto the table; it was all she could do not to bang it. "Wait, why are liars you're favorite type of people?" She lifted her head for the answer.

"Huh? Oh, I don't know," LeAnn sounded as if she'd already forgotten what she'd said. "It sounded good, I guess. Hey, you know what would take your mind off of this?" LeAnn's train was already leaving the station. Katya found herself running along side of it, barely able to keep up, let alone get on board. "RMs. And guess who happens to have some."

And just like that, LeAnn kept Katya's attention diverted like a playful kitten with a ball of yarn. She shared stories from her job as a professional photographer, a random dream she'd had of being chased by fairies, and a newly acquired fear of rolly pollies. By the time the duo were through laughing about the client who had to keep being told to literally keep his shirt on for a professional headshot; analyzing what it meant to be chased by mythical creatures (they deduced LeAnn was feeling overwhelmed by her life ambitions); and agreeing that rolly pollies were, indeed, creepy and could take over the world if they had a mind to, it was a little after one.

"I gotta get going. You've got this, right?" Katya cocked her head toward the check. "No more fun money from mommy and daddy. I'm a poor, starving journalist now."

"Ha! Yeah right. I know all about your trust fund, remember?" she joked. "Yes, I've got it. Get out of here and go make history. Text me as soon as it's over." LeAnn stood to give her a quick hug. "I have so much faith in you." She whispered the words with conviction.

"Thanks." Katya gave one final squeeze before power walking to the parking lot. Stepping out into the marine-layered, semi gray of that Thursday afternoon, she felt like Neil Armstrong. Getting into her car was one small step for an Assistant Reporter Level I, and conducting this interview was one giant leap for all assistant-kinds. She decided Armstrong's quote was infinitely grander.

Katya arrived in Coronado in a little under 40 minutes. The near nausea she felt made her only partially regret her decision to double down on not one, but two confection-rich meals.

She scoured the area for any sign of anyone that might be Jeslyn. The problem was she had only a slim idea of what Jeslyn actually looked like. She had scored a grainy, lo-res image of her at some event with Forbes Keith – the affectedly handsome biochemist Jeslyn had some connection to. A connection that Katya was guessing was romantic in nature.

She allowed her thoughts to dip into a pool of fantasy, wondering what it must be like to be held in esteem by a man like that. Hell, what it was like to be held by a man like that, period. Katya had been told, on more than a few occasions, that she had a 'nice personality' and a 'cute face.' Descriptions that were more condemnation than commendation, in her opinion. She'd tried to lose weight on numerous occasions. Then a donut or a day and a half of immobility after a visit to the gym reminded her why losing weight was simply not for her. Willpower in the areas of diet and exercise wasn't her strong suit. She glanced down at her small pooch of a belly.

Obviously.

Katya didn't want to stay in the car but she didn't want to get out either. She was an hour early and certain that had to be poor etiquette in some form or another. She opted to sit tight and go over her approach.

Far too many reasons shook a finger at the distinct likelihood that Jeslyn Kennedy wasn't just looking to do an interview. It was unsettling operating under that auspice; the one that hinted at the possibility that she, and perhaps *GFS Magazine* as a whole, were being played. There had to be an agenda. She didn't get the feeling it was a sinister agenda, but an agenda nonetheless. Like a good psychological thriller, Katya merely had to figure out what that was before the final scene, and without letting her adversary know she knew. Then, all that was left was to turn the tables and crack the case.

A total breeze.

Nothing more would be solved while she sat in her car, so she went over her notes and questions for the next fifty minutes instead. She then made her way into the main lobby of the Hotel del Coronado.

The Queen Anne's style architecture and iconic red roof, with its signature turrets, was only the icing on the decadent treat that was the hotel. As if the exterior wasn't enough, the swanky two-story grand lobby with its Illinois oak paneling, statement chandelier and plush carpeting underneath her feet as she stepped inside, only served to increase the magic without being de trop. It was a veritable Currier and Ives lithograph come to life. Painstaking care appeared to have been taken to create a very distinct mood, and despite the Kate Morgan ghost stories that still circulated, macabre was not the vibe she was getting. It was opulence, like tequila directly from a blue agave plant – pure, rich, undistilled opulence.

The well-heeled woman at the concierge desk seemed like she had been born and bred for the sole purpose of working there. When asked, 'how may I assist you today?' Katya explained, as instructed, that she had a meeting with Jennifer Yen.

It wasn't so much that the woman's entire demeanor changed, as it seemed she conducted the remainder of their interaction with an air of, what could only be described as, increased respect.

She picked up the phone and dialed a few numbers before announcing to whoever was on the other end of the line that Ms. Houston had arrived. Not more than two minutes later a hand was on her shoulder.

"Ms. Houston." It was a statement, not a question, but Katya responded anyway.

"Yes, that's me."

"I'm Tracy McGillan."

So, this was Mrs. I-Can't-Return-A-Freaking-Phone-Call. Instead of aggravation, Katya felt nearly euphoric.

There was a real face to put with the name, and a pleasant face at that.

Katya couldn't tell if Tracy's features were derived from Spanish, Brazilian or some other Latin influence, but they weren't unpleasant by any means. She was older than Katya, but by how much, she was uncertain. If the woman at the front desk was well-heeled, Tracy was well-everything'ed. Katya had no idea about fashion, designers or material, but she knew expensive. Her mother was a new-girl-on-the-block designer whore who had forced an appreciation for quality on Katya. Tracy appeared to be quality's mascot.

Her suit jacket and matching slacks were cream; the type of cream that seemed almost edible. Katya marveled at the ensemble, in awe at how people kept themselves stain-free dressed like that? Snakeskin taupe, black and charcoal stilettos kissed her feet as if they were grateful that *she* decided to wear *them*. A silk white camisole with lace trim stood out under her jacket. That same camisole worked diligently to conceal Tracy's ogle-worthy chest, allowing just a hint of cleavage to peek out.

Katya was immediately aware of her own spoon-shape, and a chest that could easily be mistaken for a 12-year-old girl's. She was dressed appropriately in black pinstriped Capri slacks, a crisp white linen shirt that sported statement ruffles down either side of the buttons, peep-toe black sling backs, and pearl accessories. Still, Tracy made her feel like a hobo, towering a good three or four inches above Katya's squatty five-foot-three-inch frame.

Tracy began walking to the lobby entrance and out its doors, leaving Katya to fall in line behind her (it was too stressful to walk beside her). They walked in silence, down a short path until they came to what looked like cottages on the beachfront.

She has her own house at the hotel?

Katya was not familiar with the hotel's accommodations or the fact that guest's could stay in a private beachfront villa. That was, guests who could afford to shell out upwards of twenty-five grand for an all-out luxe experience.

The svelte Miss McGillan (or perhaps Mrs., her left hand was devoid of any wedding ring or revealing tan line) walked through a gated area, silently entered one of the villas, then motioned for Katya to take the lead in front of her.

"Jeslyn's in the sitting room." She smiled curtly, then turned on her snakeskin heels and disappeared into another room that was not the sitting room.

Shit.

She might as well have said, 'there's a monster waiting to rip the skin from your bones in the sitting room.' Katya's palms became sweaty and her mouth filled with cotton.

A thousand deaths, a thousand deaths, a thousand deaths.

Katya's heart was taking running leaps and ramming itself against her ribcage. She placed her hand over it as if pledging allegiance to her runaway fear, feeling like Katniss taking the place of her sister in the Hunger Games. Somehow she convinced her body to move, putting one foot in front of the other until she reached the sitting room and came face to face with *the* Jeslyn Kennedy.

Patty at Heroes and Helpers had been right about one thing: Jeslyn was very pretty. Gorgeous. Katya had conjured up this image of Jeslyn as an older woman, perhaps even a little masculine-looking; something befitting a bootstrapping, powerhouse entrepreneur. In reality, Jeslyn looked like Beyonce and Halle Berry's lovechild – that is, if it were possible for two women to conceive a child. If she were realistically taking biology into account, then her concoction of beauty would also have a dash of Boris Kodjoe, circa 1998. A light dusting of British Formula One racing driver, Lewis Hamilton, would round out the mixture and account for her unbelievably youthful appearance.

Her cafe au lait skin held not even a trace of a blemish. High cheekbones; big, brown, round eyes prominently displaying a cluster of sweeping eyelashes, and plump full lips simultaneously clamored for Katya's visual attention. Her midnight-black, knee length, skintight, cotton dress accentuated an hourglass figure that stood out even from her seated position. Katya's eyes nearly crashed and burned in the dangerous curves created by Jeslyn's waist and hips. She could easily see Twitter topics about her being followed using the tag #knockout.

Where Patty had been mistaken was Jeslyn's demeanor. She didn't seem standoffish, she seemed downright pissed. Katya knew she hadn't done anything to upset the woman, but that didn't mean she couldn't take on the burden of feeling as though she was solely responsible for the sour countenance hanging on her face like a badge. Like some medal of honor. Like her face couldn't be more proud to look that unfriendly.

It was obvious Jeslyn could have sat there allowing Katya to stare in stupefied silence for at least half an hour. Katya, though, couldn't bear it.

"Hi, Jeslyn. Katya Houston, *GFS Magazine*. May I?" Katya indicated the chair opposite Jeslyn, but didn't wait for a reply before claiming it. The empty chair was obviously intended for her. "OK then, I'm just going to get situated here." Katya began removing contents from her Michael Kors leather messenger bag, a gift from her father a few years back.

She tried to make small talk as she set up her interim work station. More like tiny talk considering how shrunken her throat felt.

"So, do people ever call you 'J' or Jess or anything?" It took so long for Jeslyn to answer, Katya wondered if she had even heard her. She stopped momentarily to glance up at her.

"No," came the brusque reply.
OK then. This should be fun.

Katya made up her mind to conduct the interview according to her original grand design – from a position of strength. Even though her design was looking less grand as time wore on, even though her buoyancy had no buoy, even though Jeslyn was batting 1000 and Katya couldn't seem to lift her bat, and even though she hadn't figured out exactly where she was going to derive this strength from. Notwithstanding all of that, Katya was counting on a few surprises to knock the stone right off the mogul's pretty little face.

4

Jeslyn had swiped her questions. Katya tried to remain calm, but her interviewee's pithy responses – correction, response – and unflappable expression had her distressed. If it weren't for Jeslyn's eyes zipping back and forth across the paper, she could have easily been mistaken for a wax statue.

Then there was a power surge. She could almost feel the crackle of tension in the air when Jeslyn reached it. The question. She couldn't be sure, but she guessed that Jeslyn hadn't expected her to be armed with any personal information about her, perhaps with any information at all.

Take that, Kennedy!

She wondered what was going on inside Jeslyn's head and if she'd ever get the opportunity to find out. The bloated seconds struggled to army crawl by.

"This is how we're going to do this." These were the next words out of Jeslyn's mouth. She certainly didn't mince them. "I'll formulate the questions as well as answer them. I think we'll make better progress that way."

Katya could not read the between the lines of what she'd said but felt something was there.

"OK then. Am I at liberty to interject?" Confident yet humble; it was going to be a delicate tightrope to walk.

"That's fine. Let's begin, shall we?" Jeslyn leaned over and handed the sheet of questions back to Katya.

"Thank you." What Katya really wanted to say was, 'hallelujah!' However, she sensed that would not be a well received response.

"So, Katya Houston, Assistant Reporter Level I, your father is a psychologist, your mother is a Hospital Director, your older brother a surgeon and your younger sister a lawyer. What does the Houston clan make of your career trajectory?"

She had her at 'Assistant.' Was this for real? Disimpassioned, Jeslyn had rattled off the details of Katya's life as if she had a case file in front of her. There was most definitely an ulterior motive to this shtick. While she didn't know how much information about her existed in a cursory search, she was certain more than a cursory search had been done to gain that much detail about her life. That wasn't just the skinny on her; there was fat and even some bone in there, too.

Katya's resiliency began to erode. Her posture went from awkwardly casual to ramrod straight. She wrestled with her composure but tried to come off as unaffected; spirited efforts that were commendable if nothing else. She had been caught off guard, which seemed like precisely the effect Jeslyn had been aiming for. Her belief that she'd wielded the element of surprise with her Forbes question appeared to have been thwarted. Jeslyn stared her down with a look that said, 'Ah, so much to learn little grasshopper. This interview is going to happen, but on my terms.'

"They're not too pleased, actually." Katya quickly regained her equilibrium. "We haven't spoken in awhile. They feel as though I'm dabbling in a dead-end career and they're waiting for me to come to my senses. There's a strong possibility I've been disowned." Since killing her with kindness hadn't crumbled Jeslyn's Berlin Wall, Katya figured she would try TKO through TMI.

You want to know my life. OK then, I'll tell you my life. I'll tell you so much about my life that you squirm from the insane amount of intimate details. Be careful what you ask for, Kennedy.

Although an introvert by nature, Katya was more reserved than shy, meaning she could be direct when necessary although it was a secondary language.

"Since you know this much, perhaps you're also aware that my parents nearly divorced over the whole thing. My father was adamant that I attend USC and major in either medicine, law or business – USC being the obvious choice because of its Keck School of Medicine, Gould School of Law and Marshall School of Business. A perfect trio of professional achievement all on one campus, he'd said.

"Even though he was pushing for another doctor or lawyer in the family, he would've settled for stock broker, psychiatrist, pharmacist or top-level executive at a reputable company." Katya fell into a stride, never once taking her eyes off of Jeslyn's even though her muscles, taut and strained with tension, ached from the effort.

"I tried the business route, gave it a good two and a half years, but was bored to tears. Truth be told, I almost killed myself over it – un…unintentionally." She didn't want the woman to think she was suicidal. "It happened one night as I was driving back to campus. I was crying so hard, trapped in this state of depression and sheer emotional exhaustion, that I completely missed a sharp curve in the road. I drove off a steep embankment, rolled the car and ended up in the hospital. After that, I told myself I wasn't going to live my parents' dream anymore. So, I switched my major from Business to Journalism, unbeknownst to dear ol' Mr. and Mrs. Houston. Lucky for me, unfortunately for them, USC is also known for its Annenberg School of Journalism.

"My mother found out first, although right now it escapes me how. Nevertheless, she spent a few weeks pleading, threatening and trying to bribe me to switch back. I had gotten a full ride – which is an entirely different story altogether – so, it wasn't as if she could force me to do what she wanted by refusing to pay for my schooling. When it was clear I was committed to this new path, she told my father. He flipped out and they began arguing over whose fault it was I was sabotaging my life this way. Then they argued about the fact my mother didn't tell him immediately what I'd done; something about 'harboring the fugitive' mentality. I was still getting some financial assistance from them and my father got angry that my mother, who handles the family finances, was continuing to let me enjoy a 'free ride on his dime.' Yes, he actually said that."

"Was it worth it?" Jeslyn's question stopped Katya cold. Not because of what she asked, it was the *way* she asked. There seemed to be no feeling at all. Her robotic tone was almost strident in its aloofness.

"Yes." It was an answer Katya didn't have to think twice about. She noticed the subtle movement of Jeslyn unclenching her locked jaw before signaling for Katya to continue.

"OK then, um...so, yeah. Let's see." Katya had momentarily lost her stride but picked it back up quickly. "Oh yes, then came the period where no one in my immediate family was allowed to talk to me. If they did, they'd be an outcast as well. My father wasn't the ringleader on that one, surprisingly enough, that order came from my mother. The sad part is, during that time where I was essentially in exile, my parents reconciled. Somehow, distancing themselves from me brought them closer together. My brother keeps telling me that isn't true, but the chain of events are rather compelling to the contrary, if you ask me.

"Anyway, I worked all through college, random gigs here and there, made a couple of good connections and landed an internship at *GFS Magazine* after I graduated. I interned at *GFS* for nine months, did some more odd jobs on the side to make ends meet, stayed out of the nest egg I'd saved up when my parents were generous with their wallet, got hired on full time at the mag and now, here we are." Katya's meekness finally caught up with her. She instinctively shut her mouth, hoping her face wasn't flushed, knowing it was.

"Friends? Boyfriend?" Jeslyn didn't seem to mind the rambling. Katya wondered if her verbal diarrhea was taming this feisty beast of a woman; since the more Katya spoke, the less Jeslyn had to. Regret may have been too strong a word to describe it, but Katya got the distinct impression Jeslyn was not completely thrilled about the decision to do a formal interview. Even if it had been at her request.

"I have a best friend, LeAnn. I work with a lot of really great people, and a couple not-so-great people. I've got a nice-sized extended family and what not, just not a lot of time. I suppose that includes time for friends as well as boyfriends. In college it was school, studying and work. After college it was the internship and work. And now, well..." Katya's sentence was left hanging like laundry on a clothesline.

I've barely been hired on and it's been a crazy eight day countdown preparing for an interview with you.

"Anyone you've got your sights set on once this super busy life you're living slows down?" Katya could not figure out where Jeslyn's level of interest was coming from or going. One thing was certain, she obviously wasn't taking into account what Katya must be thinking or if this little Q&A segment (which was becoming more of a 'Grill & Answer' segment) was a bit too much.

"Oh..." Katya's thoughts immediately went to Ethan Peters. He was perfection. He was brainy, but in a very smooth, isn't-it-cool-to-be-this-brainy, kind of way. He was also kind, distractingly attractive and, knowing her luck, most likely unavailable. "I...well..." She didn't want to talk about her secret crush – hence the word secret. But wasn't she supposed to be making Jeslyn squirm with how intimately open she could be? Now who was squirming? "There's this guy I work with, but, yeah, no. He's, um, off limits." Katya lowered her eyes.

"Do your parents know you're interviewing me today?" Jeslyn asked.

"Do my...oh, um, not that I'm aware of. No." Katya was thrown, yet again, by Jeslyn's red light-green light conversation style. What that question had to do with the price of milk in Sudan was unknown. "I may have mentioned it earlier, maybe not, but I'm not really on speaking terms with my parents. They consider my current, how did you phrase it – career trajectory – to be sort of a slow, professional suicide. In their minds I wasted my college experience and am now intentionally throwing my life away. I believe it's safe to say they couldn't care less that I'm doing an interview."

Jeslyn continued with the random inquiries.

"Do you live far from here?"

Katya could not keep up. The woman seemed to be all over the board. Who cared where she lived, if her parents knew she was doing an inter– It was then that an irrational level of concern hit her.

Is this the part where she kills me? Is she trying to gauge whether or not anyone will miss me? I just had to go and give her every little detail of my life, didn't I? Now I'm going to die.

Katya's left-brain logic plugged the drain on her panicked line of thinking that was quickly spiraling out of control and taking all sense and sensibility with it.

Don't be silly, she argued silently. *Get it together, Houston, it's just an interview.*

"No. I live fairly close by." While not exactly true (as in, not true at all), Katya felt she should take back a smidgen of privacy. "Why do you ask?" Her voice crippled slightly, but she held her chin steady.

"Well," Jeslyn hesitated. "I've taken up quite a bit of time already. I was gauging the rest of our time together, seeing as how we haven't even begun the interview."

Relief spread through Katya like warm urine down a pant leg – soothing at first but something she couldn't enjoy, knowing it would soon become noticeably uncomfortable. "Ah, I see. No, it's fine. Like I said, I live fairly close by – well, Carlsbad actually – so, I'm good."

Chatty much?

Katya, once again, scolded herself for opening her personal bean bag and spilling the contents. Only, it didn't really feel like an invasion of her privacy. The cold apathy she'd sensed earlier had been replaced with (could it be?) a hint of interest.

"Alone?" Another random question jumped from Jeslyn's lips.

"Yes. I like it, though. In fact, when I retire, it will probably be to Bali or someplace equally remote, yet beautiful. As long as I have water and sand, I can get by." Katya smiled for the first time since arriving at the hotel. Her face felt stiff, her lips dry, and she worried her smile would come across as a grimace. To her astonishment, the left side of Jeslyn's full lips curled upward.

Katya shifted in her seat and was suddenly hit with an urge she could no longer ignore. "I'm sorry, do you have a restroom I could use?" All the liquid she had consumed that day seemed to rush to her bladder at once. Once Jeslyn had given her turn-by-turn directions to the bathroom, she excused herself quickly.

* * *

With Katya gone, Jeslyn had time to think. Her first thoughts were that Katya's replies had impinged upon her suddenly and unexpectedly. This young, entry-level reporter appeared to be a fighter, a quiet soldier. A subtle feeling of empathetic admiration began to develop inside Jeslyn and her guard, although not completely down, was no longer as adamantly aggressive.

In fact, Jeslyn found herself beginning to like this Katya person more and more. She caught glimpses of herself, glimpses of who she'd like to be, and panoramic views of someone completely opposite of her in Katya's thick-bodied package. Altogether, it was pleasant. She longed to keep their idle chit chat going but knew she had done enough inquiring. It was now her turn to share.

The situation did not call for reciprocity, only the minimum facts. Considering how anything Jeslyn divulged would end up in print for thousands of people to read, a quid pro quo arrangement was not expected nor warranted. Still, Jeslyn's frame of mind, as it pertained to the interview, was changing.

Initially, she had simply wanted to set a few records straight. She was not a murderer, a recluse or deranged, she just didn't like people butting into her business. And ever since He had come along, her life had been altered. So much had transpired with Him so quickly and then stopped transpiring with Him so quickly. She wanted Him to know she wasn't the woman in the headlines. The best way to do that was to change the headlines.

The rumor mill was so out of control it was now practically mandatory that she speak out. After all, this was the very thing that she was expressly against – negative clamor. Staying quiet in the midst of all of the hoopla was an option, just not one that would help her still-developing business platform.

Jeslyn made up her mind to give this Level I reporter a real interview; one that would wrap its hand in the frazzled hair of the media and slam it's face into concrete reality.

A twinge of something vaguely familiar infected her conscience.

Vulnerability.

Could she really do this, tell the *entire* story? There were so many sleeping dogs (and dogs in comas) that she did not want to disturb, so many rocks that she was quite content to leave unturned. Plus, how was she going to break the news that she planned to turn Katya's recording device into a confessional booth. She barely noticed as Katya rushed back into the room, muttering an apology for something she had no reason to apologize for, and settled back into her seat.

There was little time to change her mind. Jeslyn's so-called resolute decision to give a piece de resistance interview was a pot she would have to either use or get off of. She was almost tempted to ask for that stupid questionnaire sheet back, but didn't give in to the temptation. That was a coward's route. Besides, what did she have to lose?

Everything.

Despite her tendency to throw stones in someone else's glass house, Jeslyn was very much against those stones being lobbed in her direction. That was probably the case with most people; only she had taken great pains to keep the area surrounding her personal space stone free. Was she really going to dump a wheelbarrow of ammunition into the media sphere because of one young, assistant reporter (she wasn't even a full-fledged reporter for pity's sake).

Katya's goofy grin was slowly fading. Too much time was passing, time drenched in silence. Katya was waiting for her to say something, not just something, the truth. She deserved that, Jeslyn thought, even if the rest of the world – the portion that cared anyway – didn't.

"I suppose we should get down to business," she said wearily.

Katya, looking anxious for the actual interview (of Jeslyn, not herself) to finally begin, grabbed the notebook that had slid from the top of her thighs to her knees, along with the pencil she had tucked behind her ear. Since she was no longer running the show and was being spoon-fed both question and answer, she waited, mouth slightly agape, for the first bite.

"I suppose the best place to start would be the beginning."

Oh, but there were so many beginnings. Did she start with her childhood? Did she tell this perfect stranger about her family? Did she begin with Him? Her thoughts went to the first time she'd met Him in person. She had been on Katya's side of this equation, in the interviewing chair. Would she tell that story? He didn't even know that story. No one knew. Plus, what would other people think?

Screw everyone else, what will He think?

"The beginning is always good." Katya interrupted Jeslyn's internal tug-of-war with reassuring words. Her expectant, eager gaze and subtle nods were all so innocent, so bright.

If you only knew what you're about to know...

Jeslyn wished she had a vice she could reach for – a cigarette, a stiff drink. Regrettably, those were not her poisons. Hers were internal. She gulped down one of those defects now and allowed the pungent sting of it to coat her from the inside out.

Here goes...everything. Her shadowy thoughts were in stark contrast to the almost bubbly, shining face waiting patiently in front of her. Pride had always been one of the toughest pills to swallow.

5

Slow exhale. Pause. Long inhale. Katya's expectant gaze was turning into concern.

Way to put that crazy woman rumor to rest, Jeslyn thought.

Something had to be said and quickly. Katya's mouth had flopped open once already, as if she were going to speak, then reconsidered.

"Katya —"

"Yes." Overeager. Katya almost stood at attention at the sound of her name; at the sound of something, anything. Jeslyn appeared to be deep in thought. Silent thought. Perhaps talking was overrated for her. However, when you were giving an interview, especially one that was being recorded — and, so far, had only been filled with Katya's own, irrelevant back story — it was pretty crucial.

"I need to preface this with something. I'll need you to listen closely." Jeslyn's flawless, youthful features countered her heavy words.

"I'm going to tell you everything." Jeslyn allowed that to sink in before continuing. "When I say everything, I mean the most..." Jeslyn loathed the word intimate. It conjured up images of frail women and feminine product commercials. The word private wasn't much better. "...in depth..." Yes, that was more like it; very newsroom

47

appropriate as well. "...narrative regarding my current status and the history behind it."

Katya nodded politely but anxiously as if to say, 'Just get on with it already. Enough talking about talking about it.'

"I don't know if this will be what you hoped for," Jeslyn threw a glance towards the single page of questions, "but it's what I'm prepared to give."

Katya gripped her pencil a bit tighter and leaned in an inch closer in response.

"I've lived in and around Southern California all my life. I was born in Long Beach and lived there until I was about three. We moved to San Clemente when I was four, stayed there for a couple of years, then settled in Oceanside when I was seven. Everyone assumed my father was in the military; he wasn't. He had been in the grocery business most of his life – stocker, bag boy, then cashier. My mother was a secretary slash administrative assistant for various companies and we lived an OK existence, I guess." Another pause. Inside, Jeslyn was already starting to crumble. Outside, there was nothing. It may have been just a show, but it was a damn good one. When this was over, no one would ever be able to say she had buckled under pressure.

Doubt whispered in her ear that she couldn't go through with this. Even if she did, what was the point? The past couldn't be undone and the present was already sullied. Revealing the skeletons in the closet didn't make them disappear, it only made them visible.

Not true, Jeslyn contended, *it also takes away the fear, never ending stress and incessant worry that's inextricably tied to keeping them hidden.*

She was tired of pretending, hiding, and covering up. She wanted the weight of deception off of her. It had smothered her for years. Besides, she wouldn't tell anything about anyone else that wasn't necessary, only the bare minimum. She shoved aside the distraction of doubt, at least for the time being, and forged ahead.

"We didn't have a ton of money but we certainly weren't poor. Around average I would say. My life was fairly normal; it came with its ups and its downs..." A flash of memories bombarded her.

Jeslyn's father yelling. A woman apologizing. A man at the door (was he crying?) The woman pleading, her father grabbing young Jeslyn and driving away. Her father despondent. Mean words she didn't quite understand from kids at school. Retaliation from those words. Brokenness.

"...but whose life doesn't have that?" An empty sad smile spilled across Jeslyn's somber face. "I finished high school, did alright with grades and then looked for a job. A small part of that was because I wanted to help. My dad worked long hours, never really taking time off, and I would've done anything to make his life better. He was..." Pause. "...a truly great man. One of the greatest, even if I didn't always realize it. But there was a larger part of me that wanted to be out on my own, to take care of myself. Perhaps my mother was to blame for that. She was...difficult." Jeslyn left it at that.

"College was an option, but employment happened first. I told myself I would learn along the way. I was smart and pretty resourceful, which helped move me up the corporate ladder – a few corporate ladders, actually. And then college became less important. I found my professional niche in marketing and account management and just..." Jeslyn made a motion with her hand of an object taking flight in a progressively upward direction; she simultaneously made a rocketing swoosh sound. "My titles got more impressive, my paychecks got larger and my ego got more inflated."

Katya seemed mildly surprised at Jeslyn's candidness. Most people with an inflated ego didn't mention it, no matter how apparent the infliction was.

"I was proud of my accomplishments, proud of the fact that I didn't need my parents anymore. If you asked me, I would've said I didn't need anyone. I was also happy I

49

wasn't living their life. My dad was still a cashier, my mom had 'retired,'" Jeslyn made use of air quotes here, "and they were still in the same house I'd lived in for most of my life. It's like they were living life in pause or rewind. There was never any forward.

"One day, my dad took his lunch break, said he wasn't feeling well. He went out to his car to relax for a bit, had a heart attack and died." Jeslyn ran down the sequence like a grocery list. "My pops died, alone, in the parking lot of a grocery store. Not how I imagined that going."

Katya may have felt her heart constrict but she kept her pity to herself, as if she knew instinctively Jeslyn would see it as an insult.

"My mother and I already had a strained relationship and my father's passing didn't make it any better. I could tell my life made her bitter and she could tell her attitude made me want to stay away from her even more. The cycle went round and round and round, I'm sure you can imagine the drill." Jeslyn struck Katya as either being bored with this part of her story, or thinking it was an inconsequential portion of her life to bore someone else with.

"For the most part, I respectfully kept my distance from her and continued doing my thing. The problem was, my thing was just working for other people and complaining about it. I kept telling myself, 'I could do this better' or 'I could do that better,' but I never did anything at all. Until one day I finally had enough of myself.

"I was working as an Account Executive at an ad agency. The owner was some guy who had all these thriving companies that were humming along nicely while he was off in the Cayman Islands. All I could think was, 'here's an idiot who was born with a silver spoon in his mouth, and simply used that spoon to mold a platinum ladle.' He was a first class prick, too. One of those guys that you daydream about getting hit by a bus – not enough to actually kill him. I mean, I wanted him alive enough to tell me the secrets to his success. Since neither of those things was going to happen, especially the secret telling part – I don't think he even knew I worked for him – I researched him instead.

"Turns out he came from poverty and became a millionaire off the sweat of his brow." She sounded as if she wanted to add the word 'allegedly' after every fact. "After looking him up, I thought I'd check out a few other wealthy people's stories. Basically, I was looking to see if making it big was really something I could do. What began as nothing more than prideful curiosity turned into real fascination. Honestly," Jeslyn seemed to be weighing her words, "it became kind of like an obsession."

They were so measured, her words, that Katya wondered how to fix her face so that it said, 'no judgment here.' Since it wasn't something she'd practiced beforehand, she decided to simply do nothing, as she recalled how on-the-fly wasn't her thing, this time before it was too late.

"The first question I'm sure people want to know is how I made my money."

No, Jeslyn's inner voice piped up, *what people want to know is if you were schtupping a married man and then tried to kill him.*

"I can tell you how I *planned* to do it. Emulation. Plain and simple. I was going to do what the supremely wealthy did. To get where I wanted to be, I figured I would place my foot in the imprint of their footsteps and walk the same path. I really thought it would be that easy.

"I started Foxxy Red on my own." She said it like she was defending an accusation; maybe because she was. "I also started it for a specific purpose, which was initially greed. Then I realized, through a lot of...well, we'll get into that, I suppose. Anyway, I realized it needed meaning. When I did that, put meaning into it, I wound up making this beautiful mess. It was like a –" She stopped briefly, like someone had been feeding her lines and the earpiece had gone dead. Then she jumped tracks and headed in a new direction.

"The crazy part, the part that's head scratching for most people, is that what gave Foxxy Red meaning wasn't the apparel at all. That was just the gateway drug." Jeslyn's lips became a limp elbow macaroni smile. "The heartbeat developed when it went from being a crazy notion to a voice. The fact that it spoke to people – they didn't just want to wear the brand, they wanted to be a part of the brand – that's when it hit me that this is what I was meant to do. Even starting the high end apparel line and what not was mostly for fun, a way to give my creative side a little action."

Katya fell comfortably into this more upbeat stanza of Jeslyn's sentient opus. Her curiosity made her forget she was supposed to be a passive spectator.

"So, what does Matt Coleman have to do with this?" There, she'd said it. Jeslyn must've known it would come up. The man was in a coma because of a very nasty accident and the only clues so far were a racy picture of Jeslyn in his wallet and a scintillating letter to her in his office desk.

"That is –" Jeslyn looked down at her hands. Her face seemed to want to apologize for what was coming next. "That would be getting under the surface. The first question was how did I make my money. The second question I think you want to know is how the business was built." Jeslyn exhaled loudly. It had all been going so well. She had actually started enjoying herself a little bit. The surface was always enjoyable. It was the silk sheet covering the bed of nails. As long as you didn't apply pressure, everything looked and felt deceivingly smooth.

"OK then," Katya said, confused. "How did you build the business?" She didn't see how that would answer her question. Then again, she also didn't realize what she was asking. She simply saw this as Jeslyn dodging a hot button issue.

"That question is a bit more involved."

"Ready when you are." Katya smiled serenely, unprepared for anything more than either stale by-the-book dialogue about Jeslyn's startup or a politician answer.

Jeslyn got up and walked over to a mini fridge in the corner of the room, a slow motion runway walk. Each step sent her hips dramatically swaying. Katya had no sexual interest in women, but she had to admit that Jeslyn's whole put together was quite arresting.

"Something to drink?"

"Um, no, thank you." Katya ducked her head as if she'd been caught looking through Jeslyn's underwear drawer. She moved around restlessly in her chair as Jeslyn sashayed back, cold sparkling water in hand.

"I'll start with the death of my uncle." Jeslyn unscrewed the top to her drink.

"Oh. I'm very sorry to hear that." Katya wasn't expecting the kick-start to be so tragic.

"No apologies needed. I killed him." She took a slow, calculated swig. Katya was thankful she hadn't accepted the drink offer. She was sure she'd be spewing it in Jeslyn's face.

"I...I don't...what?" Katya stammered.

"He wasn't the first. I'd already offed two close family friends before him." Calm. Collected.

Katya's eyes searched the area directly in front of her, looking for anything she could use to defend herself. There was nothing but her stupid pencil.

"Now, before you run and call 911, let me explain." Jeslyn snagged a coaster from the nearby side table and placed her water on top of it. Her movements were so reserved. Katya wondered if she should bolt, scream or wait for Jeslyn's next move. She waited. "Please know I'm not proud of any of this. I will simply tell you everything exactly how it happened." Katya remained silent. "Remember how I mentioned I used to work at an ad agency? It really starts there."

6

~Before~

Jeslyn was getting 'quired' from her job – a combination of quitting and getting fired. She tried to feel fine about it, and mostly she did; the relationship had run its course. But there was a leftover part of her that wasn't fine.

As Senior Account Executive at Don Lewis Media & Marketing, one of the top digital media and advertising firms in the Western hemisphere, her head was pressing uncomfortably into the company's glass ceiling. She had reached the last possible rung of the organization's corporate ladder and was barely holding on to even that, seeing as how the company founder had hired his inept brother-in-law as President and his mistress as CEO. The trio was a sad sitcom parody of My Three Bosses.

There was nowhere to go but out. Any other available positions were either in areas that were beneath her current pay grade or not within her line of work.

She had seen the end coming for quite some time. Ever since she'd spoken up in the last executive meeting denouncing the CEO's idea to email coupons to leads, the end had started barreling towards her.

"Why don't we just hire sign spinners while we're at it?" Jeslyn had quipped. DLMM was a lauded marketing firm, not a sandwich shop.

Granted, the sarcasm was unprofessional. It was just that she had no nerves left; the last one had been tap danced on eons ago. Literally. The CEO had asked Jeslyn to take her daughter to her tap dance lesson and pick her up because she had an important meeting she simply couldn't miss. Jeslyn had returned, whiny daughter in tow, to find the woman freshly mani'd, pedi'd and more mystic orange than when she'd last seen her.

It also did no one any favors that the company's second in command had the ego of a prima donna; the intelligence of a fourth grader – Jeslyn had seen the show which pitted contestants up against the mental prowess of a fifth grader, a fourth grade IQ comparison was a compliment; skin color that resembled sharp cheddar, and the body of a cheap plastic surgeon.

Yet, here she was, in all of her plunging neckline, skintight miniskirt glory (there were times when staff members had to avert their eyes due to these wardrobe selections), reigning supreme as Cheap Eye candy Officer for a Fortune 100 media agency. DLMM had officially become an advertising brothel.

If someone had taken a disaster, poured it into a baking dish, put it in an oven and turned the heat to broil, they couldn't have made a hotter mess.

When she wasn't dropping borderline prejudice comments about immigrants or blue-collar workers, she was gabbing on her bedazzled cell phone about her trysts with the owner, Don Lewis – or MyBabyDonny, as she liked to call him. Not to mention, her favorite words were 'like' and 'you know', as in: 'I think we should, like, send out, like, e-coupons, you know, and, like, offer, like, companies and businesses, you know, like discounts.'

An actual sentence. Hence Jeslyn's quip.

The coup de grace, essentially the cherry on top of the Real Mistresses of San Diego County sundae, was that her name was Bambi. What type of coke-addled, stripper of a mother named their child Bambi? Apparently a psychic one. Bambi made sure to live up to every syllable of her name.

But Jeslyn seemed to be the only who noticed the company being NASCAR raced into the ground. Either that or she hadn't gotten the memo that said not to mention it. Her last quip was deemed by Bambi to be "confrontational." After that, her duties and responsibilities began changing dramatically.

Key accounts were reassigned to other managers and more menial tasks were delegated to her specifically. If coming to work before had been a chore, the new shift in her role had made chain gang labor look mildly appealing. Knowing that she was perilously close to the professional chopping block due to hurting the feelings of the office carrot, calling in sick or taking time off were not wise choices. She also knew that, even though she was losing her mind and needed a break like Lindsay Lohan needed rehab, going postal would most likely be frowned upon. So, she did the next best thing. She killed her uncle.

This wasn't the first time someone close to her had met an untimely end. Other loved ones she knew had bought the farm during random points in her career when it suited a purpose. Why? Because who was going to argue with death?

Grieving, travel, family time, and a funeral bought at least two, sometimes even three to four days. Devious? Yes. Deceitful? Without a doubt. It was also very effective. That is, when one got away with it.

"Jeslyn, can I see you in my office?" Brian Collins-Lewis (yes, his name was hyphenated per his wife's, Don Lewis' sister, demand) used the company's intercom to contact her. He was in the office next door. She could not only hear him over the phone, she could hear his actual voice. It couldn't have been forty feet away if it was an inch.

Without replying, Jeslyn walked out of her office, did the walkway tango with Bambi's administrative assistant who was passing by, then stepped into Brian's office.

"Have a seat, Jeslyn."

She sat.

"It has come to my attention that you took some time off a few weeks ago to go out of state for the purpose of attending the funeral of a family member."

"An uncle."

"Yeah." Brian made the word two syllables. "You see, Jeslyn, the problem there is that one of our staff members is claiming they saw you in town during that same time period."

"Your point?" Jeslyn held her poker face in place.

"Well, isn't it obvious, Jeslyn?"

She was beginning to hate the sound of her own name. "Perhaps I'm missing something." She'd spent the last two hours bidding on and monitoring bids for several eBay items for Bambi, who had then assigned her RFP creative brief to a project coordinator. 'So you'll, like, have more time, you know, to like, concentrate on winning the bids,' Bambi had said. It had been a demoralizing, exasperating blow. Now, she was counting the seconds until she could be reunited with her task.

"Jeslyn, you're telling me one thing, but I'm hearing a very different, and might I add troubling account from someone else." She hadn't realized how squeaky his voice sounded.

"I'm sorry, Mr. Collins-Lewis." Whenever possible she used his hyphenated surname. "But I'm not comfortable doing he-said-she-said." She wasn't comfortable period. This wasn't good.

"Do you have anything to prove you were where you say you were?" he asked.

"Since I'm sure you asked the accusing party for proof as well, would you mind if I took a peek at that?"

Brian looked appropriately dazed.

"I...Jeslyn...we..."

"Is that 'I Jeslyn we', I can't see the information or 'I Jeslyn we', you didn't request any proof from the other party?" She stared at him blankly. She had gotten quite good at that over the years.

"Look, Jeslyn, it's my job as the President of this company to appropriately address issues such as these if they're brought to my attention." Squeak, squeak, squeak.

"Well, personally, Mr. Collins-Lewis, I find this line of questioning rather offensive." The best defense was sometimes a 'that's offensive.'

"Offensive?" Obviously he disagreed. "Jeslyn, I know we may have our differences but this is nothing more than a standard inquiry. I need you to understand and acknowledge that." The squeaking was more pronounced now that he was agitated.

"Mr. Collins-Lewis, perhaps your inquiry is standard. But if you're telling me I *must* acknowledge that, I'd prefer that stipulation in writing. Because the way I see it, your office mole has either confused me with someone else or they've exaggerated the truth. And by 'exaggerated the truth', Mr. Collins-Lewis, I mean lied."

His wasn't an entirely baseless claim, but she wasn't going to tell him that. She had been out of town; just not out of state, and not for a funeral – unless the death and burial of her morality counted. Who the tattletale was or what had spurred a probe into her personal affairs were unknowns that she was asked to forgive, but that she wouldn't be able to forget.

The meeting adjourned with a quasi-apology from Brian but a whole new level of office awkwardness. She may have fabricated a death in her family without so much as blinking an eye, but Jeslyn did have a conscience – and it was hungry. It proceeded to eat away at her for several days after their discussion. And it didn't stop there. Every whisper, glance, subtle cough or eye shift from anyone in the office made her feel as if it were directed towards her or about her. It was a maddening sort of work existence; one that would've made a great title for a children's book. Perhaps, *Jeslyn Kennedy and the Horrible Lie* or *Jeslyn Kennedy Finally Feels*

The Effects of What Happens When You Say Your Uncle Has Died Just So You Can Get a Four-Day Break From Work and Someone Calls You On It. The last one would probably need the help of a good editor before hitting the shelves, but that didn't make it any less true.

Not long thereafter, Jeslyn finally cried uncle and gave her resignation. The formalities, including her final paycheck, were processed quickly, too quickly. During the exchange Jeslyn happened to notice a stack of papers on the HR Director's desk. They were resumes. From the looks of it, they appeared to be candidates for a Senior Account Executive.

Well played DLMM.

There was no plan B. Jeslyn walked out into the crisp air of that mid-October morning, with a closed door behind her and not one open window in sight. Her financial responsibilities were more than manageable, but that was when she'd been employed. What that looked like as an un-employee was less manageable.

There was no boyfriend, no friends she felt like lamenting to, and a no pet policy in her lease; therefore, there was no one and nothing to arrive home to except her own thoughts.

She knew the difference between right and wrong, and she knew that so many things that she had done had been wrong. But owning up to those wrongs meant she had to be sorry. And being sorry made her feel bad. And feeling bad reminded her that bad people needed to be punished. And punishment reminded her of childhood. And childhood was something that she kept under deadbolt lock and key. And what was the point of marching down all those negative steps only to end up at a locked door? There was none. It was pointless. So, to save herself the trouble, whenever it came time to feel sorry, she simply bitch slapped sorry in the face – an act that was as effective at inducing anger as Pitocin was at inducing labor. Because anger was something she could handle, it didn't make her feel weak. She was done feeling weak.

They were already looking for my replacement? The bastards. Her soliloquy turned into a rant. *Fine! With the group of monkeys they've got running that circus, it's amazing I lasted as long as I did. Good riddance.*

With frustration as fuel, she scanned several job posting sites, but found her bad mood had ruined that, too.

That would be a step down. Not enough pay. Boring industry. Lame company. Degree required...

Jeslyn didn't have a degree; she had wit, a fairly credible portfolio, an impressively high and diverse level of intelligence, and resourcefulness. However, the last time she checked, they weren't handing out degrees for resourcefulness. Schmoozing and street smarts were also not on any baccalaureate lists. She usually only lasted a few years, at most, at any of the companies she'd worked for because of one thing or another. Mostly it was her issue with authority. She was like a wild tiger in a cage that viewed authority as nothing more than an antagonistic kid with a stick. Jeslyn hated cages, and she hated being prodded.

That was Jacqueline's fault, a woman that Jeslyn hated even thinking about and usually only referred to as "That Woman" whenever she was forced to mention her at all. Jacqueline had ruined her life. Not in an episode of *Full House* kind of way, where Michelle learns a valuable lesson and everything is hunky dory the next week. No, Jacqueline had ruined her life in a *The Color Purple* or *Precious* kind of way. The kind of way that people didn't want to hear about because it was too real, too disturbing; and the kind of way that Jeslyn didn't want to talk about because of those same reasons.

Jacqueline, from what Jeslyn allowed herself to recall, had been beautiful. Beauty attracted attention and Jacqueline had loved attention. And money. Two things she wasn't getting much of these days. But she had gotten them before and Jeslyn had had to pay for it. Covering for That

Woman and her "friends" had turned Jeslyn into a cold cynic. It sometimes crossed her mind what she would've been like if things had been different. But they weren't. This was her life. And right now she had to deal with the fact that in this life she had no job.

With unemployment as her supervisor and an aversion of some kind or another to the vacant employment opportunities, she had a decision to make.

Why don't you put your money where your mouth is, Kennedy? If you're so smart and so capable and can do things so much better than everyone else, why don't you do it now? Her conscience derided her.

Talking was one thing; it was easy to talk, safe to talk. Doing was an entirely different beast. Doing would require, as her conscience had so dutifully pointed out, putting her money where her big mouth was.

She wouldn't be challenged and back down, not even by her own conscience.

I can be my own boss. Jeslyn mentally stamped her foot like an unruly child. *As soon as I figure out what it is that I'm going to do.*

Renowned marketing and media companies didn't just pop up overnight. Her pride wasn't so far gone that she dismissed the fact it took serious effort to go from nothing to something – or in Don Lewis' case, a lot of something to even more something. He must have used family money or connections to get to where he was. Jeslyn abandoned her futile job search to look up information on him. She wanted to see exactly how he had bumbled his way from easy street to easier street, figuring if she couldn't join 'em, she'd try and beat 'em.

Turned out, Lewis wasn't some Ricky Stratton silver spooner. He'd come from poverty. The discovery annoyed her. She had felt justified loathing a privileged ingrate. Seeing that he'd started with nothing but put in the necessary hard work to make it to the top only made her feel that much worse.

Jeslyn wanted to look up someone else, someone whose name didn't make her want to give her computer screen the middle finger. She continued her search this time targeting random executives. Before long, her lame interest turned into real interest as she went from looking up successful businesspersons to obsessively searching the world's wealthiest individuals.

She wasn't an adrenaline or substance abuse junkie, although she probably should have been. She'd heard there were pills and drinks that could make you forget. Maybe forgetting would have taken away the fear, guilt, and anger that had plagued her until they'd become things she now relied on. Her struggle had always been with the easy-to-conceal addiction of feelings.

Her primary emotional substance these days was either anger or arousal. The catalyst could be sexual desire or simply a titillating prospect, but it had to be something she could hold onto long enough to get a substantial fix. Short spurts of arousal sent her plummeting into depression, like withdrawals. She needed either continual or long lasting drugs. Holding rank with the world's financially elite was not a short spurt; it was a notion that was deeply arousing. And if it were this much of an aphrodisiac to simply think about, what effect would it have if she were to actually achieve it? And if she did achieve it, imagine all of the things she could do.

Like payback some of the emotional debt Jacqueline and her friends had dumped on her.

Days passed. Days of reading, studying, note taking, and absorbing her new drug. She created a chart made up of columns labeled Net Worth, Industry, and Specific Product or Service, with the purpose of looking for patterns. What skills did she possess that could raise her from her current existence to one that only a select few enjoyed? What commonalities did she and this faction share?

As she chewed this over one afternoon, post-quired status, her cell phone rang. Apparently not everyone had been made aware of her departure from the agency. The creative director for a well-known sportswear manufacturer, previously one of her favorite clients, was calling to check on the status of a few projects. Jeslyn informed him that she was no longer with DLMM but assured him she would contact the appropriate persons to make sure the items were taken care of.

It was after she had hung up that two things occurred to her: The first was that nine of the world's twenty-five wealthiest people were retail moguls – her studious research had uncovered that fact. Second, she had a ton of resources at her fingertips. That call had been with a direct connect to one of the top sports and athletic product companies in the world. The *world*. They were a powerhouse. They were also a potential asset. And they weren't the only one. Jeslyn's Rolodex was like a business Olympic Dream Team.

It was times such as these she was glad she'd had the good sense (and the silent mouth) to not set all of her bridges ablaze. An idea began to formulate. She created a list of questions for things she either couldn't figure out on her own or would need an expert viewpoint on. Once that was complete, she put in work making a few calls.

As she started skimming the moss off of this slowly rolling stone, she patted herself lightly on the back for what was quite possibly her most brilliant idea to date.

7

It had to have been her stupidest idea to date. Yes, she assumed crafting a multi-million dollar empire would have its challenges but this – this was far from a challenge. This made a challenge look like a Swedish massage. No, this was no challenge, this was an impossibility.

I'm not smart enough. I'm not talented enough. I'm not motivated enough. I'm not...enough.

Enough was enough and apparently there wasn't any more of it to go around.

Jeslyn had written a lot of checks in the weeks following her departure from DLMM – or as hindsight would have her see it: perfectly respectable, stable, full time employment. The universe must have decided it was only fair to give back. To accomplish that task, it gave her a check of its own. A reality check.

She'd had an enthusiastic start in the dreaming phase, but when it came time to make something of it, that's where the dream ended. She was left with no idea of where she was supposed to go or what she was supposed to do next. She recounted her steps.

Step 1: Quit job. It didn't help that every single thing she read expressly warned against that. 'Hold onto your day job until your hobby or business meets or exceeds the income and stability your current employment provides,' they all said. Too little, too late.

Step two: Obsessively research wealthy people. While entertaining, this had not done a whole lot of good. Even her oh-so-organized chart with its color-coded columns, neatly aligned headers, and carefully arranged rows hadn't added anything more than 'engrossing activity' to her list of completed tasks.

Step three: Reach out to contacts. This step had been worth a good half a point. But while it had been a task worth parceling out some time to, the lavish lunches with their steeply priced drinks, things she'd insisted on paying for, had been a drain on her financial resources. The same amount of information could have been gleaned from a Cabernet-less telephone call or a filet-free Skype exchange. Considering how tipsy, gossipy and, in a few instances, grabby some of her network associates had gotten, perhaps *more* information could have been obtained. Though she didn't walk away empty handed, it also opened a huge warehouse of All the Things I Didn't Know I Didn't Know.

Funding, angel investors, incorporating, distribution, sourcing, importing, vendors, fulfillment, annuities, e-commerce considerations, tax implications and exit strategies – every new piece of information brought with it at least twenty more questions. The research and answers to those questions led to a hundred more questions. The cycle was vexingly endless.

The icing on that bleak cake was that her bank account was hemorrhaging from one end with only a cotton swab of aid to stop it. In other words, she was slowly going broke. Jeslyn hadn't been a fool with her money; however, the majority of the skimpy stash she had saved was already earmarked for her empire. If she blew through that, she wouldn't even have a chance. And right now it was all she could count on.

Kennedy Rule #265: there was no borrowing or lending from acquaintances, friends or family. If either party's funds were not backed by the FDIC or a comparable financial insurance agency, pecuniary exchanges would not be taking place. She had made that mistake before. Once was enough.

Thinking about that incident – the one where she had tried to help out a family member and had discovered she wasn't helping, she was enabling – reminded her of another family member she hadn't spoken to in a while. Her mother. Not because of the money loaning incident, but mainly because life was more peaceful that way. As her mother aged, everything had either become more exaggerated or completely fabricated. Strangely enough, all of that might have been bearable and the past put to rest if it weren't for her mother's bitterness and resentment. She seemed to not-so-secretly despise everything about Jeslyn, especially the portions of her that bore resemblance to her father, someone like him or someone completely unlike him. Her mother tried to cover this with shallow conversation and occasional kind words, but it came off as phony. They both could sense it. Then something would shift, the glaciers would emerge and the disdain would come back stronger than ever. It was hard to know when her mother was going to be playful, spiteful or just plain full of it in general.

There were numerous occasions when Jeslyn would take breaks and not interact with her mother at all – zero communication. Let the chips fall where they fell. At least she knew what to expect when she didn't talk to her. Staying in contact made each interaction a curveball. Helpless, Angry, Cold, Bubbly, Needy, Doting, Forgetful – it was like having seven defective dwarfs for a maternal figure.

Jeslyn, armed with what she hoped was enough patience and a thick-skinned exterior, made the call she'd been putting off for nearly three and a half weeks. Each ring filled her with both optimism and reluctance; optimistic that her mother wouldn't answer and reluctance to speak with her if she did.

"Hello."

Jeslyn could tell nothing from the initial greeting.

"Hi, Mom." She waited.

"Oh, hey there, Jezzy." While not exuberant, her mother also didn't seem annoyed – yet. She did, however, use a nickname that Jeslyn had made known on several occasions she'd prefer not to be called.

Her father had once remarked that Jezzy was really short for Jezebel. When Jeslyn asked him who that was, he had handed her a Bible and told her to read I Kings. From what she could gather, Jezebel was a pagan and a conspirator who encouraged saints to participate in idolatry and sexual immorality.

Fine reading. Even finer association. When she brought this up to her mother there had been an entire melodramatic production in the place of a simple reply – how could she ever accuse her *own* mother of associating her *own* daughter (so many owns) with a prostitute? This was followed by an unabridged theatrical performance that centered around Jeslyn and her father's apparent need to conspire together to make her out to be a contemptible person.

There were usually tears to accompany the performance, too. On and on it went, sometimes for weeks, months, even years – it all depended on her mood. Her mother didn't hold a grudge; no, she held a congressional archive of grievances.

For now, her persona appeared to be Forgetful, so Jeslyn played along. She wanted this to go well, wanted her mother to be happy, it just seemed like Jeslyn was the only one who wanted it. Ignoring the name swap entirely, she made an attempt to keep the call pleasant, yet brief.

"I thought I'd check in and see how things are going." There was no one around to see Jeslyn's pained expression as she waited for a reaction.

"How nice of you, Jezzy. Mommy really appreciates that." Mommy? Strike two. Jeslyn was in her mid 20s, the term mommy wasn't part of her vocabulary unless she was referencing a classic movie from the 80s starring Joan Crawford. Other than that, she didn't know that she had ever used the word, let alone in reference to her own mother. Again, she set it aside. These were very minor points of objection, ones that didn't need to be addressed.

Just move on. You're getting hung up on the inconsequential. She played adult to her own immature griping.

"Mmmhmm." Jeslyn nibbled at her bottom lip. Her mind flitted from one thought to the next trying to figure out how she could end the call now.

"So, I hear you're not at that agency anymore." Her mother's next statement spun Jeslyn into concentrated awareness. How the hell did she know that?

"I...no, I'm not. Who told you?" Jeslyn tried to keep her voice neutral.

"Well, I called your office to speak with you and –"

"Why didn't you just call my cell phone?" Jeslyn could feel her 'I've-Had-It' gauge start to rise.

"It was during work hours, so I didn't want to bother you on your cell," her mother said, as if that was something they'd worked out before. "It's unprofessional to be yakking away on your cell when you're at work."

No, you know we don't have caller ID and I have to answer my office phone. That way your odds of forcing me to talk to you are increased.

Instead of voicing these thoughts, Jeslyn simply murmured something that resembled agreement.

Her mother rambled on. "When they said you no longer worked there, well, you can imagine how I felt having to hear that from strangers and not my own daughter."

Actually I don't.

"Of course, my first thoughts went to your health and safety. I hoped you were OK, but figured you were probably fine. I mean, you have all of those friends on your Face page; plus, you've got that handsome boy you're dating."

I haven't dated anyone in over a year.

68

"You've got someone to take care of you…"

Yeah, me.

"…and lots of people to hang out with. You've got all the essentials too – a nice roof over your head with that beautiful condo you live in. I mean, I haven't seen it personally…"

You've been here five times.

"…but I'm sure it's beautiful. And didn't you get a brand new car recently? I remember you saying something about that, right?"

Four years ago.

"Anyway, like I said, I figured you were just fine. I did wonder, though, if you had all that free time since you weren't working – what with the holidays coming up and everything – why you couldn't give your mommy a call."

Stop already with the 'mommy!'

"But I guess with that type of busy lifestyle..." She left her locked and loaded sentence aimed but not fired. Instead, she pressed her bayonet of words just far enough into Jeslyn's skin so that it pricked but didn't puncture.

Jeslyn tried telling herself that it was probably just loneliness and regret that made her mother say things that teeter tottered on insulting. If she could just make herself believe that, she could melt away the ice that had formed around her heart, and sweep away the sticky cobwebs of distrust that had laid claim to her. The attempts were mildly successful, if that.

Outside her window Jeslyn concentrated on the serene sounds of the courtyard water fountain bubbling and splashing against the stones surrounding it. She closed her eyes. An image of a bathtub painted itself on the interior of her eyelids.

Water splashing, the bathtub faucet turned on high. Garbled threats, someone holding her head firmly, water pouring over her face, covering her nose, flooding her mouth, she couldn't breathe.

Jeslyn's eyes flung open, her lips parting suddenly as she struggled to catch a breath that hadn't really been lost.

Her jaw clenched. Surely she could get through a phone call with her mother. She picked up her end of the conversation.

"Actually, I'm not dating anyone. It's just me, taking care of myself." *Like a grown ass woman should.* "And honestly, I haven't really spoken to anyone over these last few weeks, friends or otherwise, so I could concentrate on finding another job." It wasn't the truth, the whole truth and nothing but; however, it would suffice.

"Another job? Oh, Jezzy." She exaggerated her disappointment. "Mommy had hoped you would be in a career by now. Jumping from place to place is no way to build a professional resume, now is it." It wasn't a question. It also wasn't necessary.

"Well," *don't call her Debra, don't call her Debra, do* not *call her Debra.* Jeslyn knew that calling her mother by her first name would be a good way to knock a sizable chunk of hell loose. An ornery little portion of her wanted to raise a little hell. Wisely, the more competent side won out. "De-, Moth-Mom, it's funny you mention that."

Jeslyn would try her hand once more at a teeny tiny bit of openness, even though it hadn't worked in the past. It was obvious her mother still didn't know squat about her life; either that or she didn't care to remember the details Jeslyn shared with her. For a time, Jeslyn had tried to open up to her mother, tried to understand why the woman was sometimes so cold towards her. After pissing in the wind with those attempts and getting nothing in return she'd closed herself off. Not just to her mother, but to everyone. A person could only take being let down so many times before there were side effects. Now, her mother's lack of knowledge about her life was intentional. If she didn't know anything she couldn't do anything. No belittling, gossiping or betraying could take place if there were nothing to belittle, gossip about or betray.

"Actually, I am starting a career...of sorts. It's really more than that, though. I'm going to start my own business." She remained vague. "I've been meeting with a lot of business contacts and making some good headway. It's going to be a lot of work, that's for sure, but I'm looking forward to getting something going." Jeslyn stopped talking in order to allow her mother to comment.

"So, what's this *career*?" Her mother's voice was already spiked with skepticism.

"I'm going to start an apparel line," Jeslyn rushed to continue before her mother could interject. "That's not the entire scope of it, though; there's much more to it than that. It's hard to really put it into words."

"I see." Mom was mum.

"I'm thinking this could be huge."

"So, not a real career then?" Jeslyn could all but see her mother's lips pursed in disapproval.

"This will be a real career."

"Ah."

A pregnant pause gave birth to tension.

And this is why I don't tell you anything.

"Well, looks like it's about that time. Like I said, I was just calling to –"

"Jezzy, Mom's kind of…Mom's worried about you." Doting Mother decided to stop by for a visit.

"Why is that?" Jeslyn was on the calmer side of irritated but heading quickly to the opposite end.

"How are you going to support yourself? How are you going to take care of your family?" Jeslyn had no children and no prospects of children. Her mother was clearly referring to herself. Doting had left the building and was expertly replaced by Needy.

"Seeing as how I have no dependents, I think I'll do alright." Jeslyn's 'Had It' gauge was past the midway point.

"Don't be so selfish, Jeslyn," her mother snapped. "You have what every normal American person dreams of. And look at you, just pissing away a good life. You know, not everybody is as fortunate to be able to up and quit a job whenever they choose and chase pies in the sky all day instead."

Hello, Cold Mother, nice to see you again. Jeslyn's gauge had topped out.

"The American dream? What is that? One step out of the hole you're in now? Forgive me, Mother, if I'm not super excited about the prospect of dying with the height of my existence being a brand spankin' normal four-year-old car; a fifteen-year-old, two bedroom condo that you've actually visited *five times*; an apathetic ex-boyfriend whose greatest accomplishment was marathon-watching TV all day and an enviable legacy of Account Executive and Marketing jobs. Anyone with half a brain could do all of that. That's not a dream, that's a stupor. If that's the so-called American dream, I don't want the damn dream. I want the American fantasy. How's that?"

Perhaps those thoughts should have stayed that way. Jeslyn didn't mean to unload her frustrations, she was just done with her mother pushing her buttons and then asking in doe-eyed, Urkel innocence, 'Did I do that?'

Yes, you did that and you know very well that you did.

"Listen here Jeslyn Camille." Jeslyn had not heard her middle name used in a long time. "You will *not* talk to me that way, do you understand me? You may think your shit doesn't stink because you worked for some highfalutin companies, went to a couple of fancy little dinners, and sat in your little meetings, but that doesn't make you anything special to me. Do you hear me little girl?"

"Oh, I hear you, Mother. I hear you loud and clear."

I'm nothing special to you, got it.

"Watch it, Jeslyn. I've just about had it up to here with you and your attitude."

"You know what, I agree," she said calmly. "Why don't I do you a huge favor and not burden you with anymore of it for awhile." Jeslyn massaged her forehead with her hand and clutched the phone to keep from hurling it at the wall. "I've got to go. It's been a pleasure, as always."

And with that, she ended the call and embarked on another mother-free hiatus.

There. One problem down, only nine hundred and ninety-nine thousand more to go.

8

Jeslyn had been going strong for almost an hour without a single intermission. It was like listening to a movie. Katya sat silently enraptured as Jeslyn spoke the scenes to life. When she finally did stop talking, Katya found it hard to start.

"Oh, um, OK then." What was there to say after all of that?

Not looking the least bit ruffled, Jeslyn took another slow sip of the sparkling water that sat beside her. The condensation of the bottle had made a dark wet ring on the cork coaster it had been resting upon, and Katya was sure the contents of the bottle were not as cool and refreshing as they'd been an hour ago. Jeslyn didn't seem to mind. She continued to quietly sip and look past Katya as if she weren't there.

Katya peered down at her blank journal. She hadn't written a single thing down. At this point, it was hard to say what should be written down. This was more than she had bargained for, and yet she wondered just how she was going to go about making, what was so obviously a very personal disclosure, into a prize-winning business feature. Surely Jeslyn didn't intend to share all this with the public.

What is your game, Kennedy? Katya was finding the whole set of circumstances more and more peculiar as each question led to other questions, and each answer, although wildly captivating, only led to more mystery.

"So, has there been any reconciliation…with you and your mother, I mean?" Katya questioned, not bringing up the Jacqueline woman. She had watched as Jeslyn talked about her, like 'That Woman' was someone she hated. She left that alone – it was none of her business anyway – and

74

asked about her mom. While that, too, was none of her business, Jeslyn was making it her business. And even in the midst of her doubt and concern over Jeslyn's motives, she also knew what it was like to struggle with a dysfunctional parent.

"We'll get to that. No need to go out of sequence." Sip.

Sequence? Katya found Jeslyn's comment to be almost comical. *What sequence? I thought this was just the Jeslyn Kennedy story hour?*

"OK then. Did you want to get back into sequence?" Once again Katya positioned her still pinpoint-sharp pencil deftly over her notebook, determined this time to actually put it to use.

"No." It was an unhurried reply, like more detail would be following. None did.

"OK then –"

"Let's take a break." Jeslyn didn't need any input from Katya; the decision was already being carried out. "Are you hungry?" Jeslyn was up and at the sitting room entrance before Katya could fully register the change.

"Oh, I..." Katya wondered if she was even allowed to accept food.

"I'll have Tracy get us a snack." Jeslyn smiled. Her dazzling white teeth shining behind her perfectly glossed lips seemed to be playing to some hidden camera. Then, in a split second, her photo shoot worthy smile was gone and Jeslyn with it.

"Sure, I'll have a snack." Katya muttered to the empty room. Jeslyn was by far the most peculiarly fascinating woman Katya had ever met. Not that she had met a ton of people like her. But out of the fair share of hobnobbing she had done, Jeslyn took the prize.

It made Katya wonder, though, how deep Jeslyn's storytelling would get. She had pitched bombshells of information at her; no doubt just to watch her reaction as they exploded. But Katya didn't want fireworks, she wanted answers. Who was *the* Jeslyn Kennedy? Where had she come from, what was she after and, more importantly, what had happened between her and Matt Coleman? She would have to bide her time. A few minutes later, Jeslyn returned to the room with her right hand woman bringing up the rear.

Silently, Tracy rearranged the two small side tables that flanked Katya's and Jeslyn's chairs, and erected the portable serving stand she had brought with her into a makeshift dining area. While she was nearing the end of this, a knock came at the door. Tracy disappeared to answer it then reappeared with a sharply dressed older man whose right arm was ornamented with two small, covered, silver platters. After giving a hasty but polite greeting to all the women, he wordlessly laid out an assortment of meats, cheeses, fruit and crackers along with two serving plates. Afterward, Tracy and he exited together and it was just Katya and Jeslyn alone again.

"Don't be shy. Dig in." Jeslyn seemed more at ease.

"I turned off the recorder while you were...out." Katya said.

"Alright," Jeslyn popped a cheese cube in her mouth. "Are you going to make me eat this by myself?" She tossed a grape into the air and skillfully caught it in her mouth. "Down the hatch." She spoke to no one in particular.

Katya slowly picked at the light buffet. For whatever reason, she was finding it hard to completely relax. That constrained discomfort did not go unnoticed.

"So, recorder's off. Does that mean we're not in interview mode anymore?" It was the most informal she had been. Pop, pop, pop. More cheese, a pineapple chunk and another grape went down the hatch.

"Ah, yeah. That's...yes." Katya's head bobbed.

"So, you said that getting a scholarship was a whole other story. What did you mean by that?" Jeslyn tucked a leg underneath her and toyed with the table in front of her with her foot. Her already youthful facial features lost another few years. She now resembled an adolescent who was attempting to make a new friend.

"The scholarship?" Katya questioned.

"You. College. Your scholarship. Whole other story comment." A strip of thinly sliced roast beef dangled from Jeslyn's lips before she scooped it up with her tongue and chased it with a bite of bleu cheese.

"You want to know about my scholarship? OK then. Well, I –" before she could continue, Jeslyn cut in.

"What's with the 'OK then?' You say it quite a bit." Jeslyn's attention was directed toward a slice of honey ham wrapped around a tiny wedge of sharp cheddar.

"I do?" Katya had not been aware.

"Yes. Is it a nervous habit? Are you nervous?" It was at this moment Jeslyn focused her full attention on Katya. Her plate and both hands lowered gracefully to her knees, her big brown eyes putting a puppy dog's to shame.

"Maybe a little."

"Why?"

Katya was stunned. She would have thought it was obvious; that nervous is exactly how Jeslyn had intended for her to feel. "Well, you're very..." Jeslyn shoved a full quarter of an apple into her mouth causing her cheeks to stick out like a chipmunk's. "Serious." Katya watched Jeslyn's mouth work to hold the contents she'd just packed in it.

"Mmmmhmmm." Chomp, chomp, chomp.

"And you're a bit..." Jeslyn jumped up and padded barefoot over to the mini fridge. There was no runway to her walk, just casual clomping.

"Something to drink?" Jeslyn sucked at her teeth with her tongue before using her perfectly manicured nail to scrape something from in between her upper bicuspid and canine.

"Standoffish." Katya finished, while Jeslyn's actions mocked her descriptions.

"What was that?" Jeslyn was bent over digging through cans and bottles, her head almost buried inside.

"I'll have a diet coke." Katya's voice was quiet.

"Soda's horrible for you." Jeslyn stood and wiped at her impeccably trimmed bangs, her breathing was only slightly labored. "Here", she tossed a can Katya's way and grabbed another sparkling water for herself. Katya fumbled with the can but didn't let it drop.

"Organic energy drink. Not available on the market yet. You still get the fizz and the jolt," Jeslyn winked (an actual wink) "but without the high fructose corn syrup and other crap. Of course water's best but, whatever."

"Um, thanks."

For the weird public service announcement on nutrition, Katya finished silently. She popped the can's top open, guzzled a quarter of the drink and tried unsuccessfully not to feel self conscious as Jeslyn and her perfect body made their way back to the overstuffed chair. She watched her pound the cushions with her fist and bring both feet up under her on the seat.

"Where were we? Oh yes, you were going to tell me about the scholarship." Jeslyn noshed contentedly.

She seems perfectly fine now. Maybe she was just hungry. Katya knew how grumpy she got when she was hungry. Perhaps Jeslyn's surly demeanor had been nothing other than 'hanger' – the anger one gets from being hungry.

"Oh, right. OK then I –"

Jeslyn touched her right finger to her nose then pointed at Katya.

"What?" Katya was confused yet again. "Do I have something on my..." Katya wiped delicately at her own nose.

"OK then." Jeslyn's mouth was full of strawberry.

"Crap! Again?"

"Yup." Jeslyn tapped her nose with her finger. They now had a sign.

"Ugh, OK th-" Katya stopped herself but Jeslyn tapped her nose, pointed and cried out excitedly.

"Nope. No. You said it. You said it!" Her eyes were dancing with merriment.

"Agghhhh, I can do this." Katya took a deep breath and placed her hands out in front of her as if steadying herself. Her barely touched plate rested on her knees. "Oh my gosh, now all I want to say is 'OK then.'" Both girls chuckled lightheartedly. "OK, here we go. So. OK." Katya's motor kept stalling. Jeslyn tapped her nose. "Hey, I didn't say it!" Katya defended herself.

"Nope, but you're going to," Jeslyn said decidedly.

"I won't." Katya was resolute. "My scholarship. Geez, I almost forgot what we were even talking about." Katya tried alternate words, words that did not begin with 'OK then'. "So. Yes. Scholarship. Whole other story. Here we go." She chewed a piece of peppered turkey and contemplated where to begin. "In high school I played softball —" Katya's story was interrupted this time by three loud knocks on the door. No one moved. Two loud knocks followed.

"Oh that's right, Tracy's gone," Jeslyn said mostly to herself. "Who's there?" She called out instead of getting up and going to the door.

"Housekeeping." A woman's voice called back.

Katya was suddenly hit with a fit of giggles. It was Jeslyn's turn to crease her brows.

"Say, housekeeping who?" Katya whisper-giggled. Jeslyn was slow on the pick up, so Katya quickly acted it out. She made a knocking motion in the air first and pointed toward the door. "Who's there?" Katya mouthed, then pointed back at Jeslyn, an indication this was the line she'd spoken. "Housekeeping." Katya mouthed silently then pointed at the door again to indicate the response. "Housekeeping who?" Katya excitedly pointed back at Jeslyn insinuating this should be her next line — a real-life knock knock joke. Jeslyn's eyes widened in delight, her nostrils flaring as she struggled to suppress laughter.

"House…housekeeping who?" She clapped her hand over her mouth as a snort escaped.

"Uh...housekeeping." The woman behind the door did not know how to more accurately clarify her title.

"Come back...later. Another time, please." Jeslyn choked back another snicker. They could hear the maid's cart as it moved back down the hall.

"That. Was. Awesome." Katya stated.

"Classic." It took a minute for their amusement to fade.

"Scholarship." Katya still had pieces of giddiness stuck in her throat.

"Yes, scholarship." Jeslyn snuggled deeper into her chair.

"Like I said, in high school I was a softball player, a pretty good one. Good enough for a softball scholarship; at least until the middle of my senior year. Cue classic Shakespearean athletic tragedy. Promising scholarship down the tubes because of a severely torn ACL. Not only that, but my grades slipped drastically after the surgery and time spent in rehab – physical therapy rehab," Katya added quickly. "There was absolutely no way I was getting that athletic scholarship after that, but I had been really getting after it with the books prior to the bang up."

It was here that Jeslyn let out a noise that sounded like a mix between a cough and a lawnmower motor failing.

"Ummm...ok." Katya looked for an explanation.

"Sorry." Jeslyn bit down on her bottom lip, a smile fought to break free.

"You wanna share with the class?"

"You said bang up." A few puffs of laughter escaped through her nose. "Actually you said 'really getting after it with the books prior to the bang up.'" Snort.

"Yeeeessss." Katya waited for the punch line.

"That's..." Snicker. "...that's what she said!" Full on laughter.

"That was so bad." Katya grinned broadly. "Oh wow, that was really cheesy. I don't even know if that one coun –" Words could not express. "That was so bad. I'm actually embarrassed for you, right now." She couldn't stop grinning.

"You're probably right," Jeslyn's eyes were moist, her golden, sugar-in-the-raw skin glowing. Katya knew her own complexion was ruddy in comparison. "I'm sorry. Continue." Jeslyn wiped at her eyes.

"Only if you're sure you have no more extremely bad jokes." Jeslyn nodded, smiling. Katya went on. "My dad has connections everywhere and he decided to grease a few wheels to ensure I got an academic scholarship to USC. The horrible part, well, it's all horrible, but what makes it that much worse is he could've totally afforded to just send me. We didn't even need the scholarship. He was just too caught up on what the full ride to USC stood for." By now the smiles had shimmied down from both of their faces. "His demented justification was that I would have gotten a scholarship anyway had I not messed up my knee and fallen behind."

"Not to sound like a jerk, but with a knee injury couldn't you have kept up with your grades? I knew a kid that got jumped by eight guys at my high school. They broke three of his ribs, fractured his nose and dislocated his shoulder and he still graduated with a 4.0 GPA. And believe me, he got the 4.0 on his own merit. His folks didn't have enough grease for their own wheels let alone enough to grease anyone else's."

"No, you're right." Katya admitted sheepishly. "I fell behind because I sort of shut down for a bit after the injury." Katya went on the hunt for the right words to explain what had happened. "I had just busted my knee, right. My mother runs to the dugout after they haul me off the field and she is crying *buckets* – I mean, genuine, honest-to-goodness, crocodile tears. But not about my knee, oh no. She kept saying 'the scholarship is gone' and 'your future is ruined.' So, there's that going on and then my dad…well, he seemed thoroughly pissed off about the whole thing. I –" Katya exhaled and wriggled in her chair a bit. "I kind of gave up, I guess."

"So, you and your family aren't close then I take it?" Jeslyn questioned.

"We are, we were...we...are. It's complicated." Katya pinched her lips together in thought. "When my brother and my sister and I were little we were close. We were happy, too; this awesome little family unit. Then my grandpa passed away, he'd been a really wealthy guy, and my dad inherited his entire estate. It was a total shock to all of us. He and my grandpa hadn't been on speaking terms before he died and my father figured he wouldn't get anything from his old man. Turns out he was the sole inheritor; he got everything. Our lives flipped upside down after that. We moved to a new house in this fancy neighborhood and immediately it as all about keeping up with the Joneses." Katya spit the last few words out as if they tasted sour in her mouth.

"Yes, money can change things, if you let it."

Before either could comment further a faint buzzing sound came from some unseen place. Jeslyn produced a Bluetooth headset from the bosom of her dress and adjusted it to her ear. She didn't look for the source of the buzzing and Katya didn't see a cell nearby. A wicked grin tugged at her lips, eventually pulling them into a devilish smile.

"Well, hello stranger." Her voice came out smooth, like each word was dipped in port wine. They were rich without being overpowering and, no doubt, having some type of an effect on the recipient. Jeslyn's pearly whites scraped along her bottom lip, dimpling it just barely. She unconsciously brought her long, slender, caramel fingers to her hair, playing with a few strands of it. Her conversation, although little more than murmurs of affirmations, seemed to speak volumes. Again, Katya found herself captivated by the essence of Jeslyn Kennedy. She was confidence. She was power. She was a thing of beauty. She was...flirting?

"I could easily fix that situation for you." It was an appropriate enough statement but held such a naughty implication that Katya immediately felt the heat in her cheeks rise, bringing the blotchy tell-tell tinge of blush to the surface.

Jeslyn continued her cryptic conversation with the caller who could apparently be identified by only a buzz. "We'll pick this up later when I can go into explicit detail about what the nature of that arrangement would entail." It may have been eloquently delivered, but this entire exchange made Katya feel as though she'd walked in on something very intimate. The call ended with Jeslyn saying, "I look forward to it." Another tap of the Bluetooth and it was tucked back into the fleshy recesses from where it had been retrieved.

Still caught up in their girly banter from earlier, Katya playfully inquired about the call. "That was certainly steamy." She was met with a terse smile, but took it a step farther. "So, was it Forbes?"

A silent glare can be delivered in such a cold manner that it's almost physically debilitating. Jeslyn gave Katya one of those glares now. The subzero annoyance was instantly felt. It jaggedly tore through Katya's punchy raillery with such intensity her breath caught in her throat as if she'd been forcibly flicked in the esophagus.

"I...I'm sorry. I didn't mean to pry." Katya watched the heat die down in Jeslyn's eyes. It was like watching the hair lower on the back of an angry mastiff. While there was still the danger of being mauled to death, it wasn't as imminent.

"Let's get back to the interview shall we?" In an instant, the fun-loving Jeslyn was gone, replaced by *the* Jeslyn Kennedy. Katya's heart sank.

Little did she know the sinking feeling wouldn't last long. While she sat trying to figure out the inconstant Kennedy woman, and failing miserably, a whirlwind of chaotic activity was unfolding that would wreak havoc on the carefully constructed arrangement that had been struck between the two.

9

~April 26~

      When they initially spoke, one of Jeslyn's (many) rules of the interview had been no cell phones. Katya had left hers in the car and hadn't given it much thought. If she would have brought it with her, she'd have seen eighteen missed calls and over twenty unanswered texts that had come through in the last hour and a half.

      Something that had started out simply enough had since created an avalanche of pandemonium that was barreling toward Katya and Jeslyn at a rapid pace while they unwittingly played the role of sitting ducks.

*   *   *

      Sara Jensen was tired. She'd had too many long days filled with caffeine, antacid, tight deadlines, a few big breaks, some bigger losses, and not enough respite from it all. She had looked forty dead in the eye two years ago, but felt as though it had been at least a decade. With one failed marriage under her belt and a long (too long to even bother recalling) line of disastrous first dates, second dates and, couldn't-even-be-called-relationships in her rearview, she wasn't interested in being with anyone, but tired of being alone.

She stared out her office window at the blindingly bright April daylight and concentrated on the San Diego skyline. She could hear the bells and pings from incoming messages but gave herself five minutes to zone out. Just five minutes. She deserved that, didn't she? The fact that it was a question only served to dampen her mood.

But downtime wasn't in the cards. David Sims burst into her makeshift sanctuary, all slick and urgent. Like a slimy seed inside half of a juicy lemon, he shot through her door as if some unknown force had popped him out of his citrus confines.

"Sara, oh, I'm so glad I found you!" He panted.

Sara was used to David and the commotion he created; commotion that was usually the result of inconsequential events that David found more fascinating than anyone else. Being that she practically lived in her office, she figured this first commotion du jour that began with, 'so glad I found you' (*where the hell else would I be Sims?*) would prove to be just another Sims-ism; a term synonymous with over exaggeration. This time Sara was wrong.

"This isn't good, oh boy, this isn't good." David paced the small space in front of her desk and massaged his forehead with his hand, taking care to not muss his stiff hair. Sara waited, looking more patient than she felt. "This is really not good. I don't know how it happened and I can't get in touch with Katya."

At the mention of Katya's name, Sara perked up. It was time to stop with the 18th century hand wringing and peasantry wailing and get down to brass tacks.

"David, sit!" Sara's drill sergeant command was heeded instantly. David sat. "Look at me." David looked. "You've got thirty words to tell me what the hell is going on. Go!" David went.

"Katya's interview with Jeslyn got leaked. Everyone's up in arms trying to find out where they are, how we got the exclusive, and what's going on. It's bad." Two words to spare.

Sara didn't realize she'd raised herself out of her chair into a standing position until he'd finished and she found herself looking down at his chin. It was clean shaven and angled upward allowing his eyes to lock fretfully with hers. She eased herself back into her chair and let the information soak in before speaking. "Leaked how?"

"At this point, we think via Twitter."

"When?"

"The post was made at around 3 o'clock on some random account."

"What've we heard from Katya?"

"We've tried calling, texting...nothing."

"Damage?"

David took a deep breath; his words came out in a rush during his exhale. "The pandemonium is in full swing and a shit ton of questions are hitting the wires. Phones are crazy. Emails are pouring in. They all want the scoop."

Sara figured the situation was probably drawing attention, but she simply couldn't rely on Sims' account of the whole ordeal. His propensity to lean toward the dramatic in virtually all instances made him a loose cannon – in virtually all instances. David stared at her bug-eyed, his tongue darting out in lizard-like fashion to moisten his lips. He also kept flicking his nose with his thumb in an annoyingly compulsive way, like some rehabilitated junkie.

She doubted David was, in fact, a rehabilitated junkie, but he didn't seem to be able to leave his nose alone and it was distracting.

"David, do you need a tissue?" She asked bluntly.

Maybe it was something he heard often, or maybe she had been the first to make him aware of his aggravating twitch, either way, David shook his head and sat on his hands instead. Sara ignored him and looked up the number for the Hotel del Coronado. She called, conveyed an urgent – 'but not life threatening,' she made sure to mention –

message to the concierge, then prayed for a speedy return call.

"You are excused, David. I'll call you if I need you."

David looked as if she'd just told him he was going to be spending the next six months in Alcatraz. He dejectedly rose from the chair, gave her a sad nod and walked out. Sara then set to work trying to ascertain the extent of the damage while simultaneously checking emails and voicemails. Multitasking for her was like a sedative. It was when she had too much time on her hands that she felt anxious.

Unfortunately, David was right, things didn't look good. A few breaking news reports – this was actually being categorized as breaking news – were cropping up on smaller news sites all over the web like brush fires around a dry wheat field. Tantalizing headlines were the winds carrying them into even more dangerous territory. At the nucleus of that potential fire storm was *GFS'* name. Normally, any exposure was good exposure. The magazine had received negative press before, but that wasn't the problem here. The problem was Jeslyn had made it very clear that if anything got out prior to the official story being released or without her consent there would be a heavy price to pay. Sara knew *GFS* didn't have the kind of collateral that price would exact.

She reached for a bottle in her desk drawer, not caring if it was antacid, aspirin or rat poison; she could use all three. Speaking of rat, she searched the Twitter feeds for the initial leaked post. She found the mention within minutes. @BatteryPowered had made the post at 2:55pm which read:

@GFS Mag scores #JeslynKennedy exclusive interview Apr 26 at 3p PST.

The @BatteryPowered Twitter account only had a total of four tweets and the account itself was only three months old. That last piece of information was at first a relief. At least the perpetrator, whoever he or she was, hadn't established the account after the call from Jeslyn had come in, Sara thought. Then, considering it further, realized that offered little solace; the timeframe meant nothing. In fact, maybe it was a bad thing. Perhaps it meant this leak had been premeditated by someone from Kennedy's camp, or someone who had inside information beforehand. It could be *GFS* was being toyed with and this was one of those clues that would prove to be the clincher later on.

She took a screenshot and saved the image in a newly created desktop folder. Just in case it disappeared, it would be good to have on file. Now, she simply had to find a way to put out all of these pesky fires before the blaze burned too ferociously to do anything about it. Her mission, she thought bleakly, would be easier to carry out if Katya would call her back.

*　*　*

Jeslyn had not been pissed before; Katya took Patty's side once again. The look on her face when she'd first laid eyes on her actually had been standoffish. Now, she was pissed. And that put Katya on pins and needles. It had happened when Tracy made an appearance and whispered something in her ear. Even the whispering had seemed foreboding. Plus, Jeslyn did not seem like the type of woman who suffered interruptions graciously. Katya's self fulfilling prophesy began to play out.

"Thank you." Jeslyn dismissed Tracy before redirecting her bristled attention to Katya. "I find myself on the verge of outrage when I watch movies, TV shows, or hear stories where one character observes an event from a distance, then automatically jumps to an incorrect conclusion, causing the rest of the plot to be irreparably ruined by a simple misinterpretation."

She stared at Katya, menacingly – what Katya thought was menacingly. It was really just direct, but Katya was jumpy again and everything had become menacing. The shadows in the room were menacing, the stillness outside of

88

the room was menacing, even the leftover meat and cheese that sat unappetizingly in front of her was menacing.

"Had one or two direct questions been asked," Jeslyn continued, "and the other party given ample time to respond, I bet that over fifty percent of the entertainment choices we now have at our disposal would cease to exist. Either that, or producers would actually have to start crafting better storylines."

Katya shifted warily in her chair not knowing where Jeslyn was going with this. And not even sure she wanted to know.

"That being said, I'm going to ask you a few very direct questions. I will hear your response in its entirety, then we can go from there. Are we clear?"

As mud. "Yes." Katya felt as if she'd just been caught sneaking in past curfew. What in the world could this inquisition possibly be about?

"First question," Jeslyn cracked her neck, pulling her sinewy muscles and veins taut beneath her skin. The sound was like the crack of a whip to Katya. "Besides your immediate superiors and select office staff members, who else knows about our interview?"

Katya's thoughts had positioned themselves against the cinderblocks of her memory waiting for Jeslyn to ask the first question. Now that the question was out there, those thoughts began to race. As far as she knew, no one else besides the parties Jeslyn had just mentioned was privy to the knowledge of their meeting. Katya voiced this out loud.

"Question two," Jeslyn didn't acknowledge Katya's reply, so she didn't know if it had been accepted or if Jeslyn was simply waiting until all of her questions had been answered before she went off. "Have you or anyone you know posted any details about this interview online?"

"No." That was an easy one for Katya to answer. She felt secure in her honesty despite the fact that her voice wobbled nervously. After all, Jeslyn had said not to talk to anyone about the interview aside from those who absolutely needed to know. There had been no one who hadn't absolutely needed to know that Katya had –

Oh no! There was one. Her best friend LeAnn. *No, no, no, no, no.* Katya had expressed quite emphatically that the information regarding this interview not go any further. LeAnn was a steel trap. She wouldn't have. She didn't. *But what if she did?*

"Question three." Jeslyn was moving on but Katya knew she had to speak up. Her stomach lurched at the thought of it. Knowing it was the right thing to do didn't stymie the feeling that she was about to show Jeslyn her partially digested breakfast and lunch.

"Wait!" Katya snapped her eyes shut as if she were bracing herself for the impact of an oncoming vehicle. "I...there was someone else. I told someone else." Katya let the words fly out of her mouth quickly for fear she wouldn't have the nerve to say them. When she opened her eyes she was greeted with Jeslyn's stare. Another unfeeling, unnerved stare that, right then, felt worse than the most severe tongue lashing she'd ever received. "My best friend, LeAnn. I told her. We talk about everything and I mentioned I had an important interview coming up and –"

"I'm not worried about LeAnn."

Katya's gasp hitched, like a fist had grabbed it in the middle and cut it off before it could finish reporting her bafflement. Her head swam trying to grasp the meaning behind those words.

Was Jeslyn saying she wasn't worried that Katya had told her best friend about the interview? Or – and this thought filled her with more trepidation than any other – was she saying she wasn't worried about LeAnn because she'd already checked LeAnn out? Meaning, she not only knew all or most of the people in Katya's life, but she had investigated them as well. If her opening act was any indication – *your father is a psychologist, your mother is a Hospital Director* – the latter scenario was probably the nail head hitter.

90

Unaware, or at least unconcerned, she'd just cracked and scrambled Katya's brain, Jeslyn continued. "Question three: Are you aware of a post made via Twitter that mentions your magazine has scored an exclusive interview with me, giving the specific date and time..." Katya was fully prepared to answer 'no' but Jeslyn hadn't finished. "...posted by at Battery Powered?"

This was when her heart dislodged itself from her chest and catapulted itself somewhere else. It wasn't beating, it wasn't racing, it wasn't doing anything. Her heart had left her body leaving Katya wondering if this was what death was like. If it wasn't, she was probably about to find out. If Jeslyn didn't kill her, Sara most definitely would.

While Katya hadn't been aware of the leaked post, she was aware of the handle. @BatteryPowered belonged to her.

10

It had been over twenty minutes. In the media world, where minutes were like dog years, this was a century. Sara had instructed the entire office to respond to any and all inquiries regarding the Kennedy interview with two words and two words only. No comment. This had made things worse. And it was no wonder. This was a story a lot of people wanted. To not talk about it could mean only a few things; the top two being either: A) *GFS* was making the entire thing up (this accounted for the majority of the claims). Or, B) something illegal or underhanded had transpired that had allowed *GFS* to obtain the story.

Gray Flannel Suit Magazine was known for keeping its nose clean as a company, for the most part. The monthly glossy was also recognized as much for its stunning design and editorial layouts as its hard truth business journalism. Trashy exposes, fluff pieces and sensationalism were not the rag's modus operandi. Therefore, the foul play outcries, although making the rounds, were more background babble than foreground pageantry.

As the speculations swirled, Sara waited. It killed her to feel this helpless. She remembered signing her divorce papers, looking across the kitchen table at her ex and asking the age old question, 'Where did we go wrong?' He'd looked at her with those weary eyes of his and said, 'You figure everything else out on your own, Sara J, I'm sure you don't need me for this one.'

Well, here she was in need. If she could, she would've bottled this moment and saved it for the next time someone insinuated she didn't need anyone. It would be evidence. 'Look!' she'd cry, 'I was in need.' And when they asked when, she'd hold up her bottled moment, wave it in front of their face so they could get a good, hard, long look. Then, she'd smash the bottle over their head, whoever the unlucky idiot was. Everyone needed someone at some point in time. How moronic to assume she was any different than the people she crossed paths with.

Speaking of crossing paths, she needed to cross paths with Katya and find out what was happening with that damnable Jeslyn Kennedy interview.

*   *   *

This was bad. Very bad. Jeslyn was waiting for an answer, and from the looks of it she wasn't pleased in the least that it hadn't arrived. Before Katya, who felt as though she had one foot in her career grave and one on a banana peel, could once and for all bury herself professionally, Tracy walked back in the room. More whispering. Jeslyn's face revealed nothing more than it had before. She held out her palm and Tracy placed Katya's cell phone in it. Tracy placed Katya's cell phone...

"That's my phone." Katya spoke out loud the words that were being screamed in her head. It was impossible. Her cell phone had been left in her car. Her locked car.

"Your boss needs to speak with you." Jeslyn extended her hand indicating Katya should take her phone. She numbly grabbed it. She could barely concentrate. How had Tracy gotten a hold of her phone? Her cell phone that had been left in her car. Her locked car.

Katya shot a glance at her messenger bag and saw the familiar glint of silver in the outer zip pouch. Her car keys were still in her possession. Was this some kind of joke? What exactly was she dealing with here?

Katya was agitated. "How did you get my phone?" Tracy exited the room leaving only one person left to deal with her outwardly benign, inwardly raging conniption.

"You have calls to make. I'll leave you to it." Jeslyn stood up, smoothed her hands over the front of her dress and made to leave. Katya stood up, too, heart pounding wildly and blocked her path.

"How did you get my phone?" Her voice was uneven.

"Tracy had a locksmith open the vehicle." Simple. Eerily simple.

If Katya had been omniscient, she still wouldn't have known what to say. She felt as though she'd just been violated. That was because she *had* been violated. She was angry and confused. She looked at her phone, the same phone that had been in her locked car and was now in her hand. Why couldn't she smell burning skin? Her whole body felt like it was on fire. The flames of indignation lapped at her face and burned through her powers of deductive reasoning.

"Special circumstances. It won't happen again." Jeslyn stood there only long enough to see if Katya would say anything further. When she did not, Jeslyn disappeared through the double doors of the sitting room, quietly shutting them behind her.

Katya fumed over Jeslyn and her weird control antics. Then she began fuming about the Twitter account. How had a message about the interview been posted through Twitter using an account she set up?

She skimmed through the missed calls and texts, checked her email quickly then called Sara's cell phone instead of her office line. The editor answered on the first ring.

"Tell me something."

"Sara, I'm going to have to ask you to trust me." Katya's was working to piece this puzzle together and she felt she was just shy of figuring something out.

"Katya, you need to tell me something. It's a tad bit hectic around here right now. I got jammed phone lines, reporters in the lobby and a newswire that's spewing out some pretty interesting stuff. What's happening with our lady of mystery?"

"Not much. She's —" Katya tried to think of the best way to describe Jeslyn's demeanor, "reservedly pissed." *And controlling, and infuriating and, and, and.*

"Reservedly pissed? What does that mean?"

Obviously, it hadn't been descriptive enough. "She's not happy, but she hasn't called off the interview. She just wants to figure out what's going on first."

"Speaking of 'figuring stuff out,' have you figured out what's with this crazy secrecy?" Katya knew Sara was not only referring to Jeslyn's demand to keep this particular interview under wraps but also her connection to Coleman.

"No. But what I've surmised so far is that she likes her privacy. She also likes her publicity handled a certain way." She knew this wasn't what Sara wanted to hear.

"So, what's next?" Sara asked.

"I'm going to have to call you back with the answer to that. I'm pretty sure I can get to the bottom of this fairly quickly, but I need a minute." Katya also needed to make another call.

"Katya Houston, you have ten minutes tops. Otherwise, I'm going to handle this myself, how I see fit." Katya doubted Sara had worked out that 'see fit' plan yet, but she was sure the woman could come up with something.

"OK. Ten minutes. Got it." Without offering a formal farewell, Katya pressed the end button then immediately dialed another number. This time the person didn't answer as quickly. After four rings Katya started to panic. She needed him to answer.

Ring five.

It didn't look good.

Ring six.

Even worse.

"Hi, Katya."

Mercy (noun): Compassion, pity, benevolence or kindly forbearance shown toward an offender, an enemy or other person in one's power.

Thank heaven for mercy.

"Oh. Hi, Ethan." She'd been so preoccupied that she'd completely forgotten how his voice gave her five-year-old-child-night-before-Christmas anxiety. "I was wondering if you could help me look at a this...I mean, really quick at something for a minute...if you could."

Botched.

"I'm sorry Katya, I think you might be breaking up."

"Sorry. Let me try that again." Katya tried to un-fluster herself which was a lot like trying to unlearn English. "I was wondering if you could do me a favor. Before you agree...or...or not, I just want you to know that the request isn't exactly on the up and up."

"Not on the up and up, huh? I'm listening. What do you need?"

Man, she liked this guy.

"Do you remember the training I put together a few months ago for some of the people in the office on social media?"

"Yeah, the Tech Savvy-less Geriatric Justification Training Course?"

"That's the one." Katya smiled, relishing (much too heavily) in the fact that Ethan remembered something about her.

He'd stopped by her desk to ask if she'd been invited to that month's writers' and editors' meeting. She was still interning, which apparently meant she wasn't allowed to actually do anything that would be relevant to the job she was looking to acquire. Instead, she'd been assigned to put together a series of training courses on social media for some of the staff.

When she'd looked over the roster of who'd be participating in the training, she realized her students were comprised of mainly older (ancient) staff members as well as staff – some executive level even – who seemed to be allergic to new technology. She had told Ethan that, no, she hadn't been invited to the meeting; she was responsible for creating and delivering a Tech Savvy-less Geriatric Justification Training Course. She couldn't possibly be bothered with superfluous things like journalism and writers' meetings.

She had only said it that one time. He'd remembered.

"Anyway, I was wondering if you've also heard about the little Jeslyn Kennedy Twitter leak via the account I created for that course?"

"Little leak? Ha! That's an understatement. Yeah, I've heard about it. What are you thinking?"

"Well, I know this sounds very double-oh-seven of me, but I think it was an inside job."

"Me too."

You do? Katya didn't know why exactly, but his response shocked her. "Oh, OK then." With that out of the way, it was time to take the level of difficulty up a notch and explain exactly who she thought was behind the mayhem. "Well, I also have an idea of who it might be."

"OK." Ethan waited.

"Look, Ethan, I need you to know I don't go around accusing people. I really thought about this." In reality, it had taken her all of thirty seconds to come up with a suspect.

"You don't have to justify yourself to me, Katya." He said it like someone standing up for her instead of someone who was about to follow it up with, 'tell it to the judge.'

"Thanks Ethan. Now for the not-so-above-board part – I need you to check someone's computer for me. Not...not just their computer but their internet history log."

"Katya, not to bust your Blue's Clues bubble or anything, but don't you think if he were smart enough to make a post on Twitter using the training account you set up, he's smart enough to delete his internet history?"

Ethan had said 'he.' Katya hadn't mentioned a gender. She'd specifically kept her accusation gender neutral until she could assess Ethan's position on the whole thing. It was going surprisingly well; especially considering this was only the second time she'd ever called him on his cell phone. The first time was when the hard drive on her old laptop had crashed. She'd been lamenting to a coworker about it and Ethan had overheard. He'd given her his personal number and told her to call him after work and he'd check it out; he was somewhat of a closet IT guru. Like a musical prodigy, computers were his thing – just not his career thing. He preferred to fiddle with CPUs, processors and interface cards as a hobby.

"Possibly." Katya spoke the word slowly, as if she were a wind up doll on the last rotation of her crank. "Then again, sometimes cockiness has a way of making some people feel as though they're beyond detection or suspicion."

"OK."

"OK?"

"OK. Give me a few minutes and I'll call you back." Ethan seemed prepared to hang up.

"Ethan?"

"Yeah."

"Aren't you going to ask me whose computer I need you to check?"

"If you'd like me to, I can." Ethan was acting as if it were a redundant formality. Katya didn't know how to proceed. She'd never heard Ethan speak ill of anyone, at the office or otherwise. Her call to him was coming pretty much out of thin air, and yet he was behaving as if they'd been working on this case for some time now – tracking the same lead.

"I'm going to put it out there and say I'm a bit confused."

Ethan sighed audibly. "There aren't too many bad guys here in Gotham City, Batman. So, when you bump into one, they tend to stick out."

"Oh. OK then." Katya still felt unsettled. Part of her wanted to believe Ethan was gunning for the same target, that she could go ahead and let him get started with his P.I. duties sans any further discussion. The other part of her – the cross your t's and dot your lower case j's part – needed to know they were both on the same page. Her tormented silence must have come through loud and clear.

"Although *GFS* is a big organization in theory, it's very small when it comes to dirt." Ethan filled her in on what he meant by this. "So, a little over a week ago, a call comes into the office and all of a sudden there's this buzz going that the new girl has landed an amazing feature story. Not just any story either – a high profile whopper. So, of course everyone's interested. The only thing is, this high profile whopper of a story is very hush-hush. *GFS* is known for laying all its cards on the table, so the secrecy is a big head scratcher for a lot of people. For one person in particular, this secrecy is an unacceptable affront. For one person in particular, it's been reason to openly gripe and complain. I figure where there's smoke, there's probably fire and Seltzer has been doing a lot of smoking lately."

There. He said it. Katya realized she'd been scrunching her muscles together in anticipation. She relaxed them before replying.

"Ethan, I owe you one."

"Don't worry about it. Now, the big question is, what do you want to do if our suspicions pan out?"

Katya tried to not be affected at the fact he'd said 'our suspicions.' But anything that paired her and Ethan together was cause for her temperature to spike. She clung to her wits by a silk thread.

"I haven't figured that part out yet. Perhaps we could find a way to let Sara know who the culprit is without divulging the tactics used to discover said culprit." She knew she was compromising Ethan's integrity on a host of different levels, but it felt good to have a cohort in this. Besides, it didn't appear he minded all that much.

"That could be arranged, actually." Ethan spoke carefully. "Can you hold on for two seconds?"

"Absolutely." Katya's blood rushed in her ears as much from the thrill of all this mad capering as the thrill of working with Ethan.

While they were chummy office mates, this was by far the most intertwined their work partnership had been. Still, she knew her affections for him were one-sided diversions.

Katya had become BFF with the 'he's-just-not-that-into-you-if-he-wanted-to-ask-you-out-he-would-he-only-thinks-of-us-as-friends' realities that most women ignored. She didn't fool herself with gilded lies about how she was too intimidating, or he really liked her but was waiting for an opportune time to ask her out. She'd been at *GFS* for nearly nine and a half months. Several opportune times had come, asked him about his day, given him kind smiles, mooned over his perfection, and gone.

As for intimidation, Katya was the most approachable person she knew. Not only that, she practically salivated anytime Ethan was in her line of sight. A lobotomy patient could have picked up on the fact she was smitten by him. No, this was her crush to bear alone. Katya was mature enough to take it for what it was and leave the fantasies of what she'd like it to be completely off the table.

"You still with me?" Ethan sounded slightly out of breath.

"Yes." Was she ever.

"So, Major Anya Amasova, let's see what we have here." Katya could hear Ethan clicking away on a keyboard. Her heart double thumped at his reference to her as one of the James Bond series' most liberated Bond girls. Some even considering the character an equal, in skills and abilities, to Bond himself. Ethan's innocent pairings of the two of them was turning Katya's insides into warm oatmeal. As she so often did, she stuffed those emotions into her back pocket until she could appropriately deal with them at a later time and place.

"Did you already look at his computer?" Katya's heart raced.

"Nope. Looking...now." Ethan sounded distracted.

"You're at his desk?" Katya gulped. The cubicles that hemmed in their desks gave little to no coverage, especially for something this covert. Ethan was sure to get caught.

"No, I'm at mine." More typing.

"I'm dying here." Katya could no longer conceal her exasperation. What was going on?

"While we were talking, I logged into my computer at home. I have a program that, when installed on a device, mirrors its activity. I downloaded that program onto a flash drive and uploaded it onto Seltzer's computer. Wasn't too difficult; I just walked over and asked him if he had the files from last November's issue on his computer because mine had lost access to the network for some reason. He didn't suspect a thing. I popped the flash drive in and presto!" Ethan's words were punctuated by enthusiastic keyboard clicks.

The man was brilliant.

"So, what do you see?" Katya gnawed on the inside of her cheek.

"He's definitely been on Twitter. There's nothing to suggest that he was the one who accessed the training account...yet." Ethan continued to mine for data. Katya's confidence sagged. Perhaps she was barking up the wrong tree. She'd been wrong to assume Brandon Seltzer was behind this in the first place. Nothing good ever came from blindly accusing –

"Hold on a minute." Click, click, click. Katya held. "Looks like someone isn't as dumb as he seems. Our boy used an anonymous proxy server recently." He might as well have spoken to her in Japanese.

"What does that mean?"

"It means, he was more than likely visiting places on the web that he didn't want anyone to know about, so he used a proxy server to hide his IP address. Basically, he was trying to cover his online tracks for some reason or another. While it's not a smoking gun, I'd say it provides reasonable doubt."

Katya knew reasonable doubt wasn't enough. She'd been hoping that Brandon *was* as dumb as she thought him to be and had left himself wide open. No such luck. Now, with the mention of servers and proxys and hidden IP addresses (oh my), she was even more discouraged.

"Well," Katya filled her cheeks with air that she pushed out forcibly, a small part of her resolve blowing out with it. "Thanks, Ethan. Sorry to have dragged you into this for nothing."

"It wasn't for nothing and you didn't drag me," he argued. "You and I both know he did it, we just don't have the evidence yet. Believe me, there's probably no one who wants to see that guy go down more than I do. He's a complete ass. Something will come up; if not now, at some point."

"You're probably right. For now, though, I have to squelch this insanity."

"Any ideas?"

"A couple."

"Well, I'm always here if you need me." Ethan's friendly offer made Katya's insides clench.

"That's very kind, thank you. I'll let you know." She had used him enough for one day. Katya let Ethan go, then set to work herding the cats that had been set loose with that one Twitter post.

If one post could do all of that...

Katya logged into the training account. She then posted a salacious, and terribly false, tweet from the @BatteryPowered profile that said the *Wall Street Journal* had scored an exclusive interview with Jeslyn Kennedy at 7:00 p.m. PT. She then logged into the magazine's HootSuite account and scheduled three more similar posts, five to fifteen minutes apart, using the names of other top news publications.

Next, she called Sara back and instructed her to put out a release that said it appeared a spammer was targeting several news publishers and that *GFS* was looking into the matter. She was careful to point out that in no way should the interview with Jeslyn be flat out denied, simply not mentioned. Keep the attention on being spammed and, if possible, reference any other cases where something similar had happened.

Lastly, she sent LeAnn a text that read, 'RM - this whole f-ing JK experience/nightmare.'

As if on cue, Jeslyn opened the sitting room doors with a flourish and entered the room. She sat in the same chair she'd been occupying since the interview began and made a Groundhog Day reenactment of regarding Katya silently. Katya, who had paced all over the room while she cleaned up the mess made by the leak, and had ended up on the far side by a bay window that overlooked a terrace, continued to sift through her texts and emails. She was over Jeslyn's intimidation-through-silence mind rape. If she wasn't going to open her mouth and say something, Katya wasn't either.

"Thank you." After what seemed like forever and half an eternity, Jeslyn's voice brought life to the dead air.

"For?" Katya was having a hard time losing her edge. She still hadn't forgotten the cell phone retrieval incident.

"Everything." Jeslyn met Katya's gaze. "I know this is a lot to deal with. I see, now, that you weren't responsible for the fiasco…the leak of this interview. I also see I've upset you. While not my intention, it happened nonetheless. So, thank you for being gracious and for honoring our agreement."

Katya softened. "You're welcome." The apology trimmed with gratitude threw her. It was a pull-your-hair-out-and-slap-the-pope test of grit dealing with Jeslyn's hot/cold, soft/steely personalities. One minute she appeared to be stereotypically self-righteous, and the next she seemed doggedly remorseful, if not insecure. She'd only spent a few hours with her, but Katya didn't know if she could make it through whatever sudden plummet, twist or loop the rest of the Jeslyn roller coaster ride had to offer.

"If you're still interested, I'd like to finish." Jeslyn spoke softly, almost demurely and her features turned angelically serene.

"Of course. Yeah, let me just –" Katya fired off a text to Sara to keep her apprised of any changes in the Jeslyn Gate affray. Then she went back to being a passive inquisitor.

"Before...everything," Jeslyn made a slow jazz hands gesture to indicate the leak situation, "you posed a question."

Katya racked her brain trying to remember what that last question had been. There was the bit about the cell phone retrieval. *No, that was after the melee.* Beforehand she had asked about…

"Forbes?"

The beguiling side smirk that Jeslyn effectuated so well made an appearance. "While his story for the sake of talking about him is not mine to tell, the part of him that deals with my story is."

Katya moved her lips, silently repeating what Jeslyn had just said. On first hearing it, she was struck with 'Who's on First, What's on Second, and I Don't Know What That Meant' confusion. "I'm sorry. Come again?"

Jeslyn laughed. A soft, light laugh that Katya was certain could help bring about world peace. Katya fished her self-respect out of the water and reeled her girl crush back in. After examining it and realizing it wasn't a big enough issue to hold onto, she let it swim free, and allowed herself to feel excitement that she was once again invited into Jeslyn's private realm. She was going to talk about Forbes. This should be good.

"What I'm trying to say is, I will tell you the entire story but I need you to understand this is from my perspective. I'm sure he sees the entire thing quite differently."

Sees. She didn't say he 'saw' the entire thing differently. Did that mean...? Katya held off asking any further questions even though that is precisely what she was there to do.

"Unfortunately, he had no idea what he was getting himself into. I'm sure if he'd had any warning beforehand, he would've run in the opposite direction."

Jeslyn would let the story divulge itself. There was no use poisoning the well if you were getting ready to tell the villagers you'd poisoned it. Katya would learn soon enough why it was best to steer clear of her raging emotional rivers and any sources, metaphorical or otherwise, attached to it.

11

~Before~

One month and two days. She had already been unemployed for that long. The dispiriting part of that realization was that she wouldn't have been able to explain how she'd spent her days and weeks in that span of time if she'd been asked. Thankful for her, no one asked.

The Thanksgiving holiday was quickly approaching with Christmas holding onto its heels like a twin trying to enter the world concurrently with its sibling. Jeslyn had barely noticed either one. Aside from casually keeping in touch with acquaintances, she had mainly been keeping to herself. Without a nine to five, days had begun to melt into each other like a watercolor painting left in the rain. With nothing on the horizon and very little progress on her millionaire mission, weeks began to do the same.

As she sat at her dining room table early one morning taking part in her only pastime – scouring online sources for information on the world's wealthiest people – she came across a picture of a young, attractive CEO. It looked as though the photographer who'd been lucky enough to snap his image captured him seconds after he'd been told an amusing joke. Genuine happiness seemed to be etched across his face like initials carved into bark.

Jeslyn knew countless attractive men; maybe not personally, but the world was full of actors, models and everyday guys that could turn heads. Beauty was in the eye of the beholder. One woman's Adonis was another's Average Joe, she got that. However, she knew this profile picture would behold to a very large percentage of the population. The pale green eyes, like two memories of mint, peering at her below thick, dark brows, grabbed her hand and forced her to click the link.

Forbes Keith. She instantly connected with the name. It was both unusual and at the same time commonly sophisticated. She read the bio. Several images of him were included for her viewing pleasure. Forbes' serious face. Forbes' professional shot. Forbes at a speaking engagement. Forbes laughing casually, head slightly tilted back, eyes looking straight to camera.

Jeslyn wasn't one to swoon over just a picture, but she did appreciate beauty. Forbes' winsome features, which hinted at a delicate mix of ethnicities swirled into his metro-rugged Anglo American-ness, were fetching. If nothing else, it beat the leathered old codgers and fake-n-bake cougars whose pictures were normally in the lineup of the world's most affluent.

He was a biochemist. Jeslyn knew very little about biochemistry, only enough to know that a high level of intelligence was required to be successful in the field. She assumed a mind-boggling amount of intelligence must be required to achieve the level of success Mr. Keith enjoyed.

That was intriguing. Brains and beauty were not often bedfellows found in one person. Split between a couple? That happened all of the time. There was no shortage of beautiful creatures who had attached themselves to homely brainiacs. A beautiful brainiac? That was a diamond in the rough. Jeslyn indulged herself with more information on this shiny gem.

An Ivy League college graduate (naturally), originally from Chicago and currently residing in San Diego County – a SoCal transplant. Wealthy, respected parents; charity donor; former lacrosse player...his bio read like a formulaic perfect-on-paper curriculum vitae. With her interest petering out, Jeslyn went to click the back button but something caught her eye. Forbes' favorite quotation was listed. While there was nothing noteworthy about having a favorite quote, his quote in particular made her do a double take.

"Don't complain about the game and what ruins it. We are the change we want to see - Solutionists. In the heart and mind is where revolution is. And in life and on mics is where we're showing and proving it." ~ Sojourn

It was a tailored version, most likely tidied up to pass without question for inclusion in profiles such as these, but those were definitely the lyrics from a song by a local underground hip hop artist. This clean-cut, multi-millionaire biochemist was quoting hip hop. Jeslyn stared at his picture.

"What's *that* about Forbes Keith?" She spoke aloud to the room of one.

The thing with obsessions is there's always a trigger. Something that pulls the pin of the synapses back and then forcefully plunges it into the primer of desire, igniting the powder of compulsion and projecting the obsession into whatever agitator instigated the episode in the first place. Forbes Keith was now pulling on Jeslyn's trigger finger. An attractive face and a fat wallet were a dime a dozen. Forbes, however, showed an edge; a quirk hidden in plain sight that hinted at the possibility of there being more to him than initially met the eye.

That was only the beginning.

A few minutes, turned into a few hours, which turned into nearly half a day of sporadically Googling, YouTubing and Wikipediaing Forbes Michael Keith.

Every article, press release, image and php/wordpress/java mention plunged her deeper into insatiable engrossment. Like an alcoholic promising himself just one more drink, Jeslyn couldn't stop after her lips brushed the bottle.

She told herself it was for fun, then she told herself it was for research – she would have told herself it was the cure for cancer if she needed to.

This latest fire in her belly prompted her to seek out information on creating a business plan. What she found was the tools to make the business plan creation process easier were scarce. Either that or she was too preoccupied with her Forbes fixation to find and decipher them. Undeterred, Jeslyn got started on her future.

*   *   *

Light socializing kept a number of things out of Jeslyn's sight and, therefore, out of her mind. This included the holidays that had finally arrived.

It was late in the morning on a Thursday when Jeslyn's phone began to chime incessantly. There were dozens of Happy Thanksgiving well wishes and follow up responses of what people were thankful for.

A knot began to form in the pit of her stomach that was bound by two distinct strings of thought; the first being a question of her priorities. How was it possible that a person could forget such a momentous occasion like Thanksgiving entirely? The second string of thought was more like a noose. Jeslyn's thoughts drifted to her mother.

It wasn't a rarity to be spending the holidays apart from her mother; that was actually normal. Family gatherings stopped being something Jeslyn participated in after her dad died. Spending the holidays with relatives was never really a part of her immediate family's repertoire anyway – too much drama. They had occasionally gathered together as a small family unit, but each year the number of those discomfited gatherings dwindled until they faded completely.

No, it wasn't the fact that Jeslyn wasn't with her mother on Thanksgiving, it was the thought of what her mother would be doing without her. Would she seek out people to spend her time with? Would she go on a self-sabotaging spending or drinking spree? Would she show up, unannounced, at Jeslyn's front door demanding she spend the day with her? Her past erratic behaviors left the possible scenarios hanging in the air like weightless dust particles.

Jeslyn tried to tell herself that she didn't care. She had been riding high on thoughts of Forbes and a life of luxury – one she planned to establish on her own – and thinking about her mother was a buzzkill. It was said money couldn't buy happiness. While that may be true, she was sure it made suffering a hell of a lot more pleasant. She would much rather be depressed in a posh chateau located in the south of France. But there were no posh chateaus in her immediate future, so she quashed any thoughts that were set on bringing her down. This Thanksgiving she would be thankful to not be burdened with anything that could not be changed.

And people that couldn't be changed either, she reminded herself.

She forewent checking the shriveling balance of her bank account since that, too, would have been an albatross on her disposition. Instead, she propped herself up on her sofa with a paper notepad, her tablet, her cell, and a cashmere blanket that she had gotten years ago at a company Valentine's Day party gift exchange.

One entire notebook had already been filled with random ideas, thoughts, doodles, numbers and a few personal notations. She looked it all over feeling as though she was reviewing a child's scrawling. This half-ass approach wasn't working.

She had worked for and with enough high level executives to know that you didn't need brains to be rich or successful. Several pauper-to-king and did-it-on-a-dime startups told her you didn't need to start out wealthy to increase your wealth tenfold. So, if you could start out poor and stupid and parlay that into insane affluence, it wasn't beyond the realm of possibility that she could do the very same thing.

She wasn't penniless – she had a small amount of money saved up – and she certainly wasn't stupid. Her idea was solid, the desire was there; the only thing missing was a solid how-to plan to get her from point A to a million or more.

She grabbed her tablet with the intent of looking up more business planning information but found her screen was still displaying the latest article she'd read on Forbes Keith. Unable to resist the slight rush he provided, she abandoned her business plan search in order to feed her online voyeuristic appetite.

The more she visited then revisited sites on Forbes, the more she studied his picture, the more she learned about him, the more she yearned to know. He was becoming more and more attractive with each pixel and not just his physical features, but his obvious intelligence and the contrasting dichotomy of that, coupled with his hobbies and interests.

The Sojourn lyric he'd semi-quoted had interested her. Reading about his perfect date (dinner at a burger joint, followed by drinks at a craft brewery; or enjoying a concert featuring the musical styling of anyone from Mos Def to Metallica), trapped her. She didn't think she'd mind being in his captivity.

She also learned he wasn't just a donor, he was a hero for the charity. A hero. He was the yin to his own yang. More photos she'd found showed he had a few discrete tats. Then, there was a completely different image of him dressed to the nines in a crisp, stark white, button down shirt and blazer, his hair styled in tousled-yet- tame perfection, sipping champagne in a ballroom. An 'At Home With Forbes' article featured a black and white of him in loose-fitting cargo shorts and a Bob Marley T-shirt posing with his two dogs – Lance and Layla. Lance was a yellow lab he'd had for eight years and Layla was a six-year-old, gray pit bull that he'd rescued from a shelter.

He dabbled in poetry, had an extensive gun collection and liked to go shooting every once and awhile.

He was, in essence, the quintessential man. Jeslyn wondered if all of this was just well crafted self-marketing. He was too...everything. He was *that* guy. The guy most men claimed they wanted to be and most women claimed they wanted to be with.

"He's a damn fairy tale is what he is," Jeslyn muttered out loud. Talking to herself had been happening more and more lately.

This riddle needed solving. It was the only way to scratch this devil of an itch. It was also a flagrant lie that she was telling herself just so she could go from swimming to drowning in her unhealthy preoccupation.

She didn't do well with thoughts of something – or in this case, someone – being out of her reach. But it wasn't as if she wanted Forbes, she didn't even know the man. It wasn't like she was some deranged fanatic. She simply wanted to put the niggling assumptions, questions and thoughts of him out of her mind.

By meeting him.

*　　*　　*

Resourceful.

It wasn't merely an apt description of Jeslyn and her capabilities, it was an innate part of her makeup. Unfortunately, honorable wasn't. She had made up her mind on Thanksgiving that she would arrange a meeting with Forbes Keith. She then spent the next couple of days devising a way to make that happen. If nothing else, he would serve as a nice quill to add to her slip of contacts. Anytime thoughts of her mother's well being bubbled to the surface of her mind, she popped them by devoting even more mental energy to this new plan.

When the Monday after Thanksgiving rolled around, Jeslyn was prepared to put her planning into action. The domino effect began with a simple phone call to local newspaper.

"Features, this is Scott."

"Hi Scott, my name is Mandy." Jeslyn began walking the line between youthful and seductive. "I'm a senior at Torrey Pines High School and I'm planning to continue my education by majoring in Biochemistry at Stanford next fall. The reason I'm calling is because I read an amazing article you wrote on..." here she paused for effect. "Keith Forbes. No, no, I'm sorry, Forbes Keith. Is that right?"

"Yeah, I wrote a Forbes article." Scott sounded wary.

"Wow. You're really a great writer. I've read quite a few pieces on Mr. Keith, but I've gotta say, your article was amazing. You captured the details so well."

"Well then, I'm flattered. Thanks. How can I help you?" Scott's wariness waned.

"No, thank *you*, actually. It's refreshing to know that great writers still exist." Jeslyn let her words massage his ego before continuing. "Well, I don't want to take up too much of your time."

"Oh, no, you're fine, you're fine." Scott was now well past wary. Having already lubricated him with flattery, Jeslyn felt it was time to drill him with her request.

"I was just wondering if you could provide me with any information on how you landed the Forbes Keith story, how you got in contact with Mr. Keith, and how you came up with the angle for your article. I have an essay that I need to write for my final on an inspirational figure in my intended career industry. I chose Forbes after reading your article. Actually, I'm kind of bummed that I didn't choose to pursue a career in journalism."

Actually, the article was dry and devoid of a strong central message. Jeslyn thought to herself. She would've pegged Scott as a stringer instead of a staff writer had she not read his byline.

"Oh, and why is that?" Scott played coy. Jeslyn played dumb.

"Well, because then I'd be able to write my essay on you." Jeslyn turned up the purr on her innocent sex kitten.

"Ah, well, I'm not really all that impressive," Scott said. 'You bet your sweet tits I'm impressive,' Is what Jeslyn read between the lines. "I'd be more than happy to help you out, Mandy. Such a pretty name by the way. You know, that's one of my favorite songs – *Mandy*, by good ol' Manilow. You're probably too young to even know who I'm talking about."

"You mean the guy who writes the songs at the Copacabana and is ready to take a chance because he can't smile without you." Jeslyn sprinkled the titles of four Manilow hits into her reply.

"Well, look at that. You're good. Young girl like you, now I'm impressed," Scott flirted casually.

"Impressed? Lucky me." Stupid giggle.

"Well, did you want to come by the office, should we meet somewhere or…?" Now Scott was the one fishing. Jeslyn knew she'd have to handle this carefully. She risked her catch wriggling off the hook with the wrong rejection.

"Scott, I am so embarrassed to say this, but I am actually a little farther behind on this project than I should be. If we could go over the information now, that'd be great. Then maybe we can arrange a time to get together later. I'd love to see if you could…" Jeslyn allowed one Mississippi to pass, "…persuade me to change my major."

"Yes! Yes, of course." His exuberance was completely unconcealed. No doubt the prospect of bringing to life his 'Barely Legal' fantasy tied up with a ribbon and bow and nothing else spurring him on.

The next half hour was spent stroking Scott's ego, listening to him stroke his own, and dropping breadcrumbs throughout his dense forest of bullshit in an effort to help him find his way back to her original question. Twenty-eight excruciating minutes later he finally got there.

"…so I say, sure I have time to do a little write up on a biochemist. The fact that he's a millionaire is like, whatever, you know. I have a net worth myself that's not too shabby. I just choose to keep it stashed for a rainy day."

"Oh, mmmhmm, of course. That's so awesome." This was Jeslyn's fifteenth 'awesome' in the last eight minutes.

"Anyway, I have my assistant track the guy down. Get this – he answers the phone himself. He's supposed to be this crazy rich bio geek with yachts and whatever else, right. But, I call his office, go through the automated phone directory, dial his extension, and get the guy right away. I was like, you've got to be kidding me!"

Jeslyn once again ignored the glaring lie in his story. The only assistant Scott had was most likely Rosy Palm and her five friends.

"That's...crazy." She was already so programmed to say 'awesome' it had almost slipped out. "Which office did you call?"

"Well, most people don't know this, but he actually owns a company called ByoKem. He doesn't put anything out there about it. It's probably some tax shelter or something. Anyway, that's how I got a hold of the guy."

After getting the correct spelling along with some other useful info on ByoKem and tons of non-useful info on Scott, it was time to disengage.

"This has been really awesome, Scott. You know so much about so many things, it's incredible. Can you – would you mind holding on for two seconds?"

"Yeah, no worries," Scott said.

Jeslyn pressed the mute button on her phone and did nothing for a few seconds. When she felt enough time had elapsed, she came back on the line. "Thanks so much for holding. My mom is here to pick me up but it was really great talking to you."

"Uh, definitely. You too." He was nudged but not derailed. "So, did you still want to get together this week, maybe, see if I can do some more of that persuading?" Scott's voice got perceptibly lower.

115

"Oh, sure. Well, I mean, I'd have to ask my dad. He's in law enforcement and really anal about who I spend time with. It's kind of lame. Anyway, let me just clear it with him first."

Scott started back-pedaling. "You know what, that's OK, Mandy. Why don't you concentrate on your project and then let's talk later. Maybe after the New Year or something."

"That would be great. And again, thank you so much." She strove for sincerity but feared she hadn't completely masked the ribbon of sarcasm laced in her parting words.

"Sure thing, Mandy. Take care." And with that he abruptly ended the call.

Jeslyn hadn't seen anything about ByoKem in her Forbes searches, but didn't have too terrible a time finding the company or its contact info.

With a telephone number firmly in hand and the knowledge that she could possibly be speaking with Forbes Michael Keith directly in a matter of moments, Jeslyn felt her confidence falter. That had been entirely too easy. She'd had more trouble getting the contact info to the customer service department for the warranty registration on her computer. Yes, she was resourceful, but this had been like shooting fish in a barrel – with no water.

Far be it for me to bite the hand that feeds the gift horse's mouth.

So what if it had been easy. This is exactly what she'd wanted and here it was, just waiting to be taken advantage of. Jeslyn glanced at the time on her cell phone. It was half past ten in the morning. Would that be too early to call? Too late? Was Monday even a good day to call? Jeslyn tortured herself with uncertainty. Then another thought crossed her mind.

What am I even going to say to him?

Jeslyn assumed someone of Forbes' stature would not be as easily misled as Ego Scott. A few words of flattery and a flimsy back story would not be enough. What if Forbes actually had a team in place to shield him from people?

Like you.

No, a dog and pony show would not be enough for this one. If she was going to do this, she would have to pull out all of the stops. Still telling herself this was a simple meet and greet that held absolutely no meaning, Jeslyn turned her planning to plotting.

12

~Before~

The art of deceit.

For Jeslyn, that meant taking a pure blank canvas of honesty and covering it with a variety of colors and brushstrokes. A skilled artist could create a masterpiece. An amateur artist could create garbage worthy of nothing more than a loving mother's refrigerator door.

Jeslyn was no amateur.

The first step for any artist, though, was choosing the appropriate medium. One could choose to cover her canvas in oil, chalk, or perhaps water color. An artist of Jeslyn's variety had to also choose appropriately. For this particular masterpiece, she decided to cover her canvas with the guise of press. Since it seemed Forbes was very comfortable speaking with and to the press, aligning herself with that faction wasn't much of a stretch. But it had to be done correctly, precisely. She would need to call in a favor or two.

It had been a few years since she'd called in any favors and she didn't particularly want to do it now. So why? If this wasn't an absolute necessity, if it was only petty curiosity, then why jump through so many hoops?

Why not?

The reasoning of an addict. Jeslyn didn't need, nor did she want, suggestions that would deter her from her ultimate objective. She only wanted the prize. Therefore, favors were required.

Marco (last name unknown, first name probably fabricated) had been incarcerated four times for computer hacking. He wasn't an Anonymous-level hacker, but he was savvy enough for Jeslyn's purposes. They had met years ago when Jeslyn's life had been less unencumbered. The chance meeting had taken place at a house party. She had known the host (a little too well) and Marco had come with a friend. He'd casually struck up a conversation with her, looking to turn casual talk into pillow talk, and in his inebriated state had gone into detail about his latest technological conquest. She had gotten his contact information as she'd been accustomed to doing when someone proved interesting or useful.

Some people collected magnets, coffee mugs, porcelain figurines, stamps, coins or even stickers. Jeslyn collected resources. This particular resource had come in handy on two other occasions. She hoped this third time would be a charm.

"Always a pleasure, J. To what do I owe it?"

"Como estas, Marco. Oh you know me, just working."

"Right. Gettin' that hustle on, baby girl. I feel you. Whatchu' got for me?"

"I need an email and I need an email."

"OK. Speak on it."

Jeslyn gave him the details of what she was looking for, in return Marco gave her an estimated delivery time.

"This ain't nothin', baby. Gimme' a few hours and I'll hook you up."

"You always come through. Thank you."

"Right. Why don't you ever let me *come through*, then?" The balancing act when dealing with the male sex was so precarious. Reject too hard, run the risk of getting blacklisted. Reject too softly, wind up getting screwed. Literally.

"Marco, Marco, Marco. You do this to me every time, papi. You know I can't go there with you. I'm not one of those hard-core chicks you hang with. I'm too soft. You'd break me into a million pieces. I'd be calling you nonstop, begging you to be with me. It wouldn't be pretty. You're so much better off, believe me."

"I'd hang up the game for you, baby girl. You know that."

"You shouldn't have to change for anyone, Marco. You do what you do best and let me admire from a safe distance."

Like putting a fussy baby to sleep, Jeslyn cooed and rocked him down gently.

"I ain't givin' up, girl," Marco said as he gave up.

"Alright. Get at me whenever it's ready."

"You got it."

Art.

*   *   *

Marco contacted Jeslyn later that evening. He'd done his job. With nearly half of the plan in place, Jeslyn set to work creating the other half. It wasn't difficult, just time consuming. Thinking of the perfect domain names, securing them, populating them with content – it all took time. But when her emotions were running the ship, time was the one thing Jeslyn always had in abundance at her disposal.

Sometimes, the most amazing masterpieces took months or even years to create. While she didn't intend for this to drag out more than a few days, she did intend to do it well.

Approximately ninety-six hours after acquiring the information on ByoKem, Jeslyn was set. A web search for 'Jeslyn Kennedy' returned two pages of scattered references. Personal social media accounts, business directory pages and a website – complete with a fake portfolio of her previous articles and press releases – while sparse with content, referenced her. It wasn't as dialed in as she would have liked, but it would do.

She then configured a POP3 account for her new email address, courtesy of Marco, that made it appear she was an employee, or at least an affiliate, of a prominent San Diego magazine publication. Granted, it was a lifestyle magazine; but there was no way she was going to spend the needed time and effort learning about biochemistry just so she could contact Forbes under the pretense of writing for a prestigious biochem mag – if such a thing even existed. Besides, science wasn't her thing. Lifestyles were. Her angle would be getting a glimpse into the lifestyle of a (handsome, successful, enigmatic) biochemist.

She checked to ensure the magazine hadn't profiled him before. They hadn't. All that was left was to put the plot into play.

Jeslyn typed up a formal email and shot it off to Forbes. Marco had successfully acquired his email address as well. He'd even offered to hack it and get her the man's password so she'd have access to his account. She'd declined at the time – out of embarrassment, not decency. She wasn't a huntress, she was an opportunist. The label did nothing to soothe her conscience, so she abandoned all labels altogether.

I am me.

It was as simple as that. The good, the bad and the opportunist. Sorting through it all would wreak havoc on her psyche if she kept it up for too long. And her psyche was already going through enough stress now that she'd officially contacted Forbes.

Waiting for his response was torture. Even though she'd put herself on this collision course, she worried over her actions. If she'd had more emotional control she would have told herself to quit her bellyaching. Then again, if she'd had more emotional control she wouldn't be in ninety percent of the predicaments she found herself in, including the one she was in now. Irony at its best was often Jeslyn at her worst.

She checked her email, sporadically at first, then began hitting the send/receive icon like a lab rat that'd been allowed to dispense crack to itself with the push of a button. She sent test emails from another email account to ensure her bogus one was working. She considered calling Marco again to ask him to hack into Forbes' email (only to see that her email had arrived safely, of course) but didn't. A 'read receipt' for her email had been requested, but she knew it could be declined. She continued to wait.

In agony.

The kicker was that it had only been about three hours, give or take a few minutes. Obviously, patience was not her virtue.

Unable to stay in her own skin without crawling out of it, Jeslyn got dressed and headed to her sedative.

She wasn't a workout kind of girl in the traditional sense. Running, bicycling, weight lifting – those common fitness practices were not a part of her repertoire. Yoga was also out. Yoga asked you to clear your mind. Jeslyn's mind was a thought hoarder's paradise. Too many lies, secrets and not enough rationality were hidden there. She risked losing it all if she tried doing any sort of clearing out, and that was a risk she was not willing to take. She went to the one place that allowed her to hold onto all of her thoughts, even utilize some of them to her advantage if necessary, while keeping the effects of them at bay. The cage.

If she were hooked up to a polygraph and asked if she were tough, Jeslyn would have answered 'no.' Her body was racked with the desire to flee every time she walked through the doors of the mixed martial arts gym. But no one would suspect it watching her enter. Her black hoodie, black skull tank, black fitted shorts and gray mood camouflaged her in the open 12,000 square foot space like a walking leaf insect in a jungle.

Several stations were set up offering everything from grappling to kettle bell training. Jeslyn's areas were the far back corner and the cage in the center of the room.

An ex, more like a fling, from long ago had turned her on to the pleasures of MMA. He'd turned her on to the pleasures of a hell of a lot more, but MMA had been something that had stuck. He was a Taekwondo fighter who had slipped effortlessly into the mixed martial arts scene.

Initially, Jeslyn would only watch while he trained. Then he taught her a few moves that she picked up decently. Her background in dance had aided her movement and dexterity capabilities, but it was obvious she was better suited for con work than floor work. Her discomfort at not being good at something was upstaged by the chance to become good at something new that could ultimately give her more power over another person or situation. It was an opportunity to not be helpless. Survival of the fittest overrode fear or discouragement. Jeslyn was programmed to survive.

He'd taken her MMA virginity sweetly at first. As she proved herself, the sessions became more difficult. She would never be half as good as he was or half as good as anyone at that gym. In her first sparring session she'd gotten her ass handed to her by Tanya – a deceivingly small, deceivingly young looking girl with long blonde hair that had been pulled back into a tight bun. It had felt like mortal combat instead of sparring; though nothing had been cracked or broken, just severely bruised and beaten.

Just?

Jeslyn wanted to throw in the towel after the first thirty seconds, but spectators had gathered around the cage and stayed there as the two went at it for almost two rounds. Apparently, newbies didn't last a full round with Tanya.

"Then why the hell would you put me in the ring with her?" she'd asked after the bell sounded for the end of round one. She was wheezing, wishing she could die and get it over with. The answer scared her more than anything else.

Tanya was the least experienced fighter and the only sparring partner they had to offer up for Jeslyn.

She didn't usually gravitate toward the ubiquitous three letter abbreviations that were mainstays of her generation's intercommunications. As she thought about the fact she had never written a will, along with all of the things she should have done differently with her life, because she was sure she was about to meet her maker, Jeslyn found herself with only one thought going through her head at the start of round two.

FML.

She made it halfway through that round, but her body gave out before her pride. A few scattered claps could be heard as she lay on the mat staring up at the stars that were putting on a dance show for her. According to her ex, that had gone well. Her second and third fights weren't much better, but by her fourth fight she was beginning to get the hang of things. She'd studied Tanya while the lethal amateur fought others. No studying took place when she was actually in the ring with her. When she was in the ring, Jeslyn could only concentrate on two things: Not getting pummeled and her ex, either in her head or on the sidelines, barking out orders. So used to his commands, she'd once woke herself up mumbling 'circle left, circle left, work your jab.'

Tanya had grown accustomed to Jeslyn's fighting style after only three matches. She knew what to expect, when Jeslyn would grow weary, when she'd give up, when she'd move in, when she'd retreat. Therefore, the element of surprise, by definition, would not be expected. After two standard rounds of predictable blow-by-blow interaction, Jeslyn entered round three with an agenda: Get Tanya on her back and get her to stay there. She saw Tanya did not guard her kidneys or the right side of her face, mainly because there was generally no need when the two of them were duking it out. This breach was Jeslyn's focus. There was little time to mess around. Once Tanya realized that Jeslyn had changed her game up, she too, being a more experienced fighter, would switch tactics. This had to be a clean kill. Get in, hit hard, get out.

The art of distraction.

The two women walked to the center of the mat and Jeslyn affected the kindest, most heart-warming smile she could muster around her mouth guard. A smile was like Halley's Comet in the gym, especially in the cage. It didn't come around very often. The rule of thumb being: If you wanted to smile, go to the dentist. If you wanted to fight, come to the gym.

Tanya's brows lowered ever so slightly in confusion, enough to throw her off for a millisecond after the bell. And with that same awkward smile stamped across her face, Jeslyn connected her foot with Tanya's kidney using enough force to send her opponent stumbling to the side. Before awareness kicked in and motivated her to react, Jeslyn circled left and worked more than a jab. Her fist pounded deftly and with a sickening thud against the right side of Tanya's face, then another deafening kick to the kidney. One. Two. One. Not frequently acquainted with blows of that nature, force, or location, Tanya fell to her knees, tight bun slightly askew, before collapsing face first onto the mat. And she stayed there.

While not her back, Jeslyn was satisfied. She knew she'd have to work harder in the future – giving up a win was another thing Tanya wasn't frequently acquainted with. But for that match, Jeslyn was the victor. A 'Rocky' style celebration did not ensue. Only a few more claps than her last so-called triumph could be heard bouncing off the walls. This wasn't a showboating arena. If you wanted to showboat, become a reality star. If you wanted to fight, come to the gym.

Today (oh, especially today) Jeslyn wanted to fight. She worked out a majority of her anxiety on the speed bag and the body bag in the back corner of the room before heading to the cage in the center. Two guys were sparring and she watched them intently, determined to keep her focus here instead of letting it wander to disconcerting places.

Two and a half hours in the gym passed quickly enough before Jeslyn retired back to her condo. A shower and the preparation and consumption of a light snack ate up another hour. This was good. She decided she would wait until tomorrow before checking the newly acquired email address. If Forbes hadn't responded she'd spin herself out again. If he had, then waiting for a reply wouldn't be the worst thing in the world that had happened to him. Not by far.

There were a million and one ways to avoid checking her email. Jeslyn knew herself well enough to know that she would ignore every single one of those deterrents if she didn't stay away from her computer, so she opted for mindless entertainment.

Zoning out panned out better than anticipated. When she glanced at the clock on the microwave above her stove and saw that it read 8:30 p.m., she allowed a smug grin to play across her lips. Dinner and a BluRay movie concluded the evening. An evening without email. Overcoming that small battle gave her a small measure of peace. Unfortunately, it was peace that could only be cherished for a few hours. Because when she woke, the war that was her life would resume.

13

~**Before**~

Liquid anxiety woke Jeslyn from a restless night of pseudo-sleep. It flowed throughout her body, from her prickling scalp down to her legs, which felt as if they'd been struck with RLS.

Jeslyn practically jumped out of bed to promptly check her email. Her already accelerated pulse quickened when she saw the notification for an unread message. She accessed her inbox with more enthusiasm than she'd given to several other more deserving life experiences and was adequately rewarded. There was a reply from Forbes Keith. Without hesitation she opened it.

Ms. Kennedy,

Funny to see that written out, I feel like I'm addressing a member of the American royal family. Thank you for your email. Yes, I'd be happy to speak with you regarding your prospective feature story. Feel free to send me more details.

Regards,
Forbes Keith

Jeslyn felt light headed from the near delirium that was causing her jaw to clench then rhythmically unclench. She carefully contemplated her reply before submitting it:

Dear Mr. Keith,

Funny to see that written out, I feel like I'm addressing you by your first name. Thank you for your prompt and personal reply. I had expected to coordinate the logistics of the interview with a member of your staff. Hearing from you directly is a welcome surprise. I'm available either via phone or I can arrange the interview to be conducted in person at a location and time that is convenient for you. My only prerequisite is that the interview take place within the next two weeks as I have a submission deadline to uphold. Other than that, I am very flexible and amenable to working around your schedule.

Warm Regards
Jeslyn Kennedy (no relation)

Playful yet professional. Jeslyn felt her aim, as it pertained to the tone she wanted to strike in her response, had been pinpoint accurate. She hit 'send' with a high level of confidence, wondering only briefly if giving him a two-week window was a good idea or if it would backfire. She would have to wait and find out.

Back to waiting.

Having already made it through the most nerve wracking portion of the plot, waiting this time around wouldn't be as hard. And patience not being as limited seemed to make time fly by. Within a few hours after sending her second email, she received another reply.

Dear Queen Jeslyn (that feels better),

You drive a hard bargain but I believe a date and time within the next two weeks is possible. My schedule gets a little hairy around the holidays but I'm sure we can figure something out. It would appear that setting the exact date and time rests in my hands so I'll get back to you on that asap. As for assistants, I like to handle personal details on my own, if I can. I prefer connections as opposed to formalities. A quirk I guess. I've been called down-to-earth (I've actually been called worse, but that's an entirely different story). As for in person vs. phone, I'll leave that up to you and what best suits your needs. Touché on your

opening line. I see I'll have to keep my eye on you. You're a quick one.
I like it!

> *Regards,*
> *Forbes (first name) Keith (last name)*

A smile broke across her face as she read then reread the email a dozen times over. She was in communiqué with Forbes Michael Keith. He seemed personable and warm, witty and charming – everything that fueled what logistically should have been squelched within her.

There was no turning back. Jeslyn was a deceiver of the most distressing sort; one that had started to believe her own lies. She was the artist who believed her painting was real, her sculpture was alive, and her dreams were actually memories. And now, she was completely wrapped in her own marred fairy tale. Only a hard dose of reality would open her eyes to the fact that writing lies across her skin didn't make her part of the story, it would simply force her to cover more of herself all of the time to prevent being read like a book.

She wasted no time in her reply.

> *Dear Duke Forbes Michael Keith, of the fair windy city de Chicago, Illinois (that feels about right as well),*
> *Yes, it would serve you well to keep your eye on me. That being said, I opt for in person. I look forward to your response regarding a date and time as well as a specific locale or a general geographic area you would prefer. I'm glad you enjoy getting personal; this will make my job a whole lot easier.*
> *Warm Regards,*
> *"Princess" Jeslyn Kennedy*

It was happening.

It was best if she didn't think to long about why and how it was happening. Besides, she was a good person; a bit misguided, slightly warped, uncharacteristically dubious, but a good person nonetheless. Right?

Sure, as long as no one knows the real me.

And just like clockwork, Forbes – unaware of the real Jeslyn Kennedy – sent over another response:

> *Dear Princess Kennedy (color me surprised),*
> *I've completely changed my schedule to accommodate you, Your Highness. I am available next Tuesday at 11am. Anywhere in or around the La Jolla area would be best because I have a prior engagement after our meeting. If the date, time and location are all well and good, let me know. I'm actually looking forward to being interviewed by a Princess.*
> *Sincerely,*
> *The Duke*

Jeslyn was not so lost in herself as to be struck with delusions of grandeur, but his reply came off as enticingly sportive, no doubt emboldened by her coquettish replies.

It was all she could do to contain her excitement. Friday to Tuesday now seemed decades away. Then again, she thought, it would also allow her time to prepare. This nothing personal, simply curiosity encounter would not only be something he could look forward to, it would be something for them both to remember for a lifetime.

*   *   *

The art of disguise.

Minus horn rimmed glasses and her hair in a conservative bun, Jeslyn embodied a typecast, no-nonsense journalist. Tuesday had come sooner than she'd expected; something she'd been grateful for.

Arriving at the designated meeting place fifteen minutes earlier than scheduled allowed her ample time to get a lay of the land. Despite the storm of emotions that she weathered internally, Jeslyn looked and operated under the auspice of a woman who was unperturbed and completely in control. Just the way she liked it.

Presently, there was a fad circulating in the world of female fantasy that painted the ideal woman as an inexperienced, clumsy creature with low self esteem who had no idea why any man would look twice in her direction. This same pathetic depiction of a woman then turned out to be the only person in the world that powerful, handsome, beautifully flawed, insanely wealthy men (or supernatural entities) wanted. This inexplicable allure also meant that these every-woman's-wet-dream male heroes incessantly fawned over the dowdy-but-suddenly-daring females. In the end, the guy broke all of his rules in order to secure the ugly-duckling-turned-heroine's eternal love and unwavering devotion.

Bullshit.

While she may have possessed certain insecurities, Jeslyn recognized the fact that she was quite easy on the eyes (even if she happened to be quite taxing on the heart). Her body, blessed by nature more than effort, bordered on dangerous. Cafe au lait skin, long legs, and a slender yet curvaceous physique that rarely went without notice was enough to make men sin. Not that most men needed much prompting.

High cheekbones, dense lashes, almond-shaped hazel eyes, mouthwateringly full lips, a nearly flawless complexion and long hair the color of overripe strawberries plated in caramel with natural honey highlights didn't do her any disservices. Her ethnicity was hard to accurately define at first glance, which only served to earn her frequent glances. She was attractive and acutely aware of it. Yet, this was only the exterior.

Jeslyn's intelligence could easily have been classified as profoundly sharp or masterfully clever. Not pursuing a formal higher education didn't mean she wasn't smart. Learning, for her, was simply a constant labor of love that took place outside of university confines.

She was the type of woman you wanted to get to know, wanted to please, and wanted to be cautious of even if you weren't sure exactly why. Jeslyn made people feel a thousand different ways depending on what she wanted or needed from them at the time – best friend, worst enemy, most passionate dalliance, and most frigid association were all part of the Jeslyn Kennedy experience. The outcome was almost always determined by Jeslyn herself, unless she deemed it advantageous for it to be otherwise. Even if you believed you had guided all courses of action, you were generally wrong. And unless she wanted you to know you'd been played, you were more often than not left in the dark as to why things had not panned out more in your favor.

It was how she established stability in a life where so much of it had been forcibly ripped from her. It was not always pretty, it was not always nice, and it was hardly ever ethical.

Jeslyn assessed her surroundings at the Hyatt Regency La Jolla at Aventine hotel as she stood in the lobby waiting in line to speak with the concierge. Sunglasses framed her face and she held her mobile to her ear even though she was talking to no one. She didn't want to be bothered and a couple of older gentlemen stood off to the side doing a horrible job of pretending they weren't waiting for an opportunity to approach her. Jeslyn dashed any possible opportunities against the porcelain lobby floor as she clicked by in her heels.

After explaining her purpose there, the concierge directed her to a bay of elevators to her right. She would be meeting Forbes in one of the hotel's twenty-four suites. A quiver of delight shot through her as she made her way to the elevators and up to the designated floor.

Her impeccable timing delivered her at the front door of the suite five minutes before their 11a.m. appointment. She tried not to telegraph her anxiety.

Mind over matter. Her thoughts repeated words her father had said. *If you want to lift your right hand you lift your right hand. Unless you have a disability, you're in total control of you.*

She was in total control – mostly.

She lifted her right hand and rapped on the door three times. She clenched then unclenched her jaw in anticipation as she heard heavy footsteps approaching. A fleeting smirk played at her lips as she heard a man clear his throat and let out a short, forceful whoosh of breath before laying hold of the door handle.

Was he preparing himself? The fact that he could possibly be even the slightest bit jostled was stimulating. Then the door opened and Jeslyn's entire plan changed in an instant.

This was no longer curiosity.

He was beautiful. That went without saying. His tall, muscular frame in the doorway was only half the assault on Jeslyn's senses. He smelled like midnight – not early morning fresh or end of the day stale, but that bewitching hour when possibility either calls it a night or is just getting started. His scent was a start and it nearly made her lick her lips from pure, unadulterated desire. It was also enough to dampen the silk panties she sported beneath her frame-hugging, navy blue linen skirt. She did not allow her features to belie her provocation.

"Duke Forbes Michael Keith I presume?"

"Ah...uh, yes. Yes." He was visibly flustered – in a good way, she hoped.

"Princess Jeslyn Kennedy. May I come in?" She was already assuming control but would cede the semblance of it to him once they were settled. Making him feel confident and powerful would do wonders, she assumed, sizing him up quickly.

"Yes! I'm sorry. Of course." Out of the corner of her eye she saw him slide a palm down the leg of his slacks. With her back to him, he couldn't see the triumph that flashed across her face. She deliberately swayed her hips as she walked past him over to the sitting area, claiming a spot on the settee. "Can I get you something to drink? Water, soda, coffee?"

"Oh, no thank you." Jeslyn smiled modestly. "I'm on the job. Wouldn't want you to slip something in my drink and then take advantage." She let the highly inappropriate insinuation simmer before steering it out of the gutter. "I've got a top of the line laptop here that I saw you eyeing. I know your type. You bring a poor defenseless girl up to your suite then, bam! You've taken her technology and ran." She broadened her smile.

"Ha ha," he seemed relieved. "You've got me. I am a sucker for technology." He also seemed more at ease as he copped a squat in one of the high wing backed chairs catty corner to where she sat.

Jeslyn considered how to play her hand. She absorbed Forbes with as many senses as she could. He was a delightful sight to behold and she found herself struggling to not grin incessantly. Mere curiosity and nothing more had flown the coop. She now wanted him and she wanted him to want her. Without even starting the interview, she knew she wouldn't be happy until she had conquered him in some shape or form.

"So, right out of the gate, I've got to be honest with you. I didn't exactly get permission from my editor for this feature. It's just –" she pretended to falter. "It's just that I've wanted to do a write up on you for a very long time. Your work is beyond incredible. I figured it was either now or never. I hope you don't mind." Jeslyn tossed flattery, general interest and interest of another sort altogether into the ring.

"No, sure, that's fine. Believe me, there's enough write ups out there about me to last me a lifetime. I just wanted to do this for you...er...for your magazine. So, yeah, shoot." He was not the cocky, overly confident, unaffected millionaire that would rip her clothes off and have his way with her in every prepositional position and on every surface in the suite. Who on the planet (in their right mind) would? But it didn't stop Jeslyn from allowing the scenes to roll footage in her head anyway.

"Ok. Well, thank you. I struggled with whether or not to tell you that and figured it was best if I did. Alliance between kingdoms and that sort of thing." She played one last hand on their inside Duke/Princess joke. "Before we start, let me just say you are a formidable man. I already have a deep respect for you without knowing all that much about you. That's a first for me."

"Wow, thank you. I appreciate that." He accepted the compliment graciously.

"Second, I want you to tell me everything you feel like sharing about yourself and I'll guide you from there. I simply want our readers to get a feel for who you are when you're not changing the world through biochemistry." Jeslyn had taken her laptop out of its case and was powering it up as she spoke. She came across as efficiently professional and did her best to sound intrigued. Her exploitation knew no bounds.

"OK. Well I —"

"Wait." Jeslyn interrupted. "Would you mind if I recorded this?" She looked him in his eyes then chanced a glance at his perfect pout of a mouth. What she would give to gently suck on his bottom lip.

"No, that's fine." Forbes' tongue discreetly moistened the very area she was studying. Had he noticed her noticing? If he did, he kept the knowledge to himself.

"Please, continue." Jeslyn took a small section of her own bottom lip between her teeth and held it there as she stared into his soft green eyes. She needed him to know there was interest, but she had to be careful not to come off like some lovesick teenager. He was, after all, a very attractive man of means. Women probably threw themselves at him on the regular. This had to be broached with caution.

She actively listened as Forbes began telling her about himself. She even typed out notes as he spoke. True to her word, she guided him with questions of her own, "for the readers' sake." All was going well, until…

"...so, I decided that since biochemistry was such a passion, I might as well make a living from it." Forbes was chatting amiably, any previous awkwardness a thing of the past.

"And how did you –" Jeslyn's question was interrupted by the sound of a card key activating the door to the suite. She hadn't even heard housekeeping announce their presence; she'd been so wrapped in his every syllable. Only, when the door opened, it was not a maid. Sex walked into the room.

She looked like a lingerie model. Actually, she looked like Them – only older and made over. Like what They would have been if they hadn't been middle school adolescents. Like only the best parts from each one of them had been taken and fashioned to make her.

Her long, impossibly shiny, brunette hair, with its delicate auburn highlights was flat-ironed to perfection. Stony emerald green cat eyes were perfectly offset by exquisitely sculpted brows. She was a barefoot 5'7" but her heels easily made her 5'9" if not taller. Her turquoise crocheted dress was visible under a slick, beige trench coat. Spessartite garnet hued jewels dangled from her ears and adorned her throat then dove into her ample cleavage – granted, that cleavage looked to have had a helping hand from a surgeon and not mother nature, as did her full lips. Nevertheless, she had an air of aristocracy about her that made Jeslyn feel like a nouveau riche imposter by comparison. Expensive matte black, glossy pink, and opaque frosted shopping bags, and a leather Chanel clutch were draped over both arms and in her hands.

"How did it go?" Forbes rose from his seated position and nearly jogged over to the vixen.

"Good. It was fine. Am I interrupting?" She asked as if she hoped she was.

"No, of course not." Forbes kissed her cheek and Jeslyn's soaring heart plummeted into her high heels.

136

"We have to be there at 12:30, Michael." She couldn't have sounded more aggravated.

"I know, babe. Don't worry."

"I'm not worried, Michael, I'm just telling you!" She snapped.

"Did you eat already? I can have room service —"

"Michael, I'm perfectly capable of taking care of myself. Yes, I ate. But there's going to be food there, so I just got a snack. Is that OK with you?" She asked the question sardonically, as if she were implying he would somehow not be OK with her dietary decisions.

"O...K." Forbes seemed at a loss as to how to soothe his obviously flustered suite mate. Jeslyn looked on, perplexed and annoyed.

And why did she keep calling him by his middle name?

"Jeslyn Kennedy. Would you care to join us?" Jeslyn had walked over and was now extending her hand to Satan's daughter. The woman accepted the proffered hand as though it were smeared with feces. Her limp fish handshake, where she barely touched the ends of Jeslyn's fingers, seemed to cause her physical pain.

"Gisele. Pleasure. How long is this little thing going to take?" She made it sound like Jeslyn was teaching Forbes the alphabet.

"Not long at all. However, I can also reschedule if this is an inconvenient time." Jeslyn was addressing Forbes. Only Forbes. What she'd wanted to say was: "I can reschedule after you've ditched this nightmare and it's just you and I."

"No, no, no. This is fine. It's good. We're good?" He looked at Gisele for confirmation.

"Fine. Let's wrap it up then." Gisele, not as graceful as her svelte body would have one think, clumped in her stilettos over to the sitting area. Jeslyn sauntered behind her and Forbes trailed both women. When Forbes sat, Gisele plopped herself in his lap.

You've got to be kidding me. Jeslyn watched the territorial display in utter disbelief. Granted this whole interview was fake, but Gisele didn't know that.

A part of Jeslyn felt smug superiority at the fact Gisele all but urinated on Forbes to mark him as hers. That meant she felt threatened.

As you should.

Showing that weakness had not been a wise thing to do and Jeslyn went out of her way to prove that as the interview wore on.

"I'm sorry, Forbes, I didn't quite get that last part. You seem to have a bit of a sound barrier." Jeslyn's comments came after Forbes attempted to answer a question with his lap dog positioned so that she was practically hiding him from view. "Not to impede on your comfort, Gisele, but would you mind scooting over just an inch or so? The mic needs to be able to pick up his voice in order to be effective. Or perhaps you'd be just as comfortable in a nearby chair."

Gisele narrowed her eyes until they were nothing more than smoldering slits; she held her ground for a few seconds. Jeslyn smiled and waited like a kindergarten teacher waiting for a stubborn student to put her toy away and join the rest of the class. Gisele begrudgingly adjusted her position.

Forbes stayed quiet during the two women's exchange, almost as if he were mystified by it. It was painfully obvious Gisele was not used to being told what to do. Was this really the type of woman that appealed to him? Aesthetically, Jeslyn got it. Gisele looked as though her middle name was photogenic. But there were a million beautiful girls in the world, girls that didn't possess that snake venom attitude, not to mention a complete disregard for social etiquette.

Really Forbes?

Perhaps she'd misjudged him. Everything else about him was exactly as Jeslyn had envisioned. He was as remarkable as he came off in print and pictures – a brilliant, sexy man who didn't seem to know the full extent of his allure.

He'd mentioned he'd been a shy kid and chubby until he was about eight or so. His family had raised him to be humble and polite and he'd had to work for everything he'd ever wanted. Life had not been Ferris Wheels and kettle corn simply because he was a genius or because his parents were wealthy. Perhaps Gisele was merely the chubby kid in him going after the proverbial ice cream. Can't stuff your face? Bag a hottie instead – exchange hard candy for arm candy.

As the three of them concluded the interview, Jeslyn tried to get more info (dirt) on what else might have attracted Forbes.

"So, Gisele, what do you do?"

"What do you mean?"

The question was glaringly obvious, but perhaps clarification was necessary. "I mean, how do you either contribute to the gross national product or productively enhance the social and or economical fabric of our society." Jeslyn cocked her head to the side and watched the woman's eyes glaze over.

"If you're asking where do I work, I don't do the job...thing." Gisele's mouth curved into a frown as if the word job had a flavor and the flavor had rotted. "I do some modeling and acting and help out with charities and shit."

This is not happening. It was Jeslyn's turn to be struck dumb. She had found it. This was the chink in Forbes' armor. Was he incapable of spending time with an intelligent woman or was his relationship with this simpleton not established enough for him to care? Maybe Gisele was a rebound. Whatever she was, it was apparent she was not worthy of the man's time or attention, though she was in possession of both.

Jeslyn's slight competitive streak became as wide as a four lane highway. Gisele would simply not do, if for no other reason than she was an impertinent nitwit. Jeslyn realized she wasn't winning any awards with her own unemployment status. That would have to change, too. Changes were coming. Jeslyn would make sure of that.

14

Obsession could drive a person insane; especially if that person had driven herself partway there already. Jeslyn had been non-stop obsessing over her idealizations of prosperity and over Forbes. It invaded her dreams and filled ninety percent of her waking moments. Pretty much the only thing it wasn't filling was her bank account.

Christmas and a new year had come and gone, yet Jeslyn's situation remained relatively the same. Stagnant. And the less she accomplished – and she had not accomplished a lot – the less she felt she was capable of accomplishing. She irrationally thought that Forbes would have been enough of an impetus; that meeting him would have jump started a creative frenzy that resulted in overnight success. Negative. The only thing her meeting with Forbes had done was drive her mad with a deep seated craving she couldn't shake.

Pride or no pride, she needed a job. While that revelation did nothing to uplift her spirits, it did give her something else to concentrate on.

Score one point for rationality.

Jeslyn had talent, knowledge and experience, which were all wonderful ingredients in a recipe for good fortune, but she was missing a staple. The one thing in short supply was gumption. Whether it was the fear of achievement or the fear of failure – it felt like good ol' fashioned laziness –

remained undefined. What was crystal clear, things were going to go from uncomfortable to unbelievably wrecked if she didn't figure it out. And quickly.

Perhaps Gisele was right, only in her view that the word job did taste a little overripe. Just a little. But what if she could use the job listings and companies posting them, companies that were now looking like perfectly respectable organizations, as a key instead of a cage? What if they could be a stepping stone instead of an anchor? What if she could do this thing, this idea that had started fizzing and popping in her head, as a temporary way to stave off poverty and homelessness – that was a bit exaggerative – to stave off collections, and, at the same time, stay out of a 9-to-5 rut? Then, she could work on her empire (it needed a new name; calling it an empire was beginning to sound like a puerile fantasy) on the side.

Jeslyn pondered this. She'd done marketing and account executive work for dozens of other companies and clients; surely she could do those same tasks without a CEO, COO or any other C-level supervision. She would be her own boss – a prerequisite that had been overshadowing wisdom as of late.

Her contemplative mood required a fitting ambiance. She fired up Pandora and selected a classical channel. Bach's 'Cello Suite No.1 in G Major - Prelude' wafted from the speakers and into her soul. Flashes from late in her childhood crackled through her memory.

Yelling. Arguing. Doors slamming. Glass breaking. The din of noise being drowned out by the soothing sounds of a cello. Fingers sliding up and down the strings. A melody coaxed to life by a bow. A haven of harmony amidst the sounds of domestic war.

Bach's enchanting piece, her favorite composition of his, continued to provide a soundtrack for her memories. She closed her eyes and let herself fall still. The introduction sounded like grace or forgiveness; a reprieve. The coda was a pardon from life itself, from several lifetimes, including the current broken but patched one she was still trying to make it through. It was an escape; one without the running and without fear. It was an escape to a future good place, as long as she was still.

The piece reminded her of *The Red Violin*. An instrument that had traveled through centuries, and had played a role in various stories and courses of human existence.

She felt like that Red Violin.

Only her story – more personal – was deeper and richer. The higher octaves of the violin did not reach the core of her human existence. Her story would more aptly be titled *The Red Cello*. That had a nice ring to it. Jeslyn tried it out on her tongue, "Red Cello."

Bach's Suite came to an end as her eyes slowly opened. Her aimless musings kept going as Beethoven's 'Moonlight Sonata' started up. Red Cello. It fit – it wasn't too big or too small, too much or too little.

Pragmatic as always, she checked the WhoIs database before following through with what was already half drafted in her head. The domain name was available. She secured RedCelloMarketing.com, not able to think of anything more suitable, more fitting. Then, she set to work – real work this time – creating the other half.

*   *   *

The downfall of Jeslyn's highly creative nature was that while ideas came to her at a mile-a-minute pace, it took time to bring them to fruition. She wanted results to occur at the same breakneck speed. That was simply not reality. It was indisputably evident that reality was not something Jeslyn dealt well with.

Reality meant certain things didn't work out, feelings got hurt, loss occurred, challenges had to be overcome and obstacles had to be faced. Understanding these things was not her issue. Suffering through them was.

She'd sent out an email blast and posted meticulously worded and beautifully designed advertisements on appropriate sites. She pieced together an impeccably detailed and SEO-friendly templated website, and updated her (real) professional social media page. Having recessed into solitude for weeks, she began reconnecting with acquaintances and ex-colleagues. She even attended a few networking events despite the fact that she loathed them. Jeslyn did all she could to kick-start her fledgling new business venture.

And then watched as nothing happened.

Weeks passed. Slow, interminably, agonizingly long weeks. The lack of activity during those weeks was so sparse it was not worth mentioning. Panic began to nudge its way in. Doubt, always at the ready to rear its ugly head, also made an unwelcome appearance. Doubt pushed around her capabilities, kicked her ideas in the shins and spit in the face of her future.

If she couldn't even start a small marketing business – something she actually knew how to do – how in the hell was she going to create something bigger? Jeslyn was easily wrapped up in her own drama and continued digging deeper into the self-imposed depths of despair. She was not concerned about anything other than her own pathetic worries. Life decided to lend a helping hand in refocusing her attentions.

Feeling as though she was barely keeping her head above water, the last thing Jeslyn was expecting was a call from her mother. She considered answering it then decided against it – the first time. When her phone rang a second time, not two minutes later, she picked up.

"Hello, Mother."

"Jeslyn?" Her mother's voice sounded weak, like she was fighting a cold and losing or had just woken up. Or something worse.

"Mom, what's wrong?" Jeslyn kept her voice even. She was not yet alarmed but she was treading cautiously.

144

"I...I'm not sure." The raspy voice was so soft it was hard to make out the words. "I came to and I was on the floor. I don't remember much. I'm just so cold."

"Came to? What do you mean came to? Did you pass out?" Jeslyn tried to gather facts.

"I think so. I'm not sure. I didn't know who else to call. Oh, Jeslyn!" She began to sob softly, or at least make sobbing sounds.

"Do you need to go to the hospital?"

"I don't know!" She sounded like a petulant child who had misplaced her favorite doll.

Where did you last see it? Adult.

I don't know! Petulant child.

"Well, what is it you'd like me to do?"

Silence. Not even the sound of crying could be heard. The doubt that had so easily woven itself into Jeslyn's thoughts about herself now wound through her thoughts about her mother.

What game are we playing now?

She resisted the urge to sigh (or curse) and continued to wait it out.

"Yes, maybe I do need to go to the hospital." It sounded as though she was speaking through clenched teeth.

"Did you want me to take you?" Jeslyn asked.

"Yes." Her mother's clipped tone no longer sounded feeble.

"I'll be there in half an hour."

Jeslyn pulled on a pair of comfortable leggings, fleece boots, and a long sleeve scoop-neck sweatshirt that hung off one shoulder. She grabbed her coat, along with her wallet and keys, and headed out the door. A feeling of dread coated, then hardened in her stomach like a piece of fruit dipped in warm chocolate, then set out to cool. More than likely her mother was fine and using this as a way to...

A way to what?

The two hadn't spoken in quite some time, but Jeslyn could think of a half a dozen other ways for her to break the ice than a bogus health emergency. Adages about black pots and kettles and apples falling from trees bounced around in her head. She promptly bounced them right out. Perhaps they did share similarities. That didn't mean she had to acknowledge them – if they did indeed exist.

She made the trek to her mother's house in record time, figuring the sooner she got there the sooner she could deal with whatever this was and be on her way. Steeling herself, she rang the doorbell and stood on the porch for an eternity, rubbing her hands together to keep them warm from the chilly air. But it was what she saw when the door opened that made her stop short.

Occasionally, people would compare the two of them, mother and daughter, even though they looked absolutely nothing alike. There couldn't possibly be anything to compare now. It looked as though her mother had lost weight, a lot of weight, too much weight. Dark circles outlined her bloodshot eyes and a bruise painted her sallow cheek. A stitch of guilt pierced Jeslyn.

"Can I come in?"

There was no verbal response. Instead, her mother just shuffled away from the door and back inside the house. Jeslyn took that as her cue to follow.

It was like walking into a lair. The blinds and curtains were shut tight. The only light was the dim brightness of the muted TV.

A plate of food, that looked more like someone had pushed the contents on it around instead of eaten it, was sitting on the kitchen counter. A slew of medicine bottles crowded the space around it. If someone had told her that her mother had robbed a pharmacy, she wouldn't have had a hard time believing it. After taking in the bleak surroundings, Jeslyn was ready to leave. She had never seen the house or her mother in such a dismal state.

"So, are you ready to go?" Even to her own ears her voice sounded cold.

"Why are you here?" At first the thought hit her that her mother had lost her wits completely and had forgotten they'd just spoken less than an hour ago. The mist pooling on her lower lashes threatening to spill over onto those sunken cheeks let her know that wasn't the case.

"I'm here to take you to the hospital."

"Why. Are. You. Here?" Her bottom lip quivered. Jeslyn clenched then unclenched her jaw and shifted her weight from one foot to the other. She pinched the bridge of her nose between her thumb and finger trying to summon whatever it was this situation required.

You don't have to feel it in order to do what's right. Jeslyn's father's voice was clear and present in her head. *If you wait until you feel like doing it, you're gonna' be waiting a long time. You need to let your actions lead your emotions, not the other way around.*

How many times had he told her that? One hundred? One thousand? Her propensity to react or not react based on her emotions had gotten her into trouble quite often as she was growing up. She still had not overcome this acute inability – refusal would be more accurate – to appropriately control her emotions.

"I'm here to take you to the hospital, Mom." The kindness and warmth that had been absent, not only for this interaction, but for the past decade or more forced its way awkwardly into her reply.

"Well, let's get going then." Her mother quickly swept her hand over her eye, erasing any remnants of the tears that were building there. She did not put up a fight; instead, she let Jeslyn drive her to the nearby urgent care center. Once there, they waited in silence, neither one attempting conversation. Jeslyn knew conflict would seek them out soon enough, why go looking for it.

Tests, blood work, monitors and paperwork, so much paperwork. Jeslyn could've sworn an hour was spent just going over her mother's medication. Was there a pill she wasn't taking? That was probably what they should have asked. It would have saved time. One would have assumed her mother had a life threatening disease based on sheer quantity alone.

She took something to help her sleep and another something for anxiety. There was an arsenal of pills to help stabilize her mood, combat her high blood pressure, fend off migraines, minimize allergies, and something to help with nausea because this entire drug cocktail was making her sick.

After all was said and done, the medical professionals could provide no clear answers. The results from the blood and urine samples wouldn't be available for another day or so, but the results from the MRI and EKG were inconclusive.

Jeslyn gave it the appropriate label: They couldn't find anything wrong. Even the symptoms her mother gave were hard to assign to a particular problem. Blackouts, shortness of breath, disorientation, dry mouth, sudden heart palpitations. There was no pain or convulsions, no memory loss (aside from the occasional convenient ones), no clots, obstructions or blockages. Her heart, head and lungs appeared normal, healthy. By all accounts she was fine. Jeslyn did not bring up the possibility they were visiting the wrong type of doctor. That perhaps a more conclusive analysis could be found with the help of a psychiatrist instead of a general practitioner.

The two left the facility with no more insight than when they'd entered. As they approached her car, Jeslyn's cell alerted her she had a message; it was a text notification from her bank. She received alerts when funds were credited or withdrawn, or when her balance dipped below a certain level. The alert she was looking at now reported a dip. Unlike the results her mother had received, this message was very conclusive. An expletive fell from her lips.

"What is it?" Her mother sounded genuinely alarmed.

"Nothing." It was Jeslyn's go-to response whenever her mother asked her a question; it rolled off her tongue like a habit. She sunk into the driver's seat.

"Nothing, nothing, nothing." Her mother mocked her with a scowl on her face. "It's always nothing with you!" The irritation was so thick it felt like a physical presence crowding the small space in the vehicle.

"We just left the hospital, Mother. I didn't think burdening you with my life was important." It hadn't taken long for conflict to find them.

"I'm a big girl, Jezzy. I think I can handle your little *life burdens*," she spit out.

Jeslyn tried to recall something she'd read once about sudden mood changes and strange behavior being a precursor to something serious. A stroke? Alzheimer's? Or was it dementia? She couldn't quite remember.

They were still sitting in the parking lot. Something had to be said in response, but she wasn't sure what that was. Sharing details about her life with her mother was never good. Too many times it had been used against her in some way or another. She remained silent. As she started the car her mother started in again.

"And don't pretend you're concerned about me now. My health and safety wasn't a concern for you last month or the month before that."

"Mother please." Jeslyn felt her energy drain. "Don't do this. I really don't think it's beneficial."

"I'm just trying to be a part of your life, Jeslyn. You're my daughter and I know nothing about you. You shut me out! You just shut me out like I'm nothing, like I'm nobody. I raised you, I took care of you..."

Here we go.

Her mother droned on, rattling off every motherly thing she'd done, conveniently leaving out the things a mother should never do, while Jeslyn tuned her out. She hadn't RSVP'd to this pity party – or was it an anger fest? Possibly it was both.

Jeslyn wondered if her mother's spikes and plummets, hot and colds, ups and downs were from fighting truths, the ones she claimed she couldn't remember. When it came to owning up to the past, her mother's memory bank was always empty.

Bank. Money. Doubt.

Jeslyn's thoughts circled back to the present and doused her in ice-cold reality. Her mother was still going.

"...ever asked is that you tell me what you need. I did the best that I could. I've always tried to be there for you, through thick and thin; even when you abandoned me. All I've ever asked is that you talk to me. But no, I can't even get that."

"I'm going broke, Mother." Jeslyn wrenched the steering wheel to the left, roughly pulling the vehicle into her mother's driveway. It was almost over.

"What was that?" Hearing something other than 'nothing' must have been a surprise.

"You said you wanted to know what was going on. Well, I'm going broke; that's what's going on."

Heavy silence. Thick, heavy silence.

The car's motor hummed quietly. A cat mewled in the distance. Jeslyn trained her eyes on the garage door in front of her and suffered through the nothingness. It was some time before her mother spoke.

"So, is that why you came?"

"Is what why I came?" Jeslyn continued to stare straight ahead.

"I do my best to be there for others. I sacrifice and I give."

Jeslyn's eyes were now on her car's ceiling, her head leaning against her seat as she tried to make sense of what had just been said. She couldn't. "I'm sorry. I don't understand where this is going."

"I don't hear from you, I don't see you, I get nothing from you. But now. Oh ho, now! Now I see why you're here." She was nodding her head as if she were agreeing to something.

"What are you talking about?"

"*I'm broke.*" She whined the words. "You can't call me, but you can sit here begging me for money?"

"What!?" Jeslyn whipped her head around to face her mother. "I am *not* asking you for money, let's make that clear right off the bat. You! *You* called me. *You* asked me to come get you. *You* asked what was wrong. *You* wanted to know what was going on in my life. *You* demanded I tell you, so I did. I don't want *anything* from you!" Jeslyn was close to yelling. Close.

"You can't tell me this isn't about money, Jeslyn. I see right through you, right through all of this. You're not going to leech off of me like you did your father. He knew what you were. And you know what he thought of you? He thought you were selfish. He thought you were selfish and a mistake! You know why? Because you are!" her mother bellowed.

Camel. Straw. Back.

She and her mother had been in this pattern for as long as she could remember. They didn't belong together, not even in the same room at the same time. Their being together was like seeing Clark Kent and Superman in the same scene – it wasn't right. Jeslyn had thought there were no more lows her mother could sink to. She was wrong. The below-the-belt comment, whether true or not, became an ache so sickeningly strong that Jeslyn feared she was actually going to be sick.

Restraining herself – face of stone, heart of granite – Jeslyn raised a finger and pressed the unlock button. The car door locks clicked. Her mother wanted a reaction out of her but Jeslyn wasn't in a giving mood.

"Jeslyn, wait." The woman's voice was still too stern. There was no remorse, only an attempt to renege on her own harsh words. Jeslyn didn't wait. She jerked her door open and walked to the other side of the car where she jerked the passenger door open. Her mother stepped out and began babbling. Jeslyn could no longer hear her. She pressed the lock on the passenger side door before slamming it shut, then walked back around to the driver's side.

"Jeslyn, you need to stop right now and listen. Hey! I am talking to you!" Being unable to assume control of the situation was making her mother angry all over again.

"You need to get inside. It's cold out here." The possible double meaning of her words was lost on her mother. Jeslyn shut her door, buckled up and backed out of the driveway with a screech, not even looking to see if the woman in the driveway had heeded her advice. She didn't care.

The farther away from the house she drove the more speed she picked up. She was doing seventy on a fifty mile per hour road. A red traffic light beamed brightly from an intersection. Its luminous command was ignored. By the time she hit the I-5 freeway, she was barreling down the slick asphalt at ninety miles per hour and still applying pressure to the gas pedal. She wove between the cars and only decelerated when she reached her exit.

Fighting the tightening in her chest, she knew she wouldn't be able to hold back for much longer.

She sped to her condo, nearly crashing through the back wall of her garage before slamming on the brakes. Scrambling from the car, she half speed walked, half jogged to her front door, fumbling with the keys in the lock as she tried to get it open.

When she was finally inside, she closed the door gently then turned and slid her body down its glossy-painted finish. Tears rolled in unison down her face. She didn't allow her muscles the relief they ached for, to completely scrunch together in agony. She didn't allow her vocal chords the release they burned for, to cry out in anguish. She only allowed the warm, salty flow of tears to course over her cheeks and drip from her trembling chin.

She was an idiot. Trying to do things the right way, playing on the safe side of the street; it had only left her broken and vulnerable. No more right, no more broken, no more tears, Jeslyn promised herself. It was time to cross back to the other side.

15

~Before~

Dredging up the past was a tricky sort of thing, especially her past. And especially because, although it was familiar, it was a place she'd at one time (more like a dozen times) sworn she'd never sink or return to.

But sometimes she would sneak back to it, like a dog returning to its own vomit to lap at something that maybe could have been good but wasn't – not in the beginning and especially not now.

There was a certain familiarity to it that was almost comforting. She knew what to expect from her past and what was expected from her in return. It was stressful trying to pretend she had nothing to hide, all the while struggling to keep things hidden. And there was always the possibility that her past could sneak up on her instead of the other way around. She didn't want that. If anyone or anything were going to be doing the surprise return, it would be her – her terms, her rules, her way.

An eerie sort of calm settled over her with the first call to associations she had long stopped associating with. And for good reason. There were certain things and certain people who were out of her league, but Jeslyn never liked to admit that. So, she suited up and placed herself in the bullpen. It didn't take long for a turn at bat to present itself. In circles like these, it never did. Just her reemergence was blood in the water. All the sharks came out to see what chum had been dumped in their territory. Sharks like Willie.

"Where you been hiding at, Jezzy?"

"Not hiding, just living." She snuffed out the first spasm of regret.

"Living, huh? If you say so. You ready to work?"

"Yes. But not what you're thinking." Best to be straight with him upfront.

"And how do you know what I'm thinking?"

They both knew his question didn't warrant a reply.

"OK, so what exactly is it you're trying to do?"

"Make money."

"Doing what?"

"Tidying up your operations. Upstairs, not downstairs."

"And who says my operations need tidying?"

Jeslyn said nothing, only sniffed like she was tired of him beating around the bush, because she was.

"Tomorrow. Noon. *Upstairs*." He drawled the last word like an eye roll.

"Today. Four o'clock. The pizza joint across from Blue's."

"You call the shots now, J? Is that with this is?" He didn't sound impressed. "My date, my time."

"I have a prior engagement tomorrow. It's...personal," she said.

"Prior engagement, huh?" He mulled it over. "Fine. Today. Four thirty."

"Across from Blue's?"

"Fine, whatever." One foot was already in the deal. She didn't have anything further to say so she hung up.

And just like that, she was back.

*   *   *

She knew Willie had said four thirty just so he could feel like he was running the show. She also knew he'd be there at four, which is why she arrived a few minutes before then. Willie strolled in five minutes later – like clockwork. He twisted one side of his lip into a frown of disapproval but bought her a beer anyway before heading to the back corner booth where she was seated.

"Did you order?" He handed her the bottle.

"Not hungry." She took a drink.

"Then why the hell are we at a pizza joint?"

Another long pull from her drink was the only answer he received.

"When do you wanna start?"

He wasn't putting up any resistance; that was a shock. "I started fifteen minutes ago." Better to ask forgiveness than permission.

"Oh really?" He chuckled. "And what rate am I paying my new employee who started fifteen minutes ago?"

"A set one. I only do retainers."

"You got a lot of nerve, J." He consumed a third of his beer in two big swigs.

"Well, last I heard, you don't work with spineless cowards who don't know their ass from a hole in the ground. Maybe I heard wrong." She leaned back in the booth, draping one arm over the top of it and polishing off the rest of her beer with the other. She didn't look at Willie – not out of fear, but as a way to let him know she could take this or leave it. She gave her attention to two guys defiling the sport of billiards near the front of the restaurant instead.

"What I *need* is brains."

She shot him a disapproving look of her own.

"Not what you're thinking," he added with a smirk. "Actual brains. And someone who's got pull and can run game on a certain investment cat. I got heat breathing down my neck and I need someone to get them off. I hear you're just the girl I'm looking for."

Jeslyn studied the middle-aged man sitting across from her. He didn't look like a Willie. She always thought of the country music icon when she heard the name. This Willie was nowhere near country.

A well-fed, Pacific Islander with pock marks dotted across his bloated face, and an impressive array of tattoos splashed across his neck (necks) and arms was what this Willie was. His skin was a muddy brown, a dismal caricature of the golden brown complexion typically associated with his race. The ashy tint that dulled his features was probably directly tied to his "honest living". The same honest living that was undoubtedly behind the unwanted attention – heat as he called it – that he was receiving.

His wavy hair hung down his back and lay limp and heavy with grease on his shoulders just below his collarbones, or the spot where his collarbones would have been if they weren't concealed under a puffy coat of fat. He also had a lazy eye. Extremely lazy. Jeslyn wondered if the eyeball, which seemed to be on delay whenever his other eye moved, wasn't made of glass.

Yeah, you need brain alright, you just couldn't get the paper bag thick enough for me. Jeslyn reached for her bottle, only remembering she'd already drained it of its contents after she picked it up.

"You want a refill?" He made a move as if he were going to stand up. Then again, it could have just been his fat rolls undulating.

"I'm good." She kept the look of disgust off of her face, just barely, as he shoved a stocky finger up his left nostril and took his sweet time exploring the cavity. "So, why the heat and who's the suit?" Jeslyn asked.

"The heat's because of the suit. He's got it in for me."

"Who?"

"Matty. I hear you know him. Matty Coleman."

Time stood still. Everything seemed to freeze, for what seemed like minutes, then time was speeding to catch up with itself. If thinking of Jacqueline caused her blood to boil, thinking about Matt Coleman turned it to molten lava.

157

She knew him all right. Knew how he had been fooling around with That Woman and how he had ruined her life. How he had bribed her to stay quiet about a certain affair and then threatened her to stay quiet when she wouldn't accept the bribes. She had been just a kid. But she wasn't a kid anymore.

"What's he have to do with anything?"

"We went in on a deal together. Deal went south. Not my fault, but Matty's still a little upset about it. Since he's Mr. Corporate Big Wig, he's trying to use his influences to bring me down without getting his hands dirty. He knows that if I try and bring him down, I get put on front street and all my shit gets put out there, too. I don't like people in my shit, J. I need somebody that can get him off my back."

Meaning, you want me to get my *hands dirty.*

"So? Can you do it or what?"

Could she do it? She thought about everything that could go wrong, how she'd probably have to see Coleman again, and how much she really didn't want to do this. Then she thought about something else, a way to give Coleman and That Woman a taste of their own foul medicine.

"If I couldn't, I wouldn't be here." She clamped her molars together then released them.

"You gonna let me in on your plan or are you gonna keep giving me these little smartass answers?" Willie crossed his chubby arms over his chest, which resulted in a cavern of man cleavage.

"I'll have something for you by tomorrow." She already wanted to be done with this. Thankfully there was no need to drag it out. She knew exactly how to get Coleman to fold.

"Im'a need proof you did something, sweetheart."

"I'll bring it to you before my...thing." Jeslyn grabbed her cell off the table and slipped it into her jacket pocket. She slipped her sunglasses on next, then folded her hands on the table and stared at him.

"What?" He wiped what might have been beer but could just as easily have been saliva from his chin with the back of his hand.

"I don't work for free, Willie." It was now or never.

He let out a loud sigh, but made a production of reaching into his pants pocket. It was a cringe worthy feat watching his belly crush against the edge of the table as he huffed and puffed his way to his money clip.

"Here." He tossed a healthy amount of bills her way, scattering them in the process. She cocked her head to the side and waited a beat before collecting them. "If I don't see you tomorrow, I'm gonna come looking for my money, Miss I-started-fifteen-minutes-ago."

Jeslyn scooted out of the booth and rose to her feet. "It's Miss I-started-over-a-half-an-hour-ago, now." She stuffed the money in her back pocket and walked away from the table and the foul man who still sat there thumbing through his large wad of remaining "pocket change" – probably because he was too out of breath to follow her.

She wasn't happy, she wasn't proud, she wasn't anything except nearly three grand less broke than she'd been over half an hour ago. She'd been briefed on Willie's dilemma before he contacted her, but hadn't been told Matt Coleman had anything to do with it. Upstairs in his Pacific Beach office Willie ran a windshield and glass repair business, a fairly profitable one at that. The downstairs operations of that same building were a whole other story. Downstairs was a sewer.

Jeslyn knew he dabbled in a deplorable mix of barely legal and completely illegal activities, but never inquired any further than that. Sometimes *not* knowing was half the battle. At first she thought that the stench of activities from his cess-pool must have tipped someone off. Going with that idea, she had told her informant she could help Willie out. Hearing that she'd have to deal with Matt Coleman, the scum that had been the start of her changed life – a change to bad, not good – made her realize just how awful this decision was.

There was no acceleration of the beating of her heart, no adrenaline spike or feelings of nervous energy as she drove back home, grabbed the shoebox and drove across town. There was only the unexceptional feeling of numbness.

Why she still had it was something that she hadn't ever had to answer. She just did. And right now she was glad she did. The shoebox sat on the passenger seat unopened. She didn't need to open it; she'd memorized everything inside it, then memorized it again when she'd made copies of it all. What she had with her now were copies. She wouldn't have to tell him that, he'd be able to see it for himself. Whatever Coleman had on Willie wouldn't matter after this.

His house looked the same. Like someone had flown it in from a plantation estate in Virginia and dropped it in the middle of this Carmel Valley neighborhood. She parked right across the street, not caring if he or anyone else saw her, hoping he would. The note she'd taped to the box had seemed clever when she wrote it, but now she wished she'd written something profane and threatening. But that was his style, and she wouldn't give him the self-satisfaction of thinking she was trying to be like him in any way.

It was after six and already dark. She placed the box on his doorstep, rang the doorbell and walked away unhurriedly. She had just gotten back into her car when the door opened. She had secretly been hoping for his wife, but saw it was him. The numbness evaporated. He picked up the box, a casual smile on his face like someone had left him a present, and then she saw him read the note.

Fear.

That was all she needed. The years of seething hatred and loathing didn't disappear, it would take more than a look for that. But seeing the horror in his eyes, even from a distance, was enough for now. He looked around frantically, but never at her. Her tinted windows must have hid her from his sight. When he'd gone inside, she started the car and drove away. Music blared from her speakers as she drove back home. She couldn't hear it; she could only feel bass, and energy, and contentedness. She had put fear in Matt Coleman's heart. She almost didn't need Willie's money; that had almost been payment enough. Almost.

She did wonder, hours later, as she let the near scalding water from the shower rain on her back, what it was that Coleman had on Willie. When you slithered through your entire existence as Willie had, it was a crap shoot as to why someone wanted to dig their heel into the crown of your head. It could be a million things, but Jeslyn had a feeling it was something very specific. Call it intuition or a gut feeling.

It was nearly three in the morning when she finally succumbed to dreamless sleep, something she hadn't been expecting. She had anticipated nightmares of unthinkable terror torturing her all night long. After all, she'd given her subconscious thoughts a lot of fodder over her lifetime and now she was exhuming the graves of bad decisions.

*   *   *

Morning came all too soon. Jeslyn woke up early, as if she'd gotten a full night's sleep. She hadn't. Three and a half hours lying in a crime scene position on her couch had not been sleep; it had simply been long stretches of stillness.

She was antsy as she assembled the file she was going to drop off at Willie's office that afternoon. He may have been hilariously fat and disgusting, but he was serious about his money, and he was speaking the truth when he said he'd come looking for her if she didn't have something for him by the time she said she would. She wiped at her brow distractedly as if there were sweat there. There wasn't. It was just her skin tingling from the brief thought of what Willie was capable of when a truly sour mood hit him. She quickly banished it; nothing was going to happen. She would kill before she let Willie or his hooligans violate her in any way.

As she continued her preparations, a message came through on the email address she'd acquired for communication with Forbes. She'd contacted him again after the last run-in with her mother, deciding to go all in on him, too. She wanted him. In what way she wasn't certain. She knew her desires could be temporary and capricious at best, vengeful at worst. In/out, hot/cold, fascination/indifference, admiration/disdain. The direction of the wind could change her feelings in an instant. This instant, the forecast was hot fascination.

Jeslyn didn't believe in hard to get. When she wanted something, she made herself available to the opportunity. She did, however, believe in the notion of hard to read. There was a difference – for her anyway.

Her email to him had thanked him for his time and asked if she could shoot him. His photograph would accent the article nicely, she'd written. The email had also simmered with innuendo, but could have been interpreted as completely innocent if it became necessary to offer an explanation. His response would let her know whether or not she'd have to. His email back to her was short – *Would love to. When and where are you thinking?* – but sweet. She would have to consider that. When and where indeed.

Jeslyn tabled her response to Forbes, finished compiling the file for Willie, then put the finishing touches on a presentation she'd created for a possible client. She'd received her first lead for Red Cello the previous day. A company by the name of Good Feet had contacted her, but she didn't want to jinx anything with high hopes. Cautiously optimistic, that's what she was. After that was done, she started on a personal project.

Next to nothing was what she knew about him, but from the little she did know, she felt Gisele had to be a mistake. There was no way their fling was serious. She refused to even think about it as a relationship. Forbes was smart, successful, polished and distinguished. Gisele was...not. Snipping the thread of their connection would be easier than taking candy from a baby. She simply needed something sharp to cut it with.

All Jeslyn had to go on was a first name. The lanky sexpot had said she modeled. Well, that would be an exercise in futility. The wrong results would certainly crop up if she searched 'Gisele model'. What else? Perhaps there was a link between her and Forbes. 'Gisele + Forbes Keith'.

That was the ticket. Gisele Marie-Claire Le'marchal. That was quite a mouthful.

Jeslyn had a pre-established account with an online background service agency – the original reason for it was out of the picture, but it came in handy now. There was a record that listed Gisele's name as Mary Marshall. Could be an inaccuracy, could be information. Jeslyn searched it.

After a few seconds a pop-up appeared on her computer screen. 'XXX Fun With Busty Beauties.' Three more equally salacious pop-ups appeared. Then two more.

Spam.

Jeslyn had neglected to update her anti-virus software but had thought she had a spam blocker installed. Whether she did or not, it wasn't doing its job. She cursed this minor derailment and set to work eradicating the virulent cookies and spambots that had infected her computer's network. Then it was time to head to Willie's office, promising herself she'd continue this latest enterprise when she returned.

*   *   *

The drive took longer than expected. Although they hadn't agreed on a specific time, Jeslyn had that appointment later in the afternoon that she couldn't be late for. She walked into the office and stood waiting as the front desk girl, who looked barely old enough to drive, smacked her gum, giggled and murmured sweet nothings in Spanish to a young kid with a buzz haircut and a pair of red lips tattooed on his neck. Jeslyn cleared her throat. Nothing. It was as if she didn't exist.

"Perdon. Donde esta tu jefe?" Excuse me. Where is your boss?

Jeslyn got a scowl in response from the girl and an appreciative look from the pimply-faced boy.

"Como podria soberlo?" How should I know?

A saucy thing this one. Jeslyn briefly wondered just how flippant she would be nursing a split lip and two black eyes. She wasn't here to play games.

"Utilazando la cono en lugar de su cabeza, no vas a saber." Like riding a bike, she had picked up foul language again easily.

Her eyes never left the girl's face as she walked past the stunned-to-silence couple and over to the door leading to the underworld. She grabbed the doorknob. The girl mumbled something dismissive but quickly diverted her eyes and shooed her amused looking suitor away before turning back to her computer.

Jeslyn casually stepped into the coolness of the stairwell. Her heeled ankle boots echoed in the space and she tried to silence them as best she could. For some reason, she didn't want to announce her arrival. It didn't matter, cameras poked out from the corners of the ceilings like black orbed guards.

She knew, even without trying the handle of the door at the bottom of the stairs, that it was locked. There was no need to knock or otherwise announce her presence because she also knew that whoever was behind the door was already aware she was there. A loud click signaled her permission to enter. She snapped her poker face in place before walking in.

Without the luxury of windows, the cavernous recesses of the underground area seemed darker. The artificial lighting, with its buzzing fluorescent bulbs, only barely dispelled the gloom. A huge wooden reception desk hulked in front of her with a diminutive, scantily clad Filipino girl manning it. The word 'girl' could not have been more accurate. If there was a passing puberty scale, like the height scales for certain amusement park rides, she may not have passed.

Two monitors and a phone decorated the desk. That was all. The girl never lifted her eyes from her cell phone screen as she pointed to a long hallway to her right, Jeslyn's left.

Although it looked like a hallway in someone's home, walking the long corridor made Jeslyn feel like she was a convict on death row escorting herself to the electric chair. There was a wall to her left painted in a rather pleasing shade of beige up top. A chair railing and wainscoting covered the bottom two thirds. Framed pictures of Willie with music artists, Mafia-looking men, bikini-clad women and even some government officials were arranged neatly on the wall's surface. Closed doors stood as wooden sentries to her right. Only one door, at the very end of the hallway directly in front of her, stood open. She made her way to it, folder in hand.

Willie sat inside the room in an oversized recliner looking like Jabba the Hutt. His shirt was off even though the temperature indoors was set on Antarctic. More girls, wearing next to nothing, lounged around him on chairs and a leather sofa.

"Well, well, well. Look who we have here." Willie smiled big, too big, and wriggled in the recliner like a dying worm on a hook.

"Here." Jeslyn half handed, half tossed the envelope – which held another set of copies of what had been left on Coleman's porch inside – at his lap. His smile disappeared. Maybe he didn't like her discourteous behavior being exhibited in front of his harem.

"Kiki!" Willie yelled. A bleach blonde Asian girl swung her head woozily to look at him. He clapped his hands twice as if to say 'chop, chop.' She stumbled to her hooker-heeled feet, then, like a zombie, dragged herself over to where Willie sat and lost half her arm into the pocket of his shorts. He barely made a move to aid her progress. After retrieving a tiny key, she stumbled to a metal cabinet in the corner, unlocked a drawer, accessed a safe within it and retrieved an envelope. In the same stupefied fashion, she walked over to Jeslyn and handed the envelope to her. Jeslyn knew without opening it that there was money inside. The thickness of it told her it was a lot of money.

"Don't you want to look at what's in there?" A slight feeling of panic rose in her chest. Willie hadn't even touched the file she'd brought to him.

"I will, I will." Willie's smile returned as the girl clumsily stuffed the key back into his pocket. He pulled her onto his lap. Jeslyn's stomach writhed with nausea. She was done here. As she turned to leave Willie called out, "I'll be talking to you soon."

It sounded like a threat.

She quickly made her way back down the hallway hating the clicking sound of her heels as she went. She paused, mid stride and contemplated removing them. In that short tick of silence she heard a noise, a few whimpers. It was coming from behind one of the closed doors. Jeslyn knew without looking that cameras were also installed here. And if there were cameras, there was sure to be someone monitoring them. She cleared her throat softly, the whimper came again. Willie's laugh rumbled in the distance behind her. He was occupied.

Clearing of the throat. Whimper.

Again. Response.

She started down the hall and located the door she was pretty sure held whatever or whoever was making the noise, then she clutched at her chest.

Not wanting to alert Willie that she was still in the hallway, she made movements as if she were having a coughing fit, but no sound actually escaped her lips. She pressed her hand against the door as if for leverage, then let it slide to the doorknob as she continued to pantomime cough-choking. With a slight turn of her wrist the door inched opened. Jeslyn cut her eyes inside the room and almost truly started choking.

A girl – no, a *child* – sat huddled in a corner of the dark room on a blanket. Three other children lay on the floor around her. They were chained.

They. Were. Chained.

Like a string of code, pieces of intelligence began lining up in rapid succession. A split second later the code was cracked. Willie was engaging in human trafficking. She didn't care if she wasn't completely right. You didn't chain children up inside a room for any reason. The puzzle was crystal clear. This was Willie's heat, what Coleman must have been holding over his head.

What had she done?

She silently shut the door, wiped at her eyes like she was recovering from the coughing fit and continued down the corridor as if nothing was wrong.

When she got back to the opposite end of the hallway, the girl at the desk flicked a nervous glance in her direction. Jeslyn returned it with a bored look of her own. A familiar click and Jeslyn was freed from Lucifer's Lair.

She unhurriedly made her way back up the stairs to the street level office. Any prying eyes would not have noticed a change in her exterior demeanor. Inside she was seething. Inside she was sick. The envelope of money dug through the lining of her pocket and into her skin like talons.

Something had to be done. Alerting the authorities was not an option.

Something had to be done. She couldn't be tied to this.

Something had to be done.

Another favor.

16

~Before~

Jeslyn pulled into the parking lot of the Carlsbad office at twenty past four. Her thoughts were swirling and trying to collect them was like trying to collect loose leaves in a tornado. Every second she did nothing, those children suffered. Now that she knew what was literally going on behind closed doors, she was an abettor rather than an aide if she didn't do something. But she couldn't do anything about it at the moment; it would have to wait.

Even though this response from Good Feet had come through for Red Cello, Jeslyn's enthusiasm was blunted. She needed to repurpose the indignation that she felt for Willie, the indignation that rolled and churned inside her like a concrete mixer; just for a few hours, until after the meeting, or risk spoiling this opportunity. She needed this opportunity.

The woman at the front desk was pleasant and accommodating, nothing like the girls Willie employed. Jeslyn made sure to compliment her. There was no way to know who had influence over what, so it was best to treat everyone like a decision-maker.

The meeting itself started out well. She'd always been outstanding under pressure, orally impressive and quick on her feet. That combination, in conjunction with the polished presentation she'd put together, turned an initial discussion with the company's Operations Manager into a formal negotiation with the company's CEO.

Good Feet was a manufacturer of arch supports. Initially, she had considered turning the lead down – what did she know about manufacturing. Then, she'd done some research on the company, both on their GoodFeet.com website and by reading industry reports. The results yielded a plethora of marketing opportunities – one of the first being that their products were made in the USA. The company also claimed that they didn't produce over-the-counter, one-size-fits-all inserts, but premium, personally-fit orthotics that eliminated, or at least drastically alleviated, everything from foot pain to back pain and more. If their claims were true, her job would be a cinch. Regardless, she was interested in getting a look at these alleged prefabricated miracles.

The CEO proved to be a no-nonsense negotiator. His business acumen was fierce, his numerical calculations pinpoint accurate, his requests firm but fair, and his ability to weed out quality from crap well above average. He was slow to speak and seemed to carefully analyze each piece of data Jeslyn provided him. Meeting with him was like being a contestant on *The Apprentice*; he might have even been able to give Trump a run for his money.

There was no back-and-forth indecisiveness; the man knew what he was looking for. There were only direct questions which demanded immediate and intelligent answers. Jeslyn gave it her all. Two and a half hours later she had her first client.

Had the weight of Willie and his debaucherous dealings not been so heavy on her mind, she would've probably contacted an acquaintance or two to celebrate – something she hadn't done in quite a while. As it was, she didn't feel like celebrating; she felt like heading back to Pacific Beach chaining Willie up in a room, locking the door, and throwing away the key. She'd barely made it to her car and out of the Good Feet parking lot before she was on the phone.

There was a non-spoken rule, even among thugs and thieves: Don't mess with children. Get as down and dirty as you want, but leave children out of it. When word got out what was going on in Willie's underground playpen, she doubted he would have a leg – or a cankle – to stand on. He thought he had heat before? Jeslyn would see to it that Willie got an inferno.

*   *   *

Another date and time with Forbes had been set. Jeslyn saw this second meeting going much differently. This would be a foray into the art of seduction.

It wasn't as if she'd never seduced a man before, but the problems with this scenario were threefold. Number one, Forbes was involved with someone. Regardless of how inappropriate or inconsequential she viewed that involvement, he knew she knew he was involved. Number two, she was supposed to be interviewing him, not trying to seduce him. And number three, whenever she took the lead with a man it was because she knew he was interested. It was a way to flash a thumbs up sign if her hard to read tactics had left her target completely illiterate. Jeslyn had no idea what Forbes was thinking in regards to her, or if he was thinking of her at all.

Her last meeting with Willie had netted her six thousand dollars. Because he hadn't looked at the file and because he knew damn well why he was getting unwanted attention, she knew he would be looking for something else from her. That meant she'd been given a loan, not a payout. Willie wasn't going to shell out just shy of ten grand for information he was already well aware of. He wasn't that stupid. He just assumed that she was. He assumed incorrectly.

Despite the source, meaning or implications, sleaze money spent just as easily as honest money. A limo would be picking Forbes up at an address he'd provided and taking him to an estate that had been secured for the occasion. Working with high-level designers, photographers, and media companies during her marketing and advertising stints meant she knew a thing or two about how to put together a production. And the best part was the fact he would be solo for this rendezvous. She'd made sure of it.

Jeslyn: *Do I need to make arrangements for anyone else in your party or just you?*

Forbes: *Just me.*

Everything was set. Jeslyn took a cab to the location so that they could share the limo afterwards. Her failsafe in case she didn't reach her goal during the photo shoot and her treat in case she did.

It was stupid to say that she missed him. Her drug. Foolish to think of how she missed the look of his face, the sound of his voice and his way — that je ne sais quoi charm that was as much a part of him as his pelvic-contracting smile. She would not admit that she missed being in close proximity to him and the headiness that proximity created.

A text from the driver let her know she would be receiving a Forbes injection in just under five minutes. She visited the powder room for one last sweep of her person to ensure she would not offend any of Forbes' senses. Hair, makeup, teeth, breath — all systems check and go. She heard the creaking of the wrought iron gate and the crunch of tires on the gravel path leading up to the circular driveway. The driver knew to escort Forbes in, so she busied herself with checking her DSLR camera's exposure triangle settings.

She was, for all intents and purposes, a novice when it came to operations behind the lens. There was enough knowledge to get her through this shoot, but not enough to wax poetic about it. Therefore, she would need to keep the topics of conversation on other things, like him, him, and him.

"Right this way, sir." The driver was leading Forbes to her. In mere seconds he would hit her bloodstream, which was already gushing from her heart like it was being dispensed through a fire hydrant pump.

"Hello Jes..." He stopped short.

Jeslyn purposely had her back to him. She had dressed to seriously maim in short, silk black cuffed shorts, translucent pearl gray pantyhose and thigh-high black leather boots. Up top, she sported a sheer black, long-sleeved, button up dress shirt that hugged her torso. Underneath it was a low-cut, lavender camisole trimmed in black lace. Her balconette bra turned her sufficient handful into two plentiful hills flowing with honey butter skin. She wore her hair down with side swept bangs and big voluminous curls. It was daytime so she went light on the makeup and, as always, light on the perfume. She preferred the hint of body spray to the punch of musk.

It didn't matter if he was involved or not. It didn't matter if he was a priest. The man had eyes and a libido.

"Hey Forbes, thanks so much for..." Jeslyn barely looked at him. She tinkered with a light stand before completing her sentence. "...coming out. I know I'm putting you through the ringer and this isn't even a sure thing. You don't know how much I appreciate this."

"Oh, no, it's no problem at all." His eyes scanned her quickly, like he thought she wasn't looking. She was.

"You look amazing by the way." She finally gave him a tablespoon of her attention. "Thanks for making my job so easy." She cat walked to where he stood and placed her hand on his arm. "I will have you on your way in no time." A squeeze to his bicep, then release. Before he could respond, even though his lips were unsealing from each other in order to do so, she took the few steps over to where the driver stood. "I'm sorry, I didn't catch your name." Jeslyn also reached out and touched the elderly gentleman's arm.

"George, ma'am."

"Please, George, call me Princess." She tossed a wink in Forbes' direction. "I'm kidding. But please do call me Jeslyn."

"Sure thing, Miss Jeslyn." The driver smiled broadly. Jeslyn linked her arm in his while Forbes looked on.

"George, would you like to stay or would you like to come back to collect my extremely handsome photography subject?"

"I can come back, Miss Jeslyn." He adjusted the cap that covered his thick head of white hair.

"Whatever suits your fancy. And can I just say, I love how you say my name. Miss Jeslyn. You're a real peach." She pinched his cheek lightly before unlinking their arms, and walked over to the foyer table. George followed. "Here you go." She handed him an envelope with a handsome tip inside. "We'll see you in a few hours." After he left she turned to face her quarry.

"You know you just made that man's entire year." Forbes smiled. Jeslyn's pelvic floor contracted.

"Hardly. I was simply being nice to a nice man. Come here."

He came.

She slipped her hand smoothly into his and led him into the sunken family room. "I'd like to do you here first." She pulled her hand away then reached up to stroke both of his cheeks, the bridge of his nose and forehead. "Do you have a problem with makeup? Your face is a little shiny. I'm concerned it might look a little hot in the light." She scrunched her features as if seriously considering the possibility of that.

"Ah, no." Raspy. Clear throat. Try again, "No, not at all."

"Good." Jeslyn clicked her tongue twice as if she were encouraging a horse and brushed past Forbes to the makeup bag she'd brought with her. "Sit." She pointed to the sofa.

He sat.

Jeslyn walked right up to him, nearly crotch to face, and worked to open a compact of powder. "See, still new," she said as she tore at the insanely over-packaged product with her teeth. When she'd finished grinding her enamel down on the recycled plastic, she knelt before him as if she were a liege kneeling in devotion before her lord. He followed her movement with reverent eyes.

"A brand new compact all for me? Wow, I must look worse than I thought. How much of this stuff are you going to use?" He grinned lopsidedly, seemingly amused at his own joke.

"Oh stop it. Look at my face. Can you even tell I'm wearing foundation?" She leaned in close to him, resting her hands lightly on his lower thighs. They locked eyes for two glorious seconds before he trailed his eyes over the rest of her face. Like a shooting star across a night sky, she felt the warmth of his scrutiny everywhere his gaze fell.

"No," voice barely audible, "you're perfect." Then with recognition of what was said, "Your skin," his voice got louder. "Your skin is perfect."

Jeslyn laughed softly. "Actually, that wasn't fair." She smiled conspiratorially, glancing to her left and right as if she were checking to see that they were alone.

They were very much alone.

She lessened the distance between their bodies by several inches and placed her lips a hair's length from his ear, her cheek nearly grazing his. "I'm not wearing foundation." *I'm not wearing panties,* could have been read between the lines of her whisper. She backed away quickly. "Now, close your eyes."

"Ha ha." His was nervous laughter as she popped open the case. "So, you're the interviewer, writer, makeup artist and photographer, huh?" He made an attempt at small talk.

"Yup." She coated the brush in powder then tapped it to release the excess.

"Impressive."

"Not really. When you're freelance, you're generally not given a lot of resources. So, you learn to make do." She took a moment to absorb him with his eyes closed. The shutter of her mind's eye clicked, capturing his features for personal use later. She swept the powder over his skin carefully, as if she were applying it with her lips instead of the delicate hairs of the makeup brush. She used the soft pads of her fingers to smooth out his eyebrows – molesting him as blatantly as she could, until she could keep up the guise no longer. There was only so much powder a face could hold. "And you're done." She tapped the brush on the tip of his nose. "Voila!"

By the time he opened his eyes she had already stood and grabbed the camera.

"So, am I presentable?" He motioned to his face.

"Forbes, you are..." Jeslyn heaved an overly dramatic sigh.

"I'm what? What's whheewwwww?" He mimicked her exhalation.

"It's best if I keep my thoughts to myself." She looked down at the camera knowing he wouldn't drop it, loving that he wouldn't drop it.

"No. Out with it, *Miss Jeslyn*." He was teasing her. If he only knew how he was teasing her.

"It's not like it's a secret, Mr. Keith. You know you are –"

"I am...?"

"Really? Seriously?" She managed an eye roll. "Does it please you to force people into divulging their secret thoughts?" No need to wait for an answer. He clearly wanted to hear this as much as she wanted to say it. "Fine. If that's what floats your little boat." Jeslyn moistened her lips. "Forbes, I think you are extremely (*insanely*) attractive. I understand I'm meeting with you under professional circumstances, and I will remain a consummate professional, I promise (*I'm lying*), but yes, I am taking great pleasure in my (*completely made up*) job right now. There. Satisfied?" She kept her expression serious, almost stern. As if she were terribly disturbed that he'd forced her to admit this.

She was not.

"Wow. And here I thought I was your worst interview of the year the way you bark out orders, throw out your questions, then run." He smiled to indicate this was just more ribbing. Then the smile compressed into something more earnest. "But, thank you."

"You're welcome. Shall we?"

"You know –"

"Yes?" Jeslyn interrupted hungrily.

"You're very attractive yourself." It was said more like an offhanded observation.

"Well, thank you. If I thought that could get me somewhere...shall we?"

"Wait. You keep doing that."

"Doing what?" Feigned innocence.

"Where you say something but don't say it. Just say it."

"What are you wanting me to say, Mr. Keith?" Jeslyn already knew. He wanted his ego stroked, which was just fine with her. She was fully prepared to stroke his ego and so much more.

"I want you to say exactly what you're thinking. I like transparency."

"How about this, I will never be able to photograph you, much less speak to you again, if I am fully transparent right now." Truer words were never spoken. "So, if you let me get what I came for, I will be as transparent as you'd like and then I will go and die from mortification. Deal?"

"Always the negotiator, Miss Jeslyn, but you have yourself a deal." His grin, that was like a signature for his face, John Hancocked itself there now. Jeslyn felt warmth pool in her abdomen and course slowly to her desire train's central station.

Concentrating was hard. She found excuses – searched for them like hidden treasure – to touch him.

Position his body, angle his face, adjust his clothing, apply more powder. Every touch was like a tiny hit. By the time they were finished she was high on Forbes Keith.

"So, Jeslyn."

Showtime.

"So, Forbes." She started assembling her equipment.

"Anything you care to talk about?" He had dropped himself on the sofa, partially sitting, mostly laying. One arm was lounging on the armrest, the other slung across the back. She imagined crawling into his lap and hovering her body over his like a UFO waiting to claim a planet. What exactly would he do? A blink brought her back to the here and now.

"I assume you're referring to my private thoughts as it pertains to you?"

"Well, when you say it that way, you make me sound like a pervert." He smiled cockily.

"Are you? A pervert?" She continued gathering her things.

"No." He practically scoffed in response. "Just...curious, I guess. Maybe I shouldn't be." His words seemed to water his conscience, helping it to grow.

"Curiosity is simply part of human nature. It's ok." She tried to dehydrate his voice of reason. "I mean, I'd be lying myself if I said I wasn't interested in your thoughts at the moment." He'd already shifted into a complete sitting position, forearms resting on his thighs, hands locked together. "As for my thoughts," she continued as she turned to face him, "I find you captivating." Jeslyn tilted her head to the side, studying him. "I think you're extremely attractive, obviously, but there's something about you that intrigues me."

Although she was cutting herself open, she kept her voice strong and direct. "I wish I knew more about you. Not biochemist you, although I'm sure that's absorbing as well, but more about Forbes. The man that quotes Sojourn lyrics." His eyebrows arched up in surprise. "And the man who flirts shamelessly, even though he has a girlfriend?"

She presented this to him in the form of a question. Yes, she was shaming him a bit, putting the onus of moving forward on him. And with that, she made herself officially hard to read. *I want you. Aren't you taken?*

"Interesting." If he was uncomfortable it no longer showed. He seemed empowered, his earlier displays of awkwardness chased away by interest. "Yes, Gisele and I are seeing each other."

Dismissive much? So, he was a playboy.

"I didn't realize you'd take transparency to heart. And what do you know about Sojourn?" His segue was said amusingly.

"I know quite a bit actually." She didn't want to talk about music. Was he bringing them around to safe territory?

"You're a surprise, Jeslyn, you really are." He spoke the words like an afterthought. Then he pulled his phone from a bag that he'd brought with him. "Do you mind if I make a few calls, or did you need me for something else?"

Jeslyn's stomach went cold. This was not the route she'd intended to take.

Assume control, assume control. Her life's motto was on repeat in her head.

"No," she said.

That is not assuming control!

Her emotions and logic waged a violent war within her.

"Thanks." He rose from the sofa and left her field of vision, dialing as he went. She could hear his muffled voice checking in with someone about blasé business matters.

George would be back in a few minutes. She took the time she now had alone to check her own phone. Another email had come in for Red Cello. Joy. The vibrancy of her mood felt like it had been splashed with a coat of matte gray paint. A little of it must have gotten on her sleeve, the same place where she seemed to be wearing her heart.

"Why the long face?" Forbes had come back into the room.

"Oh, I'm not sure." Lie.

"Is everything OK?"

No. "Yeah, everything's fine. How about with you?"

"Good, good."

Awkward silence.

"Listen, Forbes, I'm really sorry if I said something I shouldn't have. I can see I've made you uncomfortable and –"

"Jeslyn," he interrupted her firmly.

"I just...yes?"

"You didn't make me nervous." His features softened. "Just...pensive."

"Transparency, Forbes." Her heart exited the city streets and entered the autobahn of anxiety with no limit to clip its pace.

"You've just given me some things to think about." He put his fist to his mouth as if he were concealing a burp. "I'm not as good at transparency as you are, but I'll give it a go. Ah, let's see. Jeslyn." Pause. "I also find you intriguing." His words seemed stuck, like he had to pry them loose from somewhere before he could get them out. "You're a very beautiful woman, but you are also very...there's something unique about you. It's hard for me to explain. Yes, you are correct, I am seeing someone." Another pause. "However, if that weren't the case," he swallowed with some difficulty. "I would like to get to know you better as well." He shrugged as if to say, 'yeah, I said it, what are you going to do about it?'

Vibrancy reinstated. Jeslyn walked over to him, slowly and deliberately, until she stood so close that one big inhale from both of them would cause their bodies to touch. She searched his eyes intently.

"You're perfect at transparency." Just above a whisper. "Thank you for giving me something to think about, too."

"And what would that be?" His voice was low and thick with expectation.

"If your situation changes, and you find yourself in a position to explore new opportunities, I would be more than happy to divulge that information." It was a blatant call to action. "Until then, I hope you keep in touch. I meant what I said."

In her peripheral she could see George coming up the porch towards the door. She hadn't heard the gate or the car. It was all she could do not grab Forbes' hand and lead him off somewhere, anywhere, where they could continue this cat and mouse non-foreplay. Instead she walked over to the front door to let the punctual driver in.

"Am I too soon?" George inquired innocently.

"No, George, you have impeccable timing." Jeslyn went about prepping for their departure as if she and Forbes had not just pseudo sexed each other's emotions in the foyer.

Both men assisted with lugging her equipment to the limo and loading it in the trunk. She was already inside, staring out the window when Forbes slid in beside her. She felt him watching her, but he didn't speak. When they had left the neighborhood and were cruising through a business park, she chanced a glance in his direction.

"Still thinking?" He looked at her with somber eyes.

"Yes." For once, the truth.

"Is it wrong that I really wish I knew what you're thinking about?"

"No." She could spit out truth all day with inquiries like these.

"Will you tell me, then?" A shard of hope broke from the smooth glass of his expression.

Jeslyn's heart began to racquetball itself against her chest.

The truth, Forbes, is that the entire premise upon which meeting you is founded is nothing more than a dubious machination.

"I was just thinking that..."

I am a fraud, playing you for a fool, all for a good...

"Forgetting the actual reason for our communication and interaction, I mean, putting all of that..."

Sham. That's what this is. And all because of that stupid quote. Well, that and the fact you're a fine piece of...

"...aside, I'm really having a wonderful time just hanging out with you. You're..."

Trouble. You're also sporting a size twelve shoe, which means you probably have a very nice...

"Packaged differently than what I expected."

"Different good?" He sounded worried.

"Yes." She turned to look out the window again.

"Hey." He ran the back of one finger down her arm to get her attention. The contact made her involuntarily cross her legs. She faced him again.

"Yes?" They stayed suspended in each other's eyes like aerial acrobats for a few seconds. Jeslyn could see conflict pass over Forbes' face like a cirrus cloud passing across the sky, creating the slightest hint of a shadow.

"I like hanging out with you, too." He offered a weak smile that seemed more conciliatory than anything else, like he was seceding.

She scanned his face, taking in every detail, while inhaling his scent inconspicuously. He watched her watching him. "I hope I get to see you again, Forbes." She nodded her head solemnly, like a goodbye.

"I hope so, too." His words could have given hers a flat tire, they came on the heels of them so quickly. The limo slowed to a stop indicating they'd reached their first destination. "This is me. May I?" He extended his arms. In that gesture was the universal symbol for a hug. He wanted a hug.

He. Wanted. A. Hug.

Wordlessly, Jeslyn scooted over to his side of the plush leather seat. She slid her arms around his neck, pressing as much of her body as she could against his given the constraints of their respective angles. He took his time sliding his hands over the side of her body, letting them travel leisurely around to her back. Her cheek pressed firmly against his ear, her chin cradled by the side of his neck. Against her will she sighed. It came out more like a soft moan. She felt his forearms and biceps constrict, forcing her deeper into his sturdy frame. One hand slid to the nape of his neck. Another hand slid to her shoulder blade. He pulled his head back slightly, hers followed suit until they were cheek to cheek, then chin to chin. Their embrace had slackened but not by much. Then...

"Here you are, sir." George swung Forbes' door open. A cold draft of air blew away the heated 'almost' that had been about to nearly happen. Forbes released her slowly, collected his bag and stepped out of the limo. George, ever dutiful, continued to stand at the door. Forbes ducked his head back inside.

"Thank you."

Thank you? For what? For the hug, the fake interview, the even grander but equally as fake photo shoot?

"For everything." He answered her cyclonic thoughts. "We'll speak soon, yes?"

"Yes." Jeslyn let him borrow a smile. He used it to mirror her expression, then stepped back as George shut the door.

Jeslyn didn't turn to get a final glimpse of Forbes Keith dropping out of sight. There was no need. She was confident they'd be seeing each other again and she didn't want to ruin the image of him in her head with the actuality of him fading from view.

She pulled her cell phone from her purse. A small red light was steadily blinking indicating she had messages. A weepy voicemail from her mother was one of them. She blubbered through an explanation – not apology – that her father had never said she was a spoiled brat; she'd just lashed out. Jeslyn gritted her teeth in frustration as she listened. Her mother then droned on and on about how she'd always been a good mom, but she's had a hard life too – yada, yada, ya-delete.

Jeslyn began to make a list. 'Get Mother professional help' was placed at the top.

The next message was another prospective client for Red Cello. This made the third inquiry in a week. When it rained...

Jeslyn added, 'contact Red Cello Marketing clients' and 'develop company philosophy and objectives', to her list.

She scrolled through texts, coming across a number she didn't recognize. All it said was:

it's done.

Jeslyn figured it was a wrong number. As she considered that, a new text appeared from another number she didn't recognize. This one flooded her senses.

This is my #. Feel free to use it if u need to get a hold of me. Talk soon princess.

She held off on a reply, but hugged her phone to her chest and smiled self-satisfactorily.

Oh yes, they would be seeing each other soon. And when they did, there were only two words she wanted to hear him say. Gisele who?

17

Katya didn't realize she'd been gnawing on her lip until the raw sting bit her back.

"This is incredible." It was the first thing that came to her mind.

"What?" Jeslyn sounded as if she was coming out of hypnosis.

"This. Everything. Your story. It's incredible."

Jeslyn shrugged noncommittally. "It's life."

"Not everyone has a life like this, Jeslyn." There was a 'don't you realize that?' tickling the back of Katya's throat that she swallowed away.

Another shrug, this one in resigned agreement.

"So..." Katya hesitated. Perhaps there was more. She wanted to hear more, but didn't know how to lure this bee back to the nectar of her own story. Unless there was no more story. Katya hoped there was more. "Anything else?"

"Anything else?" Jeslyn's was a perplexed echo.

"Is there anything else to share?" There had to be. There were too many, 'so-what-happened-with,' cliffhangers.

Jeslyn sighed. "You mean is there any more ammunition to take out of the gun fight?"

That was not what she meant because she had no idea what Jeslyn was talking about. "What?"

184

"It's from this story, a parable. My dad used to tell it to me when I was young. It never even made sense for me until I got older; and even then I didn't do much with that knowledge."

"What's the parable about?" Katya pressed.

"Guilt. Pride." Jeslyn seemed to consider the simplicity of that statement before offering, "Truth."

"Can I hear it?"

"Hear what, the story?"

"Yeah."

Jeslyn turned away, like she was expecting her father to appear and tell the story for her, or give her permission to tell it herself. When he didn't appear, she spoke.

"OK. Hopefully I get this right. I've never actually told it before, now that I think about it. I've only heard it told to me"

Katya relaxed into her chair as Jeslyn brought the parable to life.

* * *

What many today call magic or even witchcraft was simply a way of life to the people of the Bhuuntua Village, the first people of the earth. Eternal Spirits — the beings that were and are and ever would be — watched over the sacred land of the village and its inhabitants from the heavens. Every ten years, when the star of Ga'sethi passed over the sky, marking the Day of Shaf'hil, the Spirits descended from their celestial dwellings, walked among the people, and offered their wise counsel.

The Bhuuntuan people had lived in perfect harmony for many centuries. But after a time, they began to groan inwardly and the Spirits saw the desires that beat in their hearts. They yearned for oneness; yearned for the Spirits to walk among them and dwell in the village as their daily guide. But this was not possible.

And so it was then, when the sun was still a new creation, and the moon had just been conceived, the Spirits gathered a small group of men together. The Spirits needed men who were pure in heart

185

who could serve as leaders incarnate for the people of the village. They bestowed upon the men the power to see and know a portion of what they themselves were able to see and know. They also promised to bless them abundantly and breathe eternity into them and any woman they took as their wife and any children that came from that union. Anyone not joined to the men in marriage, fathered by them through that union, or a descendant of those offspring would eventually taste the bitter sting of death. However, the blessing was given under one condition. The men were ordered to protect and serve the village for all of eternity and keep violence and bloodshed far from it.

The group of chosen men solemnly swore to adhere to the laws passed down to them in exchange for the blessings.

The men then asked the Spirits to show them how to protect and serve the village along with its abundant resources. For you see, the village was rich with rare flora and fauna that cured disease, rare gems that increased wealth, and rare natural water sources that sustained youth. Outsiders who had learned of these resources, wanted to find and inhabit the land for themselves. The men knew that neither violence nor bloodshed was permitted. This was to keep the land pure. For it was said that if human blood that was shed in anger reached the soil it would unleash the demons of greed, envy and war, and all would surely die.

The Spirits, pleased that the men intended to do as they had said, caused a deep sleep to fall over every living man, woman, child and creature who lived in the village. While they slept, the Spirits grew a hedge around the village made of thick ivy and briar. The ivy produced tiny beautiful red flowers that would release a mist of sweet smelling perfume should anyone try to pass through it. This perfume would cause a person to forget everything they knew. The briars produced tiny sharp thorns that were full of venom and would instantly strike a person blind. When the protective hedge was fully grown, the Spirits awakened the villagers and the creatures from their slumber. They reminded the men again that they were to protect and serve the people and encourage all to live modestly and with humility. They promised them that if they did, they would want for nothing from now until eternity.

One chosen man by the name of Y'Juntdo was distressed. He had not always lived in the village. Many years ago, when he was but an infant, he had been found alone in the woods. A young village woman named Mi'Yja, who could not bear children of her own, heard his cries and rescued him. She and her husband had brought him back to the village and raised him as their own. Y'Jundto wanted to know why only a select few had been chosen and why others had to die. The Spirits' only response was that it was done in order to fulfill the prophecy. This bothered Y'Jundto greatly, but he said nothing further.

For years, the men protected and served the villagers and guided them in the way the Spirits had advised. They encouraged the people to live with modesty and humility, and they prevented violence and bloodshed, which kept the demons of greed, envy, and war away.

As the years wore on, the chosen group of men, along with their wives and their children, did not taste the sting of death. Death did, however, come to visit those who had not been a part of the chosen few. Each wail announcing the passing of another villager, each burial that marked the loss of a loved one, made Y'Jundto more angry.

Why did anyone have to die? Why had he been chosen? He had not been born in the village. He did not know where he had been born, yet he had been raised by these people as if he were their own. He watched his mother and father, sisters and brothers, friends and loved ones cross over into the afterlife. Each death produced more anger within him. He knew their deaths were simply because they had not been chosen. It could easily have been him.

Years passed. Then many more followed.

Death had not visited the village for centuries. The slender dark children – descendants of the chosen – who ran happily through the tall grass of the fields and played at the river water's edge knew of death only in myth. Tales told in the late evening, using the wispy gray plumes of smoke and crackling kindling of fire as a backdrop, spoke of death from many, many years ago. But they were only told as ghost stories; a way to frighten unruly children: "Stop breaking your toys. If you don't, I will send Death after you." Or by older siblings to scare their younger brothers and sisters into submission: "If you don't give me your sweet bread, I will call Death to come and claim you."

Y'Jundto heard such a threat from his older son one day and admonished him harshly. "You do not know what you speak of! Never let me hear talk of death come from your lips again, do you understand?" The boy nodded obediently before slinking away.

Y'Jundto knew he had to do something. His heart had become hardened due to so much loss and centuries of guilt. He did not enjoy his life. Instead, he mocked his blessings and cursed his immortality. Soon, his anger consumed him so completely that one day he traveled to the eastern edge of the village to the black waters of the Kwanta'hil'ni River. There he dropped to his knees and cried out in frustration. He sliced his palms using the sharp flint that jutted out over the river's cliffs and cursed in anger at the demons of greed, envy, and war.

He cried and wailed for many hours until finally he lost consciousness, his blood seeping into the dark, moist earth. In his unconscious state he saw a vision. When he came to he rushed back home. The vision had shown him a way to become greater than the Eternal Spirits and steal all of their powers, including the power to bring the dead to life. He thought of his mother, his father, his sisters, his brothers, and friends who had been dead now for many, many years. He wanted to defeat the Spirits and be reunited with his loved ones. Then, there would be no more blessings for only a select few. All would be given the breath of eternity. He knew that this was what was best. He mocked the spirits for their poor judgment.

Becoming greater than the Spirits required Y'Jundto to collect the thorns of the briars and the flowers of the ivy the Spirits had grown around the village. With these things, he could fashion the weapons that were needed. It was a dangerous task, and even though he was blessed with immortality he still found his memory and sight affected.

He paid it no mind.

Using the vision he'd received as his guide, Y'Jundto spent many days and many nights creating various weapons that would allow him to carry out his plan. As he worked, his memory and sight became worse. Fearing he would forget completely or go blind entirely, Y'Jundto carved the vision onto the hide of a leopard and hid it in a clay jar.

In two weeks' time he'd completed his task. It was the Day of Shaf'hil, the day when the Spirits would come to walk among the people. Y'Jundto's family helped the other villagers prepare. There would be a ceremony and a feast. Y'Jundto did not take part in the preparations. This did not go unnoticed.

"Why do you stand around scowling instead of helping to prepare for the Shaf'hil ceremony and feast?" B'Ntabwu, another of the original chosen, had asked. "After all that the Spirits have done for us!"

Y'Jundto scoffed. "All they have done for us? You mean killing our family and friends, separating us from the world, forcing us to live for eternity in their prison?"

"Do not speak in such a way," B'Ntabwu scolded. "Do you not know why we were chosen? Only those who were pure in heart, those who would not grow to bring death and destruction to the land were blessed. With pure hearts we selected mates and bore children who would also share the same pureness of heart. This is what allows us to live in eternal harmony.

"As for your talk of prison, have you seen what lies beyond the protective hedge? The demons of greed, envy, and war leave poverty, disease, famine, and pain in their wake. We have been spared and given a life of peace, serenity, and plenty. Prison indeed. May you come to fully understand what you speak in such ignorance about." And with that, he walked away.

Y'Jundto began to think. Had only the pure in heart been chosen? Would the rest have truly brought sorrow and destruction to the land? Surely his mother and father had been pure. After all, they had saved him from certain death. Did the protective hedge keep them safe instead of imprisoned? What if these were all lies? Y'Jundto's thoughts warred with each other from the time the sun was high in the sky until it began to lower beyond the western mountains.

When it was time for the great ceremony before the feast, all of the villagers gathered around. The spirits descended before them.

"Before we begin," the Spirits spoke collectively, "we must address a threat that has come upon this peaceful village." Everyone began to murmur excitedly. "Does anyone know if an outsider has broken through the protective hedge?"

A scatter of no's went up in response.

"Does anyone know what the threat might be?" The villagers looked at each other in confusion. No one knew. The Spirits continued.

189

"The soul of a Da'ahntur, one the land's most agile and swiftest creatures, soared to our celestial dwellings with a message from the demons scrawled in its flesh.

Gasps could be heard throughout the crowd.

"If anyone knows why this might be, please come forward."

No one moved.

Y'Jundto shifted uncomfortably. He stared at the ground, but did not come forward. "Y'Jundto," the Spirits called him by name. "You, who were one of the first chosen, do you have any knowledge of this threat?"

"I do not." Y'Jundto lied.

"Y'Jundto, if you have any knowledge, reveal it to us. The threat will be removed, but the blessings will remain and the offense absolved."

The villagers began to take a greater interest in Y'Jundto and wondered why the Spirits had called him by name.

"I have nothing to reveal."

"Y'Jundto," the Spirits tried a third time, "hiding the truth will not prevent it from being discovered; for the truth is light and can only be concealed in a light as bright as itself. You can not conceal light in darkness. It will shine through, exposing itself."

The villagers now looked at Y'Jundto with concern.

"I said I do not know!" Y'Jundto answered in anger. He then excused himself from the ceremony. Had he stayed, he would have heard the omen the Spirits spoke to the rest of the villagers.

"We must rid the land of this threat. Darkness and deceit have no place here. Wherever the truth hides let it come forth. Let the threat against the people reveal its true intentions by carrying out its intended purpose on the one who gave it life. As we have spoken, let it be done."

The ceremony and the feast continued without incident. When the festivities were nearing their end, Y'Jundto's wife went in search of her husband since he had not reappeared to join the villagers.

It was then that a wail could be heard. The sound, which had not been heard for centuries, rang out across the village. The people came running to find out what had created such agony. When they found Y'Jundto's wife, they saw her prostrate on the floor next to Y'Jundto who lay in his bed clutching the hide of a leopard. Ten weapons protruded from his body and his blood spilled out from the wounds.

B'Ntabwu carefully pulled the hide from the dead man's hands. He read the words inscribed there to the people.

It was a letter written in the hand of Y'Jundto's mother, Mi'Yja. The letter told of how she had stolen Y'Jundto from a woman wandering through the woods outside of the village, then left the lost woman to die. It told of how she had spent all of her life trying to conceal her dishonesty from the Spirits and the people. It also revealed that she had hidden her secrets in the only place she had thought they would be safe — her son's heart.

There, the secrets had festered for many years, finally consuming his heart whole, causing him to cry out and shed his own blood in anger. When he had become unconscious, she had sent him a vision. For in her selfishness, she had wanted him to join her in death.

The people were deeply saddened. Instead of coming forward and letting the Spirits cleanse his heart and restore his blessings, Y'Jundto had allowed himself to be killed by his own lies.

The people of the village learned from Y'Jundto's mistakes and passed his story down for generations.

*   *   *

Katya waited for the haunting feeling to pass before she spoke. "That's quite a story; especially for a child."

Jeslyn shrugged, dismissing the idea.

"So, essentially, the guy killed himself with his own lies and the truth was revealed anyway."

"Yes, that's one takeaway."

"What are yours?'

"Oh, let's see..." Jeslyn sighed as her eyes met the ceiling. "There's the ever-popular, 'be careful what you ask for because you just might get it.' There's also, 'appreciate what you've been given'; 'everything happens for a reason, whether or not we understand it' and 'don't let the lies you, or even someone else has placed on your heart, control you.'"

Katya thought about that. There was a span of silence, so she filled it. "Are you ready to continue?"

"Depends."

"Depends? Depends on what?" Katya was confused – nothing new there.

Jeslyn eyed the recorder. She wanted it off. That meant whatever it was she had to say, she didn't want it on the record. Katya leaned over, picked up the device and did more than turn it off. She took the batteries out and placed everything back on the table.

"Now, are you ready?" Katya didn't know if she was asking this of Jeslyn or herself.

"Sure, why not."

"So, what's next in the sequence?" Katya smiled in spite of herself.

"Next in the sequence," Jeslyn volleyed that smile with a soft half grin, "is one of the lessons I just mentioned, I guess."

"Which one is that?"

"Be careful what you ask for because you just might get it."

18

~Before~

It was an uncharacteristically warm day, even for February in San Diego. Perspiration gathered in Jeslyn's hairline as she sat baking in her car across from Willie's office. The windows were down and a breeze teased her skin, but the heat was ever present in more ways than one. The place was swarming with cops – and possibly some robbers too.

Officer Kevin Luby had been inside the building for what felt like hours. In actuality, it had only been about 15 minutes. Jeslyn surveyed the area, which was littered with police cars, pedestrians, and the rotation of nosy bystanders who constantly had to be asked to continue on their way. It was hard to convince people there was nothing to see here when yellow caution tape snapped against temporary barricades, orange cones peppered the sidewalk, and road flares hissed on the asphalt like sparklers on a sheet of birthday cake.

She had called Kevin the day she discovered the children in Willie's building after leaving her meeting at Good Feet. There were four things she needed him to do. First, was getting the children out of Willie's building and somewhere safe. She told him exactly what she had seen and exactly what she figured was going on. As they spoke on the phone, she thought she'd heard something being smashed

193

on his end of the line, later he told her he'd punched a wall. His actions were completely in line with her feelings. He'd said he would immediately arrange for the children to be placed in protective custody, but they had to be rescued first; which led to item number two. Second, she needed Willie handled. She told him she'd let him decide how and left it at that. Third, she told him about the safe, and lastly, she'd asked for one more small favor – a little digging into someone's background.

It would have been an easy call to make had her intentions been totally kosher and her history with Kevin untarnished. As it was, she rarely called people just to call them and her past with Kevin was riddled with debris.

He was someone she had known in high school; he'd been a campus patroller at the time. Not that her high school was crawling with nefarious activity, not at all. The majority of the school's students were from well-to-do families and most of the rest did their best to play the part. As campus patroller, Kevin's job was simply to ride around in a golf cart and deter, detect, and discharge improper student behavior. It was a fairly cushy position.

Jeslyn had caught his eye, not for improper student behavior, but more for improper campus patroller thoughts. Nothing had happened while she was in high school, but after she graduated he'd tracked her down and asked her out. His feelings were stronger than hers and she'd ended up damaging a piece of him that he claimed he didn't actually possess once he became a full-fledged police officer.

He had lied.

She found this soft spot of his on numerous occasions – mainly when she was in trouble or needed his assistance – promising to treat it with care if only he'd help her. In the end, though, she always returned his heart back to him in pieces even though he had trustingly given it to her fully intact. Whether he was looking to prove each time that 'this time would be different,' or whether his impaired judgment overran his emotions (a disorder Jeslyn was all too

194

familiar with), Jeslyn never heard 'no' from Kevin. Even when, like now, her request could cost him his entire livelihood.

Asking him to save the kids and handle Willie judicially was fine, he had even said he was glad she'd contacted him about it. Even asking him to get her an in depth background profile wasn't too bad of a request. It was her interest in Willie's finances, a portion of which he kept locked away in a safe, that presented a problem.

She knew he kept the key to the drawer that housed the safe in his pocket, and she knew the Asian girl with bleached hair and black roots had the combination. Maybe she was the only one of the drugged out wenches who had it, maybe not. She also knew Willie would be able to hear and see an unwanted intruder coming from a mile away and clear out or lock down anything he didn't want found. Dropping in on Willie unannounced and without detection was like taking a shit on the White House lawn and expecting no one to notice – especially if you were a cop.

Lucky for her, Officer Luby had not always been an officer. There was a time when he had been a little street. And as they say, you can take the officer out of the street but you can't take the street out of the officer. He was far from ghetto, but he had enough swagger to allow him to fit in there if need be. And there were far more bridges that he'd left standing than burned when he turned PD, and those bridges did not support the trafficking of children.

It also didn't hurt that Luby's father had been a mayor at some point in time and still had significant pull with influential people, pull that could come in handy should the need to barter arise.

It would have been a messy affair if word of all the reasons she needed Willie incapacitated had gotten out. Everyone would have been gunning for him just so they could get their hands on his stash. So, the only reason for wanting the job done (the only reason that was leaked, anyway) was Willie's inappropriate love for babies. When you put it that way, it was reason enough.

Kevin didn't let her know the person or persons who had handled Willie, or exactly what they'd done to him, and she didn't care to know. It was information above her pay grade, or below it, depending on who had taken care of the situation. All she knew for sure was that he was still alive, although barely, and allegedly handcuffed to a hospital bed with police detail outside his room. Perfect.

With Willie unable to properly conduct business as usual and his loyal flunkies out of sight, having ditched him at the first hint of trouble, it was as easy as pick-pocketing a dead man to go in and retrieve the booty. And since Kevin had been the one to receive an "anonymous tip" that there was some type of trouble down at Willie's Windshield and Glass Repair Shop, he was assigned to the case. There was, after all, no better way to stay abreast of the developments of a case than to be part of the team investigating it.

As for the safe itself, the contents had been emptied and distributed between Jeslyn, Kevin and anyone else Kevin had felt inclined to reimburse. Jeslyn didn't ask what the safe had contained. It didn't matter to her how much loot or other spoils there had been to start with, she was quite satisfied with her five digit payout.

As if to remind her that not all money came easy, her Red Cello cell phone vibrated in her center console. It was Good Feet. They were looking to set up a meeting between herself and a media production company that handled the company's TV commercial productions. She was spreading herself too thin in too many unsavory directions and not spending enough time taking care of her honest responsibilities – those that didn't involve thugs, robbery, assault, obstructions of justice and coaxing an officer of the law to conduct acts of malfeasance for her personal gain.

What she was doing wasn't right and she vowed to change that immediately. And by immediately, she meant right after she found out whatever dirt there was to find on

Ms. Gisele Marie-Claire Le'marchal – thus, the stakeout position across the street from the scene of the crime. She had asked if they could meet anywhere else, but Kevin was working and had said if she wanted the information quickly, she would have meet him there. She wanted that information.

A figure jogged across the street in uniform, head down, cap shading the man's face. Jeslyn did her best to relax her posture even though a jolt of panic hit her.

"Ma'am, I noticed you've been parked here for quite some time. Do you mind if I ask you a few questions?" Kevin leaned into her car window.

"You might as well handcuff me and take me in, Officer," Jeslyn joked, then immediately regretted it. There was a familiar flicker of longing in his eyes.

"I'd be more than happy to handcuff you and take you."

Subject change. "What do you have in your hand?" She was careful not to ask 'what do you have for me,' or 'what's that you've got there' or any other possible double entendre that would lead them down a path that she would have to march them out of.

He held up the large manila envelope. "Your friend is a bit kinky. This was actually fun. So, thank you for that."

"Kinky? What do you mean kinky?" Jeslyn snatched the envelope and immediately tore into it. Inside were racy photos and pages upon pages of both typed and handwritten documentation on Gisele.

Jeslyn's eye tripped over a name on one of the papers. Known aliases: Mary Marshall. Underneath it was a picture of Gisele. All of Gisele. If Jeslyn had ever wondered whether or not she preferred full or partial Brazilian waxes, the answer was revealed there, unequivocally, in high-resolution precision.

"I see." She fastened the clasp back on the envelope and set it on the passenger seat. "Looks like you enjoyed yourself, Officer Luby."

Kevin looked down the street to his right. "It was a favor for a friend that I didn't mind handling, I'll say that." He didn't look at her as he spoke. His barely sun-kissed brown skin tinted slightly. Thanks to a Puerto Rican father and a Caucasian mother his face didn't glow red when he blushed. Jeslyn found herself looking too long at that face, the dimple pitted into the left cheek and the thick, dark fringe that made up his eyelashes. Her libido chose that time to make itself an unwelcome third party.

"So, now that you're all ramped up, Officer, how are you going to release your pent up...aggression?"

What are you doing?

Kevin's attention jerked back to her. "I don't know, Ms. Kennedy. You got any ideas?" The muscles in his forearm rippled as he adjusted his position on her window frame. His chiseled arms were massive and she knew from past experience they connected to a chest that resembled two beveled dresser drawer panels. To say he was in shape would be doing his body a disservice. Athletes were in shape. Kevin was in construction.

You should not be doing this.

"I could think of a few."

"Like?"

Stop now.

"You're too far away to hear what I have in mind."

Kevin leaned further into her vehicle.

If you have any sense at all you will not do what you're about to do.

Jeslyn skated her hand around his tree stump of a neck, pulled him even closer and pressed her lips to his. She waited for the action to register, for him to deepen the connection. She didn't have to wait long. His hands found then firmly held the side of her face. An intense but brief enmeshment of lips, tongues and teeth left more than just her mouth tingling when she pulled away.

"Like that." She delivered a delayed verbal reply to his question.

"Do you know what you do to me?" His hands were still locked on the side of her face.

"I know what I'd like to do."

You're heartless.

"When do you get off?" she asked.

"As soon as you get to my place tonight." There was no more amusement. He was dead serious. His hands had fallen from her face but his fists were clenched, dangling over her window frame just millimeters away from her chest.

OK, point proven. He's still into you. It's gone far enough.

"What time?"

"Eight."

"I have to get back home at a decent hour."

"You could stay the night."

Jeslyn gave him the look.

"After all this time. After all *this*," he said, motioning towards the throng of activity going on across the street. "You won't sleep in my bed?"

"I don't sleep very well in other people's beds."

"Then I'll come to your house."

"I don't sleep very well with other people in my bed, either."

"Some things never change, Kennedy."

Good, maybe now he'll do the sensible thing and call this bad idea off.

Kevin sighed heavily and dropped his head onto his arms.

"Six thirty." His voice was muffled.

"What?"

"I'll see you at my place at six thirty."

"Done."

You could still call it off later. It's not even noon yet.

"And don't do the thing where you call me later and tell me you can't make it; or the thing where you don't call at all and just don't show up. If you're going to play that shit, just tell me now." He squinted as he looked up the road again.

199

There went that.

"Hey," she hooked his stubbled chin with her finger and forced his bare eyes to her sunglass shielded ones. "I'll be there."

You've gone and done it now.

"Alright." He relaxed his fists. Then he grabbed her by the neck suddenly and pulled her mouth to his, devouring her lips for a few desperate seconds before releasing her just as abruptly. "Alright," he repeated. His open palms pounded lightly on the window frame a few times as he stood up and adjusted his cap. "You remember where it is?"

Jeslyn gave him a wicked one-sided smile. "Oh, I remember."

Kevin checked for oncoming cars before backing up into the street. He pointed at her, his chest flexing beneath his tight polyester shirt as he lifted his arm.

"Six thirty, Kennedy."

She nodded and turned her key in the ignition. Watching him walk away dumped a pile of coals on her already smoldering urges. As she pulled away from the curb, she told herself she wouldn't hurt him this time. Before she merged into traffic she came to terms with the fact that she already had.

Her personal cell phone lit up with her mother's name. Kevin had fired her up and her mother added icicles to the flame. She answered the call unenthusiastically steamed.

"Hello, Mother."

"Jeslyn, I've been calling you, I even left messages, but I didn't hear from you."

"Well, you got me. What's up?"

Try harder.

The thought came to mind unbidden making her wonder if she was referring to her mother or herself.

"I...I just wanted to tell you that I'm sorry. I know I don't always do or say the right things, but I'm sorry for hurting you the way I did."

Jeslyn was unmoved but uninterested in arguing at the moment, so she said, "I forgive you, Mother. I also think –" She hesitated, not sure how this request was going to go over. "I would also like for you to talk to somebody."

"OK, who?" Her mother sounded eager to please.

"A professional."

"A professional what?" Less eager.

"Therapist."

"Oh." Eagerness M.I.A.

"I would pay for it, of course. If you don't have insurance or if there's a co-pay or something." Jeslyn's words leap frogged each other. "I just think it would be helpful for both of us."

"Are you talking to a therapist too?"

"What? Me? No." Jeslyn threw the words out as if the mere idea was preposterous.

"Well, you said you thought it would be helpful for both of us."

"Oh. Oh that. I just meant –" How could you tell someone that they were solely responsible for the breakdown of communication and the deterioration of a healthy relationship?

You couldn't.

"I mean...I might." Was that true? Would she actually go to see a shrink? It had never occurred to her to speak with a mental health professional herself. Considering her life over the past few months, it didn't seem like that implausible of a suggestion.

"If you think it would help us, then, OK."

The slogan for the big box office supply chain instantly came to mind.

That was easy.

"So, when would you like to get started?" Jeslyn spoke slowly, carefully.

"When did you want to get started?"

She didn't know how to respond to her reverb. "Can I make a few calls and get back to you?"

"OK."

"Alright, I'll give you a call, maybe tomorrow."

"OK then. And Jezz– Jeslyn," she corrected herself.

"Yes?"

"I love you."

Jeslyn played opossum. "OK. Talk tomorrow. I got a call coming in that I've gotta take." The words themselves weren't altogether unpleasant, it was just the initial shock then skepticism of what the words were or what they truly meant that made her uncomfortable; like someone sneaking up on you and pouring something warm and gooey down your back.

The dichotomy of her mood was disturbing. Kevin's mouth had left a phantom kiss lingering on her lips while her mother had left an odd sort of phantom pain lingering on her heart. She struggled with the conflict.

To deflect, she followed up with clients as she drove and made a pledge to herself to go home and get right to work. And by right to work, she meant right to work poring over each piece of paper tucked neatly in the manila envelope laying beside her.

Jeslyn was blown away that Gisele's X-rated side gig hadn't been found out already. By the looks of the dozens of pictures Luby had printed out, she wasn't the only one who'd been blown. It made sense now why searching the name Mary Marshall had infected her computer. Those triple X pop-ups weren't the result of a failed spam filter.

Even before she reviewed all of the salacious details, she wondered how she would expose this information to Forbes. He couldn't possibly know that he was dating an amateur adult entertainer, could he? Jeslyn kept trying to make him out to be the victimized saint in all of this, but perhaps she was casting him wrong. The truth of the matter was, she had no idea what role he should play. Two face-to-face meetings, a dozen emails back and forth and a few online articles did not a solid knowledgeable foundation of a man make. The only thing it did was create a pleasant shield she could put up anytime she wanted to block out something she didn't particularly care to see.

Maybe plastic and smutty was his thing. Jeslyn felt the acidic dregs of a fierce insecurity rise up inside of her like bile. A feeling she hadn't felt, or allowed herself to feel, rather, for quite some time. Her mind became a stereoscope, clicking through images of memories, some distant, some incredibly close.

A huddle of children laughing, someone pointing and whispering, crying alone in a bathroom stall, a fight, a crowd of kids chanting in rhyme.

The hot prick of tears poking at her ducts forced Jeslyn to shift focus. She made a pit stop at the bank then headed home, determined to not think about how the past held her back but only about what the future held.

Sitting on the bar-stool at her kitchen counter, documents arranged in a haphazard collage in front of her, the future seemed to hold the key to Gisele's undoing. Like Forbes, Gisele was also from a blue-blooded blah, blah, blah upbringing. Jeslyn's interests were buried beneath her pedigrees.

Ms. Le'Marchal had done some modeling alright; soft core porn from the looks of it. Did mommy and daddy know about this little hobby? Doubtful. She scoured the pages for clues that would tell her whether this was a long-ago foolish mistake or a nascent venture that was being secretly cultivated. Jeslyn found herself hoping for the latter.

An hour passed, then two. She had once again gotten lost in trivial pursuits and forced herself to set the Gisele project aside and repurpose her energies to Red Cello. The two newest clients simply wanted her for short term projects. The contracts were three months at best. Good Feet looked to be a more long term deal, but even that wasn't a certainty. None of it worried her at the moment. Poverty had been foiled by theft, even if it had been a foolish thing to do. It wasn't until his text came in that she was reminded of yet another of her foolish mistakes.

Where r u?

It was almost seven. She was supposed to have been at Kevin's place already. Dread filled her, a sensation that usually didn't come until she was slipping silently out of his bed and out his front door as he slept. She knew what would happen if she went to him. A reel of their previous meet-ups rolled footage in her head, the soundtrack a slow steady death knell. An hour or two of pleasure – *don't think about the pleasure, don't think about the pleasure* – for an as yet undecided amount of time of guilt. She texted back.

Still working. Sorry.

His reply was instantaneous.

I already knew. Knew it before u drove away. U take care of urself Kennedy.

Her hummingbird breaths became deep inhales and exhales of relief. Maybe he had solved her problem for her. It was better this way. She waited for the contrition of letting him down to henna itself on her – not permanently, just long enough to remind her of her ever-present deficiencies – but it never came.

With her evening free and her mind in shackles, it seemed like the perfect time to research therapists and psychologists for her mother. The final selection would have to be determined through visitation trial and error. After jotting down a few candidates, her attentions were once again diverted to the mess of papers that lay strewn across her tiled countertop.

She rock, paper, scissored back to the conclusion that he couldn't possibly know about this. No man of Forbes' caliber would be down with this.

Would he?

An answer to that question could only be satisfied by one thing and one thing only. She had to be sure he knew.

19

~Before~

When Frost spoke of the road less traveled, he assumably meant the higher road; the road that most people refused to take only because it wasn't as winsome as the path worn slick by the sheep-like trudging of followers. It was doubtful he meant the road that had been marked off by chains, ropes, and other portents to warn would-be travelers of the dangers of the restricted area. The very path Jeslyn was merrily skipping down as if it were the way to grandmother's house.

Providing Forbes with knowledge he may or may not have already been wise to was a delicate affair. One couldn't just send a courier with a folder of evidence to his door with a note that said, 'P.S. your girlfriend's a whore.' That's something a covetous woman would do. Jeslyn was not covetous, she was interested. The differences were spider web-thin.

There was a better way, had to be. It was just waiting to be discovered. The intricate framework of her interconnected neurons began sifting through previously stored Forbes data. Her long term memory bank coughed up reserves from things she'd seen, heard, read, interpreted or imagined – Biochemistry. Chubby. ByoKem. Chicago. Green eyes. Thirty-two. Guns. Poetry. Music. Sojourn. Michael. Sister. Charity.

Bingo.

Forbes was part of a charity organization, Heroes & Helpers, that paired adults with underprivileged youth. Kids and porn did not mix. If a concerned individual were to report that a boy had gotten his hands (eyes) on Forbes' girlfriend, and had associated the connection between the two, there was the very high likelihood that charitable organization would contact Forbes to address the issue. Even if he was aware of Gisele's extracurricular activities, the embarrassment from having it pointed out to him by someone from the non-profit organization wouldn't go over well. She could disguise her voice and make the call herself, she thought. Not to him of course, that was too risky, but to one of his office staff. She could pose as a representative of the organization, and save herself the time and headache of wondering if he'd ever been contacted. Decisions, decisions.

In the end, Jeslyn chose the former evil. The authenticity of an actual staff member contacting Forbes directly was priceless. Besides, her voice disguise plan had holes, and she couldn't risk one of those holes tunneling back to her. She did, however, need Forbes contacted directly. In an effort to ensure this happened, she requested to speak with an executive at Heroes & Helpers. Her conscience was napping – more like hibernating – when she got someone on the line. It was all downhill from there; a fast tumble to the bowels of her morality.

A how-could-this-happen-what-kind-of-organization-are-you-running-there-is-this-what-you-call-a-hero outrage, and a demand that something be done immediately – *and I mean immediately,* she heard herself say – started the call off. Stressing firmly that a follow up call would be made to ensure someone had contacted Forbes brought the call near its end. And warning that if someone didn't contact him directly, and do it immediately (she didn't repeat herself this time), this would become a public issue

206

instead of the private issue it currently was concluded the call. Somewhere in between, the conversation ping-ponged back and forth on exactly when contact would be made. She was assured it would be dealt with *immediately*.

Disturbing or amazing, it was difficult to tell which would aptly describe Jeslyn's ability to transition from calculating conspirator to purported business woman in a breath. After stirring the cauldron at Heroes & Helpers, an entire morning was devoted to putting together an outline for Good Feet's latest product launch, creating a social media calendar for a brand awareness push, and drafting a proposal for a promotions campaign that would drive traffic to a SaaS e-commerce site for her other clients.

Lunch was spent reviewing graphic design portfolios for product packaging ideas. Dinner was a hastily made cup-of-noodles slurped down while typing out notes on multivariate testing. The later evening hours were devoted to her dream business venture – not the one that was currently allowing her to look the part of a conventional, hardworking member of society.

Red Cello was no longer a do or die undertaking. Money woes had been placed on the back burner thanks to Willie's stash padding her coin purse; a windfall that felt as natural as a paycheck. Stealing and lying shouldn't have felt so natural.

Although financial worries may have been pushed aside, nightmares were a different story. Willie was her Elm Street protagonist who waited for her to fall asleep, then terrorized her while she slept – chasing, chaining and suffocating her, causing her to wake up panting and clawing at sheets and pillows in the middle of the night until she was able to unhinge herself from the dream and connect herself back to reality. Everything had its costs. Jeslyn dragged herself to bed every night asking what the price would be of a good night's sleep; then remembering, if you had to ask, you couldn't afford it.

Sleep deprivation absconded with her focus. She had forgotten to call her mother with the therapist recommendations. Late one morning, not long after she'd made the suggestion of counseling, she placed the call and felt her blood pressure drop when the answering machine picked up. All of the details for Jeslyn's preferences about who to call and the contact information for each were left in the message. There would be a return call, no matter how explicit she'd been, to go over who her mother had selected (if she even went through with this). It was also a shot in the dark as to whether therapy would do anything, change anything, make any sort of difference or not, but it was a shot nonetheless. It was either therapy or excommunicating her mother for good. There was no way to continue the relationship like it was. The acrimony was growing too strong and Jeslyn's determination to preserve the tie too weak.

Jeslyn's heart seized at the recollection of her mother during their last encounter. The haggard appearance, the cold words, the reflection of a child lost in the haze of years of suffering swimming in her eyes; then realizing it was her own reflection.

The thought of pursuing a therapeutic session for herself crossed her mind for the hundredth time. She made a motion to investigate her options when a text came through.

Can you do lunch?

Two seconds of her life were lost as her heart ceased its rhythmic cadence then started again. It was Forbes.

When?

It honestly didn't matter when. She counted the millenniums until her phone chimed again.

Today. Later is better. 2:00?

Two o'clock would work.

Where?

She responded immediately.

My place. I'll order in. Do you have a food preference?

His place?

208

Not picky at all.

Before she could hit send another text from him came through.

I meant my office. Sorry.

She smiled and sent her MMS message letting him know that she was open to his menu choice. He sent her an address and ended their communication with, 'see you then.'

Suddenly, her smile was gone and a flurry of thoughts swirled in Jeslyn's head like artificial snow in a shaken up snow globe. He wanted to meet. He wanted her to come to his office for lunch. Had he been contacted by Heroes & Helpers? Did he somehow find out she was involved? Did he find out the magazine article was a fabrication. Elation turned to alarm as each question caused her to face her own deception. She was stupid if she assumed he simply wanted to see her. This would be an interrogation, no doubt. She was done for. Her rickety house of cards would finally come crashing down.

She felt as though she were going to be sick. Her stomach churned and her saliva thinned, the viscosity resembling that of watered down baby oil. It was eleven. She had three hours to suffer. A deliberately long shower followed by meticulous hair and makeup preparations ate up two. She paced and tried to come up with a defense to an attack she was blind to until twenty minutes past one, then she headed to his office.

Her fingers drummed the steering wheel; her knee bounced causing her left foot to tap against the floor mat. This was maddening. The relatively short drive seemed to span several hours and thousands of miles. Familiar stretches of highway became unrecognizable blurs of overpasses and exits. He had instructed her to park in the building's parking garage and she felt like Jonah being swallowed by a big fish when she entered it. Concrete walls became a belly of doom as she navigated her car into a parking stall then walked to the elevators which would take her to her fate.

The elevator doors opened into a quiet hallway. A security guard was walking towards her and she felt the support of her meniscus nearly give way. He gave her a passing nod and was gone. It felt like a close call. She continued down the hallway until she saw the suite number that Forbes had given her stamped on a wall placard which held no other identifying info. The placard for the suite next door read ByoKem. Was she at the right place?

The knob of the door turned easily in her hand and she stepped out of the hallway and into what looked like a studio apartment/office. It was one large open space divided unequally by a frosted glass partition that jutted only partially out of one wall, allowing easy passage into the area beyond it. An espresso leather couch, with matching ottoman and club chairs, a white shag rug, and a 60-inch flat screen TV, apartment-ized the entrance. The rest of what she could see was designed for business, not pleasure.

The scent of sushi and wasabi made her mouth water in a Pavlovian manner. A figure moved behind the frosted glass. Forbes. Her chunky-heel, camel-colored suede boots clicked along the smoke gray porcelain tile that was etched to look like wood. She was sure her heartbeat could be seen through her white blazer that was cinched at the waist with a thick brown belt that almost connected with the wide linen lapels. She wore a bra underneath her blazer and nothing else – slightly provocative but not indecent.

"Jeslyn?" Forbes called out before she came into view.

"Hi." The sight of him struck her immobile. He would have to make the first move.

"Hey, good to see you again." He smiled, then crossed the room to where she stood and held out both arms. Standing, they were able to connect the full length of their bodies. His radiated heat. His thigh barely pressing between the both of hers was suddenly an overwhelming sensation.

"You too." They released each other. Jeslyn reluctantly.

"Are you hungry?" He stepped away, closer to where the food was. "I got sushi. I didn't know what you liked, so I got a bit of everything. Almost everyone I know loves sushi, so I figured it was a safe choice."

"Yes." She wished he would get to the point.

"So."

"So?"

"Did you want to eat?"

Was he stalling?

"OK. But first," there was no way she could enjoy their time together if they continued to ignore the gigantic elephant in the room. "Was there a specific reason you invited me to lunch?"

"Oh. Wow. OK. You certainly know how to deliver an icebreaker, don't you?" He laughed softly through his nose and raked his fingers through his hair. He wiped at his mouth. He looked at the sushi sitting on the small glass dining table in the corner of the room. Finally, he looked at her. "I wanted to see you." She waited for more. More was late.

"You wanted to see me..." There had to be more.

"I wanted to see you. I just...I wanted to see you."

"Wanted to see me how?" She took a step towards him.

"How?" He swallowed forcefully. "I don't know. See you...like this. For lunch."

"For the interview?" Two more steps.

"No."

"Then how?" One more step.

Perhaps the curse left his lips, perhaps she imagined it. "You're killing me, you know that?" He groped for words. She wished she were words. "Lunch. You and me. Talking, getting to know each other."

"What about Gisele?" She said it quickly, like ripping off a bandage – made of super glue.

211

"We're not together."

"When?"

"Recently."

"Why?" Jeslyn fired out the questions.

"Not a good fit."

"And now what?" She was two steps away from him.

"And now I'm having lunch with you."

"To get to know me?" One step away.

"Yes."

Jeslyn looked past him and eyed the sushi. Knowing she wasn't being interrogated, knowing he'd called off his relationship with Gisele, and knowing he had called her here just because he wanted to see her had summoned her appetite. She could hear his breaths. Deep. Slightly faster than normal. Aroused?

"OK. Let's eat." She brushed past him and took a seat at the table. He leaned his head back, like something tall and massive had appeared in front of him and he was looking up to take it all in. He stood there like that, back to her, showing her the crown of his head for a few seconds. Then he joined her.

"You're something else." He was seated now, watching as she poured soy sauce into a small bowl, then eenie-meenie-miney-moe'd her first selection, trying a piece of a roll topped with salmon.

"This is good." Ignoring his watchful eye, she stacked her plate with spicy tuna, fresh yellowtail, avocado, and masago cut roll pieces. "Aren't you going to eat?"

"Not hungry." He stared at her.

"Hmm!?" She exclaimed as best she could with a mouth full of rice and fish. She swallowed before asking, "You're seriously going to make me eat this all by myself?"

He nodded slowly, grinning.

"Nope. No. I don't think so, sir." Jeslyn snatched the napkin from her lap and pushed her chair back. She assembled a few pieces of sushi onto a clean plate, stood and rounded the small table to where he sat. She towered over him plate in hand.

"What?" He looked up at her amusedly.

"Scoot." He scooted his chair away from the table.

Gingerly, she lifted one long leg and crossed it over his body, then sat in his lap, her inner thighs hugging the outside of his.

"Open." She held the chopsticks up to his mouth, a bite of spicy tuna dipped in soy dangling from the end. Silently, he opened his mouth and she deposited the food inside, waiting until his lips clamped over the stick before she pulled it away. "Good?" He nodded, eyes darting back and forth searching hers. "Still not hungry?" He chewed but shook his head, no. She shifted on his lap, just barely, just enough to remind him of where she was. "For anything?"

She didn't know where his hands had been previously, but she felt them now as he placed them on her thighs and slid them up to her hips. She could feel his fingers adding pressure to her skin. She turned at the waist, deposited the plate of sushi onto the table behind her, then turned back to him. A few fingers slipped under her blazer and grazed the skin above her waistline. Her arms became lithe scarves around his neck; she sank deeper into his lap then leaned in to Eskimo-kiss his nose with hers. He inhaled sharply through his teeth and dug his fingers into the taut muscles of her obliques. Then it was her turn to inhale his slow exhale, wrap her arms tighter around his neck, and pull him firmly against her, no gaps. Her fleshy chest crushed against his iron one.

His hands recalibrated so that his thumbs could push back on her hips, and the rest of his digits could reverse the movement. He pulled her in then pushed her away creating a rhythmic grind. Her fingers tangled together as she moved in to take the lobe of his ear between her lips. The fine vellus hair lining his ear barely registered against the tip of her tongue as she lightly applied pressure to her lobe with her teeth. What did register fully and completely was an unmistakable distention straining against his slacks, expressing its presence between her legs. The middlemost area of her body became considerably bedewed in response.

His legs shifted underneath her, a motion that escaped her attention until he was standing, cradling her in his arms, her legs wrapped around his hips. Effortlessly, he carried her over to an upholstered chaise that sat several feet from a desk that looked more like a piece of handcrafted art than a catalogue-selected piece of furniture.

He laid her down gently as if she might break. One hand had never lost contact with her posterior and he used it to tighten his hold and jerk her downward so that she was directly underneath him. Their lips had remained fairly passive, nearly uninvolved in the erotic fracas. Forbes expunged their neutrality, lowering his mouth to hers and all but consuming her bottom lip. An inferno ensued; heat burst through Jeslyn's body. Like a fever eliciting erratically delirious behavior from the afflicted, a grappling instinct possessed her, causing her to hook one leg around his torso, one arm under his shoulder and flip him to his back. The move was unexpected for him and she pinned him easily.

"Holy shit!" Forbes' exclamation brought her to her senses.

"Sorry. I'm sorry." She was nearly breathless, but not from the exertion of the pin.

"No, it's fine. I just...wow. That was a new one for me."

"Sorry about that."

"Please, don't apologize. Not for that." He grabbed the back of her head and forced her mouth to his once more. She accepted his advances more than willingly and acquainted herself with the silky smooth feel of his tongue. Her knees squeezed the sides of him as she ran one hand up and over his stomach, past his chest to his throat. Her hand curled around his neck and she bore down gently. This time the utterance of profanities was clear. He tugged at her hair which hung loose, framing their faces together. She bit down on his lip. He dug his fingers into her back. She intensified her grasp on his neck until she could feel his carotid artery pulsing wildly in her palm. He lifted his hips off of the cushion as her free hand wrestled with the buttons of his shirt.

"Forbes." The sound of a voice in the room startled both of them. "I have Gisele holding for you." It was his phone's intercom speaker.

"Thank you, Gail." Forbes called out, winded, to the bodiless voice. Jeslyn released her hold on him and stood up. Her lips were raw and her body ringing from the awareness of recently being semi-ravaged.

"I'll let you get that." Jeslyn made a motion as if to leave.

"No. Wait. Just wait a second." Forbes looked annoyed as he stood, adjusted himself, and stomped over to his desk. He grabbed at the phone, snatching the receiver from its cradle as if he were ripping a weed from the ground. "Not a good time, Gisele. What is it?"

Jeslyn couldn't make out exactly what was being said on the other end, but she could hear the whiny timbre of crying and pleading.

"Gisele, I don't care, that's the point. No. No. I don't care." Jeslyn watched as Forbes' face transformed from aroused, to apathetic, to agitated. Forbes' pissed off face. She added the image to the mental album she'd collected. "What about it? Believe me, that's the least of my worries. No. Because I can't even look at you, don't you get that? I can't even *look* at you, right now. What does that tell you? Well, what the hell did you think was going to happen? Huh?" More high-pitched wailing. "Do your parents know? Why don't you go tell them about your little side jobs. Look, I'm at work and I have someone here. I can't do this. Because there's nothing left to say, Gisele. No. No. I have to go. Don't call here. I'm hanging up now. Goodbye." Forbes returned the receiver to its holster, this time with less vigor. "Sorry." He stared at his desk.

215

"Don't be." Jeslyn waited, debating whether or not she should ask him if he wanted to talk about what had just transpired during his phone call. She decided against it. Plus, she already knew what had happened. "I should get going. Thank you so much for lunch." She backed up a step.

"Wait." He made his way over to her, his shirt half unbuttoned revealing a trail of smooth skin. When he was inches away, he reached for both of her hands and clasped them in his. "I want to see you again. I know that," he motioned to his desk, not the chaise, "was awkward. And I'm sorry. But that's all I'm sorry for." His meaning was not obscured.

"You don't think you need time to clear the air from your..." It was Jeslyn's turn to nod toward the desk. Forbes dropped her hands. A boulder in the shape of her heart dropped in her stomach.

"Maybe." His eyes found the floor, then her feet, her legs, up her body, her chest, her neck, a lingering pause on her lips, and back to her eyes. "But I don't want to." His hands slid smoothly over her hips and he tugged her into him, smashing the boulder into smaller, more manageable pieces, and setting her heart back on the shelf of her ribcage from where it had fallen. "Unless you want me to back off."

Jeslyn shook her head. Her silent answer was rewarded with a slow, deep kiss. After he worked his mouth over hers, like it was his full time job and he was looking to put in overtime, he pulled back just enough to examine her face. He seemed to be taking in every detail, every pore. "You're not like anyone I've ever met, you know that."

Ain't that the truth. "Mmmhmm," was all she said.

"You're so different, so...unique. You're intoxicating."

Jeslyn had no words. It was all happening so quickly. He had been a biochemist on a computer screen, a millionaire in an online article; and now, he was a man in her arms, holding her, kissing her. She had successfully manipulated her way to exactly what she wanted – it wasn't the first time – and yet her balance was off. This wasn't real. Things like this didn't happen. He should have scores of assistants, and assistants' assistants, and security detail preventing any possibility of contact with him while he holed himself up in some luxuriant Onyx tower awaiting the damsel-in-distress cry of a real Princess. He shouldn't be so easily accessible by phone or email. And he certainly shouldn't be so easily duped by a calculating opportunist with a contaminated past who would probably contaminate both of their futures. Jeslyn worked all of that over in her head like a calculus equation. He didn't seem to notice she had gone mute.

"I have a weekend or two free...now..." he let the sentence remain fractured and Jeslyn repaired the break wordlessly.

Now that you're no longer with Gisele.

"And I would like to see you. If you're not busy, it'd be great to spend some time together."

"I'd like that."

"Perfect. I should get back to work, but can I call you later? We can figure something out."

"Of course." With her dry responses, one would think she was agreeing to a merger instead of a date.

He let her go. She retraced her steps back to her car, out of the parking garage and back to her condo. Time seemed to be rewinding. She felt like she was doing everything in reverse only for time to begin again, forcing this whole situation to pan out differently. Much differently. In the revised scenario, she would drive to his office where she would be greeted by an angry Forbes, a sneering Gisele, and maybe the security guard from the hallway who would threaten to report her to the appropriate authorities should she ever contact him again.

She sat in her living room waiting for the clock to turn back to eleven, when she'd first received his invitation, but it didn't happen. Time moved forward not backwards. She had spent two and a half glorious hours with a man that delighted each one of her senses. The sight, smell, touch, sound, and taste of him was, as he had said in reference to her, intoxicating. He was three flutes of champagne on an empty stomach and she found herself bubbly and dizzy from guzzling him down.

Her mother called and was pleasant. That, too, was as surreal as anything had been that day. She had selected a psychologist by the name of Rosalyn Parker and had made an appointment to see her next week. She wanted Jeslyn to accompany her to her first therapy session. Jeslyn felt it was the least she could do and agreed without hesitation. Her mother even thanked her before hanging up and the call ended without incident.

Afterwards, she checked her email. There was correspondence from Good Feet. They were thoroughly pleased with her product launch ideas – that's what the email had read, 'thoroughly pleased.' Their latest arch support product, an athletic performance support, had tested well in the R&D phase. The fact that it, too, was made in the U.S. was also a huge deal; a lot of manufacturers took their business overseas. With that knowledge, she'd submitted a marketing plan which included heavy mentions of Made in the USA messaging. In addition, she had advised them to put out a survey to people who represented their core demographic to discover what they loved about performance products, what made them buy, and what dissuaded them from buying. She had assembled the survey questions for them and sent them over along with her I.P.C.I. strategy – a term she had coined to describe her marketing process – and what that meant going forward.

It was the same foundation she used for all of her clients. Identify. Plan. Create. Implement. While the work and outcomes of each phase were different for different companies or different projects, the overall blueprint was the same. She would begin with 'Identify'. This was going over the project in detail: What were the goals? Resources? Who was the target? Was the market viable for this product or service? What is the company's niche? Who are the competitors? What are the challenges?

After this initial stage she moved onto 'Plan'. That entailed drafting plans of action to either reach the goals that had been established, modify the goals or a plan to discover the goal. Some clients, believe it or not, had no idea what their end game was, they were simply after an undefined measure of success. She would also evaluate whether or not there were enough resources available to meet that goal. It wasn't uncommon for there to be a lack of staffing, production or even money to meet the goals clients had come up with on their own. Until everything was down on paper, it was not clear to them they'd go broke trying to carry out their over-zealous ideas.

Once the identification and planning phases were complete, the creation phase began. This was her favorite part – the designing, building and physically creating of whatever had been discussed in the planning phase. And lastly, there was the implementation. The identified, created plan put into action.

While simple to explain, it was a lot of work; work that most people outside of marketing, and even a few marketing professionals themselves, failed to execute properly if at all. A lot of executives figured marketing was either A.) Some magical elixir. B.) Throwing together of a bunch of random projects and waiting for the money to roll in; or C.) Sales. The last was Jeslyn's pet peeve. If she had a quarter for every time she had to explain that marketing was the process by which a company correctly identified, attracted and retained consumers, she could afford to purchase a small country. Yes, marketing encompassed sales, but the two arms of business were not interchangeable by definition any more than cooking and eating were.

She wrapped up with work realizing she actually felt content. It had been a productive day; a day that left her staring up at the ceiling as she lay in bed that night. If she closed her eyes would she wake to find it all a dream? Her body spasmed with desire at the remembrance of Forbes' lips, his tongue, his hands on her body, tangled in her hair, gripping her skin. She needed a release. Sliding her hand into the fabric of her pajama bottoms she found it.

20

"Jeslyn!" Her name was a chorus shouted at her by faceless figures. She couldn't register the voices. Was that her mother? Her father?

"Jeslyn!" They blended together like one person with a dozen vocal chords.

Then she was running. She couldn't see the danger but she could sense it, and if she didn't run she would die. But her feet felt like lead, her chest burned from the exertion, and she couldn't breathe. She couldn't breathe because now she was nearly submerged in a pool of water, her head bobbing just above the surface. She was in a steel room with no windows or doors, only a metal plug on one of the walls. It looked like the inner workings of a clock or a bank vault or a safe. Willie's safe. She was locked in Willie's safe and now she was going to drown. The lactic acid in her muscles set her arms and legs on fire as she worked to keep her head above the water. When her strength expired she floated beneath the surface, accepting her fate wearily.

It was only then her lungs remembered an instinct she was not aware they knew. She could breathe. The murky water was dimly lit and she could see a man swimming towards her. As he got closer his features sharpened.

Daddy.

"Why Jeslyn? Why?" His mouth didn't move but she could hear his disappointed words as if he were in her head. "You used to make me so proud."

She was crying, her chest aching from the pain she had caused him, but the tears were absorbed by the water. She wanted to cry out that she was sorry but was afraid to open her mouth, afraid of the water rushing in and choking her. She could only stare at him, her face contorted into grief. Then the edges of her vision blurred into a new scene. She stood, dry, in the middle of a living room. Her father and Jacqueline were arguing in the bedroom. She could hear them yelling, her father accusing Jacqueline of doing something awful. The woman had hurt his baby. Jeslyn didn't want to hear this. She covered her ears with her hands because her legs refused to move, her eyes were squeezed shut. Then a warm hand gently touched hers.

"Let's get out of here." Forbes. He was shirtless and beautiful and leading her outside. She glided, not walked, after him. His touch allowed her to fly. They moved to a field where flowers gave way to grass, grass to dirt, then dirt to rocks. Now, they were standing at the edge of a cliff. "You'll fall."

She didn't understand, but didn't question it. His hand was so warm and he was so pleasant to look at. She wanted him. Would he let her kiss him?

"Why Jeslyn? Why?" Forbes' face was still before her, but it was her father's voice she heard. Then he released her hand. She didn't realize she had been standing over the edge of the cliff, her feet floating in mid air, until he let go.

And she fell.

Forbes' face leaning over watching her fall became a speck in an instant. She knew she was about to hit the ground and realized with sudden clarity it would all be over. She wanted to scream, but couldn't. She didn't want it to end; not now, not like this. She clawed at the air, her arms and legs flailing uselessly. She was going to die. She craned her neck to try to see her imminent demise but only saw blinding white light behind her.

Then impact.

*   *   *

222

Jeslyn's body jerked awake. Her cheeks were moist and her T-shirt clung to her, damp with sweat. A dream. It had just been a horrible dream. Light poured into her room as if the sun were a pitcher of radiant energy in the sky that had been accidentally knocked over. Birds chirped outside, somewhere gardeners were leaf blowing and hedge trimming, the sounds of their labor faint. Her chest still ached as the visions of the dream began fading to nothing.

She got out of bed eager to be a part of the daylight hours that were a bastion for her thoughts. During the day, the incubuses that tormented her in her dreams retreated to their hidden crypts waiting for their REM resurrection. They could be held back more easily as long as the sun was out. As it was now.

Even though she went about her tasks dutifully, Jeslyn found herself checking her phone during every activity. She was anxious to hear something from Forbes, something to tell her that he, too, hadn't been just another element in the succession of images and emotions that had passed through her mind and ricocheted through her body as she slept. She heard nothing and that nothingness turned her into an anxious mess. Maybe he had come to his senses. Maybe he and Gisele had worked things out after all. The maybe's continued all day and all evening until it was once again time to place herself at her subconscious' mercy.

That night her dreams were mild, but still she woke the next morning thinking of Forbes with a hollow sort of sadness that seemed way too severe given the circumstances. There was nothing she should expect and no reason she should feel such a strong sense of longing because of her own stupid, and now dashed expectations.

She considered crawling back into bed and letting her nightmares have their way with her, but instead, she spent half a day actually working. There was more than enough to keep her mind and her devil's-workshop hands busy so their idleness didn't lead to more trouble. It felt good to concentrate on something productive, something healthy and something that allowed her emotions to rest; they needed it. Today, she felt as though neither her mind nor her body could withstand anymore ragged fluctuations.

As if to prove her wrong, her phone alerted her to an incoming text.

Are you busy?

Of course he would choose this time to make a reappearance. Just when her roller coaster had cruised to a near halt and she was readying herself to step off the ride, there he was, propelling her to the top of her own free fall.

Just working. What's up?

It was a paltry reply, but all she could offer.

I'd like to see you.

Instead of the giddiness she expected to feel, a deep irritation filled her.

Oh, would you now? I don't hear from you for a whole day after a very intense "lunch" and now you're all 'la dee da, I'd like to see you.' Just like that?

She decided to remain impassive. Responding defensively or dismissively would just come off as psychotic. Lord knew he didn't need that much truth. She would play it cool if it killed her. Something she feared had a real chance of happening.

I see. And what would the meeting be in regards to this time? :)

An emoticon concealed the barbed wire in her words.

I need to talk to you.

That was never good.

Aren't we talking now?

There was a delay of quite a few minutes before his response.

I'd like to talk to you in person.

This accelerated her heart rate.

That sounds...serious.

Another maddeningly long delay.

Sorry. Ur right. I'd LIKE to talk to you and see ur face while I do it. How's that?

Her system's warning lights ceased their internal beeping and flashing.

Yes, better. Can't do lunch today, though. Sorry :(

His next reply was a request for dinner that evening. Her schedule was as open as a twenty-four hour diner.

Tonight and tomorrow are out, too. Sorry.

There were few things more pathetic than a woman who was always available. She would be available (not hard to get), just not at his beck and call (hard to read). Five minutes went by, then ten, then another twenty. Finally, over half an hour later he texted back.

I have to go out of town for a few days. Really wanted to see you before then. Anyway I can?

Nope.

So sorry. My schedule's just really tight right now. Let's reconnect when you get back.

And then her phone rang.

"Hello?" It was less of a greeting and more of a question.

"If you're not going to let me see you before I leave, you're going to have to come with me." His voice sounded gruff, demanding almost.

"And hello to you, too." She gave a weak laugh. He had to be joking.

"Never mind dinner. You're coming with me." He was being serious.

"Forbes, I can't go out of town with you." She gave another weak half laugh, half sigh. Almost as if to say 'can I?'

"Sure you can. It's only two days in San Francisco. You'll be back before you know it. There's Wi-Fi, office space, Skype, any and everything you need to carry on with work if you need to or you can just hang out. Consider it a mini vacation."

"Forbes –"

"Don't make me beg, Jeslyn." His authoritative tone sent a flood of warmth to discrete places. "Maybe you're busy, I can understand that. Or maybe you think it's a bad idea because you're afraid of what I'll think of you. Or maybe you're blowing me off. That would suck, but it's also good information for me to have. So, which is it?"

The truth always made her uncomfortable no matter how open the other party was being. Right now, it felt like his openness was just a lure into a false comfort that could be snatched away at any time. But, oh how she wanted to be lured. And he was doing such a fine job. His voice was a siren call and she was ready to throw herself over the edge because of it.

"It's just that this is all a little...I'm concerned about being —"

"A rebound?" He interrupted with what she was thinking, but not with what she was going to say. Was he a mind reader now too? She hoped not. Her graveyard of a mind didn't need visitors. Let the dead rest.

"No. What I was going to say was, I'm sure you're going out of town for business. I don't want to distract you from that. We can just catch up when you get back."

"And if I say that I don't want to wait until I get back, what then?"

"You can't always get what you want"

"No, but I can try. And I want you...to come with me."

To properly melt a Jeslyn, simply mix honesty with a touch of cockiness and add heat.

"I see."

"And you know you want to." He may have been teasing her, but he was spot on. "I can hear you caving. Just go ahead and cave, I won't let you fall apart completely."

If you still find her to be tough, a dash of tenderizer should do the trick.

"Why are you doing this?"

"Why are you being so stubborn? You turned me down for the next two days. OK, pride officially wounded.

226

Don't keep turning me down." His bedroom voice made it difficult to properly concentrate.

"Says the guy who waited a whole day to call me." Then that came out.

"Ah," he said as if he had just figured out something profound. "You know, I thought about it – calling you, contacting you yesterday. And then I thought, no, let her process. She seems like the type of woman who needs space and time to process things. But maybe I made a mistake?" A question. Possibly of her sanity.

"I only meant that you'll be fine without the immediate gratification you're so keen on obtaining."

"Come with me."

Gladly. "Forbes, be reasonable. You're not helping."

"Actually, I am. I'm helping my own cause. Jeslyn, I don't care about conventional rules or stupid societal standards. And this isn't some rebound thing. If you knew the whole story you'd understand. I'm not asking you to marry me or to have my babies – although, two boys and a girl will be fine, I guess." She could hear him grinning. "I'm asking you to accompany me on a business trip. It'll give you more crap about me to put in your article. We'll go as colleagues, how's that?"

Ah, yes, the article. That would have to be dealt with soon as well.

"You're very charming and very convincing, but I'm still going to have to decline." Her teeth ground against each other in nervous anticipation but her voice was steady. "It's not because I'm not interested. I just have to tend to some personal and business matters that require me to stay in town."

"Fair enough."

"When you get back, please call me."

"But not good enough. Whatever you have going on tomorrow night, cancel it."

"You're incorrigible."

227

"Nice word choice. I can pick you up at seven o'clock. Text me your address and wear whatever you like."

"I don't like surprises. You're going to want to tell me exactly what you have planned."

"What? Who doesn't like surprises?"

A woman who's had a lifetime of unpleasant ones and doesn't trust that even well-intentioned surprises will be enjoyable.

"Consider it a quirk." To say the least.

"Well, spoil sport, it's just dinner. I'm thinking Italian."

"OK."

"So, you're accepting my invitation I take it?"

"I am."

"Wonderful. I look forward to seeing you."

"Likewise."

They ended the call soon after that and Jeslyn found herself grinning idiotically. It was a grin that kept cropping up over the next thirty hours and refused to sequester itself when he rang her doorbell the following evening.

Only when they were settled in his car did he provide her with more details.

"Dinner's at my place. I hope you don't mind." He stole a quick glance at her.

"Your place, huh?" She pretended to be disturbed by his words, but the goofy grin that had temporarily disappeared was back. "Hopefully I can trust you."

"You can't." He smiled devilishly.

"You're unbelievable, Mr. Keith." She shook her head in mock disbelief.

"As are you, Miss Kennedy." He took his eyes off the road again to give her a long, hungry look. She turned and held his gaze. She would not let him see her squirm. He was forced to break eye contact first in order to operate the vehicle, and for whatever reason that felt like a win.

They conversed easily and arrived at Forbes' handsome La Jolla digs in what seemed like no time at all. The home was tucked away down a very narrow, windy road at the end of a private cul-de-sac. The tires of the car made virtually no noise as Forbes directed it onto a glassy smooth, sealed concrete driveway. The abode attached to the driveway mirrored its owner perfectly. Buttery light filtered down from several large unconcealed, glass window panes. The design of the home, which was modern and understatedly elegant, was the perfect mix of inviting and stately without being pretentious. Its angular lines, untextured beige stucco and natural stone exterior provided the masculinity, while the lush landscaping of the front yard added warmth.

Jeslyn waited patiently as Forbes exited the vehicle and came over to open her door. He then led the way inside where they were promptly greeted by Lance and Layla.

"I hope you like dogs." Forbes laughed as Layla weaved herself between Jeslyn's legs and Lance pawed at her excitedly.

"I do." Jeslyn squatted down to pay them the attention they were seeking. When he saw Lance trying to wriggle himself onto her lap, Forbes, who had been trying to wrangle in Layla, turned his attention to the seventy pound lab.

"Lance! No! Down!" Lance immediately backed away and sat down. Layla, noting Lance's sudden inactivity, plopped herself down next to him. "Sorry." Forbes directed the apology to Jeslyn and extended his hand to her. "Come on."

She placed her hand in his as they walked out of the foyer, through a great room and into a cozy den. The dogs stayed put.

"I also hope you're hungry, there's a lot of food." He had let go of her hand and now stood a few paces away, facing her.

"You like to feed me, don't you? Lunch, now dinner. What's next?"

"Breakfast, if you let me." Jeslyn felt her face flush, her complexion expertly concealing it.

He'd transformed her appetite into a craving of an entirely different nature, and now he just stood staring at her, no longer seeming unsure of himself. Having her there in his home and on his terms seemed to give him the fortitude that had escaped him during their first two encounters. She gave him a wayward smile which he RSVP'd to promptly. Suddenly he was too far away. She wanted him closer, much closer. Her eyes traveled to where her mind was – his mouth. That glance was all the incentive he needed. In two strides he was where she wanted him to be.

One hand slid behind her neck, the other around her waist. Her arms floated to his shoulders as he stooped to connect his mouth with hers, gently at first. Then, as their holds on each other became tighter – fingers clutching, bodies pressing tightly together like two palms pressed together in fervent prayer – their mouths responded just as passionately. Her teeth bit into the soft pulp of his bottom lip then she sucked away the sting as his tongue went on the hunt for hers. Her jacket was quickly discarded and idly fell to the floor, the external heat between them affecting her internal temperature. His hand, which had lingered at her waist, then her lower back, slid further down and he dug his fingers firmly into her flesh. Jeslyn wound one leg around his and, using his broad shoulders for support, hitched herself up his sturdy frame as if he were a pole and she a dancer. With her legs wrapped around his torso he sunk to his knees, his gravity pulling her with him.

He palmed the back of her head, shielding it from making contact with the plush rug where they now found themselves lying. Their mouths remained fused together as he crudely kicked off his shoes. Her cowl neck cashmere sweater became an obstruction that Forbes deftly removed by sliding his hands up the length of her body and over her head. He then tugged at his ribbed V-neck pullover sweater until it, too, was out of their way. Jeslyn began working on undoing the buttons of the shirt he'd worn underneath it as Forbes worked on undoing her reserve by massaging her breast and trailing kisses down her jaw to her neck. When he'd been freed from the confines of all his upper body garments, she urged his body away from hers to give herself access to his belt. Her nimble fingers unhooked it single-handedly, followed by the button and zipper of his loose-fit, dark denim jeans. He continued his southern trek down her body to her chest. He camped out there for a while, the location helping to create a tent in his pants.

One hand fumbled with the clasp of her bra, after two attempts he unhooked it. She brought her knees up and reached around him to remove both her boots and her socks before crooking her big toe into the band of his jeans and shimmying them down his legs to his ankles. He wriggled out of them completely and lowered his body back down to hers. Her skin-thin leggings provided little barrier to the feel of him. Her hips pushed off the floor and her hands left his body to slide her leggings down and whisk them from her legs completely. When her silken skin met his he bit down barbarously on one of her puckered nipples. This elicited a cry of lascivious pleasure from her previously silent lips. That cry was Forbes' undoing. He tugged at the last remaining fabric separating their bodies.

"Wait." She clutched at his hand, the lace of her panties halfway down one hip.

"What is it?" He raised his face to hers revealing eyes drunken with desire and lips tinged with color from libidinous activities. He continued to rub against her, slowly.

"Protection." It wasn't sexy to mention, but she would be an idiot not to. She was horny, not stupid.

"Shit." He lowered his head in defeat and let his forehead drop to the plush valley between her breasts. His heated breath warmed the skin below her sternum. She plunked her head down to the floor and wrapped her fingers in his hair holding him to her as they breathed heavily.

His iron hard member twitched involuntarily as she massaged his neck and shoulders. They lay in that position for a minute before Forbes peeled himself away from her and, rising to his knees, stretched toward the nearby couch and grabbed a blanket from it. He pulled her into a half-sitting position under him, forcing her to contract her abs so he could drape the blanket over her shoulders. Scooting backwards and resting his back against the couch, he tugged her towards him and motioned for her to sit on his lap. The puzzle pieces of their bodies locked together seamlessly as she faced him and he hugged her ribs. She placed soft kisses on his forehead, eyes and cheeks before brushing her lips against his. Forbes' arousal pressed against her and she gyrated her hips, deriving intense pleasure from the friction against her throbbing female bud. He kissed her deeply, the swirl of his tongue matching the rhythm of her grinding. As the movement continued, he clutched the top of her buttocks and forced her harder into him, then faster. His breathing quickened and she realized she was about to satisfy his carnal urges. He moaned into her mouth making it hard to decipher where the sound had originated. Her thrusts became more isolated, focused on meeting his immediate need. Her breasts rubbed against his chest and he grabbed at one roughly. Their united kiss became lips barely touching, then connecting briefly as hot bursts of air passed through them. He was mumbling inaudible affirmations letting her know his peak was fast-approaching. His groping quickly turned to fingers pinching and twisting the aching peak of her nipple and she bit into his neck causing him to tremble violently underneath her. A warm moistness spread between them as his body shook uncontrollably and he grunted spasmodically into her hair.

Eyes closed, his hand still cupping her breast, he kissed her gently and repeatedly. This lasted until she crawled off of his lap and jerked her head toward a hallway she assumed led to areas where he could freshen up. He obliged.

When he returned he was wearing baggy sweatpants and nothing else. He found her in the kitchen in his shirt which was only halfway buttoned, sitting on a bar stool, one leg tucked beneath her devouring a slice of pizza.

"This is good Italian," she said between bites.

"Thank you, it's homemade." He shooed her out of the seat, lifted her onto the cold granite, then sat down in the barstool and settled himself between her legs.

"What are you thinking?" He asked as she licked pizza sauce from the corner of her mouth.

"Did you steal my vagina," she replied, then took a bite of pizza.

"Wait, what?" He was chuckling, confused.

"I'm wondering if you stole my vagina," she swallowed, "cause only chicks ask things like, 'what are you thinking?'" She mocked him with an exaggerated deep voice.

He punished her dig and her mocking by grabbing her thigh and tickling her mercilessly.

"Is that right?" he asked as she laughed, squealed, and tried to wriggle away from his firm grasp. "I try to be nice, ask the lady how she's doing and she calls me a girl." He continued tickling her while she breathlessly screamed her surrender.

"I give! I give! I'm sorry."

"Say I'm the man." He was now attacking her ribs.

"You're the —" Her words were cut off by squeals and shrieks of laughter.

"I didn't hear you. Say I'm the man."

"I'm going to pee on your counter!" she cried out, laughing uncontrollably, tears starting to slide down her face.

"Jeslyn, did you steal my penis? 'I'm going to pee on your counter?' That's something a dude would say. That's just nasty." He stopped tickling her suddenly, and grabbed her in a bear hug, just in case she planned to retaliate.

It took several moments for her laughter to die down. He held her the entire time, breathing heavily into her now wild hair, chuckling every so often.

"You're a jerk," was the first thing she said when she could speak without gasping.

"Thank you," his bear hug loosened.

"Only a jerk would think that was a compliment." She smiled into his shoulder.

"Well, you're not a jerk." He pulled back to look at her. "You're kind," he wiped a strand of hair from her face. "You're funny," he kissed her cheek. "You're beautiful," he kissed her mouth. "You're a classic vinyl in a world full of duplicate mp3's."

She laughed softly and wound her arms around his neck. "Forbes Michael Keith, I do believe that is the most amazing compliment anyone has ever given me." Nothing could take the smile off of her face.

"You're going to think I'm crazy," she doubted his words, "but I really want you to come to San Francisco with me."

"You're right; I do think you're crazy." She raked her fingers through the sides of his hair. "But you're also brilliant," She kissed his forehead. "And charming." She kissed each eyelid. "And unbelievably handsome." She let her kiss linger on his mouth. "You're like a drop of bright red blood on new fallen snow. You're vibrant, mysterious, impossible to miss, and a sign that life is real and it exists, but only because of you."

"That was like…it was like poetry."

"You're like poetry." She grinned at him. He just stared.

"Why are you so different? Why are you instantly so unlike anyone I've ever met?"

"Maybe you've been hanging around only one type of person."

"Maybe. Or maybe there's no one like you."

Let's hope not. Jeslyn kissed the bridge of his nose. "Maybe." She let him have that one.

Conversation flowed easily for the next few hours. When only one slice of pizza remained and the conversation had found a comfortable lull, he asked her the question that had been a wanton suggestion earlier.

"Will you let me make you breakfast?" What he was really asking was for her to spend the night.

She ran through a dozen reasons in her head why that was a bad idea before answering, "I'd love to."

He didn't have a stash of condoms or an extra toothbrush ready and waiting, which meant he wasn't automatically prepared for overnight guests. That thrilled Jeslyn nearly as much as anything that evening had. She finger brushed her teeth beside him at the sink, crawled in bed beside him, soaking up the hint of cinnamon and light woodsy scent of his room, and fell asleep beside him wearing one of his T-shirts. Her sleep was dreamless for the first time in weeks.

21

~Before~

      Forbes had been gone for two and a half days. He'd left for San Francisco early the next morning after their first night together, but had been texting her frequently. During his absence she spent her time counting hours – hours until his return and hours until therapy.

      Her mother's first therapy session – essentially her first session, too – was now only a day away. Jeslyn wasn't as burdened with anxiety as she'd been previously. While she and her mother weren't poster people for a happy, healthy, mother/daughter relationship, they also hadn't butted heads since the last incident. Thank heaven for small miracles.

      Work was another thing she was grateful for. It was going well, and since she had a nice sized nest egg that shielded her from destitution, she was able to enjoy it. It was also a constructive use of her time. A lot of her time. Even still, as busy as she was, her thoughts drifted to Forbes constantly and she found herself feeling more and more content with each one. He seemed smitten and the feeling was mutual. Guilt assaulted her from time to time, but she combated it with promises to redirect her desires in exchange for this idyllic trend to not only continue, but for her to come out of it unscathed. Much like a desperate sinner promises God their soul, their first born and a lifetime of piety in exchange for one favor, Jeslyn promised to be an honest woman if only things would remain as they were.

She had decided she wanted back on the safe side. If Forbes was a part of the equation, a straight-laced life wouldn't feel like a straight jacket. The yellow house, white picket fence, two and a half kids American standard could be her future. She would bake pies, go to soccer practice and dance recitals, the whole nine. She would grow Red Cello into a slightly larger operation and let that stand as her legacy. Everything else could be set aside, which was fine because there wasn't much to set aside anyway. Her life would be complete with homemade pizza dinners, charity events, romantic dates and pleasant vacations. It's what she wanted.

Correction: Would want.

She was still trying to convince her heart of what her head was already planning, her heart promising to catch up with these intentions in due time. Right now, she was simply compiling the list; capitulation would come later.

Forbes' time away got extended by another day and he let her know he wouldn't be back in town until Tuesday evening. He was working on what he simplified for her as a science fair type of project. An agricultural company had him consulting on the benefits of using traditional soil planting methods versus hydroponic methods for a variety of different fruits, vegetables and flowers. After his explanation, he told her he missed his Princess. After that, her heart belonged to him.

Tuesday arrived on schedule and at four in the afternoon she met her mother at the office of Rosalyn Parker, Ph.D. It could have been any psychologist's office – a ton of books, comfortable seating and colorful, abstract artwork on the walls summed up the space. Dr. Parker, who preferred to be called Rosalyn, was a plump older woman with thick, short, jet-black hair and a kind face. She looked like someone's younger but very wise grandmother; a woman who wouldn't patronize or criticize. Jeslyn instantly felt at ease. She also liked that Dr. Parker didn't force her or her mother to air their dirty laundry (although her mother seemed more than willing to do so), she simply asked what had brought them in and then listened to their separate responses. Jeslyn let her know this would not be a tandem session each time, her mother had just asked she be there for the first one. When Rosalyn asked her why she thought that was, Jeslyn hesitated.

"I'm not sure." That wasn't entirely true.

"Are you not sure or would you prefer not to say?" She had been called out.

"The latter."

"And why is that?" Rosalyn looked as if she really wanted to know. Her mother, too, looked as if she wanted to know, but for different reasons. She could already sense her mother's defensive reply before she spoke.

"Well, for starters, I don't feel like being berated for my honesty."

"From your mother?"

"Yes."

"Why would you think I would –" her mother started but Rosalyn held up her hand indicating she should remain quiet.

"Does that happen often, being punished in some form or another for speaking out about how you feel?"

"Yes." Jeslyn answered the question but was growing more and more uneasy. This was her mother's therapy session, not hers.

"I see. And how do you feel when that happens?"

Jeslyn felt irritated by the question but couldn't identify why. This woman had been nothing but nice. "How do I feel when I'm punished, as you say, for being honest with my mother?" Repeating the question in that manner was meant to point out that the answer should have been obvious. Rosalyn either didn't get that or chose to ignore her sarcasm. "It makes me feel like honesty isn't the best policy."

"Do you honestly believe that or is that simply something you say or do for safety reasons?"

"I don't know. Both I guess. Look, I'm not trying to steal the spotlight here. This was for her." She jerked her thumb at her mother who sat beside her, lips pursed.

"I understand that. But it helps me to get a clearer overall picture of the situation if I hear from you as well. You may be able to illuminate areas that your mother is not able to recognize."

Rosalyn graciously steered the conversation to less prickly topics and then away from Jeslyn altogether. She did her best to keep her mother focused on specific root causes of issues as opposed to surface level emotional regurgitation. The hour felt like two. When it was over, Rosalyn asked if she could speak with Jeslyn alone. Her mother huffily left the room, leaving the two women to themselves.

"I think it would be helpful if I saw you one-on-one as well." She was candid from the gate. Jeslyn quieted her inner cynic that was offering the suggestion this therapist, psychologist, whatever, was simply looking for another hundred and fifty dollars an hour.

"I'll consider it." Her guard was still up.

"I'd like to schedule it now."

Cornered. "Rosalyn," she paused to consider her words. "Honestly, I don't know if I'm ready for therapy." Her molars briefly ground against each other. A trickle of unpleasant memories threatened to turn into a flood and their sudden unwelcome emergence caused tears to prick the corners of her eyes. She ducked her head to conceal the telltale glassiness. What the hell was this almost blubbering about?

"I can understand that, especially with what I've seen and heard today." This made Jeslyn look up.

"What does that mean?" she asked out of curiosity.

"I think there's an unhealthy dynamic that has been established between your mother and yourself. I also think there could be lingering effects from that, and it might be helpful to you if we explore them."

Great, another prophet; just what she needed. "Life hasn't always been perfect, but I think I'm managing fine." It was her most blatant lie of the hour.

"OK. As you know, the decision is yours but I think it'd be extremely helpful." She started gathering her papers from their earlier session. Jeslyn watched her for a moment before speaking.

"Thursdays work." She said it so quietly she wondered if she'd spoken at all.

"Evenings or afternoons work better?" Rosalyn didn't make a big deal of her acquiescence.

"Around this time is good, I guess." She felt like a sullen teenager who had been forced to see the school counselor because of 'problems at home.'

"Great." She checked her calendar and penciled something in. "I have you down for this Thursday at four. Here's my card with the date and time." Jeslyn stuffed it in her purse.

"Thank you." Rosalyn was thanking her. Shouldn't it have been the other way around?

"You're welcome," she replied awkwardly. Exiting the office, she expected to find her mother waiting to pounce, but she was nowhere in sight and her car wasn't in the parking lot. Jeslyn breathed a sigh of relief. She also saw Forbes had texted her regarding their date for that evening. She let him know their date was confirmed.

They went to a poetry slam in Encinitas. Her thoughts were on nothing but him for the five hours they spent being entertained, then dining, laughing and talking. He touched her frequently – holding her hand, stroking her fingers, caressing her arm, sliding his fingers up and down her thigh – and she reveled in it. They talked about nothing (their favorite childhood cartoons, his fear of clowns, her most embarrassing memories) and everything (his plans for the future, her marketing work, his thoughts on religion, the state of the economy) until the wee hours of the morning. He invited her to his home to spend the night, again, and she accepted, again.

As they snuggled in his bed, she hummed softly while he kissed the delicate area behind her ear and the sensitive areas on the back of her neck. Humming became sighs of bliss as his hands massaged her. They then discovered each other with lips and legs, arms and fingertips, taking their time exploring the sensual pleasures of being together. All barriers of clothing were removed and they slid their naked bodies together until they were both slick with sweat and desire; fondling each other until she thought she would melt into nothing. Then he disappeared under the sheets and kissed, sucked and licked the receptive folds between her legs. She directed him with the gentle pulling of his hair, repositioning of her body and verbal exclamations. It wasn't as easy or as quick for her to climax as it had been for him. Her body was a test of his sexual skill and dexterity. Apparently, he had studied this course before. When he had built her up to a frenzy she called out his name and squeezed her knees around his head, completely overtaken by the orgasm that was initially concentrated at her core but spread rapidly, like a radiation leak, throughout her body. Deliciously and utterly spent, she went limp and was only mildly aware of him tucking her bare body into the crook of his and whispering sweet nothings to her as she drifted into sleep.

The next morning he made her breakfast and served it to her in bed. After making a plate for himself he joined her and they chatted about the day each of them had ahead. They made plans to see each other later in the week and he let her know his schedule would be taking him out of town again soon. He didn't ask to see her that evening and he didn't ask her to join him out of town this time, two things she took no notice of until she was four hours into her workday. It was a gnat of a thought that started like the evolution theory – a tiny atom that collided with another atom – before cataclysmically snowballing into an entire thriving existence all its own. For the time being, she did her best to neglect it in hopes it would die off.

*   *   *

She didn't mention Forbes or the other things, the things she should have been discussing in her Thursday therapy session. Instead, she gave safe answers and revealed minimal concerns. She knew this wouldn't help her but she wasn't ready to face it all just yet. Things were going well and rocking the boat seemed like a terrible inconvenience at the very least and a catastrophe at worst.

Days and then weeks passed like this. She and Forbes spent time together, she worked and her mother seemed to be progressing – or not regressing anyway. Life was happening and it was good. Her two biggest concerns now were the transgressions of her past and the desires of her future. Willie's trial was a few months away and she feared her name being brought up in connection with him. This fear was muted by the satisfaction Forbes was bringing to her life. The only problem there was that the more she had of Forbes the more she wanted. And it seemed the more she wanted the less she got.

Another project was usurping his time. His communication became infrequent and their time together lessened as well. While he was full of apologies and, when they did see each other, a show of interest, a definite shift had occurred. This shift was an irrigation system for her negative thinking but it was only a sprinkle. The torrential downpour would happen later.

*   *   *

Spending the night at his place had become a fairly regular occurrence. Their comfort level had grown to the point that they would often sit in silence, each with a tablet or laptop in front of them, working or surfing the net. One morning, after being treated to one of his Secret Recipe smoothies, she propped her tablet on the kitchen counter and began replying to emails. Forbes went to take a shower. She noticed his laptop light blinking, an indication his battery was running low and she plugged it in for him. The screen came alive and his email account with it. She would have simply gone back to her earlier task if it weren't for the first message. The sender was Gisele and the subject line was 'Missing You.' She had done worse things, reading his email wouldn't top the list. She opened it.

The email chain was quite lengthy. Six or seven replies had passed between them in the timespan of two weeks. This didn't appear to be a fresh reconnect, either, as the first email from Gisele began with, 'So, I'm back in town now. Don't worry, I didn't do anything stupid'.

Don't worry? Why would he be worried about her? And why was she telling him about her in and out of town adventures in the first place? Jeslyn's stomach shrunk to the size of a peanut as she continued to speed read through their electronic conversations.

Gisele poured out her heart. Forbes thanked her for her honesty. She went into detail of what her body, heart and sole – *Seriously? Are you really that ignorant?* – was missing without him. He consoled her. She updated him on what her parents were doing and how they spoke of him often. He told her about his trip to San Francisco. She told him she missed him terribly. He replied.

I miss you too. I miss you too. I miss you too. I miss you too. I miss you too. I miss you too. I miss you too. I miss you too. I miss you too. I miss you too. I miss you too. I miss you too.

The four words were only written once but Jeslyn's eye repeated them a hundred times, a thousand times. Her chest constricted. He went on to say that this was hard for him but 'he was getting through it' and 'he hoped she could understand.' That last email was from the night before last at 9 p.m. She thought back to where she was in relation to that timeframe. She hadn't been with him; he'd been "busy." She could see just how busy now. Her head began spinning. He would be out of the shower at any moment. She hit the forward icon, entered a few random letters into the message field, typed 'sent from my iPhone' at the bottom of the message field and forwarded the email to herself. She then deleted the sent message from his sent folder. It had all been done to make it look like he'd inadvertently sent the message to her himself like a butt email instead of a butt dial.

She would not freak out, she would not freak out, she would not freak out. Inside she was freaking out. She dressed quickly and silently, scribbled a note on a piece of paper that she left on the counter and then fled, half walking, half running down his street until she reached the main road. There, she called a cab and waited anxiously for its arrival. Her inbox now had one unread message, which she left until she got to her condo. Forbes called her and, when she didn't answer, sent her a few texts asking if everything was OK. Her note had been vague. She assured him everything was fine (it wasn't) and they would talk later (they wouldn't).

Dread sat like a toad on a log in her stomach. Her body was physically depleted but her mind was wired and running like mad in a million different directions. She carefully read through the entire email exchange, then reread it twice more. She began going through four of the five stages of grief. Denial, anger, bargaining and depression came upon her in waves. Acceptance escaped her. This was not acceptable. She couldn't accept this. She felt like a fool and couldn't wrap her mind around what had happened. In their discussions, he had made it seem like his relationship with Gisele was forced upon him. His mom and Gisele's mom were dear friends who had plotted and planned to get their babies together. He hadn't wanted to date her at first, he'd said. She wasn't his type, he'd said. She called him by his middle name because she thought his first name was silly, he'd said. Yes, he cared for her but there was no real connection, he'd said.

I miss you too, he'd said.

Had the player become the playee? Reminding herself for the umpteenth time that she was not owed anything, nor should she expect anything from Forbes, was useless. Her heart tripped over itself in her chest and she became lightheaded. She imagined this is what the beginning of a panic attack felt like.

She had left her heart assailable and it had been damaged. While there may have been a good explanation or maybe even overreaction on her part, Jeslyn didn't care. She cared about protection and that meant she had to gird her feelings. To effectively handle the situation she couldn't be a bumbling mess. Hurt did her no good. Anger did. The burning, stinging fire of it was a forge that could shape her into something nearly indestructible. Not wilted and torn apart over a guy. She would not mention the email to Forbes just yet, there would be an appropriate time and place for that. Until that time arrived, she refused to be his plaything.

Days passed and once again a blind eye was turned to personal responsibility and promise – as in the promise a person would find the crap she was looking for sooner or later if she kept looking up the right orifice. Jeslyn's snooping, whether she initially intended to or not, had uncovered a still-warm pile of it. Remorse was also a foreign concept to her. Because of this, Forbes began getting the more frigid side of her shoulder and the gym took her heat. He started asking more and more if everything was alright and she had continued lying that it was, even though she provided less and less reasons for him to believe her. And now this was life and it was not as good.

It was a Saturday morning, one that had started with another decline of an invitation from Forbes because she was "terribly busy." In reality, she was on a double date with her cable provider and her flat screen TV, flipping through channel after channel of drivel, still sporting her PJs. Her eyes would well up for no particular reason, which would make her angry that her emotions continued to betray her.

She had tried to cauterize them in order to mitigate the bleeding of her heart, but that had destroyed something else in the process. This became Jeslyn's pendulum. It swung from stable to less so and back again all depending on the time. Only her life was more Clockwork Orange than functional timepiece.

The cackle of two women broke through her practically catatonic haze and she lifted the remote to turn the channel to something else she wouldn't concentrate on in order to escape them. It was the lower third bar on the TV program that halted her hand. In it was written: *Lara Dressler, Founder of Buti Buck. Multi-million dollar company started at dining room table by stay at home mom.* That grabbed her attention.

The hosts of a morning show were asking Lara to tell the viewers a little bit about Buti Buck and what prompted her to start the company. Lara, a plain woman who looked every bit the part of a stay at home mother, explained how she cracked through the million dollar ceiling in just a few short years:

"Thank you for having me. Buti Buck is a skin care line with high-quality creams, lotions and cleansers that are on par with the top skin care products in the nation, but only cost a fraction of the price. We, as women, spend exorbitant amounts of money on our beauty products when what we're mostly paying for is a company's marketing budget and their brand name. Buti Buck products are packaged to look every bit like an outrageously expensive brand but they only cost – yes, you guessed it – a few bucks. You can get high-end department store products on a dollar store budget.

More cackling then a few more questions. What made you start the business? How did you go about it?

"Well, I had the American dream. I had a house, a job, I'm married to a great man, we had nice cars and everything was fine. Then I stopped working to stay at home with our kids and while that was great, I was lacking something. There was this void. So, I'm slathering cream and lotion on my face one day and my husband asks, 'how much do you spend on all of that stuff?' and I start thinking about it. I had a whole medicine cabinet full of beauty products and each bottle or jar was...well, let's say I didn't get the cheap stuff. And then he goes, 'you know, you could probably make something yourself for cheaper.' It was said in jest but it totally got me to thinking. I was like, I really could make products that were just as high in quality, but for a lot cheaper. So, I started researching and asking questions and putting everything together and a few months later Buti Buck was born. After I started the company I realized this is what was missing. Buti Buck literally filled that void."

The hosts asked the audience to stay tuned; they'd be right back and would show women how to look two dress sizes smaller with one easy fashion color trick. Jeslyn turned the TV off and grabbed her tablet. What had she been thinking? Forbes was nice but it was clear he wasn't a sure thing. Red Cello was great, but it wasn't what lit a fire in her. Then there was the whole white picket fence/baking/kids lifestyle she'd tried to convince herself she wanted. Baking? She didn't even like baking. Kids? Soccer practice? She still felt like an errant juvenile herself at times, how was she possibly going to raise children? And who the hell had white picket fences anymore? This wasn't Pleasantville.

Lara Dressler's personal and company websites were easy to find. Jeslyn checked out ButiBuck.com first then began reading about the founder. There was an 'Upcoming Events' tab that listed her appearances and speaking engagements. She would be the keynote at a Women's Conference in San Diego in a few weeks. Without hesitation, Jeslyn sought out the conference details and reserved herself a ticket for the event. Then she got to work.

It didn't have to be perfect, in fact it wouldn't be. She hadn't ever managed to get past square one, so starting from the top again wasn't that difficult. An organized download of every stitch of information and task she'd compiled and completed to this point, a list of what she still needed answers to, any immediate resources required, and an estimated budget for those resources. She jotted down notes about her prospective targets, including who she wanted to reach and how she'd reach them. Then, she started to make notes about her goals – both short and long term – but found herself struggling with uncertainty. The initial reasoning behind the whole endeavor had been a knee jerk reaction and a very lame one at that. Chasing money was as meaningful a goal as chasing the wind; it was nothing to build off of because it had no substance. What she wanted now was...

The answer to that question should not have been difficult since going after wants had been the crux of her existence for years. But, she reasoned, it had all been surface level pursuits, as Dr. Parker would say. The root desire was...

Peace.

She simply wanted – no, she needed peace. She had been seeking peace by means that anyone could have seen were counterintuitive but, it was what she knew. And it had worked to some warped extent, so it had continued. But when would it end?

While she would have liked to have said 'now,' she realized if it took her decades to become this way, it would take some time and effort to undo it all. However, a start had to begin somewhere. At the top of her outline she typed out three words. It was a reminder as much as it was a statement of acceptance.

I Am Me.

It was a beginning.

22

With the way she was being constantly approached, not able to go two steps without someone greeting her and handing her something, an outsider might think she was the guest speaker. Instead, Jeslyn was merely a spectator at the San Diego Women's Conference. Exhibitor booths lined the perimeter of the space and round tables that were set up to seat 10 people each were arranged in the middle of the room. A stage had been assembled on the North wall and a clear podium was anchored at its center.

Jeslyn meandered around the room making the required small talk and graciously accepting the proffered business cards and goodie bags. Underneath the politeness, she secretly wished for an invisibility cloak, one that would allow her to browse without being seen. She hated networking; she was no good at it. The whole concept felt like a sham (something one would think she'd be extremely comfortable with) or worse, business phlebotomy. Everyone was out for blood – client blood, buyer blood, consumer blood, user blood. To her, networking events were nothing more than clandestine IV bags used to gather that enterprising life source. And while there were a few voluntary donors, they were the minority.

Another glance at her cell let her know she only had ten more minutes before she could seat herself at one of the tables and be left alone for at least a half hour while the Buti Buck queen took to her throne.

Jeslyn's heart lurched at the mental association of royalty. It had been a week and a half since she'd seen Forbes. He was out of town again and while they'd exchanged a text or two, there was no denying their communicational and emotional gap. She had a very large part to play in that, but the chinks in her own maturation armor made her view the situation in a way that put the onus on him. If he wanted to he would reach more. If he truly cared he would get to the source of the problem at all costs. It must not have meant anything to him if he was so willing to let it go so easily. Never mind her refusal to share what had instigated her frostier demeanor or the fact she continually lied that everything was fine when it wasn't. Those two facts were of little consequence to her stubborn pride.

Just as she felt an intense sulk coming on, she happened upon a standout booth that looked as if a young Audrey Hepburn had assembled it. A gaggle of women were hanging around it, causing Jeslyn to take notice. A crowd meant the potential for something interesting and something interesting meant the potential to consign thoughts of Forbes to oblivion.

"Well, aren't you pretty." An attractive blonde in a short, figure-flattering coral dress, pearl earrings and nude pumps smiled at her from behind the booth. The brunette that stood by her wearing a black a-line skirt and a taupe silk button up blouse offered a one-worded agreement.

"Indeed."

"Are you here for the guest speaker or the cheese platter?" Before Jeslyn could reply, the blonde was approached by a woman who let her know she'd chat with her later. Blondie gave the girl a hug, a smooch on the cheek, and a wink before turning back to collect an answer.

"Both." The woman's question had coaxed a smile from Jeslyn. Her first since arriving at the event.

"Good answer, friend. Christine Matherson." She extended her hand.

"Jeslyn Kennedy." Jeslyn accepted it.

"And this is my business partner extraordinaire, Pamela Nolan." The brunette broke from a recently begun side conversation to greet her.

"So, what do you guys do?" Jeslyn prepared herself for "the pitch."

"In a nutshell, we're a complimentary online business resource for entrepreneurial women. Outside of our shells, we're just two awesome chicks who help other awesome chicks kick butt in the business world."

Jeslyn eyed a magnet that read, 'Hey Gorgeous, Opportunity Called. I Sent It Your Way.' And another, 'Well Behaved Women Seldom Make History.' And yet another, 'Entrepreneurs With Style.' Each sported a Chic-CEO.com website at the bottom. The two energetic women were unconventional if nothing else and, so far, she didn't feel the prick of the networking needle being forced into her prospective consumer vein.

"So, what kind of resources do you offer?" Jeslyn fingered a turquoise postcard on which was printed information for some trendy looking event called SAVVY hosted by Chic CEO.

"Everything," Christine said simply. "At Chic CEO, we believe women should have all the business and entrepreneurial knowledge and support they need right at their polished fingertips. Our website is a one-stop-shop business resource for all the amazing women we know or have met who either didn't know how to fully implement their ideas or were too afraid to take the plunge."

It was then that the heavens parted, a light filtered through the clouds and a dove descended upon them. That was a lie; there was no dove. Jeslyn was momentarily thrown. If there was anything more fateful than the explanation that had just come from Christine's mouth, Jeslyn didn't know what it was. Here was a free online business resource for women who were stuck or too afraid of the height from where they stood on the diving board to entrepreneurship to take the leap. It could not have been a more perfect connection.

"And what's this?" She grabbed the SAVVY postcard.

"Oh, that's our lady-networking event," Pamela offered.

"It's actually a fabulous soiree we like to throw once a month for lady-preneurs, mom-preneurs and business babes." Christine leaned in and lowered her voice as if sharing a secret. "Because, come on, let's be honest, who really enjoys networking events? Ninety percent of them basically feel like purgatory."

"Yeah, MLM purgatory," Jeslyn muttered.

"And there's nothing wrong with MLMs." Christine affected an angelic smile, hinting that her last remark may have been a glib one.

"OK, not all of them," Jeslyn agreed. "But I, for one, am all candled, vita drink'ed and independent team regional vice president of absolutely nothing'ed out. There are those companies out there that give MLM a bad name; names like 'Make Less Money', 'My Life's Mediocre' or 'My Low Morals'."

"That is both positively brilliant and freakin' hilarious." Pamela typed something into her smartphone. "You just made next week's blog, gorgeous."

"Here." Christine placed a magnet in her hand as the moderator took to the stage to get the room's attention and begin the program. "Let us know if we can help you become fabulous." She gave Jeslyn her very own wink. Jeslyn willingly grabbed a Chic CEO business card and sought out a seat at a nearby table. Christine had given her the 'Opportunity Called' magnet. As Buti Buck founder, Lara Dressler, was introduced, Jeslyn had only a one-word thought, an echo of Pamela's earlier acknowledgement.
Indeed.

*   *   *

Driving aimlessly was not helping. Jeslyn had just wrapped her Thursday therapy session with Dr. Parker and was scheduled to meet Forbes for dinner later that evening. Clips from the session skipped and repeated in her head.

"...I don't know. That's just my definition of success I guess. Maybe it's something I learned, maybe it makes me feel important. Maybe it's just what I want. There, that's my root cause."

"Why don't you feel important?"

Had she not been listening? Jeslyn felt like snapping her fingers in the woman's face and telling her to wake up and pay attention. She didn't do that, though. They'd discussed her 'inappropriate reactions stemming from sheer frustration' earlier when she'd explained she felt angry or annoyed in some way most of the time.

Jeslyn parked down the street from the restaurant. She did not want to have this dinner with Forbes in public. She thought about texting him to tell him as much but figured this way might be best and for her own benefit, even if it wasn't the benefit of comfort. She felt on edge and unsure of the evening's pending developments, which caused her thoughts to spin and her nerves to run amuck. An attempt was made to put into practice what Dr. Parker had instructed her to do when an overabundance of emotions threatened to overwhelm her.

"Think of your mind like a gym and your thoughts like muscles. They need to be exercised."

Jeslyn mentally adjusted some letters and swapped the fitness term for the religious one. Her thoughts needed to be purged from the clutches of evil more than they needed a workout.

"And just like exercise, it's going to take some work. It's going to be tiring and difficult and at times you're not going to want to do it, but the results will be worth it."

What was she supposed to do, put barbells on her head?

"When a negative thought, what I like to think of as unnecessary weight, pops into your head, I need you to work it out with a positive one. Now, this isn't as easy as it sounds."

Didn't sound easy at all, actually. Jeslyn just nodded in agreement and continued to let her unnecessary weights deliver their one-liners in the otherwise silent gym of her head.

"You're going to find that replacing negative thoughts, especially deep-seated ones, with positive thoughts is challenging. But just like an exercise regime that you keep to consistently, you'll find that challenge becoming less and less difficult. Change your thoughts, change your life."

Jeslyn, who'd finally begun opening up a bit to Dr. Parker in order to receive the help she knew she needed (and was paying for), took a stab at that Mr. Miyagi-esque philosophy now and switched her thoughts from Forbes to business.

Along with work-work, she also now had homework. She'd reached out to the Chic CEO ladies a few days after seeing them at the networking event. Turns out, they had a wealth of knowledge and a bevy of professional resources including a three-day Chic Start program which was helping her firm up her business plan and craft her mission statement. They were also amazingly supportive and complimentary about her burgeoning efforts. Christine noted that Jeslyn's marketing background put her way ahead of the curve for a lot of entrepreneurs and told her what she really needed was contacts. The chic CEO promised to get back to her with a few that might fit that role. A reminder was doled out as well.

"Sometimes it's not what you know but who knows you," Christine said, putting a spin on the popular adage, 'it's not what you know, it's who you know.' They'd further explored that concept with Pamela commenting that sometimes a plan just needed to catch the eye or ear of the right person.

"Success could be as close as a pupil or eardrum away," she'd said before going on to caution that that wasn't to say it was all caviar-and-champagne easy to launch a business.

"Although it should be, shouldn't it? Can you imagine? 'I'll have caviar and champagne please. Oh, a successful business comes on the side? Fabulous!'" Christine added jokingly.

Caviar and champagne or no, both women expressed confidence that she had the brains and the brawn to pull off a multi-million dollar venture if that's what she wanted to do.

Later, as she went over her first day's Chic Assignment, a filament of an idea was sparked to life by the 'who knows you' concept. It remained a hot spot of mental activity, and Jeslyn planned to take action on it after she put a few other ducks in a row. A week and some change had passed since then – a busy one at that, full of fresh planning and progress that had been lacking previously.

Dr. Parker had been right; shifting thoughts was helpful, but also a huge challenge. Before she realized it, she was back to wondering (worrying) if she had the mettle to face Forbes. It had taken everything within her not to hit up Marco for access to the man's email account. Knowing if he was still communicating with Gisele and what those communications did or did not entail were enticing baits.

She sat in her car for thirty minutes outside of Sushi on the Rocks in La Jolla. When she climbed the stairs to the rooftop restaurant and was escorted to a table for two, she was still twenty minutes early. She had gone over the pros and cons of showing up before Forbes versus after him and had somehow decided that arriving first was best. He must have shared her logic because he walked in a few minutes later.

Or he simply arrived early because he lives in La Jolla and it isn't that far of a commute.

Healthier rationalizations were safer.

Their initial exchange of hello's felt forced. They'd seen and touched nearly every part of each other, yet determining whether a hug, kiss, handshake or stiff nod was the better opener seemed to present a challenge. They settled for a stiff hug, cheek pecks and sake.

The burning sensation in her chest and the loosening of her rigid inhibitions aided in providing a much-needed atmosphere relaxant. They talked casually, ordered more sushi than they could possibly consume and over indulged in the warm liquid courage. When it became impossible to delay the inevitable any longer, Jeslyn bit the bullet and dove right in.

"So, I think it's a good idea if I share a few things with you that I have been having on my mind…lately." That came out horribly.

Jeslyn, not having given a ton of thought to what she was going to say beforehand, was winging this one. So far, she was highly unimpressed with herself. The sake wasn't helping, either; neither was being in Forbes' presence again. His face was more of a distraction than she remembered. Even though they were in La Jolla, the Beverly Hills of San Diego County, where beautiful faces frequently popped up out of nowhere like Wack-A-Models, Forbes was a standout to her.

She was further snapped out of focus when he reached across the small table and gathered her hands in his. For a moment, they both just sat watching his definitively masculine fingers caress her smaller feminine ones. His gesture weakened so many of her senses while her sense of touch was amplified exponentially.

"I got –" She attempted speech as he trailed two fingers along the back of her hand. "You sent –" He lazily repeated the movement on the inside of her palm. "You sent me the email you and Gisele were having." She wasn't slurring her words, but she certainly wasn't expressing herself eloquently. His fingers froze.

"What?" His brows bunched closer together.

Jeslyn pulled her hands from his and took her cell phone out of her purse. The email had already been pulled

256

up, so when she entered her passcode, it was conveniently the first thing on the screen.

"This." She passed the evidence to him.

Forbes scanned the email, his eyes moving back and forth rapidly, taking in the words and sentences neatly stacked on top of each other on the phone's small screen. He scrolled down, then back up before handing the phone back to her.

"Looks like you've had that for a while." He must have been referring to the date she'd sent it to herself.

"Enough time, yes." What did that even mean?

Forbes took a sip of water. He sat the glass down then reached for her hands again. There were remnants of condensation on his fingers and he transferred some of the cold moisture to her. "Tell me what you want me to say." He pinned her to her seat with an intense gaze.

"I can't tell you what to say." Jeslyn felt disappointment fall on her like a pile of damp rags.

"I'm at a loss for words, then. I mean, what do you want to know?" The question was rhetorical and he barreled along without waiting for a response. "Yes, I still talk to Gisele." The words 'still' and 'talk' smacked Jeslyn in the face. "We dated for a year but we've known each other for a long time. Our families hang out. It's not a romantic thing, it's just a —" He looked at her helplessly, apparently unable to define exactly what 'it' was.

"You don't owe me anything, Forbes." The mantra she'd been repeating to herself sounded hollow and robotic spoken aloud. "Not even an explanation. You're a nice guy, I enjoyed getting to know you and I thought you should know I saw the email." A half shrug. She was going for detachedly unaffected but felt she'd missed her target and bull's eyed cavalier instead.

"Enjoyed?" How was it that he could say exactly what he was thinking and still come off as the stronger one? When his word choice had chafed her she'd just stewed internally. She envied his confidence.

"Enjoy, enjoyed; semantics, really. What should I say instead?" She lobbed the ball back into his court as he'd tried to do with her. What she was really doing, though, was unsophisticatedly girlish. She wanted him to plead, to confess his undying love and devotion to her and beg for her forgiveness. While that heavily embellished scenario was truly just that, she did want to know his feelings and wanted to hear him express that they were strong and positive for her and her alone.

"You should say what you're feeling." He was too placid for her fired up tastes. Could he not see that she was an invalid when it came to saying how she felt?

"I'm feeling like, maybe...I mean, we should..." She said a whole lot of nothing. Her plan coming in here was to break it off. She'd lied to get him and now she was lying to keep him. He hadn't sent her that email; she'd sent it to herself. There was nothing he should feel guilty about. He was a mouse in her twisted maze looking for a route to something that didn't exist. He was blindly being subjected to more walls, more twists, more dead ends and less chance of survival. To be with Jeslyn was to live the life of Truman Burbank. At some point, he'd realize it was all a show and discover that nearly everything had been done in artifice.

Nearly.

"Maybe we could just go to your house right now and not talk." She affected the practiced cast of confidence, leveling him with her eyes, almost daring him to turn her down.

"OK."

The check was paid, his valeted car retrieved and she followed him to his place. As soon as the front door shut Jeslyn found herself pushed against it roughly. Labored breaths were the only sounds they made. Lance and Layla ran to welcome their master home, but seemed to understand the gravity of what was unfolding and backed away before leaving the foyer entrance completely.

Forbes kissed her with fervor, ravaging her lips with such intensity she thought he might bruise them. The pain was delicious. He grabbed her wrists with both hands then pinned them with one above her head. When she tried to lower them, to touch him, he clamped down and held her firmly in place. His hand slid under her shirt and she pressed her body into him as every nerve in the vicinity of his touch sizzled to the point of mania. She needed him, all of him and it had to be now. He still hadn't let her go so there was little she could do to express her need with her hands, but she put her all into every action of her mouth and her body. She was able to express this desire effectively and he released her wrists to scoop her up and carry her to his room.

He placed her in the center of the bed then stood to remove his clothing. She slid off the side and stretched her hands above her head. After removing everything but her barely there lingerie, she bent at the waist, stretched to touch her toes, then worked out the muscles in her neck by leaning her head side to side. Then she clasped her hands behind her back, stretching her chest and shoulders in the process.

"What are you doing?" Forbes was on the bed watching her. A foil packet lay on the nightstand to his left.

Jeslyn removed the last swaths of silk and lace covering her body before grabbing the protection from the nightstand as she crawled onto the bed towards him. "That," she climbed on top of him and carefully ripped the packet open with her teeth, "was foreplay."

Raw and uninhibited. That's how they merged their bodies together and continued to please each other well into the late hours of the night. Jeslyn didn't remember falling asleep but she woke up feeling the aftermath of their inhibitions the next morning. Forbes was still passed out beside her and she took the opportunity to simply watch him sleep. Her stare or simply some internal clock roused him and a grin pulled at his lips.

"Well, good morning."

"Not yet, but it could be." Her hand found him under the sheet; she didn't have to wait long for him to respond to her touch.

"Are you always this feisty?" he asked as he rolled over on his side to face her.

Jeslyn pulled the sheet up to her mouth before she spoke. "Only in the beginning. After I've had my fill of you, you're worthless to me." He thought she was joking. She was not. It was a sorrowful truth.

He laughed softly as he tugged at the sheet. "What's this? Are you hiding?"

That elicited a soft laugh from her as well. "No, Mr. Keith. I'm not hiding. Contrary to what the fantasy world would have people believe, there is such a thing as morning breath."

"There's also such a thing as morning wood." He poked her hip with his erection. Her reply was a soft murmur of approval. "Oh, wait, do you need to stretch first?" Mirth danced in his eyes and his nostrils flared as he tried to suppress laughter.

"Oh, you're funny." Jeslyn tickled his ribs and under his arms but he didn't flinch.

"Not ticklish." He gave her a propitiative smile for her efforts.

"Maybe not there, but I'll find it." Her hands went roaming over his muscular body. She braided her fingers briefly in his hair then ran them softly down his face. She traced his lips, then his ears and down his neck. One palm worked its way down his forearm and back up again. She cupped his shoulder then moved to caress the smooth skin of his chest. Her thumb stroked his puckered nipple before she replaced her digit with her mouth, licking and teasing him with her tongue. Purposeful kisses were placed on his stomach and her hands roamed freely over his thighs and calves. She kissed and nipped at his lower abdomen and lingered there until he framed the side of her head with his hands and urged her further downwards. Flicks of her tongue and the gentle sucking of his manhood had him sucking air into his mouth against clenched teeth. She increased the efforts of her mouth and brought her hand around the base of him as an aid. Her jaw burned from the exertion and her neck muscles stiffened but she kept the momentum. He reached down to touch her and heighten the experience using her body as his very physical, in-person erotica. She allowed him complete access to wherever his fingers could lay claim and he allowed her to bring him to a staggering climax.

It was a happy ending for him – in more ways than one. Jeslyn collected her clothing and belongings and left Forbes, smiling and replete with contentment, a few hours later. She did not share that she would not be coming back, that she planned on weaning him from her life altogether. Her curiosity had been indulged, gorged actually, and to continue further down this road with him would only lead to trouble. Karma was a wicked, vengeful woman, not a peaceful paragon of justice. There would be no getting out of this unmarred. It was either quietly fall on the sword and suffer the pain of disembowelment on her own volition now or wait for karma to slice her open publicly.

Jeslyn chose to leave quietly.

She had kissed Forbes' cheek as she said her goodbye, then, realizing that wasn't the lasting image she wanted in her head or his, she had pulled him to her, locked him in a crushing embrace and kissed him with reckless abandon. Then she left. It would be awhile before he came to the realization that goodbye had been her last.

23

Time.

Jeslyn's time was now measured in Forbes. First, it was how long it had been since she'd last seen him, then since she'd last spoken to him and finally since she'd last heard from him.

The slow erosion was not his doing, it was hers. When she'd left him that morning, she'd already erased his contact information from every electronic device that she owned. She didn't reach out to him, ever, and when he would call her she would ignore the calls. Her responses to his texts became less and less frequent, yet it wasn't until his texts and emails began to go completely unanswered that the need to ignore them was no longer a necessity. He was not a man without options, she knew that, so for him to have put up with her rebuff for the nearly three weeks it took before he finally got the message they were done was a surprise. She'd assumed it would've happened sooner.

Even though she'd instigated this infinite separation, it didn't matter to her emotions. And now, four weeks and four days since she had last seen him she was still feeling the withdrawals.

She typed out texts she didn't send, emails that remained drafts, and nine of the ten stubbornly memorized numbers to his cell before setting her phone down again.

Turning back now was not an option. While there were a million excuses she could give him regarding her taciturn behavior, nothing would be good enough; and of course there was the matter of a future with him. That, too, was an impossibility. She knew they wouldn't last, couldn't last, and the end would come sooner rather than later. So, she figured, why not control it instead of waiting and wondering until it happened.

And it would have happened.

He did not get discussed in therapy, but she used therapy on him constantly. Since he was the totality of her overwhelming thoughts, he was her first choice (her only choice), for practicing her mental shift exercises on. Thinking about him was painful. His very name lampooned her heart to such an extent that she stopped using it altogether and took to thinking of the man she'd gone through such great lengths to get to know as simply 'Him.' She told herself he wasn't someone special, just another 'Him'. Her mind accepted this rationale; her heart did not.

Jeslyn's already lean frame lost even more of its softer edges thanks to an increase in gym visits and a decrease in food consumption. Alcohol consumption, nighttime rituals, and social interactions, however, were on the rise.

A glass of wine each night to help her fall and stay asleep soon turned into nearly an entire bottle. She also played the same movie each night as she drifted off and left it on, like an electronic dream catcher, to occupy her subconscious thoughts. Along with that, every hour of every day was filled to the brim with something. Her social life picked up considerably as a result.

With all of the bustling activity it was easier to stop the train wreck of emotions that had her either staring at blank walls, missing out on sleep or fighting back tears she refused to shed. Crying over Him was not a luxury she allowed herself. She and her heart had an understanding, and that was that tears were reserved for meaningful events, not pity parties or quasi-breakups with men she'd known for less time than her mail carrier. There were only two other roadblocks that still needed resolution. She approached the Chic CEO team about the first.

"Hi Christine, it's Jeslyn. How are you?"

"I'm good, what's up?" Christine's voice sounded chipper over the phone and Jeslyn wondered how long it would be before she was able to feel that way again.

Jeslyn proceeded to ask her if she knew anyone with editorial decision-making clout at the prestigious magazine she'd feigned employment with in order to get close to Him. She figured if anyone had an in with the publisher it would be Christine or Pamela. She was not incorrect in her assumptions. Christine directed her to Pamela who informed her that one of her boyfriend's very good friends was a senior editor there. Jeslyn explained truthfully what she was looking to do and not so truthfully why she was looking to do it, saying only that she'd promised a charity organization she'd try to get an article published on one of their VIP members. Pamela made a few calls and set a meeting up between Jeslyn and Senior Editor, Mike Sheffield. They met for lunch at a Thai restaurant in downtown San Diego (he'd offered sushi, she'd requested anything but) and she showed him the prepared article she'd written on Him. He wasn't familiar with the biochemist, but said he was interested in her write up.

Whether he was interested as a favor or truly interested was anyone's guess, although she would have bet money it was the former. Either way, he told her he'd run it. She would have to give him a few weeks, though, because the current issue was already a wrap and he wasn't sure about the availability for the next. That worked for her. She emailed him her article and crossed that item off her list before tackling the next.

Willie's trial had gone from months away to now only days away and she cursed herself for how she'd handled Kevin. Not going to his house had been a good idea, but the kiss. Had that kiss really been necessary? It was a question that would have put Sherlock Holmes out of business with its obviousness. She knew she could call Kevin to find out what was unfolding, but 'could' and 'would' were separated by more than first letters in this circumstance. Besides, she trusted he'd reach out to her if he saw or heard anything about her in conjunction with the scandal. It wasn't as if he hated her; quite the opposite.

What she didn't trust was random information swirling around, online or otherwise, that gave away information about her, primarily information she didn't want laid bare. She'd received a handsome chunk of change from Willie and, in turn, she'd done work for him, leaving a box of photocopied memories on Matt Coleman's doorstep – two things that didn't come without strings. Who knew all the ties that not only linked her to this current storm of corruption, but also several other storms from long ago and not so long ago. They all needed to be examined and either severed or dealt with.

She thought about how easy it had been to get to Forbes – and she was no professional at tracking information down. What would that scenario have looked like if a true professional had been on the job? What would they have uncovered? And what would happen if their expertise were unleashed on her? She needed an identity wipe. What was a fleeting thought years ago and a strong notion months ago had become an imperative in recent days with reasons that spanned farther than Willie's reach. She could see its tendrils snaking out, lightly brushing her future, threatening to taint something that still had yet to come to fruition, but was evolving day by day.

Under Chic CEO's tutelage and Chic Black Book of contacts, Jeslyn had not only been able to finalize her business plan and put together an outline of next steps that would take her from now to a launch; she'd also connected with a retired textile maven who had taken her under her wing thanks to a good word from Christine. The fact that this pursuit had begun to not only take shape, but also grow legs and move forward was huge. She still had three clients with Red Cello, but it was a struggle to keep up with it all at times, and getting five or less hours of sleep each night was a recurrent theme. But being overworked was a burden she could not have been more satisfied with. Tackling multiple projects at a time and seeing results from those efforts, results that she had created and that served her purpose, not some abrasive CEO's or ungracious owner's, was truly gratifying.

This was life and it was fulfilling.

Before she'd been underwater and had occasionally gotten sucked under the tide. Now, she was treading water and land was in sight. A meeting was in sight as well. Jeslyn got ready and headed out to meet Ynez Martinez, the textile retiree, and a colleague of hers whom Jeslyn had already spoken to and met with a few times before. The meeting was to go over the croquis and fabric samples that had been assembled based on their earlier meetings and conversations. After that, Jeslyn had an online meeting with a freelance web designer she'd hired to build both her general and e-commerce websites. All the content for the sites along with their site maps had been in the works for some time and she was almost done putting together the elements that would coincide with it.

It was happening.

To make matters that much better, the Chic CEO team had invited her to become a Chic Siren – a members only program that provided elevated entrepreneurial resources and coaching – and they promised to blast her business launch out to their fifty-thousand plus subscribers, 'because she was pretty,' Pamela had said with a grin before adding with a wink, 'and maybe because we believe in this.'

Jeslyn believed in it as well...mostly. But like any fledgling undertaking, there were those pesky doubts. Was she really just starting a clothing line? Saying it that way seemed so anticlimactic. She knew from experience that every business had to have a niche, something that set it apart from others, especially competitors. And while Ynez knew the rag trade like the back of her hand and was giving her solid advice and direction, it all seemed a bit naive, a bit too starlet-esque. What was she going to do next, create a fragrance line and join a girl band? The more she considered it, the more callow it felt. Yes, the fabrics were high quality and yes, she had an extremely adept designer that was executing her unique vision flawlessly, but the question that looped around her mind like a never ending merry-go-round was, did the world really need yet another apparel company? She considered the many malls, outlets, department stores and boutiques in her city alone then multiplied that by the thousands. Cramming another rack full of more *things* – that's all it felt like she was doing – was more deflating than dynamic.

Dr. Parker had touched on this very tendency, the one where she let the air out of her own balloon and wilted her ideas to nothing before they even got started instead of finding a way to overcome the disincentives.

"Why do you think you do this?"

Jeslyn clenched her jaw then quickly unclenched it remembering how the side of her face had been stroked softly by Him and a comment made about how often she did that. A quick mental shift focusing only on her present surroundings saved her.

"I don't know." She followed her astounding revelation up with a sigh. She was tired of the questions. With Dr. Parker it always led to a deeper and healthier understanding, but the road to those understandings was a weary one.

"Well, I'll give you time to reflect then." Rosalyn never let her off the hook.

So, Jeslyn thought and thought about it before offering, "I guess it's an easy way out. If I give up I never have to face failure or hardship or challenges and I can just tell myself it wouldn't have worked."

"Or success." Dr. Parker arched a brow. "Which comes with scrutiny and judgment and fears of its own. Do you fear success, Jeslyn?"

"Well, first off, I don't know if I'll even achieve it," she was doing it again, "but I've always thought of success like a magic wand. Like, after you get to the top, everything falls into place and life is just...better." That was a stupid answer. Once again the feeling of being an immature adolescent in the company of a knowing, probing adult fell upon her.

"Let's say you do achieve success, what exactly does that mean to you? Is it a way to be seen, to be noticed, recognized or appreciated?"

"Well, yes I want that, doesn't everybody?" Obviously.

"No." Dr. Parker completely dried up the 'duh' that had been soaked in Jeslyn's reply. "Some people prefer complete anonymity, actually. Now, this is something I need you to really think about, Jeslyn. You want to be seen, which is part of your vision of success, yet you don't want the challenges. And when success is achieved, you feel your life will be better. I need you to think about what it is you're truly looking for. Can you tell me that?"

The question echoed inside Jeslyn's brain like bat screeches off a cave wall. She'd sat mute until their time together expired, never answering Dr. Parker's question. Yes, she wanted to be appreciated and noticed, but she'd choose exactly what got noticed.

And what did that make her, some sort of desperate attention-seeker?

Jeslyn bit the inside of her cheek as she searched the web for online reputation management firms, private investigators, and background security agencies. It wasn't nerves that had one leg bouncing anxiously as she sat at the barstool of her kitchen counter, it was concern. Thoughts, like boomerangs, circled in her mind but always came back to the same conclusion.

This was paranoia.

She pushed and shoved at the thought and tried throwing her mental shift exercises at it but it wouldn't budge. It sat like a statue in her head, heavy and immobile;

and not just any statue either. It was a gargoyle that sneered at her derisively as if to say, 'yes, Jeslyn, this is how it begins.'

Despite the taunting concern, she forged on with her search. The idea was to hire someone as a way to protect herself, her past really; the sides of her she wasn't interested in people knowing about. Dr. Parker had told her that her past wasn't something to be ashamed of, but she didn't know what was in Jeslyn's trove. Dr. Parker also said that it wasn't something to judge herself for or let other people judge her for, but again the woman spoke out of ignorance. She had no idea all the sediment that Jeslyn had stirred up and the residuum that clung to her now because of it. How could the well-intentioned therapist know that Jeslyn refused to even keep a diary lest it fall into the wrong hands? She couldn't. Because it had never been discussed and if Jeslyn had any say in the matter, there would be no say about those matters at all. She wanted her past locked away, banished to a never-to-be-seen-or-heard-from-again oubliette. Since erasing it from existence completely was not an option without a science-fiction fix, an oubliette was the next best thing.

The realization that she couldn't get rid of it all was not lost on her, but she would do her best to keep all those skeletons in their respective closets. Even thinking about them felt dangerous, like she was conjuring them into existence again.

"Stop, just...stop. You're going too far, J." Jeslyn sucked air into her mouth then slowly blew it out as she talked herself down from the ledge she feared dropped off into insanity. "Not you. It's not going to be you."

Having had her fill of technology for the time being, she stepped away from the computer and withdrew to her office for a little arts and crafts time. Sitting Indian-style on the floor, she selected the closest magazine to her, along with a pair of scissors from the desk nearby, and picked up where she'd left off on her collage. The girls at Chic CEO were huge proponents of dream boards.

"Visualization is really powerful," Pamela had told her one day while she toured their office. There were boards on several walls covered in single words, quotes, pictures and artistic designs. "Those," Pamela pointed to the different ones, "are our dream boards." She smiled.

"A dream board." Jeslyn swished the words around in her mouth like mouthwash before letting them slide slowly out as she examined the boards.

"Next assignment, make your own board...za." Pamela added the pluralization at the end. "Doesn't have to be just one, you can make several. I would encourage several, actually. And here," she turned and picked up a stack of magazines from the table behind her, "are some mags to help you get started."

"And here," Christine came up behind her so quietly Jeslyn hadn't noticed she was there, "is a glass of wine to help you get started." After handing Jeslyn the stemmed glassware filled three quarters full with a deep red merlot, she walked away humming a jazz standard to herself.

Jeslyn smiled before taking a sip of the wine. Her eye caught on a slip of paper with the words 'I Love Chic CEO' printed across the back of it. She couldn't have agreed more.

Cutting and pasting lasted for hours. Inspirational words, random splashes of color, images that reflected her personal visions and interesting business ideas were carefully carved out of magazines and affixed to the poster board while music in the background kept her company. She sang along, tapping her foot to the more enthusiastic beats and swaying her body in time with those whose rhythms had less haste. The night could have ended perfectly if it weren't for the next magazine in the pile.

An issue of *Forbes* magazine stared up at her from her now paralyzed fingers. His name taunted her, poking her in the heart and reaching in to clutch her insides and twist them around their bold, serif typeface. Logic and reason would have had nothing to do with what happened next. Logic would have scolded and reason would have calmly stated that it was absurd she should break apart because of

Him. Logic would have told her that he was never hers to begin with and reason would have given her "the face", the one that said, 'Honey child, puh-lease. It was a few months of fun and an amicable parting of ways, not a forty-year marriage and a divorce.' But Jeslyn wasn't interested in either logic or reason and it was because of this disinterest that she Completely. Broke. Down.

The hiccup of a sob wasn't halfway through her esophagus before her body crumpled, falling onto itself. A boa constrictor tore its way out of her heart, leaving a burning blaze of venom in its wake and slithered to her chest where it coiled around her lungs and compressed the very air from them. She clutched her arms around her body, as if this would remove the ache that was now causing her eyes to release such a heavy flow of tears that her vision was reduced to nothing more than blobs of color. There was nothing she could mentally shift to that would blot Him out, and no amount of trying did any good. Every laugh, sigh, word, movement and look that had ever passed between them invaded her memories like a mental air raid. The explosions detonated in succession, one right after the other, like a never ending *1812 Overture* cannon finale at a Summer Pops concert. She tried getting angry, hurling insults at herself that would have made Tony Montana uncomfortable, in an effort to pull it together. Then she tried pleading with herself, which only worsened matters. Mucous mixed with tears made everything below her eyes slick and wet, and her stomach burned, and her throat felt raw, and still she bawled.

Sleep was her only saving grace.

Jeslyn woke while it was still dark with a piece of magazine paper stuck to her cheek still clutching the scissors in her right hand. The thought that accidentally stabbing herself to death while she slept would have been a welcome reprieve, crept in then right back out of her mind without her paying it much attention. She was finally numb. Except rising to her feet proved to be a challenge. Her head felt woozy, her legs shaky, and everything else a little sore from

271

lying in an awkward position for so long. She snatched the offensive magazine off the floor as she stood and dumped it into the kitchen receptacle before dumping her body, still fully clothed, in her bed.

Now that she was actually in a place where she was supposed to submit to sleep, it evaded her grasp and so she took to staring at the ceiling in an effort to bore herself there. Her breathing was slower and her body felt weak and hollow like she was nothing inside. There was no one else in her house, her room or her bed but she felt such embarrassment that she covered her face with the sheet.

Falling apart over Him was absurd and something that could never happen again. She sincerely doubted he was somewhere bawling in his homemade pizza over her. A more likely scenario was that he was somewhere with Gisele or another Gisele replacement (like she had been) living his life. And although a casual thought about why she had up and disappeared might occasionally come to mind, it was nothing that stuck with Him for any length of time. In fact, if it occurred to Him at all, it was probably a fleeting consideration that he dismissed with a shrug and never considered again. Thoughts of her did not plague Him. He did not fight urges to call her, he didn't miss her with such intensity that it caused physical pain and she would be the same.

He was no longer Him. Now, he was what he should have been all along.

He was Nothing.

24

The lights were on in the room where Katya and Jeslyn had been holed up for the past almost four hours, but the absence of sunlight funneling in from any of the windows added a solemn evening darkness to the space. Jeslyn had opened her mouth as if to say something more, then clamped it shut and turned her head to the side as if she were listening for something.

Katya, who had been silent before, didn't even dare to breathe now. She sat perfectly still wondering about Jeslyn's behavior – so many oddities had already occurred that she wondered first and saved worry as a last resort. Was Jeslyn regretting this? Was she reliving some of those personal demons she'd spoken so frankly about? Or, had she touched on a truth when she mentioned thoughts of paranoia and hereditary mental imbalances?

Jeslyn turned to her slowly and with eyes that now seemed sapped and somehow void of anything.

"I think it's time for dinner." Another already made decision.

Katya was well past distinct impressions, she knew for certain now that Jeslyn didn't do 'ask' she only did 'tell.'

"Tracy will assist you with your meal accommodations. I have some things I need to attend to. Feel free to come back whenever you're ready to wrap this

273

up." Jeslyn said it as though that could be in a few minutes or a few weeks, Katya was at liberty to decide. For whatever reason, that made Katya apprehensive. It was also said in such a way as to let Katya know they wouldn't be dining together.

"OK –" she bit her tongue before the word 'then' escaped. "Should I...actually, you know what, no need to bother Tracy, I can manage on my–"

"Unless you plan on leaving the hotel, the food choices here aren't the most economical for your budget range." Jeslyn broke in as if she hadn't finished her earlier sentence and was taking the opportunity to do that now. "I'm not saying that in an unflattering way, I'm saying it logically. Tracy will assist you with your meal accommodations." Tell, not ask.

"Sounds great." Katya forced a smile. "I'll see you –"

"Just whenever you're ready." Jeslyn walked out of the room.

Katya rolled her eyes. The way Jeslyn made her feel, like she'd done something wrong, was irritating. Then again, a person could only wield power over you if you gave it to them and Katya had handed Jeslyn the scepter to her submission the second she'd agreed to do this – whatever it was.

"Ms. Houston," Tracy said, entering the room.

Katya wondered where Tracy went and what she did when she wasn't in her presence, and how someone normal (she automatically assumed Tracy was normal) worked for someone like Jeslyn Kennedy.

"Here are the dining options available to you at the hotel. Simply tell the hostess you're meeting with Jennifer Yen and they'll take care of you."

Katya scanned the list Tracy had provided. "OK, which one?"

"Which one what?"

"At which restaurant or cafe or whatever am I supposed to talk to the hostess?"

274

"Whichever one you'd like." Tracy looked at Katya as if she'd started speaking in a foreign language.

"So, I just walk into any place that has food and tell them I'm meeting with Jennifer Yen?"

"Yes." Tracy drew the reply out.

"OK, got it." Another forced smile, this time for Tracy. This whole experience, 'The Jeslyn Kennedy Experience' as she now liked to think of it, was so quixotic it felt like a dream; like she had yet to wake up and head to the real interview, the one where she actually got to ask questions and Jeslyn was just some regular businesswoman.

Tracy escorted her as far as the front door of the suite, but then she was on her own. Katya had brought all of her belongings with her just in case Jeslyn, Tracy, and the suite itself up and vanished before she returned. Her cell phone was stuffed in a side pocket of her messenger back and she dug it out as she walked to the main area of the Del. Every communication icon was flagged with red numbers. Twenty-seven missed texts, eleven missed emails and five missed calls had all piled up in the past two hours since she'd last checked her phone.

They would have to wait.

Katya needed time to herself to reflect on everything she'd heard and dealt with up to this point. How was she going to write this story? It was no longer an article; it was practically a memoir. Then, there was the question of disclosure. Did Jeslyn really want everything she was laying at her feet to be laid out in print? Minus the portions that had been off record. Certainly not. And sure, the saga was interesting. But for Pete's sake, when was she going to talk about the Coleman scandal? Katya felt she knew less now than she did in the beginning, when she first sat down with her.

Speaking of sitting down...

Katya checked the list one more time before deciding on a restaurant. Despite her sugar laden breakfast and lunch, the Moo Creamery made her mouth salivate.

With only minor difficulty, she ignored the craving and headed towards the more sensible Babcock and Story Bakery. A slice of pizza would be fine. That is until the smell of a steak, broiled to perfection, infiltrated her olfactory senses. Like a cartoon character floating on aroma, she followed the scent all the way to the entrance of the hotel's signature fine dining restaurant, 1500 Ocean. Before she could come up with a reason not to, she was informing the hostess that she was meeting with Jennifer Yen and would like a table for one for dinner.

The same graciousness the hotel concierge had shown when the Yen name was mentioned once again reared its pleasant head. Katya was shown to a table and immediately presented with a variety of wine and champagne options she was sure cost more than what she made in a week. Katya declined the alcohol, figuring it was best to stay as sober as possible while in the company of Jeslyn Kennedy, and opted instead for sparkling water. After all, Jeslyn had said water was best. It wasn't until after she'd decided on her meal for the evening, and had gotten over the shock of the tab, that she gave attention to the missed messages on her phone.

Twenty of the twenty-seven missed texts and three of the missed calls were from LeAnn. They began sanely enough, but by the last one, it appeared LeAnn was slowly losing it over worry for her safety (or out of sheer curiosity and the fact Katya hadn't satisfied it). She fired off a quick text to let her know she was fine but still working and she'd fill her in later. Katya knew that would not suffice and that her phone would be vibrating any second with another call or text but she'd deal with that when it happened.

A text from Sara let her know there'd been no further disruptions as it related to the Twitter fiasco, and it seemed the entire brouhaha was dying down. A three text long message from Ethan seconded Sara's information in more detail, but unlike Sara's message, Katya read Ethan's texts over and over again. Just seeing his name scrawled across her screen gave her a boost of something closely resembling excitement. He was her Forbes. Only, she wouldn't be going to any extremes in order to get closer to him. If he wasn't interested in getting to know her, then it wasn't going to happen. To be honest, she was more than a little concerned about Jeslyn's rationalization and self-control capabilities. Who in their right mind would go through all of that trouble just to meet one man? And other than an uncanny knowledge of local hip hop, what made him so special?

At that moment, the hostess came into view with a tall male patron in tow. Katya's seated position allowed her to see them walking towards then past her, but the comfort of her surroundings and her preoccupation with Jeslyn's issues and Ethan's text made her unmindful of them. The gentleman was seated two tables away and would have continued being just another diner if it weren't for a server addressing him by name.

"Will that be all, Mr. Keith?"

"Yes, thank you."

Mr. Keith!?

Katya's attention was grabbed, shaken and stirred as she honed in on that brief exchange. She risked a casual glance in the direction of the voices, which had come from slightly behind her and to the right. Luck was on her side and she was able to clearly see his face, it was instantly recognizable, more so than she would have imagined. She knew what he looked like because she, too, had searched him on the Internet, although not as extensively as Jeslyn had done. Trying to remain inconspicuous, Katya kept her glances in his direction to a minimum. Was he alone? The server had removed the other place setting from his table giving off the impression that he was. Katya's mind went to work filtering through possibilities.

Jeslyn had said he lived in La Jolla. Why then would he be at this Coronado hotel when his house was nearby? Was he the phone call that Jeslyn had taken hours before?

Did he know Jeslyn was even here? And if he did, was he aware of the reason why? She tried to remember the jumbled explanation Jeslyn had given right before the part of the story that covered her relationship with Forbes. Something about his story not being hers to tell for the sake of telling it, but her part of the story was fair game. There had been a lot of rather personal details shared, would Forbes be ambushed if (when?) those details were released?

Katya's already galloping heart seemed to go into mild panic mode. The urge to go talk to him was almost as strong as the urge to get up and leave. Coincidence could not possibly be at play here, she was certain of it. Almost certain of it. There was a sliver of doubt. Perhaps there was a fifty-fifty chance. Seventy-thirty. Eighty-Twenty...

The percentages stopped making sense. Katya completely lost track of which number represented the odds for coincidence and which represented design. Thinking about how sneaky Jeslyn had admitted to being, she began struggling with paranoid thoughts of her own. Was this a trap? Did Jeslyn send him in here as a test?

There was only one way to find out.

She thought briefly through her approach tactic, what she would say, then stood and made her way to his table. The closer she got the more she realized what a completely moronic idea this had been. Something that had seemed so necessary while she was safe in the confines of her solo dining experience was now showing itself to be necessary's polar opposite. Nothing was beyond his table that would allow her to change course and make her way to it instead, she would have to go through with her brilliant-turned-quickly-dumb idea after all. So far, he'd paid her no mind even though she was walking toward him slowly like some weird creeper – an impression, first or otherwise, she wasn't interested in giving off. She picked up her pace.

"Excuse me." He looked up. "I'm so sorry to bother you. Forbes Keith, correct?"

He didn't look pissed but he didn't exactly look pleased either. "Yes. And you are?"

The way Jeslyn had described him, Katya had thought he might be a little reserved, maybe even shy or easily flustered, but Forbes was thousands of miles from shy. His strong jawline, which was only but a small facet of his impossibly beautiful face, was set so resolutely there was no denying his self-assurance. And his eye contact was direct. It was here that Katya wondered why Jeslyn hadn't gone into more detail about how gorgeous he was. People should be prepared to meet beauty this striking. Then again, she thought back to her first impression of Jeslyn, the woman wasn't too shabby herself so she probably wasn't as affected as normal people who –

He asked me a question. Forbes just asked me a question. What was the freaking question? "I'm sorry, can you repeat that?" Katya did her best not to fidget and swallowed the nervous lump that had risen in her throat.

Forbes smiled graciously, almost knowingly, as if he understood how a girl like her could be flustered by a man like him. "I asked who *you* are." Now he seemed amused.

"Oh, right, yes." Was it possible to feel like more of an idiot? Katya doubted it. "So sorry. I'm –" She stopped abruptly, having started to give him her first name, but for some reason hesitant to do so. The reasons why would come later, she was sure, but for now Forbes got her middle name. "Elise. I'm Elise." She hoped the pause hadn't been too long.

"Nice to meet you, Elise. Did you want to...?" He motioned to the seat across from him.

"Oh, no!" Too amped. "I mean yes, but no." Too nonsensical. Katya focused on her words. "What I mean to say is," deep inhale, "I would love to join you, but I'm seated right over there," cue point to table that he cares absolutely nothing about, "and I wouldn't want to disturb your dinner. I just came to say hello. I'm mildly acquainted with your work (*ha!*) and your charity endeavors." Here he nodded, giving Katya a minute amount of faith in herself. "And I really, honestly just wanted to say hello." She'd already said that. So she wouldn't repeat herself any further, she proceeded to do an awkward half bow half nod as she backed away. Forbes watched her interestedly, a half smirk still gracing his features, but he didn't speak. "I'm...you enjoy your dinner." She was grinning like an imbecile, she knew that, but his sexy-as-sin grin was bewitching and gave her the loveliest of chills.

Katya turned around before she ran into something and hightailed it back to her table. When firm contact with her seat had been established, she put her hand to her heart in an attempt to calm the wild beating of it and gulped down the sparkling water. A figure appeared beside her, then slid into the empty seat in front of her. Sparkling water had been the wrong thing to chug so quickly and a burp barreled through her chest, up her throat and right out of her mouth.

"Oh. My. Gosh." Absolute. Mortification. Katya became a huge ball of hot embarrassment. Forbes let out a light chuckle. "I am so...oh my gosh." She pressed her palm over her mouth and closed her eyes. If she couldn't see him, maybe he couldn't see her. Although that hadn't worked as a child, she prayed for it to work now.

"It's OK." The touch of his warm hand on hers made her jump.

Her eyes flew open to the sight of his dazzling smile and pale winter green eyes. And that touch. It was so brief, yet the actual feel of his hand on her hand made her swoon.

"So, Elise, what brings you to the hotel?" His world, of course, was still on its axis.

Katya had rehearsed this part for only a few moments in her head. Now that Forbes Keith was at her table, in front of her, like Jeslyn's fairytale come to life, her thoughts were scattered. "Are you...are you sitting here?" It was the only thing she could think to say. She knew her cheeks were still beet red.

"If that's alright with you. I don't want to disturb your dinner." Another smirk. He was toying with her.

"Oh, no, you couldn't possibly disturb my dinner." She was gushing. It was humiliating. Katya pinched the outside of her thigh under the table in an effort to shock her senses back to where they should be. It helped...some.

"Good. Then, yes, I would like to join you for dinner."

"OK then." That stupid grin was back, she couldn't shake it, because here he was looking at her, just staring into her eyes. It was one of the most beautiful stares she'd ever seen and he was giving it to her. Now he was arching an eyebrow. Katya got lost in the expressions that ran across Forbes' face. She could literally watch them all day.

"So...?"

But he had asked a question. Again. And she had failed to answer him. Again. And now she was at a complete loss as to what he'd asked...again.

"I am so sorry, I have so much on my mind." Nope, just a mind full of Forbes. "Would you mind repeating that?" Again.

"What brings you to the hotel?" He leaned back in his seat and waited for her answer with a look that made it obvious he was highly entertained.

"I'm a reporter." Katya did her best to pull herself together. "I'm here doing a story on a, um, celebrity...of sorts. It's kind of confidential so, can't really go into all of the details." There, finally something that didn't make her come off as the comedic relief portion of the evening.

"I see. And how do you like being a reporter?"

It wasn't a question Katya heard often because it wasn't a title she was able to give often – never would be a more correct timeframe. However, she already knew the answer.

"I love it. It's unconventional and stressful at times but I've never wanted to do anything more than I've wanted to do this so, I count myself as fortunate."

This elicited a genuine smile from him. It also elicited a continuation of easy conversation. Not only was she caught off guard by how handsome he was – Jeslyn nor the online pics had done him justice – she was also shocked by how down-to-earth he was. For Katya, millionaires were all the same: Highly unapproachable people with an inflated sense of entitlement and a disregard for the common man. Forbes was anything but.

Their respective meals came and, as they enjoyed them, the flow of conversation poured through the meal. He shared a bit about his work and a little snippet of his personal life, even mentioning his dogs. And although Katya was familiar with portions of these details, his retelling them gave the information depth. Where Jeslyn had given facts, Forbes provided meaning. Katya, in turn, gave a slightly guarded description of her family, her background and the censored version of how she'd gotten into journalism. It didn't feel as if she were in the hot seat with Forbes, they were just two people having dinner and getting to know each other. The fact that she was interviewing someone who had known him intimately, and had shared some of those intimate details about him, gave her a slight thrill.

Katya could have gone on for hours talking a little and listening a lot to this man who she could now see why someone would move mountains to get to know – hell, she was considering stalking him herself – but a phone call interrupted them.

"Mr. Keith, there's a call for you at the front." The server interrupted them. Katya's mouth automatically went up into a light sneer. She adjusted her expression quickly when she realized what her face was doing.

Forbes pulled out his cell phone and checked it before responding to the server. "OK, I'll be there in just a moment. Oh, and be sure to include the lady's tab with mine." He was referring to Katya.

"No, oh no, there's no need for that," Katya nervously replied as she considered how she'd possibly be able to explain not incurring a tab to Jeslyn. "The...my interview…it's already taken care of."

"Fair enough. Thanks." Forbes directed the first part of his sentence to her and the gratitude-con-dismissal part to the server. "Well, Katya, it's been fun. Thanks for allowing me to crash your dinner."

His choice of words was so hackneyed they were almost funny. She could imagine him tacking on a "stay sweet" or "see you next year" ending. Considering all that had been discussed between them, she smiled warmly; it truly had been fun.

"Likewise Forbes." She reached out to shake his hand, hoping he was the type who didn't do handshakes and insisted on hugs instead. All her luck had been used up, for the time being anyway, as he met her palm with his and gave it a hearty shake and a good squeeze.

"Any other final probing questions, Miss Reporter?"

Katya couldn't tell if he was joking or not but she decided to capitalize on the opportunity either way. "Uh, yeah, do you have any major regrets?" He'd mentioned the risks he'd taken in business and she figured he'd probably have a few things he wished he'd done differently. People's regrets were always of interest and she just knew Forbes would have a fascinating share.

A grave look dropped slowly over his playful smirk; like her words were the shifting of the sun behind a cloud, causing a shadow to move slowly over a once-bright surface.

"Just one." His delivery was so wrought with emotion Katya found herself looking very closely at those pale green eyes.

Forbes stood, thanked her again and left to take his call, leaving Katya alone. She waved over the server to let him know she, too, was finished. And as there was nothing to sign and nothing further to do but leave the restaurant, full from both her delicious meal and curiosity over Forbes' one regret, she did just that.

A flash of a thought suggested that perhaps the source of his regret was Jeslyn, but that was far too romantic, or too biased of an idea that was a direct result of her time with the woman, and so she halfway let it go.

She kept her eyes peeled as she made her exit in hopes she would accidentally on purpose bump into him. Unfortunately (for her), he was nowhere in sight.

Her trek back to the suite was uneventful and upon her return she found the door slightly ajar allowing her easy access. Back to the sitting room. Katya resumed her place in the over sized chair across from Jeslyn's empty one. She didn't feel it was necessary to announce her return, figuring Jeslyn and Tracy were not only aware of her comings and goings, they were also probably aware of her dinner with Forbes. In any event she was confident that one or both of them would be making another of their unnaturally silent entrances to let her know what happened next.

Jeslyn did not disappoint.

Black leggings, that looked like they'd been painted on, covered the lower half of her body. A loose, off-one-shoulder, white fleece tunic, which stopped just before those dangerous curves, as if it was afraid to touch them, hung from her lean upper half. Flashes of Jeslyn's story – mainly the parts concerning the gym and sparring – were visibly apparent in her frame.

Sometime before their dinner break, Jeslyn had pointed to her messenger bag and asked if there was a camera in it. Katya had replied that there was not. Jeslyn had then asked if photographs would need to be taken later on in the evening, to which Katya replied that a professional could handle it, if she wanted, or Jeslyn could provide the pictures herself. While she was secretly thrilled that Jeslyn would supply an image (images?) of herself, or allow newly captured images to be released, it had been a strange inquiry. Now, Katya understood.

In casual wear, her hair pulled back into a messy ponytail, her bangs brushed seventy-five percent to one side and twenty-five percent to the other, Jeslyn was the epitome of fresh-faced beauty. She looked like a friendly, girl next door, too. No Delphian oracle was required to predict something would eventually be done or said that would erase this, but until that time came, Katya allowed herself to enjoy the moment.

Jeslyn had given the OK for her turn the recorder back on and as Katya readied the device, she wondered about Jeslyn's past — the entirety of it, not just the censored clippings she was getting now. She also wondered what her relationship was like now with her mother; when Jeslyn would finally circle around and explain what had happened between her and Coleman; what transpired, if anything, with Forbes and also...

"What ever happened to Willie?" The question had been in the back of her mind, then the tip of her tongue, now it was out in the open air for Jeslyn to either bat away or actually answer. To Katya's surprise and, if she were being honest, utter delight, Jeslyn chose to answer.

25

Justice was being served. Willie had been charged with trafficking, drug possession, drug distribution, embezzlement, and, and, and – a laundry list of offenses had come to light. They'd thrown the book at him during his sentencing, Jeslyn presumed, because he'd gotten off so many times before. The final tally was 23 counts and he was looking at almost as many years in prison for each one. Surprisingly, despite the dirt she'd provided him with, Coleman's name hadn't come up. Jeslyn's name hadn't come up either.

Yet.

The word crouched around her fears, finally rising to the height of its full potential while she slept when it morphed from 'yet' to 'now'. Willie was there then, or one of his goons; threatening her, then pointing to her in a crowded courtroom right before the bailiff led her away to some penitentiary cell – and these were the pleasant dreams. The nightmares included scenes that made her wake up screaming or crying or both and unable to go back to sleep to claim even the meager five hours of it she was now accustomed to.

This was life and it scared her half to death.

During the day her fears were more sedated. She feared the outcome of her business, she feared being alone, she feared her future; but mostly she feared her weaknesses and what they would cause her to become or do. Power over them sounded nice, but didn't seem like something she could achieve. It seemed, instead, like some unicorn that people talked about, a beautiful myth that was wonderful in theory but everyone knew was really just a fantasy. Power over her weaknesses would be like having her own personal unicorn; the likelihood of which seemed just as probable.

Jeslyn knew she'd dodged a bullet with Willie's incarceration and karma seemed to be onto that fact as well. Something, then, had to be done in order to realign the scales of justice.

Her mother's name lighting up the screen of her phone didn't fill her with as much dread since she'd started seeing Dr. Parker. There still hadn't been a complete one hundred and eighty degree change, but her mother's dial had shifted somewhat so that frequent interactions were more tolerable.

"Hey there." Jeslyn answered the call only slightly distracted by an email from one of her clients asking her thoughts on their company venturing into pay-per-click advertising – an opinion she'd already weighed in on the last time they'd brought it up.

"Jeslyn." Her mother's voice sounded quiet but urgent.

"Yes?" She knew better than to settle on a reaction until she was fully aware of the situation.

"I need you to come to the house, please."

"What's going on?" The issue could be a spider on the wall or an armed intruder; with her mother it was hard to tell.

"I just need you to come to the house."

Jeslyn locked a deep sigh behind her lips and stopped herself from demanding that her mother tell her what the urgent visit was about before she even considered going over there. Mild irritation crept over her before meeting up with the apprehension in her head, where the feelings joined together, grasped hands and plunged into the pit of her stomach. Instead of dying there and disappearing, as Jeslyn would have liked them to do, they became ghosts of feelings, haunting her insides as she drove to her mother's house.

This didn't sound like an arachnid problem.

Jeslyn exited her car and walked up the short walkway to the front door and stopped to listen, straining to hear anything that would reveal the surprise before it was sprung on her, but there was nothing. She tried telling herself it was probably nothing, that her mother often over exaggerated things and that this would be no different.

Except, those damnable ghosts began wailing louder and haunting more fiercely inside of her as she raised her hand to knock on the door, chasing away the comfort she was attempting to provide herself. As the door swung open, giving her a glimpse of a person who was definitely not her mother, even the ghost emotions fled; because something bigger consumed her. And that something was panic.

*   *   *

His funeral had been more than a decade ago, so to see him standing there in the flesh was at first a shock, then completely alarming. Even though the funeral had only been in her head, and his death had been based one hundred percent on assumption and zero percent on concrete knowledge, and it should have stood to reason that there was a chance he'd show up again, someday – a chance Jeslyn had always counted as slim to none, figuring slim had left town, never to return again – her breath still stopped short.

"Well, if it isn't J.J.," he sneered. They were feet away from each other but his breath hit her hard, a smell like something putrid had died on his tongue.

"That's not my name." She wouldn't cower. A second passed, then two. Jeslyn didn't move for either one of them. He stumbled away from the door and back into the darkness of her mother's house. She followed several steps behind him.

"Mom?" She tried to keep her voice even but wasn't sure she'd succeeded.

"I'm in here." Her mother didn't sound hurt, bound or gagged, but Jeslyn had to see her, had to see for herself that the awful visions dancing in her head were not real. She had to see that he hadn't so much as breathed his foul breath on her.

Her mother was sitting at the dining room table safe, alive and untouched. As she crossed the distance to stand near her, a glint of light caught her eye. It had bounced off of a chef's knife that sat alone on the kitchen counter. She tried to read from her mother's body language what was going on but got nothing other than a look of worry written across her face as she stared at Jeslyn's half brother.

He was standing near the living room not facing them. Jeslyn calculated the time it would take to get from where she was to the knife if it came to it. Another calculation was done to figure out what she would do with the knife if it came to that, too.

He wasn't posing a threat, currently. He was, however, posing as the perfect 'after' picture in a before and after example of what drugs and alcohol could do to a person. Jeslyn couldn't tell what had hold of him now. He looked as if he hadn't slept in days, probably because he hadn't; and he smelled as if he hadn't showered in weeks, which was also probably true. His disoriented eyes rolled around in his head, then tripped over walls and chairs, then back to rolling. All of this kept his body swaying unsteadily on his feet.

Watching him that way shooed away the fear and gave ire a perfect-sized hole to fill. She was pissed that he'd found his way back into her life. From the looks of it he'd found her by way of her mother, who was ultimately responsible for his existence in the first place. There would have never been an opportune time for him to resurface, but now seemed like the most inopportune time of all. A drug binge had played Copperfield to his disappearing act ten years ago, leaving everyone but Jeslyn to wonder if he was alive or dead. Jeslyn had chosen dead and moved on with her life, but it appeared she'd chosen wrong. Now, here he was, ten years later, his body inclining from one side to the other, drunkenly, in her mother's living room.

What he wanted, where he'd been and why he was back were all questions without answers. Jeslyn tried to change that.

"So, Anthony, what brings you around?" The initial approach was to talk to him civilly, as if he wasn't a deranged basket case who'd materialized out of nowhere.

"Who wants to know?" He never looked at her, just threw the question at her with more aggression than she was comfortable with.

"I'm asking."

"And who are you?" Eye roll, eye wander, sway.

"Jeslyn."

Jeslyn who?" Here he turned to her with another of those leering grins that exposed a few yellow teeth and a few dark spaces where teeth used to be.

"Look, Anthony, you came here. I'm just wondering why."

"Did *they* send you?" Stagger.

"Did *who* send me?"

"You know who!" His yell did not echo, it boomed like a solitary explosion, making her mother jump unexpectedly. The chef's knife seemed to stand up and dance for attention. So far, it seemed Anthony hadn't developed an interest in it, although Jeslyn did wonder why it was out and who had placed it there.

Logical conversation with him was getting her nowhere. She turned to her mother hoping to fare better there.

"Why is he here?"

Her mother lifted her hands, palms up, as if she expected someone to place a serving dish in them and gently shrugged both shoulders. In other words, which were no words at all, she had no idea.

"Tell me what happened." Jeslyn spoke to her mother as if Anthony, who had now plopped himself down on the couch and was biting primitively at his thumbnail, wasn't in the room.

"He just showed up. He was at the door and when I opened it he walked inside, shut all the windows and asked where dad was. I told him dad...wasn't here." She cut her eyes over to Anthony who was still engrossed in ingesting nail. "After that, he started pacing, picking things up and holding them to his ear, and then he told me to get J.J. 'Just get J.J.,' he kept saying."

Jeslyn's jaw clenched at the name. "And how did the kitchen counter get...dirty?" The only thing on the kitchen counter was the knife.

"I was getting ready to chop up an onion right before the doorbell rang and I set it down there before I went to answer it."

"That's convenient." Jeslyn sighed in exasperation and cracked her neck.

Her half brother now had his head propped in his hands, elbows on his knees and was rocking back and forth as if he were trying to rock himself to sleep.

"Anthony!" Her sharp tone caused him to jerk his head up, eyes moving frantically from side to side. "What are you doing here?" Jeslyn wanted to get as much information out of him as possible and then get him on his way; however, if she was only allowed one of the two, getting him on his way would take precedence.

"Shhh." He raised a finger to his chapped lips and cocked his head to the side. "Do you hear that?"

Silence.

"Wait! There it is again." He jumped up and walked over to the nearest window and peeped around the side of its curtain. Jeslyn took this opportunity to grab the knife off of the counter. She held it behind her back until she could find a safer place in the kitchen to bury it, unless Anthony's actions called for it to be buried in an entirely different place. It was a thought that chilled her blood.

She and her mother were mutes as Anthony cruised from window to window tearing shutters open and curtains back to peer crazily out of the exposed window panes. Every so often, he would spit out a shushing noise or ask them if they heard something that wasn't there to hear. This went on for about three minutes, which was one hundred and eighty seconds too long for Jeslyn, until her mother started to speak.

"Anthony, why don't you come back and sit down." Jeslyn glared at her. Of all the things she could offer, she gave him an invitation to make himself at home. The woman's common sense seemed to have flown out the door when she opened it for her son, and now she had dragged Jeslyn into their drama. Anthony continued his aberrant surveillance while Jeslyn ticked off the available options.

Talking to him like a sane person was useless; he was too far gone on either a drug-induced spin-out or a permanent malfunction of his brain. She could call for professional help, but he might freak out if they showed up to collect him. That kind of ruckus was one she could live without. Perhaps it was best to fight crazy with crazy. The fact that he'd shown up here asking for her father and then her – using a name she did not ever want uttered again – was unsettling. When and where else would he pop up and what kind of damage would he leave in his wake? Loose cannons needed to be locked down and Anthony was most assuredly a loose cannon.

"Anthony, you can't be here." Her words went without a response. "They're coming. They know you're here and they're coming."

That did it.

He was across the room and standing in front of her in seconds. Her hand gripped the blade of the knife tightly as she measured Anthony up. He was taller than her by a head, but she guessed his weight to be at no more than a buck fifty if that. There were guys she'd rolled around with in the cage that were that weight if not more. Plus, she knew submission moves that would hold him while her mother called for help; if her mother could keep her wits about her long enough to call for help. She would not have to use a knife on her brother. She would not. She could not. It was already decided that she didn't have it in her. She would do just about anything else, though. A defense scenario played out in her head in preparation:

Start with a debilitating knee to the groin. When he sunk to grasp the wounded area, a chop to the throat. Then, if necessary, finish it off with a guillotine, triangle or rear naked choke until he either passed out or was otherwise subdued.

That was the plan, because he was standing much too close and his dilated pupils gave away his absence of lucidity, meaning he was capable of anything outside of his right mind.

"Are you one of them?" Quiet rage.

"How dare you ask me that!" Jeslyn yelled hoping to scare him, like yelling at a lone wild coyote. "Of course not. Are you crazy?" Perhaps that could have been phrased differently. "I'm your sister, Anthony. I'm like you (*I'm so not like you*). I'm trying to keep you safe and you're asking if I'm one of them? Fine, stay here then. Sit down like mom said and wait for them to come for you." She stared him down, holding her breath as she did because the smell of him was sickening.

"How...how do you know?" He was breaking. His hands, that had moments ago been balled into fists, relaxed.

"I had dad install a system to track them." Jeslyn backed up into the living room, never taking her eyes off of him. She picked up the TV remote and then walked it back over to where he stood looking confused. "You've got to be smarter than they are, Anthony." He looked at the remote like it was something he'd seen before, but was having a hard time remembering what it was. "You can't come back here. They know your face. They'll be looking for you here." And because the second he was out the door she planned on calling the appropriate authorities to pick him up and cart him away to some type of institution, she added, "I can send some people to help you, they'll take you somewhere safe."

He seemed to consider this. "How will I know if it's your friends or if it's them?"

Say something, anything. Jeslyn's mind searched for an explanation. "They…them…they drive green and purple cars now. My friends are in regular looking cars." Did he know a regular car from a spaceship? Probably not.

"What am I supposed to do now?" He looked as if he might start crying.

"I'm going to go make a call but I need you to sit on the floor," she could not stomach the thought of him stinking up the furniture anymore than he already had, "right over there." Jeslyn pointed to a spot against the wall by the front door. "It's a blind spot, they can't see you if you sit right there. After I make my call, I'll tell you where you need to go, OK?"

Anthony nodded his head vigorously and all but sprinted to the spot on the floor Jeslyn had designated as safe. As she watched his emaciated body move away from her, took inventory of the scabs on his arms, the extreme slackness in the pants he wore and the grunge that clung to every square inch of him, she felt her insides clench. He wasn't healthy, she knew that, and he needed help, she knew that, too. But for a split second she saw him as he'd been when he was a little boy – painfully shy with bright, round, chocolate eyes that matched his round cheeks. He hadn't been a chubby kid, just thick. One would never have guessed that from seeing him now.

Jeslyn walked to the kitchen to ditch the knife somewhere out of harm's way and grab her mother's cordless phone. She ignored the woman's silent stream of tears and pound-puppy sad face. Strength was what she needed now, not useless tears over a situation that she had, in some ways, helped create. Where were those tears when –

It was not the time or the place to concentrate on the past. She needed to focus on this situation that required her immediate and undivided attention. Anthony was still in the corner, back to biting on his thumbnail, and her mother was incapacitated by too-little-too-late grief. Jeslyn would once again have to be the one to step up to the plate and take care of a family crisis. Playing the part of chief for a forever-impaired tribe was old hat. She wanted off this familial island of misfits.

Repeating herself to the police dispatcher – she had to speak quietly to avoid Anthony overhearing her words, but had to keep him in sight to avoid panicking about what he may or may not be doing while she was on the phone – only increased her aggravation. She gave a detailed description of him and where they would (hopefully) find him. His behavior was explained, her assumptions for his behavior given and a request to have him committed made. The dispatcher explained that what happened with him after he was apprehended would be up to the authorities, but Jeslyn was more than welcome to file a formal report which would give her the ability to follow up on it.

Bureaucracy.

After the call, squatting down in front of Anthony, Jeslyn explained to him exactly what he needed to do.

"My friends are going to take you someplace safe." She had no idea where they were taking him. "They won't hurt you." They would shoot to kill for all she knew. "But you have to do exactly as my friends say." She was careful to avoid using the words 'them' or 'they'.

Anthony nodded as he continued ripping into his thumbnail to the point Jeslyn was afraid it would begin bleeding. She got him to stand up and, after cracking the front door and peering like she was checking to ensure the coast was clear, she opened it wide and told Anthony exactly where to go.

"Do you remember the park up the street, the one with that huge tree in the center of it?"

A nod.

"I need you to go there and stand right by that tree. Don't move until my friends get there, do you understand?"

Another nod. Then she was flattened briefly in the stench of his embrace before he released her and half jogged, half shuffled out the door in the direction of the park. Jeslyn watched him make his way up the street until he was only an inch tall, then he was gone and she went back inside the house.

"Do you think he'll be alright?" Her mother's question caused her to flush with livid heat.

"How would I possibly know that?" She was showing only a small percentage of the bad-tempered indignation she felt and was completely aware of it. But sometimes her mother and all of her staged or actual inabilities – whether it be the inability to be a good parent, to be responsible or to act when a situation demanded it – were more than she could handle.

Her gruff response resulted in more silent tears.

Jeslyn would let her work it out with Dr. Parker. No one was paying her to sort through her mother's issues.

Twenty minutes later, after waiting to see if Anthony would return, she left her mother's house and made a detour past the park in time to see him being escorted into a police car. He seemed calm and everything appeared to be under control. Once they got him situated, she pulled over and got out of her car.

"Jeslyn Kennedy, the one who made the call."

The cop gave a clipped introduction, asked for some identification, then provided a short briefing.

"We didn't find any weapons on the suspect, but it appears he's under the influence of some kind. Now, you're saying he threatened you and your mother with a knife?"

Jeslyn swallowed the knot in her throat. Her brother hadn't had anything to do with the knife, according to her mother's account, but there had been the possibility the cops wouldn't have gotten him off the streets and possibly to the help he needed if she'd just reported bizarre behavior instead of a threat.

"He brandished the knife."

"Did he threaten you with it?"

"He had a knife, he was waving it around and talking crazy. Was I scared? Sure. It's a deranged person with a knife. It wasn't the most comforting situation I've ever been in, but it's not like he made a motion to attack us with the knife or anything."

"Did you fear for your safety?"

The cop was just doing his job but Jeslyn had an agenda and his line of questioning was interfering with it.

"Look, I haven't seen my brother in ten years -"

"So, you're related to the suspect then? Your brother you said?"

This was getting frustratingly complicated. They were simple enough questions, but her family's history made simple answers difficult. She would keep it basic and pray it would never come to her having to defend her answers in a court of law.

"Half brother. Like I said, I haven't even seen him in ten years. He showed up out of the blue at my mother's house and was asking for my father (*that's right, I said MY father; he has no claim to him*) who's been dead for a few years now. It was obvious he was drunk or high or both and he was talking crazy saying things like, 'they're out to get me', 'I can't trust them', so on and so forth."

"Who's 'they'?"

"I asked the same question. This is where he got riled up and...and took out the knife. He waved it around a bit, started yelling that I know exactly who 'they' are and accused me of being one of them."

"What happened next?" The cop was jotting her statement down in a tiny notebook that Jeslyn thought must be part of their standard issue, along with their uniform and badge, since every cop she had ever seen had one.

"I talked him down by telling him I could protect him from 'them'." This earned her a suspicious look from the officer. "I was basically going along with his delusions since rationality wasn't working." The suspicious look was gone. "I told him to sit in a corner while I made a call to some people who would take him to a safe place. After that, I called the police office, reported what happened and told them where they could find him. Then, I told Anthony to walk down here and wait under this tree for 'my friends'." Jeslyn put air quotes around the last two words.

"Got it." More note taking.

"He needs mental help. I mean, I'm no expert, but it doesn't appear he's going to go back to normal after he sobers up, if that's even the issue here."

"Well, based on your statement and his current behavior, I can do a 72-hour hold, but right now that's all I can promise."

"Understood."

Jeslyn watched Anthony tearing into his thumb as the police cruiser pulled away with him in the back. An overwhelming desire to wrap the abused appendage in a bandage plucked at her heartstrings, snapping one or two of them and causing a reverberation that reached all the way to her tear ducts. Her mother was no longer the only one shedding silent tears.

26

~Before~

  The 72-hour hold was on its last hour. Jeslyn had spoken with staffers and then managers until she finally worked her way up to someone in a higher level supervisory position.

  "I will pay. I don't want him in some governmental facility. I'll pay for something better."

  "He has to be transitioned then."

  "And that means...?"

  "We're going to have to place him in a mental health facility approved by the state and you'll have to work with them in order to transition him to a different facility."

  "Perfect." Her headache felt like it was turning into a migraine.

  "Is there anything else I can help you with?"

  As if you've been a help at all. "No, you've done enough." She silenced a smartass comment and reined in her anger. Perhaps therapy was working. Whether it was or not, she was looking forward to her Thursday counseling session.

  Her weekly meeting with Dr. Parker had been bumped up to a late morning time slot. Despite the stress she was experiencing because of it, she had no intention of sharing the reappearance of her brother with her mental health professional. If her mother brought the subject up during her one-on-one session, that was her business; Jeslyn had other items she was confident could eat up the hour. Like her growing sense of failure.

Putting Foxxy Red together had started off with a torrent of activity. After the foundation had been secured and the framework established, a lull had settled over everything. Then the lull had continued. Now, it seemed as if the lull was tattooed permanently in place, which would effectively categorize the whole thing as a failure.

"Welcome to life," Dr. Parker said with a smile.

"Excuse me?" Jeslyn wasn't sure if she'd heard her correctly.

"Jeslyn, we've discussed your deflated balloon syndrome, where you kill an idea before it gets going. What we also should probably address is your issue with perseverance. Running away anytime something gets difficult, or in this case stagnant, will always result in failure. Successful people persevere."

These were all things she knew. What she didn't know was how to persevere; she said as much to Dr. Parker.

"You don't know how or you don't want to?"

Nailed it.

Dr. Parker continued. "I have no doubt you know how to persevere. As I understand it, you've persevered through a number of life challenges. I feel your issue is more about working through the challenge and then beating yourself up if you fall short. Like those mental shift exercises we spoke about, perseverance is also something that requires you to push through the difficulty of not wanting to continue. With this business idea, before you launch it, while you're launching and especially after you get it going, there's going to be ups and downs. During the downs you're going to need to exercise patience, use your skills, work through problems, identify solutions – the same things you'd coach your clients to do if a marketing campaign wasn't working out."

Yeah, yeah.

The oh-so-wise therapist continued on in that same vein for the remainder of the session. Jeslyn left the office feeling like she'd paid one hundred and fifty dollars to be lectured. Everything Dr. Parker had told her was true, and that was what irked her even further. Who wanted to shell out that kind of money for information they already knew?

Not her.

Jeslyn tried to recognize her own foul mood and use her mental shift exercises as she'd been instructed to do.

Nothing doing.

Over six weeks had passed since she'd received so much as a text from Him, days had passed since she'd had the run in with her brother, more days had passed since she'd had any positive news worth retelling about her not-yet-started-up start up and years had passed since she'd been in a consistently stable frame of mind. Her life clock felt like a timekeeper of disappointments.

If she couldn't shake her funk with therapy, other techniques would have to be employed. And they didn't include spending another night on the couch, alone, with a bottle of wine and the same sappy RomCom that had been replaying over and over on her TV. She also didn't care to plaster on a tranquil smile and clink crystal wine glasses with the chic squad of girls she'd recently met or sit around talking shop with her old work contacts. She wanted to put on a highly suggestive outfit, charcoal line her eyes, blood red stain her lips, inebriate her mind, drench her body in sweat on a crowded dance floor and make bad decisions.

Going out alone with that kind of game plan wasn't an option. There was audacious and then there was plain foolish. The problem was she had very few acquaintances that were of the appropriate caliber to accompany her out for an evening such as the one she had planned. They couldn't be a lush; getting sloppy drunk usually resulted in her having to babysit. They couldn't be flaky; she didn't want to have to chase anyone down when it was time to call it a wrap or worry about getting abandoned by someone who could care less about her well being. And they had to love the dance floor; nothing was worse than a chick who sulked in the corner all night or couldn't keep up.

Fortunately, her accompaniment issue sorted itself out after she sent a group text to a few of the women she had begun socializing with on a regular basis, along with some friends of friends who had occasionally tagged along. Being that it was a Thursday, the constituents with the highest desire to see and be seen were the first responders – like cream rising to the top. Jeslyn skimmed their inquiries together and formed a small party of would be roof raisers. They decided to meet at one of the young women's house at nine thirty and make their way downtown as a group, courtesy of a transportation service designated driver.

Lately, the evening hours had been something she wished would never come. Nighttime meant the solidification of her loneliness and defenselessness against her nightmares. This night was different; this night, the evening hours couldn't come fast enough, making it seem as though the day was deliberately trudging along at an excruciatingly slow pace.

Seconds, minutes and finally enough hours crawled by to mark the nine o'clock hour. Jeslyn slid her scantily clad, highly bronzed, sweet smelling body into her car and made her way to the prearranged meeting location. From there, a black town car ushered four squealing ladies, plus one coolly composed Jeslyn to the hub of the club scene in downtown San Diego.

Since she'd arranged the outing, she got to call the shots. The first was a round of kamikazes, followed by a trip down a flight of stairs to a below street level club dance floor and the start of a blur of activity. The events that played out in the next six hours could only be recalled in scenes.

Scene one: The 808 thrummed through the floor. It gave a steady rhythm to Jeslyn's feet and up through her thighs, while the high hat worked her hips, consonant chords possessed her midsection and the lyrics guided her arms.

She was music.

From behind, a hand wound around her waist and a body moved against her but there was no synergy. She turned to face her intrusive dance partner and kindly decline his advances. One of the girls handed her her second (or was it third?) shot of the night – straight tequila. Two gulps, one suck of a lime, half an eye squint and it was gone, from her mouth to her head. Then she threw away the map to the pulsating beat and got lost in it.

Scene two: His presence hit her just before her eyes found his face. His sui generis fragrance was a semi-musky patchouli, semi-sweet persimmon and jasmine bouquet mixed with warm skin. Model sensation, Rob Evans, had been cloned and suavely danced his way over to her in a tight-fit, white ribbed tank and loose-fit dark denim jeans. A T-shirt, damp from sweat, hung from his back pocket and a sultry smirk hung from the side of his mouth. He had skin that looked to have been fashioned from mocha-colored silk and hypnotic hazel eyes shaped like horizontal apostrophes. Those same eyes absorbed her movements appreciatively. His hips began to move in time with hers then joined hers in a locked grind. Strong fingers sliding delicately down her arms, encircling her wrists and bringing them up to rest on brawny shoulders tested the waters. Jeslyn stroked the back of his neck with one hand letting him know the waters were warm. He palmed her back, pressing her tighter against his rock hard physique, and took the lead. His body became the rhythm that she moved in sync to while the DJ mixed dance anthems from some hidden grotto near the back of the club.

Scene three: Evans' twin hadn't left her side (back or front) since they first discovered each other. Jeslyn's friends danced around them, then near them, then left them to their own devices at random points throughout the night and the first hour of the next morning. Two more drinks, a pink gin and an apple martini – neither being something she would have ordered for herself – found their way into her system before she called it quits. Last calls weren't her thing.

Jeslyn laced her fingers with her selection for the evening and pulled her purchase behind her as she rounded up the four women she'd started the evening with.

The women admired Chad. That was his name – a fact Jeslyn learned when an introduction of them to the beautiful man, whose fingers remained interlinked with hers, had to be made. A vague interest in how the evening would end, on her part, and a brush off of his comrades as they announced their intentions to leave, on his part, were clear signs that the quintet of females who'd arrived at the club together was being whittled to a quartet.

Scene four: Blaming it on the alcohol would have been a sorry extenuation for the actions that followed. A healthy buzz was sanding away at her reticence and keeping thoughts of Him, her mother, her brother, Coleman, Willie, her past and her cares at a safe distance. The only thing on her mind now was Chad.

Chad drove a black Range Rover; Jeslyn knew this because she'd been inside of it inhaling his signature scent. Chad lived in a posh high rise near San Diego's Petco Park; Jeslyn knew this because he'd playfully nipped at her neck with his teeth as he guided her through his front door. Chad's couch was soft, bomber jacket leather; Jeslyn knew this because she had been sprawled across it as Chad positioned himself over her, resting his elbows on the cushions at her sides and his mouth on hers. Jeslyn also knew Chad had a mole on his back, removing his shirt had revealed that. His kisses could melt platinum, she was liquefied by them. And she wasn't the first girl he'd made out with, his adroitness in that department merited nothing short of an award.

Breathlessly gathering her senses at some point during the groping, teasing, licking and squeezing that had unraveled it, Jeslyn let Chad know enough bases had been covered for the evening. In other words, he wouldn't be hitting a homerun with her. Want to wasn't the issue. It was all the shouldn'ts. This was explained to him as delicately as possible. But it was hard to convince a man you didn't intend to go all the way when you were lying half naked on his couch with your hand cradling his posterior, his hand on your breast, while he kissed you as if your lips were oxygen and he had emphysema. But Chad was a gentleman (thankfully) and slowed his pace. No thanks to her, Jeslyn's imbecilic gamble wouldn't be at the cost of her safety.

He led her to his room where his hands continued to explore safer areas of her body, his lips continued to join themselves to hers and his tongue continued the dance their bodies had been engaged in earlier. She draped herself across half of him, reveling in the silky smoothness of his skin, the heady smell and feel of him and the stimulation of his touch. She wasn't ignorant of his corporal needs, and graciously showed his hand the familiar route down his torso to his own desire, encouraging him to pleasure himself, while aiding the lustful endeavor with sensual kisses to his neck, nibbles on his earlobe and roaming fingertips.

Scene five: When he was fast asleep and had disentangled his body from hers, Jeslyn slipped out of Chad's bed, his house and his life. It was four in the morning. As the taxi drove her back to collect her car, and as she drove herself home from there, she was anxious over nothing. As was its purpose, the girl's-night-turned-girl-on-boy night had stamped out her worries, if only for a few hours. The women she'd hung out with got a response text that she was home, she was safe and she was appreciative of their company. Then she climbed in between the invitingly cool sheets of her own bed and spent the next five and a half hours in darkness.

*   *   *

His scent had changed, but she could feel Him, at least where his mouth and hands had been on her skin. A sleepy little smile danced over her face and she inclined her head droopily to his side of the bed. Slowly, her eyes peeled

305

open only to reveal she was alone. As she went about her daily routine, she tried not to let that revelation affect her, immediately going through her mantra about who he was (no one) and what he should mean to her (nothing). But something had already gotten under her skin. It was back to the fight of keeping her thoughts centered when all they wanted to do was drift and completely neglect the mounting list of to-dos.

Nearly half a dozen more calls were made to find out what would be done with her brother. Then there were calls to her mother about those calls, calls to clients, emails to clients, drafts to prepare, calls to vendors, emails to vendors – an entire day of busy work but very little productivity, it seemed.

Without warning or permission, Friday evening materialized and, again, the thought of spending it alone made her want to rip her hair out. So, at around the eight o'clock hour she showered and suited up in a classic, but eye-catching little black dress and black heels; slicked her hair back into a modish chignon; smoke-shadowed her eyes; lightly glossed her lips and headed out.

He had made a stain on her that she intended to blot out. She was dealing with her brother, her business and a new business undertaking; and while the list wasn't long, each task had about ten to fifty additional items attached to it that needed her attention. He would not be another thing, another bulleted item on the list that she wanted to place in a magazine clip and fire into her temple, if nothing other than because of how weak and stupid he made her feel. He was just some guy, and after tonight he would be nothing more than a Gotye song title.

She was waiting for someone, or at least that's what she planned to say when (if?) she was approached. This was decided as she walked through the entrance of the ritzy downtown San Diego lounge and upstairs to its rooftop bar. There were three locations she'd mapped out for her hunt, but she was hoping it wouldn't take that long to find her

306

anesthetic for the evening. Sidling up to the bar, she ordered a glass of wine and examined the potential prey. It was still fairly early. Balding, overweight men, who had to return home to wives or television sets or both, stood uselessly in groups of one's, two's and three's around the area.

Slim pickings.

After an hour of pretending to be completely engrossed in her phone, sipping her Chardonnay and explaining to men who were old enough to be her father that, no, she did not want them to buy her another drink and, sorry, she was seeing someone, she finally left location one and headed to the next destination a few blocks up the street. Action outside had picked up and fresher meat dipped in and out of club and restaurant doors.

Sitting at her second upscale bar of the evening with a Cosmopolitan in one hand and boredom in the other, she felt dozens of eyes on her. Without being obvious, she surveyed the dimly lit landscape. A lot of no-way-in-hell's raised an eyebrow, offered a smile or shamelessly gawked at her in hopes her duck, duck glances would mark them as goose so their chase could begin.

"I'll have a rum and coke." The baritone voice behind her, along with the drink order, was instantly familiar. Her spine stiffened. After a few seconds he spoke again. "You gonna sit there all night ignoring me?" He leaned in closer to her.

"I didn't see you." Jeslyn slowly turned in her chair to face him.

"Well, I certainly saw you." He looked her up and down, nodding his head in approval. "So, what's a pretty little girl like you doing out all alone on a night like this?"

She ignored the crux of his question. "What's 'a night like this?'"

"A Friday night, I don't know."

"Just having a cosmo." She raised her martini glass as proof.

"Jeslyn Kennedy, out on a Friday night, just having a cosmo by herself? I don't buy it." The bartender slid his rum and coke across the bar top.

"I'm sorry to disappoint." She took a sip and looked off as he plunked a twenty dollar bill down and told the man behind the counter to keep the change. In a place like this, there wasn't much change to keep seeing as how the drinks were outrageously priced.

"You never disappoint."

"Never?" She twisted her head suddenly, challenging him to answer truthfully.

"Maybe once or twice." He grit his teeth, pulling his lips back into an almost snarl after sampling his drink.

"That sounds about right." She dropped eye contact, asking him the next question while gazing at the cranberry colored liqueur in her glass. "So, Officer Kevin Luby, what brings you down here on a night like this?"

"Oh, you know me, just out trying to pick up chicks. I'm trying to get this one girl off my mind by using a dozen others." His admission caused her to grip the base of her martini glass a little tighter.

"If that one girl doesn't realize how great you are, she isn't worth your time." Jeslyn stared straight ahead.

"She's worth every bit of my time." Kevin inched in front of her, forcing her to either stare at his chest, which now blocked her view, or crane her neck upwards to see the sincerity in his words. She chose to focus on the buttons keeping his shirt closed.

His arm lifted with a half full tumbler and lowered a short time later with only remnants of rum and coke sliding over the ice cubes. "We're leaving."

At first she thought he was referring to whomever he'd come with and an unexpected stab of discouragement hit her. "Well, it was good seeing you, as always." Her lips curled into a half smile but her eyes remained fixed on his shirt buttons.

"Hey," he beckoned to her gaze. The movement of her head seemed to awaken the effects from the one glass of wine and three quarters of her martini. She looked up at him lazily. "I meant me and you." He held out his hand, a brave move considering all the rejection she'd given him over the years. She decided he'd received enough of it and slid her hand into his, letting him lead her outside. "Where's your car?"

"I took a cab," she said.

"Perfect."

They walked a few blocks in silence with him holding fast to her hand, as if he feared she'd snatch it away and bolt. He led her to an underground parking garage where his meticulously restored, 1970 Shelby mustang sat waiting. The shiny black muscle car looked as if it had recently been waxed and two thick red racing stripes stood out like twin tattoos on the hood, top and down the back.

It was her second stint as passenger in a man's car in under twenty four hours. This time, though, it wasn't a stranger sitting next to her in the driver's seat, and this time she wasn't too far gone under the influence of anything, other than a desire to not think of Him, to make better choices. This time, when he led her into his house – a house that looked exactly like the type of place where a bachelor cop would live, simple and older – she knew her way around, knew the smells and the layout of each room. She was familiar with the paintings on the wall, the fact that the downstairs bathroom door had no lock, that the third step leading upstairs creaked and the lamp in the guest room, a vintage Tiffany he thought looked too girly, was given to him by his grandmother.

She let him kiss her, a few tender kisses that held more meaning for him than it did for her, and she let him hold her, but that was as far as things went. He was being careful, showing her that it was alright to let him in. Even though she had no intention of doing so, she let him go through the motions of wooing something that belonged to no one.

They talked for a few hours, their faces nearly touching in the moonlit brightness of his bed, while he ran his hand up and down the length of her upper body. When she started to doze off, he kissed her forehead and pulled her close, wrapping her into him like a human cocoon. However, she was sure he didn't want her to become a butterfly that would flutter away once her metamorphosis was complete. He was perfectly content holding this incomplete caterpillar of a woman who had somehow wormed her way into his affections. And while he never said anything outright, Jeslyn knew he was over that same bright, full moon that she was spending the night in his bed. She also knew that his elation would have quickly turned sour if he knew that as she snuggled into his chest and her breathing evened, she was finding comfort by imagining the arms that held her and the bed she was lying in belonged to someone else.

27

~Before~

       Kevin took her out to dinner, to the movies, to the beach, to sporting events and even wine tasting. He helped her with her brother – his transition from police station, to rehab, to long term behavioral health facility – and one day, for no reason at all, he sent her a fresh bouquet of fruit, remembering her dislike for cut flowers. He was kind and attentive, doting and affectionate; a man intent on establishing a relationship with a woman.

       It was just that he had the wrong woman.

       Maybe she was the arrogant, foolish type who only wanted what she couldn't have. Maybe she simply wasn't that into him. Maybe she just had too much going on right then. Whatever the hang up, Jeslyn already felt smothered by Kevin's sudden attention. He wasn't overly needy or clingy, she was just under-available.

       When Dr. Parker initially asked her if she had anything she wanted to talk about, she said there was nothing in particular. So, they started the Thursday session off with a discussion about work. Some people had safe words, Jeslyn had entire safe topics. She talked about how work was going, what challenges or obstacles had come up in the past week, where was she mentally with those upsets; and on and on with similar questions. It was when Jeslyn asked her therapist to repeat herself for the fourth time in a row that Dr. Parker removed her glasses, set her notepad on her lap and asked again if there was anything specific she wanted to address.

Jeslyn knew this is what she was here for, yet it was an uncomfortably suffocating experience to have to bring up anything personal at all.

"I'm kind of seeing someone."

Dr. Parker shifted in her chair; it was obvious this isn't what she'd expected Jeslyn to say. She was probably looking to hear how her brother had shown up on her mother's doorstep or threatened to kill himself at the police station after the cops had taken him in. Maybe she was even looking for Jeslyn to confess that she was overburdened, but none of those subjects were broached.

"Go on."

"I'm not in a relationship or anything," she felt the need to say. "He's someone I've known for a long time and we've been hanging out lately."

"OK."

"I'm not sure he belongs…in my life, I mean, but I do like him as a buffer for my thoughts. So, I guess there's a bit of guilt," here she felt she used the word 'guilt' appropriately, "because it's like I'm using him."

"It's *like* you're using him?"

"I am using him."

"In what way?"

The question caused her to think of Him but he was something she absolutely would not discuss.

"For his company. He's a distraction for things I'd rather not...deal with or think about." *Please don't ask what things, please don't ask what things, please don't ask what things...*

"I'm assuming you have not discussed your feelings with him?"

Jeslyn felt as if an umpire had just yelled out that she was safe. "No. I don't really want to get into that with him. Our history should be enough of an explanation."

"What do you mean by that?"

312

"He's tried to get me to agree to a relationship with him before, several times before actually. And it's never worked out in his favor."

"So, you feel he should get the hint, so to speak, and not expect anything seriously romantic with you?"

"Correct."

"Yet, his actions are showing that he's doing the exact opposite of that."

"Correct."

"And who or what is the obstacle as it pertains to his ability to win your affection?"

Do not think about Him. "He's a nice guy, really kindhearted and everything; he's just not someone I want to have a serious relationship with. Plus, the nightmares are back, I'm trying to start a new business – I just have too much on my mind to be able to concentrate on a relationship." *With Kevin.*

"I see." Dr. Parker slipped her glasses back on. "Jeslyn, here's what I want you to do. You mentioned a few weeks ago you were having nightmares. You've also stated that you feel a sense of failure with your business endeavors, you often feel angry or frustrated with little cause, you now feel guilty about this self-serving non-relationship with a young man that you've known for awhile. You're in negative thinking overload and your mind is full. That's not a healthy combination. Our dreams are often our subconscious' way of trying to make sense of our waking hours. Sometimes it's helpful to work through disturbing issues while awake, that way dreams will have less to do."

Sounded reasonable enough. "So, am I supposed to just sit quietly and think through my problems, or meditate, or what?"

"I want you to write yourself a letter."

Red flag.

"Write myself a letter?"

"Make it from the perspective of you writing to a very dear friend that you know better than you know

313

yourself. How would you comfort her? How would you address her concerns? What would you say to her about the problems she's going through? This letter is a way to not only get things out of your head, but to walk yourself through them from sort of a third party perspective. You don't have to give it to anyone or show it to anyone, it's a letter to you for you."

How could she explain to Dr. Parker that she didn't put anything personal in writing? Ever. "Rosalyn..."

"Yes?"

She couldn't.

"I think our time is up."

Dr. Parker looked at the clock that hung on the wall behind Jeslyn. "So it is."

Jeslyn stood to leave but Dr. Parker had more to say.

"Jeslyn, you should really cut yourself a bit more slack. I know you think you should do more and be more, but what you don't realize is your fears, shortcomings and thoughts aren't very different from most people."

She had no idea, poor thing.

"And I know you're probably thinking that I don't know how you feel, what you're thinking or what you've done, but the fact that you're here in my office, seeing me on your own accord, not in jail, not dead and not strung out somewhere tells me more than you think. All I'm trying to say is you're not as bad, or as lost, or as flawed, or as unsuccessful as you think you are. But if you keep telling yourself something long enough, it will become truth whether it is true or not."

The words tried to penetrate her and she tried to deflect them. It was too much truth for a Thursday or any day ending in 'y', for that matter.

"Thank you." It was a polite response if nothing else.

At a streetlight, as she made her way home, a question hit her. Why did she feel the need to punish herself? Why was it so important to strangle herself with a constant inner dialogue of how 'un' she was – unkind, unappreciative, unrelenting, unsuccessful, unbelievably flawed? An answer piped up from nowhere.

It's your leash. Loosen that guilt, loosen that chokehold of bitterness and self contempt that's holding you together and you'll get comfortable in your deviance. You'll succumb to your basest nature if you sit there telling yourself it's OK. Then you'll wind up that jailed, strung out, dead person Dr. Parker was talking about.

But what if that weren't true? What if, like Dr. Parker said, it was a lie that she'd told herself for long enough until it became truth whether or not it actually was true? This caused a crack in her concrete wall of thinking and she could feel the pressure of whatever was behind that wall struggling to push through. The fact that she had no idea what would come tumbling forth had her busting out the plaster of negative thinking to reseal the mental fissure.

Kevin hadn't contacted her all day. Instead of relief, she felt irritation knowing that he wanted to contact her, was probably chomping at the bit to reach out to her, but trying to prove he could give her space.

Unappreciative.

There it was again, the inner dialogue that played like a broken record in the back of her mind. How could she argue with it? She was being unappreciative. Kevin was a handsome, hard working man who had been there for her on dozens of occasions. She could remember a time when he'd left a blind date early to come check on her because she thought an intruder was trying to break into her house. It had turned out to be nothing more than a crow. But that hadn't stopped him from spending hours scouring the neighborhood, installing a dead bolt on her front door and offering to buy her a security system. He ended up dating the blind date girl for a few months, and other girls before and after that one, but he was always there for her when she needed him. At one point she had asked him why he liked her so much. He had just shrugged and asked her if he had to have a reason. Now she wished she would have told him yes, he needed to have a reason, because perhaps then he would've seen there was none.

Maybe he was the type of foolish guy that wanted what he couldn't have. Maybe he was just really into her. Maybe he liked a challenge and she seemed like the perfect one. Whatever the reason, he wanted to be with her. Regrettably for him, no matter how hard she tried, she couldn't bring herself to match his level of interest.

Is that what she was supposed to tackle in her letter to herself? Jeslyn sat on her couch with a stack of college ruled paper and a pencil in hand – this felt like a pencil and paper kind of task – contemplating her assignment. Did she begin with, 'Dear Self' or 'Dear Jeslyn'?

Dr. Parker had said to address herself as if she were addressing a dear friend. Jeslyn's eyes smarted with the memory of a dear friend she'd once had, a memory that hadn't come to mind in ages. If she were addressing her, her ex best friend who had felt more like family than friend, how would she begin?

The tip of the finely sharpened pencil scraped against the paper as the words began to flow:

Dear Friend,

I know it's been forever since we've spoken. I take full responsibility for that, I'm horrible at keeping touch. It's just that I find it easier to ignore things that might cause me more pain or personal discomfort than I already heap on myself. It's a shitty excuse, I realize. At any rate, I'm reaching out to you now because I know you're struggling and I really want to be there for you.

I know you don't feel good about yourself right now. You're concerned with all the lies you've told, the hearts you've broken, the mischief you've caused, the stealing, the backbiting, the backstabbing, the way you've used your body and your mind in dishonorable, sometimes even reprehensible ways – I get it. I also know that the fact those things bother you means there's hope. Hope that you're not as bad as you think, hope that you can change, hope that what you've done isn't as deplorable as you might have led yourself to believe.

I also want you to know that it's OK to let it go. You can't change it, whatever 'it' is. You can't go back in time and make different decisions; all you can do is make a different future. And while it would be nice to read this letter and instantly feel that hope and make those changes, it's not how life works. You're twenty-six years in the making. One letter, one day, one week, maybe even one year isn't going to undo twenty-six.

Rome wasn't built in a day. You're essentially looking to build a new Rome, both in yourself and with this new business. Just remember that this is real life, and in real life starting a multi-million dollar business venture is really hard and can be really frustrating. In real life, having a crazy mother and a dysfunctional brother is hurtful and scary and maddening and anger-inducing. In real life, having a father who you miss terribly and feel you still have things to say to and ask questions of, but can't because he's dead, is hard. In real life, not being able to have a normal relationship – one, because you don't know what one looks like and two, because you're torn between wanting it and not wanting it – is sometimes depressing and sometimes difficult and all the time confusing. And in real life, not knowing what's normal and natural and what's not is enough to make you crazy.

I know you're scared of going crazy (especially seeing how rampant it appears to be in your immediate family), of being a failure, of being alone, of being hurt...of just being. But right now all you need to be is patient. Be patient with you and people around you; they're not out to get you despite what you tell yourself.

I'm cringing as I write this last part, because it's so not like me, it's so terrifyingly open and unguarded, but I need you to know this: I love you. You're fearfully and wonderfully made (that's not me, that's actually a Psalm – go figure). It might take you forever to realize it, but I realize it now. Don't give up on yourself because there's so much in you that could make such a difference to someone and something else. You have the potential to change the world, even if it's just your own. And like the girls at Chic CEO say: You're pretty.

Love Always,
J.

As she looked back over the letter, Jeslyn found certain words smudged by the wet droplets that dripped from her chin. She didn't speak ill of the tears, chastising them for providing evidence of weakness or oversensitivity. No, she let herself cry, like she would a dear friend who had been touched by these words that were so hard to read, and even harder to accept.

She read the letter again, and then again, and still again, until certain parts were memorized and other parts stuck with her as she went about other activities.

Red Cello Marketing hummed along and when she had a break in her work, stopped to have a meal or finished for the day, she pulled the letter out and pored over the words. Her website for Foxxy Red was finished, her social media pages were built, her logos were designed, her apparel samples approved and signed off on, her press releases written, her e-blast ready for launch – everything was in place. As she surveyed this new beginning, reading her letter to herself while crossing items off of her to-do list, an email came in from Pakston & Associates.

They were the private investigation firm she'd hired awhile back to investigate her. In their search they'd turned up a few things, so she'd turned to BLAKBird, Inc., an almost secret society of a company, who could all but make you disappear online, in background searches and just about anywhere else except to people with enough clearance to find anything they damn well pleased. Once she'd received correspondence from BLAKBird that their work was complete, she'd gone back to Pakston for another sweep. According to this email, their latest P.I. run had turned up nothing.

Jeslyn had expected to feel security and an overwhelming sense of relief after receiving that news, but she didn't. Instead, as she placed her letter, now a bit worn from overuse, down on the cushion beside her, she began to think about why she felt the need to disappear in the first place. Aside from obvious reasons – the unprincipled actions of her past – what had hold of her so tightly that she would go to such great measures to cut herself free, which meant she'd be in bondage to something else?

Her earlier adumbrations, which had faintly revealed her need for peace, were now more pronounced. She realized that peace and stability really meant not being ruled by her emotions, which was her own personal form of bondage. Peace meant not needing to feel that rush, not needing to be desired in the jeopardous ways she needed to now. It meant freedom from judgment or the fear of being judged. It was the acceptance of herself and, just as importantly, the acceptance of others. It was peace from the continuous struggle to build an unrealistic alter image and the freedom to just be.

Jeslyn knew she wasn't the only person to feel this way. This was despite the fact that mentally she often insulated herself in delusional cellophane. She often wrapped her mind in the belief she was the only human being who had these specific insecurities; that even though there were other lesser insecurities common to most people, no one could possibly understand or be dealing with the same insurmountable struggles that she was.

It simply wasn't true.

And if it weren't true, and if there were others who were wrestling with such heavyweight burdens, others who also wished for a BLAKBird to fly in and snatch away their identities, then perhaps there was something she could do. Something meaningful.

Three full days were spent outlining the changes required to create an entirely different mission. Not having forgotten Chic CEO's words of wisdom about 'who knows you', Jeslyn fired off impeccably written, handsomely designed letters to a few contacts who worked at or with talent and entertainment agencies. She found appropriate forums where she posted online requests for people's personal (and anonymous if they chose) thoughts on what they felt beauty was, what it meant to love, to be loved, what did success mean, what did success look like and what were their biggest fears.

Three weeks were spent altering the website, setting up a blog, redesigning the e-blasts and social media calendar, reworking the press releases and most exciting of all, going over the literally hundreds of replies she received from her posts.

Another week was dedicated to compiling those responses and organizing them into a series of online mini books that she would write based on these amazing, inspiring, funny, heartwarming, saddening and very real testimonies.

The responses continued to flood her inbox. Mostly women, and a few guys, were eager to share their fears and thoughts on love, success, life and beauty. Some views were tinted with political or religious overtones, some were stained with the effects of past abuse or loss, some were sarcastic, some were humorous, but nearly all were impactful in their own way.

That very real, difficult-to-explain and impossible-to-physically-see void inside of her began to shrink. It had been a little over a week since she'd thought of Him, even though a little over four months had passed since she'd last walked out of his home, his arms and his life.

Working during the day and parsing together compendiums in the evening, which she titled *I.a.M.*, followed by the subject it would address, knocked her five hours of sleep to three or four some nights. *I.a.M. Beauty*, *I.a.M. Love* and *I.a.M. Success* were the first three of the series to be completed. Mixing together quotes, the gathered testimonies and her own words, she sent the booklets to a graphic designer for an aesthetic overhaul.

Curling around one of the body pillows in her bed, Jeslyn found that sleep was pulling at her invitingly. She slipped easily into it and transitioned from serene dream to serene dream until images, sights and sounds led her subconscious thoughts to a bridge in the middle of nowhere memorable where her father was waiting.

His face held a smile even though his lips were silent. As she stepped toward him he turned and took a few steps away looking over his shoulder as if to signal her to keep following him. She did. The bridge was a long stretch of wooden beams and a foggy haze on either side, preventing her from seeing much other than her father's beckoning smile and the next step in front of her.

They walked together like this, him just out of reach, until the arced bridge began its downward slope. Their walk was a bit easier and quicker now, as her feet ate up two beams of space with each step. Suddenly, they broke through the haze into a blindingly bright open area. Jeslyn could feel soft grass underneath her feet and the warm dewy atmosphere on her skin. A sweet fragrance was on the wind and she inhaled deeply trying to fill her lungs with it. Her father came nearer to her now, the same gentle smile pushing his cheeks closer to his kind eyes.

He brought his hands up in front of her, a small radio dangling from his fingertips.

"It's time." He turned a dial.

"Time for what d —" Before she could finish her question a melody began to play, softly at first, then louder. A slight tremor, like a tiny earthquake, shook her body. Another followed it. Her father's smile, along with the rest of him, began to fade out of sight.

"Daddy wait!" Jeslyn reached out her hands to touch him, to keep him with her but she couldn't grab hold to anything. The light tremors continued. The melody was a tune she remembered well. Why did she remember it so well? It was…it was —

Her cell phone.

Jeslyn's eyes groggily staggered open before her mind had a chance to fully come to. It was early morning and the blinding light from her dream shifted into the less blinding but still bright light of the daytime sun outside of her bedroom window; her only alarm clock for the past decade.

Jeslyn didn't check the phone to see who was calling, she just relaxed into the soft folds of her pillow and gave herself a moment to feel the aftershocks of tranquility rippling through her post-sleep. If she closed her eyes she could still catch her father's face and his smile. The image coaxed a slow smile from her that stayed with her as she prepared for the day.

Launch day.

All the planning and preparation had come to this, letting the entire world in on her little secret. It was a prospect that both thrilled and terrified her. And while 'the entire world' was a bit of a stretch when it came to describing the audience who would be interested in her venture, Jeslyn knew that she'd put her heart into this, hadn't given up and had at least seen it through to this point. For her, that felt huge. She would work on getting the world's attention in due time. Right now, she was content in telling a small percentage of the world what she'd done and inviting them to be a part of it.

Everything went live and was sent – websites, blogs, press releases and e-blasts. And then it was once again time to wait. Days after the launch, a few orders from the Foxxy Red e-commerce site had trickled in. One of her talent management contacts, who she had collaborated with when she worked at an ad agency, ordered a few items and even sent a rather uplifting email saying she loved the concept, especially the mini books. Jeslyn's website had a few hits, her blog had a little traffic, her social media sites had a few followers and her *I.a.M.* booklets had been downloaded by a handful of people out there in the Internet-verse. She didn't blow up overnight, in fact, all the stats put together weren't much, but it was a beginning and exciting to see.

This was life and it had a scrap of peace.

She would take it.

28

~**Before**~

Another Southern California summer had arrived and the tide was shifting. Not the beach tide, although that may have been the case, but the tide for Jeslyn's interests.

Like the change in wind that signaled to the Banks children's mystical caregiver that it was time to float off by way of umbrella to another family in need, Jeslyn's internal weathervane indicated a change was in the air. Only, she wasn't interested in seeking out anyone in need, especially someone in need of her. She was ready to float off to new solo adventures and uncharted entrepreneurial territories.

Kevin's demanding schedule, which had allowed her to put everything she had into Foxxy Red for weeks without accusations that she was using work as an excuse, had since slowed. He now had time. A lot of time. Too much time. Time that he wanted to spend with her.

Fourth of July found her and Kevin lounging in the sun on a balcony patio of a Mexican restaurant in Old Town San Diego watching the bustling activity of daytime celebration in full swing all around them. She had downed her second margarita of the afternoon and sat with a dopey grin on her face that was a direct byproduct of her light food, heavier top shelf tequila lunch. Her forearm rested on the bright yellow and cobalt blue tiles of the tabletop, her fingers dangling over the edge. Kevin had adjusted his chair to sit directly next to her, so that his fingers could nestle against and slightly on top of hers. People were everywhere – in the streets, bunched together in the restaurants and on sidewalks in this sectioned off area of town.

A man and a woman, presumably husband and wife, strolled hand in hand down the street just below them. A toddler was seated on the man's shoulders and another slightly older little girl skipped along beside the woman, holding on to her free hand.

"You and I would make gorgeous children." Kevin sighed in contentment as if he hadn't just pitched a block of cement into Jeslyn's stomach. His comment smeared her grin down into a half frown.

She said nothing.

"Don't you think? A pretty little girl that's your twin and a seriously handsome boy that's obviously my spitting image. I can see that." He spoke for himself only. "Can't you?"

"No." There was no sugar in sight to coat her answer with.

"No?"

"Nope." She prayed he would drop it.

"Why is that?" God must have been too busy or too unconcerned to answer her prayers.

"I just don't see kids." *With you.*

"At all? Ever?"

Jeslyn shrugged noncommittally.

"Hmmm," was all he said.

Jeslyn's shoulders relaxed thinking he was finished.

"Do you see you and me together?" He wasn't.

No. "I don't know. I don't think about it." *Because I know it's not going to happen.*

"So, when you think about us, what *do* you think about?"

The inevitable end. "Nothing."

Now he was sitting forward in his chair. "What do you mean nothing? You don't consider the future and what that looks like for us?"

She thought back to all the movies she'd seen and stories she'd heard where guys got grilled about relationship statuses and where-do-you-see-this-going inquiries from girlfriends or girls looking to hold that position. She sympathized with them.

"I guess I'm just focused on other things." Jeslyn was thankful for the sunglasses that hid a good part of her miffed face. She scouted the patio looking for the waitress. She was either going to need the check or another drink very soon at this rate.

"Well, now that we're focused on this, what are your thoughts?"

He did not let up and Jeslyn was nearing the end of her rope. "Kevin, can we not do this?" *Ever.*

"Do what? What am I doing? I'm asking my girlfriend if she sees a future with me. As an officer of the law, I didn't realize I was committing a crime."

Jeslyn turned her head to glare at him even though her glare was shielded. "Don't." It was all she could offer without speaking her mind; he didn't want to hear her thoughts aloud.

"Don't? Don't ask my girlfriend her thoughts about —"

"Stop calling me your girlfriend, Luby."

"Luby? It's Luby now, Kennedy." The volume of his voice had attracted the attention of a nearby table.

"I'm not doing this." She snatched two twenty dollar bills out of her purse and dropped them on the table as she stood up.

"Where the hell do you think you're going?" Kevin demanded.

"Home." And without further adieu, she walked down the staircase attached to the side of the patio and melted into the sea of people celebrating in the streets. Her phone began vibrating but she ignored it. Whether it was Kevin or not, she wasn't in the mood to have a conversation.

Taxis were lined up on the perimeter of the closed off streets, their presence a reminder that drinking and driving wasn't necessary. She hopped into one and lay across the back seat as she rattled off her address.

"You have too much fun for the July Fourth, yes?" The driver's gray teeth as he smiled into the rearview mirror disappeared when she closed her eyes.

"Yup, loads of fun." He chuckled softly completely missing the sarcasm in her voice.

Her phone vibrated again and she continued to ignore it. She needed the rest of her day and evening to be Kevin-free. She considered getting a hotel room in case he decided to show up on her doorstep.

Twenty-eight minutes later, when the cabbie had dropped her off, Jeslyn drug herself inside and reclined on her couch. The sun and drinks had zapped her energy and Kevin's topic of conversation near the end of lunch hadn't helped to boost it any. Her jaw stretched into a yawn as she pulled her cell phone out of her back pocket and checked her missed calls. The first thing she noticed was an abnormally high number displayed above her inbox icon indicating she had numerous unread emails. While it struck her as odd, she didn't consider it much past that initial thought as she clicked over to her missed call log.

There were two missed calls from Kevin and one from Christine of Chic CEO. Both had left voicemails. She ignored Kevin's.

"Hey there hot stuff, it's Christine. So, just wondering when you were planning on telling me that you're in with the Hollywood elite. Ha ha! But seriously, congratulations Jeslyn, we knew you'd make waves. Call me. I can't wait to hear all about it."

Jeslyn played the message again. If it weren't for the fact that Christine had used her name, she would've sworn the voicemail had been left in error. She had no idea what the Chic CEO founder was talking about. In with the Hollywood elite? Congratulations? Congratulations for what?

She didn't want to return the call until she figured out whatever it was that Christine apparently already knew, or thought she knew anyway. Perhaps starting with the over abundance of emails would give her a clue.

It only helped add to her confusion.

Three hundred and forty two notifications from her Foxxy Red shopping cart database sat in her inbox. As she scrolled through them another two came in. Jeslyn opened a few thinking something had failed with her captcha filter resulting in an influx of spam. Each notification she opened was a legit order.

Accustomed to tempering her excitement over potentially positive situations until she knew the emotion was truly called for, Jeslyn transitioned to her computer to login to the administrative dashboard of her site. The legitimacy was two for two.

What is going on?

It was an awesome thing, these three hundred and forty-five orders (another email had already come in), but the explanation for the sudden spike eluded her.

Jeslyn grabbed her phone, prepared to make a few calls to see if she could get to the bottom of it and saw a text from one of her old colleagues.

Great national coverage on Entertainment Update. Who does ur PR?

"I do," Jeslyn said out loud. She was vaguely familiar with the entertainment show that provided news on what was going on within celebrity circles. But what that had to do with her was still shrouded in mystery.

She searched the words 'Entertainment Update' and 'Foxxy Red', holding her breath as the first ten results that displayed across her screen linked the two search phrases together in online mentions and photos.

Apparently, some young actress (whose name brought with it little recognition for Jeslyn, but seemed to be extremely popular in the entertainment industry), had scored a Foxxy Red shirt and waistlet – the belt-like purses Jeslyn had created as accessory items for her brand. She had also been photographed wearing them. There were enlarged pop outs of the purse and the logo on the shirt with captions listing the Foxxy Red brand name, website and cost of the items.

Her talent agent contact who had ordered items from her must have gifted them to her celebrity client. It was the only logical explanation she could come up with. And the rest was just pure freaking luck.

Immediately, Jeslyn thanked her lucky stars, not only for this luck by way of a star, but also for the fact that she'd had enough foresight to use a fulfillment center that tracked, housed and drop shipped her inventory for her. It'd been an intelligent move – very intelligent, actually – because in the weeks that followed an explosion occurred.

Week one saw nearly one thousand unique orders, her web traffic increased by two hundred percent and her social media following quadrupled. Week two stats beat out week one's by over thirty percent and weeks three and four increased over the first two. Jeslyn had to drop two of her three Red Cello clients in that first month. She also needed help. There was entirely too much happening too quickly for her to continue as a one-woman band. However, the help she required had to be a unique individual that not only possessed the desired professional skills Jeslyn was in need of, but also someone Jeslyn could trust with her life – her entire life.

There was no one she knew who fit that bill and she doubted a resume would reveal the characteristics she was searching for. It would have to be a referral. Asking for that referral would also be tricky. Specificity would yield better results, obviously, but it also would require her to share more information than she was comfortable with.

Catch 22.

She figured the main contact she'd dealt with at Pakston & Associates knew more about her than anyone – that was anyone who was in a position to provide a credible employee referral. Whether or not he would or even could provide one was only something an inquiry to him could suss out. It was an unorthodox request, for sure; but with her options low and her need high she figured at worst he would tell her to go pound sand and at best he would give her a name.

Tracy McGillan.

A friend of a friend of a client of a CEO's one-time executive assistant, a woman whose previous employer may or may not have been a high-ranking government official, was interested in learning more about the position.. Tracy understood business, she understood privacy and she understood confidentiality. A few days after their first meeting, she understood when she would start her new job, where she would work from and what her duties would be. A few days after that shotgun intro, her duties suddenly increased.

"Hi, Tracy, it's Jeslyn."

"Good morning, Ms. Kennedy."

"Tracy, you can –" It was pointless. She'd already explained to the woman she could call her Jeslyn but the no nonsense new hire (only hire) never changed her greeting. "Tracy, I'm going to need you to handle something for me."

"Of course, Ms. Kennedy."

"There's a lot of calls coming in and I'd prefer you to be the point person for them."

"Alright."

"Not just the point person but the spokesperson…and only contact as well."

"Alright."

"You can provide the sound bites, the quotes and company info."

"And how would you like me to respond when the request is to hear from the company founder?" Tracy questioned.

"You can tell them I'm not available for comment at this time."

"Understood." She also took orders without argument. "Is there anything else, Ms. Kennedy?"

"No. Well..." Jeslyn thought about it. Expectations that went unsaid often went unmet. "My personal contact information isn't to be given out to anyone for any reason, neither are personal details about me. The focus should always be the business. I'm not interested in being placed under anyone's social microscope."

Jeslyn had come to realize she didn't need worldwide notice or appreciation; the success of her business would be appreciation enough. There was also no more interest in fraternizing with the elite. She was content to hold rank with that clique from a safe distance. All she wanted now was to be left alone.

"Understood," Tracy said.

That understanding worked well for a long time. Just not long enough.

29

~Before~

  Something had gone wrong. Horribly wrong. Not with the business. Foxxy Red was finally coming into its own. Nearly two years after her last day at DLMM, the day her quest began; and nearly two years of sweat, blood and tears (OK, maybe just tears) the business had cracked the million dollar mark, a couple of them, in fact. It was officially a multi-million dollar company. An empire.

  Jeslyn wasn't enjoying it at the moment, though. Through the grapevine she'd learned that a very intoxicated Matt Coleman had taken a nasty tumble down the stairs at his home. Jeslyn should have been celebrating, but she wasn't. Not because she was concerned about Coleman's condition, he could die and burn in hell for all she cared, but because of the details surrounding his little spill that were beginning to circulate. Those details would be all over the news soon and, very likely, her name with it.

  Investigators had already been to visit her. They asked her for a statement and had her look at a picture that had been found in Coleman's wallet. It was a picture of a young woman. A very beautiful young woman. A woman with café au lait skin, hair the color of strawberries plated in caramel with honey highlights, long lean legs and an enticing figure. She was posed provocatively on a bed, almond shaped eyes flirting with the camera – and maybe whoever was behind the camera, too.

Then they asked her about the letter. It had been found at his office in his desk drawer. Jeslyn didn't need to read the letter, she had it memorized. She had memorized all of the letters in that box, every single word of them. Then she'd memorized them again when she'd photocopied them. She'd left a copy of each one, along with the pictures and a few other mementos, on Coleman's doorstep; had watched him pick up the box and carry it in his house. Did the idiot actually put one of the pictures in his wallet and a letter in his desk? That didn't sound like the Matt Coleman she knew. The Coleman she knew would have incinerated every single scrap of paper in that box and the box itself. He was a high profile venture capitalist. Keeping evidence like that around for a man of his position was like a man of the cloth walking into church naked. He just wouldn't do it. Then again…

Coleman wasn't the only one she'd given photocopies to. Willie's file had been a condensed version of Coleman's box, a small sampling, just a smidgen of proof to show Willie what she'd done to keep Coleman from messing with him. But the letter from Coleman's desk and the picture found in his wallet hadn't been in Willie's file. Had they? They hadn't. She was sure of it.

She looked at the photo and told the investigators the truth. It wasn't her. Yes, it looked just like her, but it wasn't her. They'd have to reexamine the photo; she wasn't about to tell them who it was. Let them do their job and figure it out. After all, it's what they were getting paid to do.

'What about the letter?' they'd asked. They were referring to the letter that had started with 'Dear J.' Again, nothing to do with her. After all was said and done, it wasn't as if they'd flat out given her a certificate of innocence, more like they'd concluded there was not enough evidence to warrant charging her with anything.

Innocence. Evidence.

Something about Matt Coleman's fall down the stairs, along with whatever had been found in his system to make it appear he was inebriated, was beginning to look more and more like intent and less and less like an accident.

It didn't matter if the woman in the picture wasn't her or that the letter, the 'Dear J' letter, wasn't written to her. People were going to talk. And talking would lead to questions, which would lead to someone wanting answers. And if someone wanted answers badly enough, they'd find them. It also didn't matter that her company was doing well. The focus would be completely locked on Coleman.

Everything from the day she haughtily decided she'd pave a new path for herself, one lined with dollar signs and no plan, to the night she thoughtfully considered making something meaningful out of her idea, had contributed to her desire to pull back into the shadows and let her meaningful creation shine. And now, the light of that shining creation was about to be overshadowed by 'who's that girl in the Coleman scandal?' gossip.

At first she told herself she didn't care. Let the rumor mill churn. The work would speak for itself. Plus, the thought of sitting down with a reporter who would feign interest in Foxxy Red, how it got started and how it was going before shifting to the real reason for the interview – what do you know about Matt Coleman? – did not sit well with her. Anything she said, no matter how innocuous, would probably get sensationalized instead of directly re-relayed as she'd originally relayed it.

It was time for another change.

Just a few months shy of a year after beginning her incredible journey, Jeslyn had packed up her two-bedroom condo and moved. Now, almost another year later it was time to pack it up again. But this time she didn't move.

She disappeared.

30

Jeslyn folded her hands carefully on her lap and relaxed back into her chair as if the weight of the world had been lifted and she was finally able to slip into a state of repose.

"And that's how Foxxy Red was born." Her simple buttoned-up ending might have been comical if Katya hadn't been so mind blown.

"So that's...? So you didn't…?"

"It is. And no." Jeslyn answered the half-baked questions then waited for Katya to say something that was hopefully more coherent.

Katya glanced down at the voice recorder to make sure it was still rolling.

"So, Foxxy Red finally takes off and then you go into seclusion. What did you do all of that time? Why did you disappear?"

"What did I do all that time?" Jeslyn repeated the first part of Katya's double headed query. "Well, I spent some time trying to get myself together, to be honest with you. I figured there was a very likely chance of me screwing something up because of everything that was going on." She gazed off as if remembering something. "It's not like I became some weird hermit or anything." Here, Jeslyn eyed Katya delicately, as if to subtly alert her to the fact that she knew those thoughts had crossed her mind. "I just took myself out of any kind of light – lime, spot, you name it."

That hadn't really answered the question. Katya would try to get a firmer answer in a moment. Right now there were other more pressing questions. "And why did you disappear? Your business was thriving, still is, and from your own account, you had nothing to do with Coleman's accident. Wouldn't it have been less trouble to stick around, say a few words to that affect and go on about your business? It seems like dropping off the face of the earth stirred up more controversy, not less. Wouldn't you agree?"

Jeslyn stretched her hands high above her head as if she needed limber muscles in order to effectively answer the question. "The short answer? Pressure. I was…overwhelmed." She seemed hesitant to admit that. "I didn't feel like myself at first, either. I mean, calls were coming in from everywhere. People I hadn't associated with since forever and people I didn't know from Adam were all of a sudden looking for me and wanting to speak with me. It was like, one day I'm this regular person, living this regular life and then a few days later I'm the most interesting person of the hour. And you'd think it would be this amazing thing, that I'd take the opportunity to use all that attention to my advantage, right?" Katya nodded. "Well, it wasn't amazing and it didn't feel like an opportunity at all; it just felt like a shit ton of pressure. Maybe that was ninety percent my own fault. As you are now well aware, I have a knack for weaseling myself into people's lives and a penchant for not always doing things on the up and up. So, it felt like it was my turn; like that angry bitch, Karma, was up to her old tricks to show me just what it feels like. I wouldn't go so far as to say I was paranoid, but I will say I was…frequently skeptical."

"So, did you leave the country or hole up in some wooded cabin or something?" Katya asked.

This made Jeslyn laugh. "No. I didn't leave the country or hole up in some cabin. It wasn't like I shut the

335

world out. I still worked, still associated with the people I needed to. I also ignored the people I needed to as well."

She was being explicitly vague.

"Let me get this straight. A few months after Foxxy Red starts experiencing mild success you move from your condo, correct?"

"Yes."

"Why?"

"I wanted a change of scenery. Plus, I wanted an address that wasn't so well known. I wasn't interested in surprise visits."

"OK. Change of scenery; business starts picking up speed; another ten or eleven months or so go by; you're working, living, doing whatever it is you do and then the Coleman issue pops up and you...?"

"You're acting like I joined Al-Qaeda and went to live in a cave. There's less drama to it than you think. I wore a lot of hats and big sunglasses. I kept to myself, rarely went out, rarely socialized, kept unnecessary phone calls to a minimum. I don't know. Things like that, I guess."

"Who did you associate with while you were...?" Katya didn't seem to know how to properly define Jeslyn's out of the limelight phase.

"Incognito?" she offered.

"Ah, yes, 'cognito. I hear it's wonderful there this time of year," Katya joked.

"I'm sorry?" Jeslyn looked rightfully confused.

Apparently, her particular brand of humor wasn't for everyone and Katya was back to feeling out of place.

"Inside joke, sorry. Just ignore that." She mentally added another RM to the list for LeAnn. "OK then, yes, who did you associate with while you were incognito?" The 'OK then' had slipped out in her mostly on-again, very little off-again nervousness.

"Like I said, I worked, which meant I kept in touch with employees, vendors and contractors; I had a few friends that I spoke with regularly, even hung out with sometime; and my family."

"I see. And when you say family, are you speaking of your mom and your brother?"

"Is this for the article or for you?" Jeslyn arched a single brow, giving Katya that look only extremely sexy or extremely intimidating people could pull off without appearing ridiculous.

"I...it's," Katya stuttered, caught off guard. She was simply wrapping everything up. It was Jeslyn who had told an epic saga of a story. Now, she was going to harangue her for tying up all the loose ends of what had happened? Unbelievable.

"Inside joke, just ignore that." She let a smile pass over her lips.

She was back to joking, was she? Katya smiled good-naturedly as well and looked up at the ceiling while shaking her head softly. There was no way she'd ever be able to figure this woman out.

"In response to your question," she replied, letting the smile trickle away. "My mom and I are still in pretty much the same boat we've always been in. I'd say the waves are less rocky, though, and our interactions are definitely less dramatic. I've accepted that she isn't going to change and she's still coming to terms with the fact that I refuse to be sucked into her drama. As for my brother, he did well for a little bit; he actually stayed in the behavioral facility for quite a few months. There was even a point where he seemed to be close to normal. But then he said he wanted to leave and live a 'real life' instead of an institutionalized one – his description of it, not mine – so, he checked out. And when he did, he fell off the face of the earth again. That's probably a bad sign. Who knows, he'll probably pop up again at some point. Or he won't." She seemed unaffected by these statements.

"Thank you...for that." Katya couldn't make herself look Jeslyn in the eye.

"For what?"

"You may have been joking, but you're right, there was no need for me to pry into that area of your life."

"Katya?"

"Yes."

"Do me a favor, will you?"

"O...OK." Katya waited anxiously for what would be asked of her.

"I need you to grow a pair."

"You...wha...what?"

That had not just come out of her mouth.

"I. Need. You. To. Grow. A. Pair."

It clearly had.

"Jeslyn, it's not that I lack...that I lack confidence," and faltering was really driving that point home. "I'm not sure if you're aware of this, but this is kind of a big story. You're kind of a big deal right now. Your company made a few million dollars in just under two years, that's incredibly impressive, no doubt. What seems to be taking center stage though is that picture of –'' Katya almost said 'you'. "Someone. Someone who looks an awful lot like you. Not to mention the highly suggestive letter to go along with it that also looks to be written to you. What people see is that you came blazing onto the scene – out of nowhere, mind you – blew it up with this scandal and then just disappeared. A lot of talk is gonna happen with that kind of pyrotechnic display, especially since you weren't talking. About either your business or the Coleman mess."

"Fine, you want the business lingo rundown? Here it is. I set an extremely high bar when it came to the company's growth expectations. And, like I told my clients, if you're planning to grow, you better make damn sure you're ready for it. So, I staffed accordingly, probably in a way that most people would have considered overconfident, if not downright stupid. I employed strong individuals who knew what they were doing, armed them with authority and set them free. Instead of remaining strictly e-commerce, which I felt limited my capabilities, I set up alternate distribution channels. Since Foxxy Red wasn't solving a problem or providing an essential staple necessary for survival – people didn't *need* another apparel line in order to live – I knew that I had to capitalize on their social need, their desires.

"What do humans desire? Well, communication is one thing; I think the proliferation of social media can attest to that. They also desire relationships, be it platonic, religious or sexual; they want art and culture and entertainment. They also want to learn more about themselves, to try to either figure this life thing out by finding out why they're here, or at least learn how to make this life thing better while they're here. I chose self-education slash art and culture as my business focus. Inviting people to contribute to the brand was huge in terms of helping the company name spread like wildfire. Of course, that one celebrity chick sporting the clothes didn't hurt the cause, either. With the mini books, the forums and everything else that spoke directly to people instead of at them – it catapulted everything into warp speed. When there was a nice buzz going, what I thought was a nice buzz anyway, I upped the ante and created the high end label. For me, it was a way to reach higher up the consumer tree and grab the attention and wallets of those who could afford to shell out more money.

"Obviously, I didn't do this all by myself. An incredible team was assembled and we built this together. I'm not going to sit here and go through every meeting and campaign and what not, but I will tell you that we probably altered the global climate with all of the brainstorming we were doing."

Katya was scribbling furiously now. Jeslyn had broken down her business in less than five minutes, yet had engaged her in a nearly five hour, personal account of what had led up to it. She had to ask.

"That was extremely concise. So, why not just give me that? Why not just bring me in here, sit me down, give me the rundown, as you say, and be done with it? Why the full disclosure?"

"Why not? For one, Foxxy Red is about imperfection. I don't know if you've gotten your hands on one of those soul baring mini portfolios, but those accounts in there are...they're unreal." There was intense passion in her voice as she spoke. "That side of us we try so hard to hide, that's actually the side that can save a life, help someone who's been wounded, repair a broken heart or spirit or soul, it's what binds us.

"I firmly believe that striving for perfection is what tears societies, families, relationships and friendships apart. People are going to hate me, like me, love me or envy me regardless of whether I'm perfect or a complete failure. There are guys in prison getting fan mail. So, what does it matter if I have flaws? I'm not the first person to have them and I won't be the last."

Katya felt her heart flood with inspiration. The fire in Jeslyn's words that flamed the heat behind her eyes gave credence to everything she was saying. This was more, so much more than just a company. She was right, it was a culture.

She had to clear her throat before she could continue. "That's amazing, I mean that. You really have something here and I'm glad you're sharing it. You mentioned that people are going to like you or love you regardless, so, can you tell me what happened with some of those people who used to love you, like Kevin Luby?"

"Good ol' Officer Luby. I'm sure he's fine. Let's see, I think I told you about the Fourth of July blow up, and then what happened?" She put her finger to her chin to aid in the contemplation. "Not much. I mean, we talked after that, had a conversation about where we were each headed and I think I told him something like: I'm going to keep breaking your heart, this isn't ever going to be what you want it to be. He was mad at me for a while which was actually good for him, I think. It was good for him to boot my ass off of that

340

pedestal he had me on and look at me from an eye level perspective instead of like an unattainable goddess or something. It was ridiculous."

"Or maybe just love." Katya felt a pang of pity for the man.

"Love isn't stupid." Jeslyn gave her a look that told her to take her pity elsewhere. "Having strong feelings for someone doesn't mean you let them ruin your life. Even an amoeba moves in another direction when confronted with something that could potentially harm them. You're telling me things without brains know to protect themselves from adverse situations, but humans don't?"

Another valid point. "True. I guess I never looked at it that way."

Crap, maybe I do need to grow a pair.

"OK, so, Kevin's out of the picture, what about Forbes?" If she was going to be confident, she was going to ask about him. After all, she'd just seen the man in question.

Jeslyn didn't react in any way except to lazily smile and say, "Forbes is...Forbes."

It was infuriatingly nondescript.

"So are you guys together?" *Does he know you're in this hotel right now?*

"Let's just say, not all fairytales end with the happy ending one would expect, and leave it at that, shall we?" A smug expression let Katya know she had hit another dead end.

"Fine." But it didn't mean she had to be happy about it. "What will become of Foxxy Red? What can we expect in the future from this game changing company?" There it was, that journalism edge. She felt like she was channeling Barbara Walters. Apparently she was the only one who thought so. Jeslyn appeared to not take notice of Katya's brilliant journalistic focus.

"I don't know. I could tell you that I plan to triple the company's sales in the next two to three years, but I won't. That's just talk until it actually happens. So, I'll say

341

that I intend to grow the company and continue to find unique ways to do so." Obviously, she felt her exit strategy was no one's business.

"Anything else you want to say about the Coleman deal?"

"Not particularly, no. I would like everyone to go on about their lives, or at the very least, allow me to go about mine without anymore talk of Matt Coleman and me in the same sentence, the same paragraph, even."

The end.

According to Jeslyn, there wasn't anything else to say. The conclusion had been reached, the trip leading to it a fantastic one. Katya thanked Jeslyn for her time and reluctantly called it a wrap.

As she gathered her things to leave, she couldn't stop herself from turning to face the beautifully flawed creature who had started, not a company, not a spark, but a wildfire.

"Why *GFS Magazine*?"

"I like your publication's approach to journalism. I looked around for and researched the best media outlet to share my story with and your magazine came up the winner."

Fair enough.

"OK, but why me?"

Jeslyn let the question dangle alone without an answer to hold it up before replying almost cryptically, "I figured you'd be the perfect person to set the record straight. Consider yourself my peace offering.

There was no way that Katya was ever going to make sense out of that, so she pressed further. "Peace offering to who? And you don't even know me, how could you possibly know I'd be the perfect person to set the record straight?"

"Katya, you have a beautiful name. As soon as I saw it on your magazine's website I had a mild hunch. You also have a wonderful heart and a great future ahead of you. That being said, I didn't just call you up completely at random. I'm sure the start to our little interview opened your eyes to the fact that I did some digging into your background. Of course, I can see your positive attributes more clearly now since meeting you, but from what I gathered beforehand, I felt you were a good choice."

It was an answer that was better suited for a fortune cookie, but it was looking like the only answer she was going to get.

"Well, so glad I could oblige. Thank you again, Ms. Kennedy."

"Thank *you*, Ms. Houston."

A handshake and the close of a door put finality to the Jeslyn Kennedy exclusive interview. Katya's departure from the hotel and drive home were filled with a million thoughts. She knew she needed to call her boss, and LeAnn was probably pacing and cursing her name by now, but she needed alone time to think through everything.

Her tiny apartment was exactly as she'd left it earlier that morning, but it felt like ages since she'd actually been there. Grabbing a spoon and a half-full pint of ice cream out of the freezer, Katya curled up on her couch to try and sort through Jeslyn's download, knowing it all now rested on her to create a phenomenal article; one that wouldn't get ripped to shreds by Jeslyn or tossed out by the extremely finicky editing team at *GFS Magazine*.

She had explicit instructions from Jeslyn to call her once the article was written. She was told she'd receive supplementary details from there. Prior to today, there had been talk around the office that someone at *GFS* who held a position that was miles above Katya's had had to sign some legal document that basically gave Jeslyn the ability to ride roughshod over these entire proceedings. It could have been just water cooler talk, but with the way things were going and the stories Jeslyn had relayed regarding her ability to get people to do what she wanted them to, it was as plausible a scenario as anything else.

Katya's phone vibrated. Another text from LeAnn. She couldn't keep her on hold any longer.

After sending a text back that she'd call her in ten, to which LeAnn responded, 'the hell you will, I'm coming over.' She called Sara to rehash everything and get the skinny on what became of the Twitter uproar.

"Nothing much happened after we deleted the post and sent out the communication that we'd been hacked. I did get an anonymous tip that I should look more closely into a certain employee's online activities. But, yeah, no, other than that..." Sara sounded bone tired.

"Well, that's good news."

"So, what's the scoop, kid? Did she tell you anything worth our time? You were with her for a long time, I hope you got something."

Did she ever.

"There's a lot to go through and I'd really like to get my thoughts together and go over it with you in the morning, if we could?" Katya nearly winced as she made the request. She was supposed to be a journalist; neither rain, nor sleet, nor gloom of night was supposed to keep her from the swift completion of an article, especially when a tight deadline loomed and that article was the feature.

"I'm sure I don't need to remind you that this is crunch time, right?"

"No." Katya's chin moved closer to her chest in marked humility.

"But you are the lead on this, and it would be nice to have a thoroughly prepared download in the morning." Sara's phrasing made it obvious she expected Katya to be ready for an intense debriefing.

"Thank you, Sara. I swear, I'll be rearing to go first thing."

"I'm holding you to that, Houston."

Their call ended only minutes before LeAnn jiggled the knob on her front door.

"Why is your door locked?" she yelled through the barrier.

"Uh, because we don't live in Mayberry." Katya went over to unlock it and let her friend in.

"Funny." LeAnn wasn't laughing. "Real cute. Info. Now."

Katya indulged LeAnn's demand, providing a detailed play by play of the extraordinary time spent with *the* Jeslyn Kennedy. Hours later, she finally had to kick her best friend out so she could organize herself for work the next day. Even then, it was close to one in the morning before she was able to cart herself off to bed.

Katya wasted no time falling asleep, she would need it. Tomorrow was when the real work would begin.

31

Jeslyn's request that she "grow a pair" had sat alongside nearly all of her thoughts the night before and hadn't moved much the following morning.

Forgiveness not permission.

If she were going to make it in journalism, or stand up to her parents, or take control of her own destiny, she was going to have to do just that.

By the time she hit the CMT Publishing building's elevators that would take her up to the *GFS* offices, she had committed to stepping it up a notch or five. The muzak that crooned pitifully through the elevator speakers wasn't exactly *Eye of the Tiger* motivational, but it didn't matter. She was on a mission. She had left *GFS* headquarters a mere girl but she was returning a new woman. The elevator doors slid open and she rushed confidently out of them and straight into the Loft Hottie.

"What. The. Hell." The word 'the' was said as if she were reciting Elizabethan prose, 'What. Thee. Hell.'

"I'm sorry, so sorry." Katya was bent over picking up the scattered papers that had flown from the beauty queen's hands. She knew she was giving anyone within a five foot radius a nice plumber's view of her backside, while the other half of the collision just stared down at her, hands on her hips.

346

"Freaking perfect." Too-good-to-help kept making useless comments like these under her breath as Katya gathered every last scrap of paper from the cold tile floor.

"Super sorry about that, really." Breathless and disheveled, Katya held out the untidy stack she'd reassembled. She got a disgusted sigh in return.

The first leg of her mission was arguably a bust; however, the day was still young. Katya adjusted her pants suit, which was feeling a bit tighter than she remembered from the last time she'd worn it, and headed to her cubicle. She could see Sara peering over the shoulder of one of the graphic designer's in the loft. Katya's arrival caught her boss' eye and she held up a finger to convey the universal sign for 'give me just a minute.' Katya smiled up at her brightly and nodded.

As she shrugged off her messenger bag, she spared a furtive glance towards the opposite side of the Pit. Ethan was huddled behind his computer looking just as spectacular as ever. A few feet away, Brandon had his feet up on his desk and was laughing with (hitting on) a girl who seemed to be enjoying his advances. Katya's nose wrinkled at the sight.

Cracking open her MacBook, she located the notes she'd typed up the night before, the entirety of which consisted of three pages. She loaded them onto a flash drive which she inserted into her office desktop computer – she didn't trust emailing the information over, not even to herself – then she stewed in a simmering pot of her own thoughts.

Jeslyn had been very specific in her request that Katya, and Katya alone, write the article. Now that the interview was done, she wasn't so sure the entrepreneur's request was going to be honored. Her fingers twitched with nervous energy as she waited for Sara to finish up whatever it was she was doing and make her way over to her.

EPeters: How did it go?

The screen on her desk displayed an intraoffice instant message, giving her nervous energy a bright and shiny new plaything.

KHouston: Good. Really good actually. How are things here?

Katya mentally smacked herself after hitting 'send'. She was here now and perfectly capable of seeing how things *are*.

You should have asked how things were.

These types of berating comments were common when she was interacting with Ethan. There was always something she felt she should have said or done differently. And while she was beating herself to a pulp over inane details, her presumed faux pas never caught his attention.

EPeters: Same ol', same ol here. I planted a note, tho. Advised the head honcho to look into you know who's online activity.

So, Ethan had been the anonymous scribe that Sara mentioned.

KHouston: Nice. Great thinking!

She stopped herself from adding fifty more exclamation points.

EPeters: Wish I could take credit. It was actually my girl's idea.

So much for growing a pair. Katya wilted. Obviously someone like Ethan had a girlfriend. Regardless of the fact that it hadn't come up before, she knew deep down inside he was spoken for. This should not have come as a surprise. It also should not have made her feel like weeping uncontrollably, like moaning and sobbing and thrashing about like a fish in a net in shallow water.

KHouston: Well then, great thinking by her. Whoever that stupid troll of a woman might be.

Katya bit down on her bottom lip and began slowly hitting the delete button, erasing the last nine words character by character. Except, she had only erased six complete words and the 'upid' in stupid when Sara popped into her cubicle.

"Sorry about that, just finishing up with a designer."

Katya yelped in surprise and got rid of the instant message the only way her stunned brain could think of in that instant – by hitting 'send.'

"You ok?"

"Yep, mmmhmm." Katya began arranging items on her desk that needed no arranging. "Nope, I'm good. You ready?"

Her speakers pinged announcing the arrival of a new message.

"Uh, sure. You want to meet in my office or the conference room?"

"Office. Your office is good." Katya tried to position herself so that she blocked her computer screen.

"OK. I'll see you in there."

"Yep, on my way." She didn't move.

Sara gave her one last uneasy look, then made her way up to the loft.

Katya dropped her head back onto her chair before checking her computer. Ethan's last message was her strike out of the morning.

EPeters: Whoever that st? Maybe you meant 'whoever that is.' Leia came up with it. I don't know if you've met her yet. Some people call her Princess Leia...or the Loft Hottie.

Of course.

Of freaking course.

Of course her Prince Charming was not only involved with someone, but involved with the most beautiful girl in all of *GFS*-land.

Katya resisted the urge to throw everything in sight; blinked back the moisture in her eyes that was gathering more moisture, which would soon form a band of tears that would take her cheeks hostage; grabbed the notes she'd just printed from the office printer and marched into Sara's office.

The door rattled lightly on its hinges causing Sara to look up wide-eyed.

"Sorry, super sorry about that." Katya had closed it just a bit too forcefully.

"It's OK, are you?"

"Me? Yeah, no, me, I'm fine!"

Thou doth protest too much.

Katya took the over enthused edge out of her voice. "I'm good. Ready?" She wanted the attention off of her wellbeing.

"Shoot." Sara looked to her to begin.

Katya ran through the day, albeit with less flair and more facts than when she'd discussed the interview with LeAnn the night before. Sara listened attentively, only interrupting to ask questions about certain parts or tell Katya to jot down notes on other parts.

"And that's basically it." Katya had made no mention of seeing Forbes at the hotel, had barely mentioned Forbes period. There was no talk of Jeslyn's issues with her mother, brother, Willie or Officer Luby, either.

"Hmmm." Sara turned in her chair and stared out her office window. "Do you think you can write it?" She asked without turning around.

"Yes." Katya felt her heart beginning to pump more quickly. This was it, the moment of truth where she would have to firmly brush off the advice and direction from her superior, put her foot down on the article as well as her position at *GFS Magazine* and grow a pair. This is when she would have to show that she'd transformed, that she wasn't somebody's pushover, that she wouldn't take no for an answer, that –

"Well, you're not doing anyone any good sitting in here." Sara turned back slowly. "You've got an article to write, Houston. Get on it."

"Yes, OK then." She felt her exuberance slacken. Sara dismissed her.

Katya hurried out of the office before Sara called her back in to let her know she changed her mind and was giving the feature to someone else. She had the early warning signs of a headache but knew the prepackaged, chocolate cupcake she had stashed away in her desk drawer (for emergencies) would help to curb it.

Brandon bumped into her, literally, on her way back to her workstation.

"Oh, my bad." He didn't even try to sound sincere.

Katya made an attempt to walk past.

"So, I hear you're a features writer now, is that right?" He blocked her path.

"Brandon?" Katya may not have been completely transformed, but it didn't mean she had to put up with Brandon Seltzer's shenanigans.

"Yeah."

"Move!" It was slightly louder than, but just as forceful as she'd intended. Her tone must've surprised him because his eyes widened and his feet seemed to shuffle him out of her way.

Back at her desk, she shut down her instant messaging program without even looking at it (no need to reopen fresh wounds), shut out her disappointment and started piecing together the afternoon and partial evening with Jeslyn Kennedy (*the* Jeslyn Kennedy). The outline she'd prepared for Sara helped remind her of the timeline of events and Jeslyn's voice, played back on her recorder, reminded her of everything else – things that made her chuckle softly, things that made her nod her head in agreement, things that made her feel sad, scared and frustrated. Things that made the story.

It took all day. She wrote, edited, rewrote, reedited, critiqued, added, deleted then added again. Sara silently checked on her, never once disturbing her with conversation.

Office colleagues milled around her. Sims had a conniption over something midday that turned out to be irrelevant an hour later. The Loft Hottie pranced – what was characterized by Katya as prancing – around the loft, doing whatever it was beautiful people did all day. Ethan (ah, Ethan) worked studiously and Brandon talked too loudly and socialized too much to have done anything constructive at all. And while all this activity bubbled around her, Katya fell back into Jeslyn's world, reconstructing it into a feature article worthy of the glossy pages of *GFS Magazine*.

When she finished for the day, she didn't run the piece up to Sara, she slipped quietly out of the building and headed home.

This was going to be huge, was all she could think, and she would have the byline. That part was still unreal. Until she picked up the next issue and saw her name in print underneath the headline, she wouldn't believe it; it was too fantastic to believe.

Katya though about contacting Jeslyn to let her know she'd finished, but the evening hour seemed to be an inappropriate time for that. Instead, she decided to spend a quiet evening at home with a plan to make contact during daylight hours. As she sat, curled up on her couch, with her hand wrist-deep in a bag of popcorn and a made-for-TV movie soaking up her attention, her cell phone rang. She went to silence it, knowing it was LeAnn and knowing she'd told her not to bug her until tomorrow because she had some serious vegging out to do. Only it wasn't LeAnn. Irritation turned to fretfulness instantaneously.

It was Ethan.

"Hello?" She tried to play it off as if she hadn't just about done a somersault over the fact he was calling her.

"Hey, Katya, it's Ethan."

I love you. Marry me. "Oh, hey, Ethan."

"Listen, this is probably going to sound stupid or a little weird, but I just wanted to clear something up with you…you know, from earlier."

Katya narrowed the possible 'something up's' down to ninety-nine from one hundred.

"I…are you still there?"

"Yeah! Yes, I'm here. Can you hear me?"

"Yeah, now I can. Anyway, when we were messaging each other today, I said that Leia had helped me with the thing, you know the, um…"

"Yeah, no, I know. OK." Katya pressed her phone to her ear with such force she didn't know if she'd be able to peel it away.

"Right. So, I had referred to her as my girl and, yeah this is probably stupid –"

"No!" She almost shouted the word. "No, please, go on."

"Well, I meant that in a homegirl kind of way, like, you know, my girl Leia. Like as in my friend girl, not my girl…not my girlfriend."

"Right. No. Of course." *Yes! Yes! Yes! Yes! Yes!*

"I messaged you back about it, but you were busy, and then you left and I never…I mean, it never got said. Anyway, it's not a big deal. I just thought you should know."

"Cool. OK then." Her eloquent retorts had returned.

"Well, that was all. I, uh, I guess I'll see you at the office?"

"Yeah, for sure."

"Unless you have any mad spy capers you need me to handle before then."

Katya snorted.

Beautiful. Way to go, Miss Piggy.

"Alright then, well, have a good night."

"You too, Ethan."

"Mmmk. Bye." She let him have the last word.

Katya placed her phone down beside her, then fist-pumped the air excitedly. If she owned a copy of it, she would have watched *Star Wars* right then.

Just because.

* * *

353

Jeslyn had given her a telephone number to use but seemed to have forgotten about it, because she wasn't picking up. Katya drummed her fingers on her kitchen counter and suspiciously eyed the fruit that sat across from her. She didn't want fruit or anything else right now. Her stomach was pole vaulting into her chest and landing with a thud in edgy disarray as she waited for Jeslyn to answer. After hearing forty-seven seconds worth of rings she hung up.

"Really. You can't be bothered to pick up the freaking phone?" Katya muttered to herself. Before hitting redial, she checked the number again. Even though she was alone, she felt her face warm with embarrassment. "Or, I could dial the correct number." Now her nerves were kicked into high gear as she started the dialing and waiting process all over again.

Jeslyn answered on the second ring.

"Oh, hi, hey there."

Hey there?

"Good morning, Katya. I presume it's finished."

"Um, yeah, er, yes. Would you like me to send it to you?" Katya rolled her eyes and silently admonished herself for her piss poor articulation.

"No. You can print it out and meet me. Today works well. Are you available at eleven?"

"This morning?" *Of course morning, stupid!* "Ah, yes, yes I am." Katya quickly recovered.

"Perfect. Is there any place that works better for you?"

"No, I'm good with anywhere."

"Alright, I'll text you an address and we'll see you at eleven. Thank you." And then she was gone.

"*We'll* see you?" Katya spoke to her cell phone as if it could provide an answer. Would someone be joining them? She guessed she would just have to wait and find out at eleven.

True to her word, a text came through with an address. Katya noted the address was located in La Jolla and wondered if she'd be crossing paths with Mr. Keith in the near future. It wasn't something she hoped against, that was for sure.

Katya informed Sara of her future whereabouts and told her she'd be in the office late afternoon. Then she waited. Time neither raced nor stood still, it simply moved at an acceptable pace closer to the eleven a.m. hour. She thought about Ethan and Jeslyn and Forbes and Willie and poor girls chained in rooms, probably scared and hungry. Then she thought about hunger and ice cream and cookies and pie...

There was a reason her muffin top had turned into a bundt cake.

She used her GPS and found herself in downtown La Jolla just before eleven. Katya stood on the sidewalk and looked up at the large, two-story office building. Jeslyn hadn't provided a suite number, so she walked through the clear glass doors that served as the building's entrance hoping she'd be able to find a directory that would guide her.

A large receptionist's desk stood in front of her with a tiny receptionist behind it who smiled at her as she breezed in.

"Katya Houston?" The petite woman, who had just a hint of an islander accent, greeted her as she approached.

"Yes."

"Go ahead and take the elevator to the second floor." That was all she said before turning her attention to something else.

Katya obeyed, wondering why she wasn't given more direction. Perhaps there would be someone to greet her when she arrived on the second floor. The elevator came to a stop and she exited gracefully – no running into office girlfriends this time. A wood-paneled wall stretched out in front of her, lining the entire length of the empty hallway which ended one hundred feet to her right and another one

355

hundred feet to her left. Handles jutted out of the wall, a seam splitting them in the middle and creating a T over head, letting her know this was the doorway.

She tugged on the heavy entrance, a task that proved much more difficult than she'd imagined it would be, and was hit with a flurry of energy. There hadn't been much that she could see or hear on the elevator side of the wall, but once she crossed over its threshold, it was as if she had entered an entirely different world. She imagined this is what the offices of the most prestigious fashion magazines looked like. Brightly colored accent walls creating forty-five degree angles with neutral ones; decor that looked like street art mixed with Shakespeare and rolled in glamour; canned and carefully placed lighting that seemed to cast 'a designer was here' light over everything, gave the open space a heartbeat.

Smiling, bubbling people walking here and there carrying fabric, folders, papers or nothing at all swished around her like the hems of dozens of ballroom gowns as she stood stock still in the middle of their cotillion.

There was another large desk; this time with a larger, five-pounds-away-from-portly young man, dressed in a slick black tie – that looked more like a thick, uniform ink stain down the front of his slate gray button-up shirt – at its helm.

"Ah, you must be, don't tell me," he squinted at her as if she were a stereogram that, if she stared long enough, would reveal her 3D identity. "Katya Houston, yeah?"

It made her smile.

"Yes."

He looked like he expected an award or at least a consolation prize.

"Glad to have ya', Kat. I'm Josh. Let me take you to our leader." He rose up out of his chair (after doing a quick, robot-like dance that she assumed was supposed to coincide with the odd alien voice he'd used when he said, 'take you to our leader') and led her down one short hallway and one longer one to an open office door. "J, I have a Katya

Houston here for you." Jeslyn looked up from her desk. "Have fun." Josh winked and left the two women alone.

Katya entered the spacious office and took a seat in one of the plush, filigree-patterned armchairs in front of Jeslyn's desk.

"Thank you for coming." Jeslyn sounded like she meant it.

"Oh, of course." Why wouldn't she come? Seriously? After everything else, showing up here seemed like a cake walk. *Mmm cake.* "So these are your...this is your...are your headquarters?" Just one interaction that didn't consist of stuttering and sputtering, was that too much to ask?

"You could say that."

She *did* say that. Clearly. Plainly. So, why did everything that came out of Jeslyn's mouth have to be cloaked in the Shroud of Turin? Katya held back a sigh.

"Do you have your article?" Right down to business.

Seeing her in this environment – a lime green wall with an abstract purple design in one of the far corners; a grayish blue reclaimed wood desk and matching bookcase; tall vases holding even taller peacock feathers and scraggly white washed sticks – Jeslyn seemed softer, kinder, not as scary.

Here a couch, there a painting, everywhere a beautiful something. Young Ms. Kennedy had an office, e, i, e, i, oh. Katya's mind hummed these words to the tune of Old McDonald after she'd handed Jeslyn the eight-page, double-spaced printout, and was able to absorb her surroundings.

A turn of a page. A minute later, another page turn. A pen appeared suddenly in Jeslyn's hand, clutched loosely by fingers that looked like they should be making ivory moan – they wouldn't tickle the piano keys, they were much too purposeful and magnificently constructed for that kind of nonsense.

Scratch, scribble, turn. Dot, scratch, silence, turn. Scratch, scratch, pen to lips, silence, stillness, back to silence (which was surprisingly even less quiet than stillness), turn. If it weren't for the sounds coming from beyond Jeslyn's office door, what sounded like a party getting ready to begin, Katya felt like a tiny piece of her sanity would have been scraped away by the awkwardness.

Jeslyn read the piece in its entirety, scratching, scribbling and dotting small changes here and there. Her face remained as placid as a spring lake at dawn; and just like that lake, something you couldn't discern whether it was warm or bone achingly cold until you disturbed it.

Katya let Jeslyn read in peace. Although, the thought did cross her mind whether or not the admittedly faux journalist had any real writing experience, enough to be providing edits anyway. There was only one thing missing – it was something a senior editor usually took care of, so Katya hadn't bothered with it. Jeslyn mentioned it now.

"It's good. Not what I expected, but good. Nice work. Other than a few minor changes, which you'll see I've made, I'm happy to let it run as is."

Katya felt her shoulders leave her earlobes.

"On one condition."

Before heading right back to the tension-filled position they'd just come from.

"I supply the headline." Jeslyn did the look again. The one that barged right into her soul and made itself at home.

Katya didn't know if she was at liberty to accommodate that request. Her whole 'ask forgiveness not permission' attitude was put to the test in the face of this perceived conflict.

"I don't see why that should be a problem." Who had said that? It had sounded like Katya's voice, but Katya's voice from far away; like Katya's voice through a down pillow.

"Good." Jeslyn whittled a string of words onto the first page of Katya's papers. Then she folded the paper, laid it carefully on the rest of the stack, and handed all eight pages back to Katya. "I hate to rush you out of here, but I have an appointment I need to get to. When will the piece run?"

Katya was having a hard time hearing, thinking and functioning all at the same time. What had she just agreed to? What had Jeslyn written on the paper? What would Sara say? What if she was fired?

What had she just asked me? "I'm sorry, you wanted to know...?"

"When the piece will run?"

Katya pulled the date from a disaster preparedness backup cloud of knowledge. Lord knew her main server was fried.

More English was thrown at her, Katya's voice from under three inches of water replied. Then life was in reverse – longer hallway; shorter hallway; 'good bye, Josh, pleasure meeting you as well,' Katya's voice from inside a motorcycle helmet said. Back through buzzing energy-filled office, practically silent hallway, elevator ding, elevator down, tiny receptionist, breeze out and back to car.

Where life resumed.

Katya opened the folded piece of paper as she sat in her toasty warm car like she was trying to peek in on a sleeping dragon, and opening the paper too fast or making any sort of noise would wake it. There were hardly any scratched, dotted or scribbled edits on this first page, but at the top, in almost calligraphy-perfect handwriting, Jeslyn had written her headline:

The One Percent Clique

32

~THOUGHT THIS MIGHT INTEREST YOU~

It was the only thing typed on the small linen card that was attached to the courier-delivered package. He stared at it for longer than he should, thinking – no, wanting – something that he shouldn't.

Could it be in this package?

He'd looked at several packages this way. None of them had been it.

After awhile of trying to convince himself it wasn't what he thought – no, hoped – it was, he picked it up, still hoping against hope. That, too, had been going on for too long, the hoping against hope, against common sense, against reason, against all the reasons. Reasons like, he had barely known her; like, she was obviously not as interested in him as he'd thought; like, she was just some chick. That last reason was stricken from the record.

Objection! his thoughts cried out, *badgering the witness*.
Sustained.

He set the card aside gingerly (in case he realized later it held significance) and tore into the thick paper. Instantly he felt disappointment swallow him completely in one gulp. He looked at the magazine contemptuously.

GFS Magazine, it said at the top. Nice. Someone was sending him a message that it was time to get back to work. There was a strip of paper sticking out from inside the magazine. What, a placeholder marking some super informative article that was supposed to suddenly inspire him? From the looks of the cover, it was probably some feminist article picked out by his mother or some other woman who thought she was doing him a favor.

She wasn't.

On the cover was a picture of a woman's face — bright red lips and a soft, golden chin was all he could see to bring him to that conclusion, since the upper half of the face was covered with a wide brim black hat. She held one finger up to her lips, as if she were telling someone to be quiet. Below the picture were three words.

One Percent Clique.

He tried to guess at what the article was about, this article that had clearly been cherry picked for him — THOUGHT THIS MIGHT INTEREST YOU — so he didn't have to actually read what was sure to be drivel.

Women are quietly becoming part of the one percent of the nation's top business owners? No, he knew the number was higher than that.

Women silence the drive of the top one percent of the nation's most successful men?

That was probably it. An article telling him that pining over a woman who didn't give a rat's ass about you squelched your potential.

That was definitely not it. That sort of article would be on some misogynistic blog, and the link would've come in the form of an email from one of his buddies with a subject line that said, 'Lock It Up' or 'Get Your Shit Together, Man.' Not some delicate linen card attached to a courier-delivered package with a cherry-picked article already bookmarked.

He gave up. Somebody had obviously taken the time to send it to him, he might as well do Mr. or Mrs. Anonymous the courtesy of actually reading it.

The magazine turned easily to the bookmarked page. He scanned the headline: 'The One Percent Clique.' Then the byline: By Katya Houston. Unconsciously, he sat up straighter in his chair.

Katya.

A memory sucker-punched him in the heart. He remembered a date, a late evening dinner. They had talked about nothing and everything on that date, including the nothing detail of how he thought the name Katya was one of the most beautiful names in the world. He remembered telling her that he almost named his dog Katya but didn't, just in case he wanted it for a different reason, a more special reason; like a name for his daughter someday. He had actually said that. Out loud. No wonder she'd run for the hills.

Now, here was that stupid name, neener, neener, neenering in his face like some schoolyard bully. He'd never been bullied in school. This must be what it felt like. It sucked ass.

His eyes roamed over the first few words of the sub headline – he'd skipped over its unbolded typeface because the name of the article's author had pushed its way to the front of his line of vision – then halted suddenly. The second most beautiful name in the world had cleverly hidden itself between other characters and spaces but was now nearly illuminated:

Opening the Closet: Skeletons and Success Unfold When Foxxy Red Founder, Jeslyn Kennedy, Reveals the Intimate Details of Her Apparel Culture

Jeslyn.

THOUGHT THIS MIGHT INTEREST YOU

Damn right it interested him. He read the two-page article while sitting on the edge of his desk; while pacing back and forth on the dark hardwood floors of his office; while thrusting his fingers into his hair and forgetting them there while he finished a paragraph, then remembering them again when it was time to turn the page or jam them into the pocket of his slacks as he continued reading.

"...I didn't start this business for the right reasons but the right reasons found me despite myself and for that I'm thankful."

To who or what do you attribute your inspiration? The next question read.

*"My dad, may he rest in peace, is still a huge inspiration for me and always will be. I'd also say Forbes Keith is quite an influencer. He's an amazing entrepreneur, very focused, extremely kind (**'and handsome, GFS contributor interjects for Kennedy'**) and yes, very handsome. He's someone with a head for business and a heart for changing the world. That's a powerful combination."*

He was being rushed to the emergency room by way of this ambulance of an article. Each word brought him closer to his cure; each word was a lift of the gurney, a swoosh through the hospital doors, a race down a hallway with light bulb memories flashing behind his eyes like the evenly spaced bright bulbs shining down from a hospital hallway ceiling. He had been fading, but now there was hope.

THOUGHT THIS MIGHT INTEREST YOU

He turned the last page, read the last paragraph, he had seen his name in print, in a quote she had given. She had spoken about him.

Someone needed to call the doctor. He wouldn't last if someone didn't call her. He had been too weak to do it himself for the past year and he didn't know if he had the strength to do it now. Plus he was scared, something he would never cop to outside the walls of his mind. She was his antidote but she'd also been his poison.

What had happened? One day she was there, in his inbox, then at his suite door, then in his home, his bed, his arms, his life. The next day she was gone.

You sent me the email you and Gisele were having.

Ah yes, Gisele. He'd accidentally sent Jeslyn their email exchange. Had that been it or was that just an easy excuse for her? If that was it, he could tell her it didn't mean anything, Gisele didn't mean anything. And this time it would be true. Before he'd felt sorry for the girl. He had feelings after all – *a kind heart, set on changing the world* – she'd said so herself. He had just been kindhearted to someone he'd known for over a third of his life. Surely she understood that. She'd made love to him like she understood that. He could still remember their last time.

The poison and the antidote.

He picked up the phone, started dialing, set the phone down again. He'd done this before – almost called, almost visited, almost reached out, until he almost drove himself crazy.

He would do it.

But what if it was too late?

No, it couldn't be. Life had always gone well for him. As arrogant as it was to think that, it was still true. Life wouldn't be so cruel as to lead a man dying of thirst to a riverbed only to have him discover it was dry.

THOUGHT THIS MIGHT INTEREST YOU

He picked up the phone again.

*   *   *

She had told the reporter everything. Every. Thing. Almost everything. She had told the reporter enough. Too much. No, enough. Yet Katya had boiled her pungent recipe down to a soothing palatable broth.

Why?

Where was the titillating expose? Where was the splashy headline? *Drug Addled Brother, Dysfunctional Mother and a Life of Lying and Near-Crime Surround Imposter CEO.* Where was the story? They'd spent hours together. Jeslyn had opened her closet. Where were the skeletons? There was nothing here that would even come close to piecing together an entire skeletal structure. You couldn't even find a stapes in the article Katya had written. Not one single thing was written that would lead anyone to believe she was anything more than an advantageous entrepreneur who had an uncanny resemblance to a bawdy young woman whose picture had been found in a dying investor's wallet.

More calls had come in, but they weren't villagers with pitchforks and torches, they were just people. People who wanted more of the regular-cloth-to-riches story. The *GFS* article wasn't even sensational; Abbess Katya had taken Jeslyn's confession and hid it under the folds of her habit. Why were they still interested?

Her penance must be this then, the dizzying confusion over why there was no bite to her article.

Her cell phone rang. It had been doing that a lot lately. Another number she didn't recognize. Another heart-stopping second where she wondered if this was it, if this is when the other shoe dropped, a shoe she'd left loose on the foot of Katya Houston.

"Hello?"

Silence.

"Hello?" she tried once more. If the caller didn't speak this time she would simply hang –

"Jeslyn?" Up. Her eyes to the ceiling, her hand to her forehead, her stomach to her throat. They all went up at the sound of his voice.

He was alive and he sounded well. Stable, calm and strong. Everything she was not at that moment.

"I need to see you, J."

He'd called her J. Not her full name, not a bad name, just J. This was good. "Of course. When?"

"Today."

"OK."

It was settled.

*   *   *

Jeslyn hadn't been to see Dr. Parker in months. Not because she didn't need to, but because she did; and she hadn't been ready. She still wasn't ready. She would never be ready. But that didn't mean she didn't need this.

The place still smelled the same, still looked the same. She didn't know if she'd expected a change, but there was none. She sat in the waiting room until she heard her name called, then she walked back to Dr. Parker's office.

"Jeslyn, it's good to see you."

Jeslyn smiled. A smile that was polite but broken in half, right down the middle of relief and sorrow.

"Thank you for seeing me."

How did this go? Was she supposed to just blurt it out? She waited for the words to come. Dr. Parker waited too; she'd always been so patient. Another thing that hadn't changed. So much was the same here, while outside of here everything was entirely different.

"I'm ready now."

"What are you ready for, Jeslyn?" Dr. Parker adjusted her glasses.

"I'm ready." The words wouldn't come. *It's your leash. Loosen it and* – She had to shut that voice up. "I'm ready to tell you everything."

Dr. Parker relaxed into her chair and crossed her legs. Every movement she made was slow and easy, like she didn't want this scared little bird in front of her with the broken wing to try and fly away before she got the help she needed. "Where would you like to begin?"

She would have to blurt it out otherwise she wouldn't be able to do it. Jeslyn felt like she was going to be sick.

"I want to fix what's broken inside of me." Her wall crumbled, she was six years old again and she was scared. There was yelling. She needed someone to help her. "Can you fix it?"

She knew Dr. Parker couldn't give her any assurances, but she needed to hear one. Her eyes pleaded. The doctor nodded or perhaps she just imagined it.

Good enough.

"I have a brother, he's a drug addict. My father is dead and my mother...you know my mother, probably better than I do."

Dr. Parker began jotting something down on her notebook. Jeslyn saw her name on a file folder. Jeslyn Kennedy.

"That's not my name."

Dr. Parker looked up. "What was that, Jeslyn?"

"I said, that's not my name." Her voice cracked.

"OK. Can you tell me what your name is?" She probably thought Jeslyn was going insane or already there.

"My name is Jeslyn Jackson, but no one knows me by that name outside of my family."

The only way to get Dr. Parker to understand was to start from the beginning. The real beginning – before the interview, before the inclusion in the one percent clique, before everything. She would have to take the good doctor back to when she was nothing more than an irrelevant member of the ninety-nine percent.

And so she began.

acknowledgements

Special thanks to everyone who has supported the book: My mom, for always telling me to "look it up" whenever I asked the meaning of a word; my brothers, for being my first fans; the women of Chic CEO; the GG crew; Good Feet, Worldwide; Sandy Kessler; Jill Tuck; John Burns; the fans and clients of RedCelloMarketing.com; Tres "Sojourn" Hodgens, musician extraordinaire; Brougham "Squid" Campbell, an amazing graphic designer; my book editor, Mike Valentino and all of the friends and family who have cheered me on during this incredible process.

about the author

Misti Cain is a marketing professional with a passion for writing, music, dance and art. Born and raised in Central California, Misti currently resides in Southern California. *1 Percent Clique* is her first published novel.